# Miracle of the Rising Sun

# Miracle of the Rising Sun

Joseph Sciuto

**IGUANA**

Publisher: Cheryl Hawley
Editor: Lee Parpart
Front cover design: Design Playground

ISBN 978-1-77180-693-0 (paperback)
ISBN 978-1-77180-694-7 (epub)

This is an original print edition of *Miracle of the Rising Sun.*

*Dedicated to my close friends for over fifty years, Howie and Eric Phillips. The memory of us shoving the snow off the basketball courts outside our bedroom windows in Parkchester is one I will always cherish.*

*Also dedicated to my lovely and precocious niece, Teresita Ann Sciuto. You give me hope that the future will be bright.*

**"The Man in the Arena"**

It is not the critic who counts; not the man who points out how the strong man stumbles, or where the doer of deeds could have done them better. The credit belongs to the man who is actually in the arena, whose face is marred by dust and sweat and blood; who strives valiantly; who errs, who comes short again and again, because there is no effort without error and shortcoming; but who does actually strive to do the deeds; who knows the great enthusiasms, the great devotions; who spends himself in a worthy cause; who at the best knows in the end the triumph of high achievement, and who at the worst, if he fails, at least fails while daring greatly, so that his place shall never be with those cold and timid souls who neither know victory nor defeat.

— President Theodore Roosevelt


Blessed are those who hunger and thirst after righteousness, for they will be filled.

— Beatitude # 6

# PART ONE

# PROLOGUE

The feeling of uncertainty was overwhelming. I got up from the black metal chair — the only piece of furniture in this lavish, sprawling room — and walked over to the sliding glass door. As soon as my feet hit the cool patio, I tasted the sea air and felt its freshness going to work on me, like a mother with a washcloth, lifting my arms to wash them and letting them drop. I couldn't help wondering what would happen if I walked straight down to the water and immersed my entire body in the sea. Would the stench of these last eight months finally be washed clean?

It was a little past midnight, the darkest hour of night. Even so, I was able to spot the man who was responsible for the improbable situation I found myself in. He stood by the water's edge, with his back to me. Even without being able to see his features, I knew he was looking up at the blanket of stars, occasionally closing his eyes and imagining the black hole at the center of the Milky Way. If I had to guess, I'd say he was seeing himself walking through it and into the future … my future. The future I had allowed him to take control of, without objection. The reason for my overwhelming feeling of uncertainty which, compared to just a few hours ago, at least gave me a glimmer of hope.

# CHAPTER ONE

Who am I kidding? I lost control of my future a good five years before setting eyes on this man.

By the time I turned eighteen, my dream of getting a PhD in English and teaching literature to fresh-faced undergraduates had vanished. Those Byron poems I memorized in high school were starting to fall out of the back of my head, replaced by the chatter of art directors, fashion designers, photographers, and fellow models.

It was the fashion industry that dictated my every move then, not this star-gazing man on a beach below, whose existence I couldn't even have fathomed.

The voices of these industry gatekeepers still ring in my head. *Lie down in the sand, sweetheart. Kick your left foot up and let the foam wash over you. Pivot your breasts a little to the left, dear.* And always, that old standby: *Make love to the camera.*

There I was again, staring out from the cover of another magazine, my face hovering next to cash registers all across the land. Beside my dewy eyes, headlines promised "Six New Ways to Drive Your Man Crazy," or the trick to dropping "10 lbs. by Summer." When I wasn't doing cover shoots, I was striding down catwalks in Paris, Milan, New York, London, Berlin, and Los Angeles, draped in the latest flesh-baring designs by Coco Chanel, Ralph Lauren, Versace, Christian Louboutin, and Calvin Klein.

Of course, the job came with extracurriculars. Coke. Sex. Money and gifts. None of us paid for the white stuff. It just showed up at parties and in the backs of limousines, along with a never-ending river of champagne, as we were chauffeured around to the chateaus, mansions, villas, and castles of politicians, movie stars, and billionaires.

I was also waking up in the beds of men thirty, forty, or fifty years older than me. The attention was exciting, and there was always something in it for us. A diamond necklace or a new watch. Sometimes the guy would leave a wad of cash on the side table as he left to go home to his wife and kids.

After five years of making loads of money, I had very little to show for it. The day I turned twenty-three I made a solemn promise to myself that this would be my last night of partying. I figured I had about ten good years left in which to make a substantial amount of money. My agent had already booked several music videos for me to be in, and he didn't see any reason why I couldn't transition from modeling into acting for TV and movies. But that was no guarantee, so tonight would be it: my last blow out.

All week I was having severe PMS, and as luck would have it, my period showed up on my birthday. I sighed, knowing I would spend half the night in the restroom. But there was a silver lining: At least I wouldn't wake up next to some lecherous old man. Being on the rag was a free pass.

In the hotel room where my agent had put me up, I snorted two lines of coke, gulped down a glass of champagne, and walked into the bathroom to change my pad for the third time in three hours.

I picked out a sleeveless black Versace dress to wear with black high heels. Considering the circumstances, black was my best option. I filled my Gucci handbag with plenty of pads and a supply of cocaine from the night before.

Some of the models I was working with were throwing a party for me at an upscale restaurant on the east side. They told me not to worry about the guest list. They would take care of it. This meant that there would be plenty of super-elites but no politicians … although the pols might join us later at one of the guest's penthouses.

After greeting the first half dozen guests who trickled in after nine o'clock, I excused myself and slipped away to visit the bathroom. I had changed my pad less than an hour earlier, and already I could feel it sagging.

I walked into a stall and closed the door. Through the crack in the door, I could see Maureen and Tina, two model friends, checking their makeup at the sinks. I hiked up my dress and sat on the toilet and immediately realized I had a situation on my hands: blood clots, the size of quarters, had turned my lace panties into a horror show. I had bought plenty of extra pads but hadn't thought to bring extra underwear. I grabbed a bunch of toilet paper and cleaned the panties as well as I could, changed my pad, and exited the stall.

When I got to the sink, Maureen noticed my red fingertips and said, "Oh honey … on your birthday! That's just cruel!"

"I know … it's been gushing out of me like an open fire hydrant."

"No extracurricular activity for you tonight?" Tina asked.

"Not unless the stud wants to wake up in a pool of blood."

"You still have a couple of orifices available," Maureen remarked.

"Please, don't go there. It'll be a sad day in hell before I start servicing some oversexed male Homo sapiens on my birthday."

"Oh, I don't know about that," Maureen said dryly. "A deed to a house in Malibu and all of my orifices would be open for business."

We all laughed as I dug into my handbag and pulled out the little bag of coke. I swung it before me and motioned for them to join me in the handicapped stall, which was big enough for the three of us. We piled in and took multiple hits from a tiny spoon that I wore around my neck, then checked our noses in the mirrors for residue and rejoined the party.

For the next two hours, I fended off ham-fisted passes from an investment banker and the owner of an upscale restaurant. By the time the kitchen brought out my birthday cake, I'd been to the bathroom three times to change my pads and clean my underwear … each time enjoying a couple hits of coke.

After they sang "Happy Birthday" and I blew out the candles, I turned to Maureen and asked her to call a taxi for me. I ate a tiny slice of cake, not to be rude, and went around the table and hugged and kissed all the guests and thanked them for coming. I apologized for leaving early and told everyone I could feel a migraine coming on and needed to get to bed early. Really I was just excited to get under the covers with a hot water bottle and a good book.

# CHAPTER TWO

I waited outside the restaurant for about fifteen minutes and still no taxi came. A limousine pulled up and two young men walked over to it. They were dressed fashionably and had been eyeing me for the better part of ten minutes. One of them turned to me and said, "If you're going uptown, we'd be glad to drop you off. Hop in."

Without giving it a second thought I said yes. I was so used to being driven around in limos that it seemed completely natural that one would just show up and take me home. I slid into the back seat, and soon I was sandwiched between the one who'd offered me the lift and the other one. Something felt a little off, but I willed myself to relax and imagined being at home in my warm bed. When the driver asked me for my address, I gave him the name of the hotel I was staying at. He nodded and raised the tinted window that separates the driver from his passengers. As I watched it go up, a little prickle rose along the back of my neck.

The guy who offered me the ride (who we'll call Asshole #1) asked, "Special occasion tonight?"

"My twenty-third birthday," I said.

"A girl as pretty as you, on your birthday, without an escort. That's just doesn't seem right. How about we all do a shot for your birthday?"

"No, I really can't. The reason I left the party was because I wasn't feeling well."

"All the more reason to have a shot. Better than any medicine." He opened a little compartment that was built into the back seat and pulled out three glasses and a bottle of vodka. He poured three shots and handed one to his friend (Asshole #2), one to me, and one for himself.

"What's your name?" Asshole #1 asked.

"Alicia."

"To beautiful Alicia! Happy Birthday!" We all drank up and a few seconds later I could feel Asshole #1's hand steadily working its way up my leg.

I froze, but managed to say, "I wouldn't go there. I'm a bloody mess. That's the other reason I left the party."

"I've fucked plenty of girls who were having their periods. Blood turns me on."

I angrily removed his hand from my upper thigh. "I said no, you disgusting piece of shit."

He laughed, as he looked at Asshole #2 and asked, "Can you believe this cunt?"

I reached over him and tried to open the passenger door, but he pushed me back and suddenly I felt a stinging blow to the left side of my face from Asshole #2, who said, "You ungrateful bitch. We'll teach you some manners."

I screamed and banged on the tinted window, and then a second blow landed on the left side of my face and I could swear that my skin on that side was literally ripped off. I felt them turning me over, and I was struggling to get free when a third blow knocked me unconscious. The last thing I remember hearing was Asshole #1 saying, "Don't kill the bitch. I don't mind fucking a bloody cunt, but a corpse is a totally different thing."

# CHAPTER THREE

I woke-up in a bright room. My mouth was as dry as a desert, and I was in so much pain that I couldn't figure out what hurt most — my face, my stomach, or my left leg. At first I was alone, but then a nurse rushed in, and soon I was surrounded by doctors and nurses checking my vitals and flashing lights in my eyes. I winced at them and tried to speak, but I couldn't make a sound or keep my eyes open for longer than a few seconds.

After a few days, as I got stronger, the doctor who had operated on me when I was first brought to the hospital came to visit me. He perched on a stool next to my bed and gently informed me that I was the victim of a sexual assault and a vicious beating. Testing revealed that there were two assailants. I had been raped, sodomized, beaten to within an inch of my life, and dumped on a side street off 5th Avenue. A week had passed since the attack.

I stared at the wall as he spoke. It was painted an institutional beige and had one piece of art on it: a simple scene of a little girl on a beach, making a sandcastle, while her parents sat on a blanket behind her. I started to cry, and the left side of my face suddenly felt like it was on fire. When I raised my bandaged hand to touch it, the doctor reached out and stopped me.

"You need to avoid touching the left side of your face," he said. "We're doing our best to avoid an infection there."

"It hurts so much," I said. "What happened?"

I could see in his eyes that he didn't want to tell me. "One or both of your assailants … may have been wearing a ring, or they may have used a weapon of some kind — the police can talk to you about this…"

He explained that the left side of my face was severely injured in the attack. The skin had literally been ripped off, and I'd been left with a deep tissue wound in the middle of my left cheek, about the size of a silver dollar. I looked at him, in shock.

"We tried a skin graft, but it didn't take," the doctor said, apologetically, "and more tissue had to be removed in the process."

I didn't know what to say. I finally asked him if it would heal, and he looked at me sheepishly.

"The damage is substantial," he said. "Given that the skin graft was unsuccessful, we're hesitant to try that approach again. For now, you'll have to wear a silver dressing over the wound at all times."

I tried to listen while he geeked out and explained that these innovative dressings release silver ions that help prevent systemic infection, bacteria, and viruses in open wounds. Then he plastered a smile onto his face and shared the "good news" that they were able to reset the broken bones on the left side of my face.

"So I have a hole in my face, and you're not sure how to fix it?"

"Essentially, yes. But at some point, when your wound has stabilized, you'll be a good candidate for reconstructive surgery."

I gaped at him and asked, "Will I ever look like myself again?" The good doctor looked down at me and hardened himself to deliver difficult news.

"There will be significant scarring, but at least you won't be walking around with an open wound that's a magnet for infection."

*Significant scarring.* I knew then and there that my modeling career was over. An acting career was probably a moon shot as well. I might be able to play the victim of tragic accidents or work for a circus freak show, but those gigs wouldn't pay the rent, let alone set me up for a comfortable future.

A few days later, two New York City detectives came to see me. They were both very kind and considerate. They brought me my handbag, which was found next to me. The female detective winked and said that everything that was in the handbag was still there, except for a bag of powder which had been discreetly deposited in the trash. Unless it had something to do with the crime, it was of no interest.

I told them everything I remembered from the moment I was knocked unconscious. I gave a description of the two assholes but couldn't remember much about the driver. There were no suspects in custody or under suspicion. The police had talked to my friends at the party, and they were all under the impression that I'd gone back to my hotel in a taxi.

The detectives pulled out the front pages of the newspapers and tabloids from that night and asked if I wanted to see the photos of the crime scene. I hesitated, but finally nodded, and the female detective held up several pages worth of coverage, followed by photos from the scene that had, thankfully, not been published. There I was, splayed out on the street, my soiled panties wrapped around my knees, my dress pulled up to right below my butt. I was bloody all over, and the left side of my face looked like it was torn off, with my cheekbone exposed. The headlines were all variations on "Supermodel Brutally Raped, Beaten, and Left for Dead."

At that moment, I knew my life would never be the same.

# CHAPTER FOUR

The first time I looked into a mirror, I wished that the assholes had just killed me. I wasn't stupid. I knew the one thing I had going for me in this world was my looks. Even though I read a lot of books, I didn't have any creative talent or skills or experience to fall back on. My whole plan had been to keep modeling and save as much money as possible over the next ten years, until the work dried up. That way, if I couldn't break into acting, I would still be okay. That plan was dead in the water, and I wished I was dead, too.

The doctors tried to reassure me that they could do wonders with new plastic surgery techniques. They talked about full thickness skin grafts, which were used to treat deep, large wounds and scars by taking layers of skin similar to facial skin and transplanting them from other parts of the body to the face. But those procedures wouldn't be made available to me until they were certain they would work. So for now, I was stuck with the silver dressing.

Maureen and Tina and a few of my other model friends came to visit whenever they were in New York. They tried to be encouraging, but they knew the game. My agent, who lived in Los Angeles, sent a big bouquet of roses and a note wishing me a quick recovery and promising to help in any way he could. I was quite sure he had already crossed me off his client list. I knew he visited New York at least once a month and yet he never came to visit, nor did he ever try to call me. Such a lowlife.

I received speech therapy to learn how to speak without a slur, and I underwent intensive physical therapy to correct the partial paralysis on my left side, below the waist. I spent nearly two months in the hospital, and the doctors, nurses, therapists, and assistants did a wonderful job putting me back together, but it would have taken a miracle to make me look like my former self. With the left side of my face massively disfigured and the right side the same as it had always been, I felt like a perfect representation of *Beauty and the Beast*.

Thankfully I had accumulated thirty thousand dollars in my bank account from the Social Security disability insurance claims I had submitted, but those bi-monthly payments would run out quickly. After collecting my belongings from the hotel I was staying at before the attack, I booked a flight to Los Angeles, which had been my home base during my modeling career. The doctors at the hospital had referred me to top specialists in LA, and they were hoping that in the next few months I would finally be ready for some type of skin graft or facial reconstruction. In the meantime, I had to keep wearing the silver dressing and change it every three or four days. I couldn't leave it off for more than a few minutes at a time because of the risk of infection.

The two-bedroom apartment I shared with a roommate in Westwood Village had been abandoned and all my belongings were put in storage by my former roommate. She couldn't afford the rent on her own and had moved back home with her parents in Bel Air. Sadly, I didn't have that option. My parents and my brothers and sisters, who lived on Long Island, had never wanted much to do with me, and to drive home the point, not one of them came to visit me in the hospital, even though it was only about an hour drive into the city.

After a short search of LA rentals, I found a one-bedroom apartment in a not-very-safe area of Hollywood. The building dated back to the early 1930s, and I was fairly sure that one good earthquake would level it, but the rent was cheap, and I had to save money. I had to hire a moving company to move my belongings from the storage area to my new home, and before I knew it, I'd spent twelve thousand dollars. I didn't have a car, which made it almost impossible to get around LA, but that didn't matter because every time I looked into a mirror I started crying and went back to my couch. I had all of my food and medications delivered, and when I paid the delivery person, I made sure my long dark hair covered the left side of my face.

The only time I left my apartment was to pick up my mail from my mailbox on the first floor. Once, after picking up my mail at some ungodly hour, my left leg went limp and I tumbled down the stairs and landed right back next to the mail boxes. I started to cry uncontrollably, and then the thought that some thug might find me there had me crawling back toward the stairs, grabbing the railing, and dragging myself back up to my apartment.

After a month, I finally opened my laptop and looked through the classifieds in my area. Lucky for me, the local supermarket needed a cashier. I applied online, and they scheduled an appointment for me in two days. It only paid $450 a week, but at least no transportation was involved.

I picked up my mail and returned to my apartment. When I looked through the mail, I came across an expensive looking envelope, on heavy paper with a visible weave. I immediately recognized it as the type of letter I used to receive as a model. It was originally addressed to my apartment in Westwood, and had been forwarded to my new place. When I opened the envelope, I found an invitation from Mr. Ronald Hess. Mr. Hess was one of the most successful real estate developers in California, and anytime he started a new project he would throw a lavish party at his ten-thousand-square-foot penthouse apartment overlooking the city of Los Angeles. He always invited a bunch of models to sweeten the guest list. The models understood that the invitations were only for them, and not a plus-one. A couple of days after the event we would usually receive a check in the mail for two thousand dollars, just for attending. If you had paid "special attention" to a guest, and Mr. Hess knew about it, you would receive another three thousand. So for many of the girls it was not only a modeling job but also a chance to play the part of a high-class hooker.

I was on the invitation list because I had attended two previous parties. The secretary probably sent out about twenty invitations in the hope that five models would accept. It was no secret that most high-class fashion models spent a lot of their time away from home. The party planner had to cast a wide net in order to secure a small supply of "model meat."

I was ready to throw the invitation in the trash when it occurred to me that all I had to do was show up with the invitation and have the person at the door check my name off the guest list, and that would guarantee me a two-thousand-dollar pay day. The left side of my face was bandaged with the silver dressing, and if anyone asked what was wrong I could just say I had a severe allergic reaction to a cosmetic product I was testing out. I still had a killer body, and the right side of my face was as flawless as ever. The other models would see right through my ruse, but I doubted anyone would say anything. They knew what I'd been through, and it wasn't like I was a threat to any of them. I just had to avoid any doctors who might be milling around at the party, or look anyone in the face for too long.

I stared at the invitation and mused on my situation. At twenty-three-and-a-half, I felt betrayed — like a victim. And why? Because my beauty had been taken away. For five years, my whole identity, and my livelihood, were tied to my physical appearance. Every compliment I received had to do with my face and body. But that wasn't always the case.

Back in high school, I was known as the beautiful nerd because I loved to read so much and got great grades. I was strong in all subjects, but my passion was English literature. My book reviews were always read out loud by my teachers and received the highest grades. I was accepted to every college I applied to and was offered full scholarships to Fordham, Yale, and USC. I was on track to study comparative literature and dreamed of becoming an English professor when a friend talked me into entering a beauty contest. At first I scoffed at the idea. Why would someone who wants to write books and essays about Byron, Baldwin, and the Brontë sisters enter a beauty contest? But I kept thinking about it, and by the end of that week, I had thrown my hat in the ring. If I won, I would use the thousand-dollar prize to supplement whichever scholarship I decided to accept.

I didn't win, but I came close, and as I was walking to the backstage dressing area a fashion agent took me aside. He told me he could make me richer and more famous than I could ever imagine, and for some reason, I listened to him. He led me to a large room filled with lights, camera equipment, and racks of clothing, and within minutes, a famous photographer was snapping pictures of me in bathing suits, dresses, and lingerie. I was apparently a natural in front of the camera, and before long, I had signed a contract with a high-level modeling agency in LA. Within a few weeks, my face started to appear on magazine covers, and I was regularly featured in ads, pitching everything from vodka to veggie burgers. Soon I was travelling the world doing fashion shows in France, Milan, New York, Los Angeles, Germany, and Great Britain. And for a couple of weeks every year, I would be flown to some exotic destination to model the year's most fashion-forward swimsuits.

It was during one of those trips, while I was lying on my stomach on a sandy beach in the Azores, listening to the clicking of the cameras as the foamy water lapped at my limbs, that I realized how far I had strayed from my original dream — and how little I cared. The idea of becoming a professor at some major university must have belonged to someone else. There was no way I would ever be confined to some classroom, or a desk, earning one-tenth of what I was making as a fashion model. The only part of the dream that survived was my love of books. I still loved to read, and did so often, in and around photo shoots, traveling, and the party scene.

Now, at twenty-three, I was facing a huge identity crisis. I knew the days of cashing in on my appearance were over, but there was one last job I needed to do.

Yes, I would go to that party, but not in some kind of disguise. I would go as myself and squeeze whatever cash I could out of the system that treated me like a slab of meat while I was beautiful, and that was ready to throw me on the compost heap now that I was not.

And I would do one better. I would get my last payday and use that money to apply to all of the colleges and universities that I'd been accepted to five years earlier. I knew the scholarships were probably long gone, but I would certainly qualify for student loans and grants, and if I had to live in a tiny dorm room and survive on Kraft Dinners for a few years, so be it.

# CHAPTER FIVE

I called a taxi to take me to the party. I was dressed in a knee-skimming cocktail dress and strappy black pumps. The shoes were already starting to hurt my feet, but I knew that for a model attending one of these parties, heels were non-negotiable. On the right side of my face, my makeup was applied the way I like it — minimal foundation and almost no contouring, but with a smoky eye and dramatic lashes. On the left side, I did what I could to conceal the redness with an opaque foundation. Of course, nothing could hide the gaping hole packed with silver. So I blew out my long, dark hair and straightened it until it fell in a glistening sheet across the left side of my face.

When I reached the Hess penthouse, I showed my invitation to the man at the door, and he let me right in. Right away I was spotted by Amanda, a friendly bikini model who I'd worked with in the Caribbean. She came over to me with wide eyes and gave me a big hug as she peppered me with questions about how I was doing and why I was there.

"You sure you're up for this? We all heard—"

I nodded from behind my wall of hair and tried not to cry.

"Okay," she said, "you stick with me." She pulled me into the party, where we found a group of other models, including two who I knew from the European fashion shows. They all expressed their shock and dismay upon hearing what happened to me, and they tried to comfort me by telling me that after I had my plastic surgery I would be as beautiful as ever. They all recommended their plastic surgeons.

My left leg was starting to feel numb. Standing around in pumps had never been easy, but now the shoes were literally cutting off my circulation, and I didn't know how much longer I would last. I whispered to Amanda that I was in agony and she guided me over to a high stool at a little table. The other models crowded around me, forming a kind of privacy curtain.

"Go ahead," Amanda said, gesturing to my feet. "We've got you." I took off my left shoe and rubbed my toes and arch until I could feel the blood circulating again. Then I put the torture device back on and rested my foot at the base of the stool.

When I looked up again, all of the models had pivoted towards the bar and were staring in the direction of a tall, handsome man wearing an Armani suit.

"Who's that?" one of them said.

"Wow, now there's a man."

I looked to see what all the fuss was about, and spotted him. He was broad-shouldered and stood at least six-foot-three, and he had the chiseled features of a warrior. In fact, my first thought was that he looked like he stepped out of the Odyssey.

Given such a polished exterior, it was a little surprising to find him leaning against the bar, chatting with the bartender about baseball, instead of mingling with the rich and powerful guests who were filling up the penthouse.

As I stood up, I forgot about my throbbing feet and aching left leg.

"He really is beautiful," I said softly. No one heard me. They were all speculating on who he was, how much he was worth, and how to get him into bed, or into a life.

"He has to be someone important," one of them said.

"Just look at him. Every A-lister at this party is going out of their way to shake hands with him."

It was true. The man happily talking to the bartender had been approached several times by people who we were pretty sure we recognized.

Just then a woman who worked for Mr. Hess came over and reminded us to "work the party, please, singly or in pairs." Three of the girls smiled their goodbyes to me as they scattered to different parts of the room. Amanda leaned in and said, "I'll check on you later."

I was alone then, teetering closer to the bar, when the numbness returned. I knew I would have to sit down or lean against something before I fell. I was about to grasp the edge of a table when my left leg went totally numb and I started to tumble to the floor. As I did, time seemed to slow down, and suddenly I was being elevated by that Odyssean hero. The man in the Armani suit had caught me in midair and was now holding me in his arms.

I was stupefied as his dark eyes locked onto mine. Then I was suddenly terrified as I realized that my hair had fallen away from my left cheek. I steeled myself for a look of horror, but his expression only softened as he smiled at me and walked me over to an empty table.

"A little soon to be out in heels, don't you think?" he said, helping me into a chair.

I was so confused that I just gaped at him, and I'm sure I was blushing madly.

"I mean, it looks like you've got a way to go. I wouldn't recommend walking around in high heels until you're completely healed."

"Are you a doctor?" I asked.

"No, but I've had a lot of experience with field hospitals and seen a lot of very serious injuries, and sadly I can spot symptoms fairly accurately. It looks like you've suffered nerve damage on the left side, possibly from an attack."

I just stared at him, unable to speak again.

"What would you like to drink?"

"Water?"

"Water, certainly, but maybe something else, to take the edge off? That is, if you're not still on painkillers?"

"No, I'm not on painkillers," I said. "I'll have a glass of champagne, please." I looked up at him, favoring my right side. "And thank you so much for saving me."

"Best catch I've made in years," he said, as he headed over to the bar. He returned a few minutes later with a champagne, a glass of water, and a beer for himself. He put the water and the champagne in front of me and sat down across from me. I drank some of the water, then took a sip of champagne.

I was having trouble meeting his eyes. I felt bashful and self-conscious under his gaze. As inconspicuously as possible, I repositioned my hair to cover more of my left side.

He took a swig of beer and said, "If you lift your leg up, I'll gladly rub it for you. It could help get the circulation going."

"Don't you think that might seem a little strange?"

"What do I care what anybody in this room thinks? I didn't even want to come to this party, but I owed my agent a favor, so I came, and now I'm overjoyed I did."

"Why is that?"

"Because, silly, I got to meet you."

That strange little term of endearment — silly — hit me like a dart. Then, like magic, my left leg went up and he started to rub my foot, gently at first, then a little harder. It wasn't long before I felt the circulation return.

"Thank you so much," I said. "That feels much better."

He stopped rubbing my foot but held onto it, warming my skin with his enormous paw, and said, "You're welcome."

He gently lowered my foot to the floor and came back up again and seemed to be studying my face. I was blushing again when he reached across and carefully drew the wall of hair aside to reveal my ravaged cheek. I froze as he gently brushed the left side of my face with his hand, taking care to avoid the silver dressing. He looked at me and said, "Why do I feel like some cowardly bastard did this to you?"

I recoiled and looked down, and he pulled his hand away.

"Two cowardly bastards," I said, meeting his gaze. He looked back at me with so much compassion that a handful of tears sprang from my eyes and fell onto my lap.

Over the next ten minutes, I told him about that night when everything in my life changed. I talked about the two men who had been dressed so nicely that I didn't see them for the monsters they were. I confessed to feeling stupid. Naïve in the ways of the world.

I didn't tell him that I felt broken — that I sometimes dreamt of myself as a doll in pieces, scattered across a runway, amid a field of debris — suitcases, clothing, people, toys, all ruined. Beyond-Repair Barbie. Or the other dream where I'm falling from the sky. There are things I can't tell anyone. But I sensed that he understood, or could at least glimpse the tip of the iceberg. He stayed with me, and the two of us clung to the icy surface of my story, speaking of facts and circumstances, avoiding the depths.

"Have the police caught the bastards?"

"Not yet."

"Those punks are probably pretty confident by now that they've got away with this vicious crime," he said. "But with a little patience and focused diligence they will be caught, and they'll pay a high price." Something in his tone sent chills down my spine.

"How do you know they'll be caught?"

"Call it a hunch." He seemed lost in thought for a few moments, but then he rallied and said, "More champagne?"

"That would be wonderful." I watched him walk up to the bar and order two more drinks. When they arrived, he opened his wallet and took out three one-hundred-dollar bills and handed them to the bartender. The server looked surprised and tried to refuse, but my new friend insisted and said, "It was great talking baseball with you." Then he shook the man's hand and took the two drinks and brought them back to our table.

"So you like baseball?" I asked, and he looked at me curiously.

"I do. Beautiful sport," he said. "The stadiums, the fields, the smell of the grass, the fans, the pitcher/batter match-up ... It doesn't matter if it's the major leagues, minor leagues, the women's leagues, or the little leagues."

We stared at each other, smiling. I was the one to break the tension.

"I used to love the Yankees when I was growing up, but I think it had a lot to do with my crush on Derek Jeter."

"A lot of girls had a crush on Mr. Jeter, but I have a feeling that if he'd met you, you would have risen to the top of his fan club pretty quickly." I laughed but had nothing to add, and I was grateful when he kept talking.

"He was great ballplayer. Smart, very clutch. It would have been nice if he'd been voted unanimously into the Hall of Fame like his teammate Mariano Rivera." When I shrugged, he said, "Maybe one day, we can go to a game together ... would you like that? I'll see when the Yankees are in town."

"I would love that," I said.

"Great! Then it's a date?"

"It's a date."

"Just one thing," he said, very Columbo-like. "You're not married or dating someone at this time, are you?"

"I am ... not," I said, then felt suddenly compelled to explain. "I never had time, but now I have plenty of time. Are you married or dating...?"

He hesitated, then said, "No."

He looked at his watch and I asked, "Do you need to go?"

"Not just yet, but I've gotten into this new ritual that's really helping..." He seemed to want to explain, but let it drop, and asked, "Did you drive here?"

"No, I took a taxi."

"Well, if you like I can drive you home."

I'm not sure how long I stood there, or whether I spoke.

"Oh, I am such an idiot," he finally said. "Of course, you can't be in a car with a strange man whom you've just met." I looked at him gratefully and he crossed his arms and said, "What should we do? What if I put you in a taxi and drive behind you? I just want to make sure you get home safely."

I looked deeply into his eyes, and saw something most of us only see once, at most twice, in our lifetime. I saw it, I accepted it, and I made a decision.

"I would love for you to drive me home. Thank you."

He held my gaze to make sure I meant it. Seeing that I did, he beamed at me and said, "Fantastic," then excused himself and went over to his friend to say goodbye. When he walked back to our table, I was starting to put on my high heels.

"Oh, no you don't," he said. "They'll only re-aggravate your leg." He took them from me and held them by the straps as we walked out the door, with him turning to wave at the bartender one last time, and took the elevator down to the basement and the valet counter.

A red Tahoe Chevy pulled up and the valet opened the door to the SUV for me as my new friend stepped behind me and said, "Let me help you. That's one big step." He placed my shoes on the roof. Then he lifted me up, as if I weighed as much as a paper bag, and placed me in the front passenger's seat. He reached over and put on my seatbelt and said, "Comfortable?"

"Very. Are you going to let the wind take my shoes?"

He smiled and reached up and grabbed my high heels from the roof and handed them to me. Then he paid the valet and got into the driver's seat. As we drove out of the garage, he asked, "Where to?"

"Hollywood. Not the nice part, but it was all I could afford…"

"I understand. You been through a lot, and to bounce back like you have says a lot about you."

"I don't know about that. I seem to spend most of my time crying."

"I get that," he said — not trying to fix me, just witnessing. I was so moved by his calm support that I decided to share my recent decision. I suppose I wanted to seem less hopeless.

"But all that's about to change," I said. "I've decided to start college."

"College!"

"That's right. Before I took an unexpected detour into modeling, I was accepted at several prestigious universities, in some cases with full scholarships … Yale, Fordham, USC."

"Wow!"

"I always saw myself as a professor, writing books and papers, going to conferences, teaching. Now I think it's time to start on that original plan."

"That sounds fabulous. Who are some of your favorite writers?"

"Ooh, that's tough. For sure the Brontë sisters. Jane Austen. Dostoevsky. Joyce, and, naturally, Byron."

He laughed and said, "Naturally," and I blushed, wondering if I'd sounded pompous.

"You read those authors in high school?" Nothing in his tone suggested that he was threatened or mocking me.

"I did. I had some great teachers."

"Well, you just named some of my favorite authors."

"Who's your all-time favorite?" I asked. Just then, we heard a police siren, and he pushed a button that locked all of the SUV's doors. In an instant, I was transported back to the bloody mayhem of that night, when the limo driver did the same thing. The skin of my neck was pulsing from a blood rush as I listened to him list his favorite authors. His voice seemed to be coming at me from the other end of a long tunnel, and only gradually did it begin to sound normal again.

"…Conrad, followed very closely by Byron, Dante, and Dostoevsky. I always carry a copy of *Heart of Darkness* with me," he was saying, when I could hear him again. "The greatest one hundred pages of literature I've ever read." While we sat at a red light, he reached into his inside coat pocket and pulled out a copy of Conrad's book and handed it to me. My hands were shaking as I accepted it and looked at the worn cover.

"Is this the first copy you ever bought?" I managed to ask.

"Yes, nearly fifteen years ago."

I flipped through the pages and glanced down at the words, which were dimly illuminated by the glow of the streetlights through the windows. I suddenly felt like I was swimming in Conrad's language.

"What do you love about the book?" I asked.

"Mostly his honesty, and the strength of his descriptions. His unpacking of the colonial project — the way he analyzes the manipulation and enslavement of an entire race of people."

"When you put it in those terms, I feel like I should try to read it tonight."

"Yes," he said with a laugh, "get cracking."

I asked, "Can I tell you something?"

"Of course."

"Nothing to do with literature or colonialism, but I feel you should know that every model at that party was drooling over you." He shot me a look of pure skepticism.

"It's true," I continued. "I was standing with them, and they all wanted to know about the mysterious man in the Armani suit, standing at the bar, talking to the bartender."

He laughed and said, "Well then, didn't I get lucky?"

"How do you figure?" In the past, I might have been fishing for a compliment. Now, with my face the way it was, it was a sincere question.

"Easy. I got the best one, and she fell right into my arms."

"Wow," I said, genuinely perplexed.

"What brought you to the party?" he asked.

"The promise of one last payday, before my services are no longer required."

"Your services?"

"As a model on the party circuit," I said. "Mr. Hess and his staff always have models on hand for parties like that one. They want to make sure there's enough eye candy in the room."

"And it pays enough to justify coming out?"

"Two thousand, just for roaming around the room, making the VIPs feel special. Three thousand more if things go a little further."

"Further?"

"If the eye candy turns into … mouth candy."

"Ah," he said, looking disturbed. "What a system."

"I only showed up so I would receive the two thousand. I really need the money."

"I understand," he said, gripping the steering wheel and staring straight ahead.

He said nothing for a few moments, and I looked at him nervously.

"I hope you don't think I'm here with you because I want to make the extra money," I said.

"That didn't even cross my mind," he said.

"Good."

"But I do have a favor to ask."

"What's that?"

"That when you receive that check for two or possibly five thousand dollars, depending on what Mr. Hess thinks we've been up to, that you'll tear it up and send it back."

"You want me to tear up his check?"

"Yes, because no young lady I plan on dating and one day hopefully marrying will ever accept money from a punk-ass pimp like Mr. Hess."

I'm pretty sure I was staring at him with my mouth open when the GPS told him to turn left. As he did, we could hear what sounded like gunfire. He flinched, but recovered quickly, and after a few more minutes of driving in silence he pulled up near my building. I pointed at the eight-story concrete block and said, "Home sweet home."

He found a spot across from my building and parked. I had unbuckled my seatbelt and was starting to put on my high heels when he opened the driver's side door for me and again took the shoes out of my hands.

I looked at him and said, "Surely you don't expect me to walk barefoot from here up to my apartment."

"Of course, not," he said. "May I?" When I nodded, he leaned in and slipped one arm under my knees and worked the other arm behind my back. Then, while dangling the shoes from one finger, he lifted me up and carried me across the street, into the building, through the trash-strewn foyer, past the dented mailboxes and a drunk guy sleeping on the floor next to the elevator, and over to the stairs, which he took instead of the elevator. As he carried me up to my fourth-floor apartment, I stared at him, not speaking except to quietly answer his questions about which way to turn and where to stop. He wasn't even winded when he gently put me down in front of my door. I opened it and invited him in, and he followed me into my dumpy apartment and put the heels on the floor next to a grate.

As we stood in the foyer, he looked around, and I fought off the urge to apologize for the state of the place. There were boxes here and there, and it was sparsely furnished, with a couch and single chair with wooden arms. He pointed to a hole in the wall next to a light switch.

"Looks like someone decided to redecorate with their fist," he said.

"Looks like it. Can I offer you a beer?"

"I'd love one, thank you." I took two steps into the kitchen and grabbed one of three beers I had in the refrigerator.

When I returned he was facing the only thing I had already set up — an old bookcase that I had wedged between two small windows facing the street. He spun around and I could see that he was holding my copy of Byron's collected works.

"Good choice," I said, and held out the beer. He smiled at me as he slid the book back onto its shelf and took the bottle.

"She walks in beauty, like the night, *and* she keeps beer in the fridge. Perfection."

I laughed and said, "This is strange, but I don't even know your name."

"Nick, or Nicky. Whatever you prefer."

I held out my hand and said, "Well Nick or Nicky, I'm Alicia." He repeated my name as though it pleased him, and we shook hands with comical stiffness. Then I said, "Do you mind if I run to the bedroom and get out of these clothes and into something more comfortable?"

"Of course not."

I turned toward the bedroom and then quickly turned around and asked, "You're not going to run away, are you?"

"No. I might even have another beer if you don't mind?"

"Help yourself," I said, and disappeared into the bedroom.

Suddenly I began to worry that he thought I meant I was going to put on lingerie, or a silk bathrobe with nothing on underneath. How could I be so stupid? Everyone knows that if you say you're going to "slip into something more comfortable," you mean something sexy. I considered going back out in my party clothes to set the record straight, but that could only make things more awkward. I could only hope that he wasn't out there getting undressed.

Then a worse thought occurred to me. What if this was all a big joke? What if I got out there and found him on the phone with a friend, laughing and whispering about the poor, sad, hideous ex-model who actually thought he wanted to date her, let alone marry her? Who states his intention to marry a girl within an hour of meeting her?

I leaned into the mirror and told myself to get a grip. "Everything will be fine," I told my reflection. Then I struggled out of my dress, put on a comfortable jumpsuit, and fixed my hair, trying to cover up the left side of my face as much as possible, without seeming too obvious.

When I walked back into the living room, I found him standing beside the bookcase again, engrossed in a book.

"What are you reading now?" He held up a copy of Toni Morrison's *Beloved.*

"Fantastic book," I said. "I can't believe I left her off my list earlier. I guess I went for the classics, but her work is amazing."

"So I've heard. Would you mind if I borrowed a few of her books from you?"

"Take all you want. Would you like another beer?"

"No thank you. Alicia, do have a suitcase?"

"Yes. Why?"

"Because you're not spending another night in this place. It's not safe. I've heard at least three rounds of gunfire since we got here."

"Gunfire," I repeated softly, not understanding what he was proposing.

"Pack at least three days of clothes, medications, and any other necessities."

"Why? Where are we going?"

"Malibu."

"What's in Malibu?"

"My house. I have so many rooms, I haven't even been in all of them. You can have your own suite. We just need to get you out of here."

"Are you serious?"

"Dead serious. In a couple of days, we can send my favorite movers here to pack up the rest of your stuff and bring it to the house. Is that okay with you?"

"Is it okay with me?" I said, staring at him. "Yes, I think I can live with that ... Nick or Nicky. Saint Nick? That will be fine."

# CHAPTER SIX

Nick placed my suitcase in the back seat, pulled out of the parking spot, and drove west and onto the highway. I started to babble about my job interview at the supermarket.

"It's in two days," I said. "How am I going to get back for that?"

"You're not."

"I'm not?"

"Let's look at the big picture for a minute. I can see you as many things — a brilliant professor, researcher, fashion model, and novelist, but I just don't see you as a cashier. Nothing against cashiers, I just don't see you as one."

"No?"

"Nope. I might not be right about many things, but this one I'm fairly certain about."

I sat in silence for a while, wondering how any of this could be happening. Finally, I said, "I don't know how to repay you for all of this."

"I don't expect you to repay me for anything."

I couldn't help myself. I muttered under my breath, "Nothing's free." Nick looked at me and I could tell he was surprised.

After a while he said, "May I ask you a question?" I nodded. "In your entire life, has anyone loved you, helped you, or cared for you without expecting something in return?"

I thought about it for quite a while and said, "No, at least no one I can think of."

"Not your parents or siblings?"

"Especially not them."

He looked at me, surprised, and said, "I'm sorry to hear that."

I shrugged.

"Well, things are about to change. All I ask is that you make your bed, clean up after yourself, and pursue whatever dreams you have."

"You're going to support me while I pursue my dreams?"

"That's the idea."

"And I just need to make my bed and clean up after myself?"

"Yes."

"Why?"

"Let's just say I have a good feeling about you. I know what you've been through, and I'd like to help get you back on your feet." Then he had a bright idea. "Think of it as an investment. I'm investing in Alicia 2.0. Getting in on the ground floor."

I laughed, and suddenly an image flashed across my mind of the two of us at the altar, dressed in our finest, ready for our happily ever after. I had to admit, this man was starting to have a powerful hold on me, and I hadn't even known him for a whole night.

As he drove, I started to relax. We chatted about the house, and he tried to prepare me for the lack of staff at his large estate. I learned that he didn't have any housekeepers working for him. "No maids or cooks," he said, "but I do have an amazing gardener who works miracles with the landscaping."

I asked him where he was from, and at first he laughed and said, "I don't know," and then he tried to explain.

"My father was a general in the Air Force, and for the first twelve years of my life we were constantly moving around … Germany, Japan, the Philippines, Qatar, Britain, and finally Washington D.C., where he was appointed to the Joint Chiefs of Staff."

"That had to be exciting, living in all those different countries."

"You'd think so, but it really wasn't. The schools I went to were all on U.S. bases, and the children were all American, so it was like being in a little America, wherever we were. I never got to meet the local kids or go to a local school."

"That does sound isolating."

"It was. And any friends I made I was saying goodbye to in a year or two."

Without prompting, he told me a bunch of things about his mother that had me sensing that there were issues there.

"She was much younger than my father, and she was always going to this party or that party, or throwing one of her own, always with the other military wives. The only time I remember venturing out into any of these countries was when we lived in Great Britain. Maybe because we spoke the same language, my mother felt more comfortable. We would go shopping and eat in restaurants quite often."

"Did things change when you moved to D.C.?"

"Somewhat. I went to the same school, grades nine through twelve, so I got to keep the friends I made a little longer."

"Was your father strict, like the military dads you see in the movies?"

"Not especially. Both my parents were more absent than strict. Let's just say that if I'd gone missing for a few days, I'm not sure either of them would have noticed."

"That's so sad."

"I guess so, yes. But I had two incredible nannies who were with me constantly — Ginevra and Francesca, sisters, from Italy, who I'm in touch with all the time, still. My parents were smart enough to hire them to raise me. And things did change a bit with my mother and father once I was in high school and we were back in the US. They might have noticed if I went missing."

"Why? What was happening?"

"I think they were having problems with their marriage."

"Ah."

"I remember walking past my father's study in freshman year, and I could swear I heard him crying. The door was shut, and my mother was out.

"The next day, I walked past his study again and I heard the same thing. I was ready to knock on the door and ask if everything was okay, but I knew that would be useless. He would have not answered or told me to go away."

"Poor man," I said. "It's hard to imagine a senior military officer crying like that."

"I know, right? He was basically Air Force royalty, but he was miserable."

"So sad."

"Then he started acting differently. I remember him waking me up at six in the morning on a Sunday and asking me to go to mass with him. Of course, I said yes. I got dressed, and we drove to a nearby Catholic church. Before this, I never even remembered my father mentioning religion.

"We stayed for the mass, and as we were driving back to the house he suddenly got very talkative. He asked me if I was happy at my new school. I said yes, and he went on this tangent where he tried to warn me off a career in the military. He said I could expect nonstop heartbreak and tough decisions that would haunt me for the rest of my life. He parked in front of the house, and I got out. He told me he had to go to the office to catch up on some work. As I was walking away, he called out to me and said he loved me. I told him I loved him too."

"Did he go to his office?"

"No. He went to Andrews Air Force Base in Prince George County, Maryland. He told the director he was there to check out a new fighter jet. He was nearly sixty-five years old and had no business flying a fighter jet. It had already been on several test flights and performed perfectly, but what was the director going to tell the Chief of Staff of the Air Force, 'No, sir, you're too old to take this baby up?'"

"He couldn't say a thing. He was outranked," I offered.

"Exactly. My father took the plane up, and halfway over the Potomac River his plane did a nosedive into the water. I knew it was a suicide and the Air Force knew it too, but the Air Force protects its men. Especially a man like my father, who fought in two wars and received every medal imaginable. The final report stated that there was a malfunction in the computer system that caused the jet to nosedive."

"My God, that had to be devastating for you."

"It should have been, but I really didn't know the man. My father was basically a stranger. The only time I remember him telling me he loved me was the day he died."

"How did it affect your mother?"

"It's hard to say. She played the grieving wife to perfection, but I've never been able to say for a fact that she's able to distinguish real life from fantasy."

"Did she remarry?"

"Yup. About a year after my father died, she remarried a high-ranking guy in the Navy."

"That was quick."

"It was. But I was used to her doing off-the-wall stuff," he said. "My parents gave me all of the essentials a child could hope for — food, clothing, shelter, an education — but little to no affection or love. They were probably never meant to be parents."

"Well, I, for one, am overjoyed they had you," I said as he smiled appreciatively. "Do you keep in touch with your mom?"

"Yes, actually, our relationship has improved quite a bit. We actually say 'I love you' on a regular basis, now. Can you believe that?"

"Amazing."

He paused and looked at me and I asked, "What's wrong?"

"I was just admiring how beautiful you are."

"Are you sure your eyesight is okay?"

"Quite sure. The more I look at you, the more beautiful you get."

"Thank you," I said, and as I blushed, I felt a stinging sensation in the wound, and my heart sank. How long before this man came to his senses and lost all interest in me?

I forced myself to sound upbeat, and said, "It's great that you're getting along with your mother so well now."

"It is. And she's been very generous, especially since my father died."

"How do you mean?"

"My father left her a big nest egg, and she would always offer me large sums of money, but I never took it, even though she did pay for the one year of college I attended."

"What was your major?"

"Journalism."

"And why only one year?"

"Because I got a job with a small media company that was looking for an assistant for the one wartime journalist they had on staff, and I realized that I could learn by doing."

"Did you work in war zones?"

"I did. For ten years."

"That's a long time."

"It was. My first assignment as an assistant was in Iraq in 2007. Have you heard of the 'surge?'" I shook my head and he said, "President Bush had just increased the number of combat troops by twenty thousand, and the fighting was intense. On my third day there, the journalist I was working for was killed. The company needed someone on the ground right away, so they gave me a chance, and I became their war correspondent.

"I spent the entire year covering the surge. The campaign was hailed as a success, but there were heavy civilian causalities ... probably triple the number of American causalities and double the number of Muslim insurgents lost. It was literally door-to-door combat.

"After a year, I came back to the States and received the Pulitzer in journalism for my coverage of the war. Someone at the company had submitted my stories and paid the entry fee without my knowing. I was shocked to win, and I sent the fifteen-thousand-dollar prize money to my mother to put into a bank account for me, with her name also on the account in case I was killed. She told me I was slowly trying to kill *her* by doing this type of work. I was actually touched and shortly thereafter went back to Iraq for six more months.

"The fighting had drastically decreased, and now most of the causalties were from suicide bombings, booby traps, and sniper fire. When I went back to the States, I was hired by a major newspaper that not only paid more but also gave me much more protection."

"Was your mom pleased?"

"At first, yes. Less so when the paper sent me to Afghanistan."

"Oh dear."

"Yeah. It didn't help that I was in Helmand Province, where the worst fighting was taking place. I was bunkered down with U.S. marines and infantry, and never in my life was I so scared. It was like being on death's door every moment of your life. It was so bad, I sent most of my news crew home. It wasn't worth all our lives to try to get to the bottom of this story."

"That sounds absolutely terrifying."

"It was. The Taliban fighters would cross over from Pakistan and attack at any time, day or night. Then they'd cross back into Pakistan and our soldiers weren't allowed to pursue them. Pakistan's policy was that any incursion of NATO forces into their country would be seen as an attack on the people of Pakistan.

"What made it even worse were the opium farmers in the hills of Helmand province. They would pretend to be NATO's allies during the day, while secretly safeguarding Taliban fighters who attacked U.S. and NATO forces at night. It's no surprise that so many young service men and women who survived Helmand came home and committed suicide."

"Tragic."

"Utterly. And I benefitted from this mess. Back in Kabul, I learned I had won a second Pulitzer for my reporting on the fighting in Helmand."

"Two Pulitzers," I said. "My God."

He was silent for a long time and then I said hesitantly, "You sound like you feel guilty, but you were just doing your job." Nick shrugged.

"How could I not? Everyone else was dying or going mad and I won two major prizes, and money, for telling their stories." I watched the light from the highway move across his face in blocks as he drove.

"Did you ever contemplate suicide?"

He didn't answer, but said, "I jumped into another assignment. This time Syria. Just in time to see Bashar al-Assad and the Russians kill hundreds of thousands of innocent civilians and watch the United States turn its back on its most trusted ally in the region, the Kurds, so that Erdoğan of Turkey could slaughter thousands of them and claim they were terrorists.

"After that I went to Sudan, Yemen, and finally Crimea, where I was only walking along the beach, not even covering the war in the Donbas area, when I was arrested by the Russian separatists and thrown into a Russian jail for nine months and accused of being an American spy."

"This story gets crazier by the minute."

"I know. But at least I made the best of my time in that hell pit by writing two novels."

"Amazing. What are they about?"

"A newspaper reporter — a war correspondent — who ends up taking sides in the conflicts he's covering and helps the people fighting for democracy and freedom."

"Wait a minute. This is all sounding very familiar. Were they the two books about the guy—"

"The Jack Bell series. *Liberty Bell* and *Freedom Rings*."

"Those books did incredibly well, as I recall. Weren't they on the *New York Times* bestseller list for about a year each? No wonder you haven't been able to visit every room in your house yet."

Nick laughed and said, "The books did well, yes, but it was really the movies that pushed me into the one percent. Well, the movies, plus a sizeable inheritance from my father."

"Of course. Now I remember. I haven't seen the movies, or read the books, but I know a lot of people who love the franchise. Aren't they a bit like *Indiana Jones*, but with a heroic wartime reporter instead of an archeologist?"

"That's a very apt description, for someone who hasn't seen the movies."

"You know how these huge cultural events trickle down. You don't have to see the movies to know about them," I said, looking across at him. "I can't believe I'm sitting next to the author of the Jack Bell franchise."

"I sometimes can't believe I *am* that author. I'm still amazed at how the whole thing worked out. 'From gulag to gazillionaire' is how my friend and editor describes it — though gazillionaire is off by a few zeroes."

I laughed and asked, "He edited both books?"

"That's right. He's also the one who got the note from my agent about the party and asked me to go to it. He's a really good guy, and now I have him to thank for meeting you."

"I feel like I should send that man a fruit basket," I said, and Nick laughed. Then I added, "So the Russians just released you? No trial, no nothing?"

"Well, if not for my mother, I might still be there. She made it her mission to get my father's friends to petition the president and the Pentagon, who in turn petitioned the Russians, who let me go at a price."

"How many times were you shot, covering all this insanity?"

"What makes you think I was shot?"

"Because you favor your left side. I might not be a reporter, but as a model I'm very conscious of people's movements. You favor your left side the way I try to cover up my left side. So how many times?"

He stared at me. "Once in the thigh and once below my knee."

"And are you writing a sequel to your first two novels?"

"I'm just about finished with the third and final novel in the series."

"So not only are you a famous, award-winning journalist, but you're also a best-selling novelist and a Hollywood big shot."

"If you say so."

"I do," I said. "Was it worth it?"

"If you don't mind living with nightmares the rest of your life, I guess it was."

"Are they awful?"

"Pretty bad."

"I wonder if that's what your father was trying to warn you about, when he said all that stuff about living with haunting memories and regrets."

"You know, Alicia, I've thought about that a lot over the years. But there's a big difference between our jobs and responsibilities. My father not only fought in wars, but his decisions and the orders he gave were life-and-death choices. God only knows how many young men and women were killed or wounded because of his decisions. I think it was their faces, smiles, and laughter that haunted him.

"When I thought a situation was too dangerous and yet I wanted to report on it, I always had my crew stay back. If I was too stupid to ignore the warnings of the soldiers in the field, that was one thing, but I never put my crew in more danger than they signed up for."

"Was the story that important to you, or did you just have a death wish?" I asked hesitantly.

"It was the soldiers' stories and the unbearable conditions they were fighting under that I felt the world needed to know about. Just like it was the story of those poor civilians — children, elderly men, and women — who were killed indiscriminately that I felt the world needed to know about. It was never about me."

"I never said it was about you," I said as he turned into the driveway of his estate.

"Well then, I apologize for misunderstanding you."

# CHAPTER SEVEN

He parked adjacent to a beautiful garden filled with red and white roses and blue hydrangeas. Although it was night, I could see the colors clearly in the glow of the landscaping lights that spotlighted the plants closest to the front door. Nick opened the driver's side door for me and helped me down. When he saw me staring at the flowers, he said, "The gardener works miracles with these plants, especially when you consider that beneath the dirt it's all sand."

"It's beautiful. Do the colors represent the colors of our flag?"

"I imagine they do. It's a military house, through and through."

He explained that the U.S. military bought miles of land along the Pacific, right after World War II, and that they still have several bases right around Malibu. "All day and night, fighter jets take off and land. They move so fast that you're lucky to see them cross your field of vision. If not for the thunderclap sound they make, you might never know they're flying past."

Instead of going inside, we walked around the property and came to a patio table with matching chairs. He pulled out a chair for me and I sat down, even though I was freezing and just wanted to go inside. As soon as I had that thought, he took off his Armani sports jacket and draped it over my shoulders. I was swimming in it, but I warmed to the familiar feeling of a couture fabric against my skin. Nick sat down across from me as I looked out over the ocean and up at the stars and the half-moon "It's so beautiful here," I said, and immediately felt unoriginal.

"Yes, it is," he replied as I looked back at the house, which was really a mansion.

"I can't even imagine how much this place cost," I said in a light tone.

"How much do you think it cost?" he said.

"I have no idea … fifty million?"

"You're only off by forty-eight and a half million."

"So, a hundred million? My God, those novels and movie deals really paid off."

"They paid handsomely, but nowhere near the amount I would have had to put down as a down payment for a house like this. No, the house cost one and a half million."

"No way … you're joking."

"Would I joke with you, Alicia?"

"Yes, you would."

"Okay, maybe I would, but that's how much it really cost."

"How is that possible?"

"I got a call from my mother, who told me she was taking a million and a half dollars out of our joint account to buy a house for me in Malibu. I asked her if I should at least take a look at it first, but she replied, 'No, there's no time,' and she said, 'Believe me, the house and property are worth way over a hundred million dollars.'

"It turned out the house was owned by the Pentagon, and they were putting it up for auction. Her husband, my stepfather, arranged a sweetheart deal. We just had to come up with a million and a half dollars, that day, and the house would be mine. So my mother took a million and a half dollars out of the bank and gave it to him. He gave it to the bursar lady at the Pentagon, and a few hours later I received a bunch of documents and a non-disclosure agreement by fax. I signed and returned everything, and the following morning, I received the deed to a house I hadn't yet seen."

"Incredible."

"Yeah, I wondered if it was too good to be true. So I asked my mother if this was all legal. She yelled through the phone, 'Your father gave his life for this country. I'll be damned if I'm going to watch some spoiled billionaire who never sacrificed a moment of his time for his country walk in and buy that house for ten million.' Then she congratulated me on my new home and informed me that because she brokered the deal, I should expect her to come visit anytime she likes and stay as long as she wants."

"How do you feel about that?"

"Well, for over ten years she was worried sick about me while I was working overseas. So I figure she's earned the right to come and visit whenever she wants."

"Sounds fair."

"She said she's very proud of all my accomplishments, but that none of them was worth losing me over. So if I ever get an inkling to go back to my old job, she'll have me arrested for espionage. Then she said, 'Love you!' and hung up."

He looked at his watch and said, "Time for my little ritual. Care to join me?"

"I think I'm going to have to pass."

"You're freezing, aren't you? Freezing and bored. Sorry."

"Don't be silly. I want to hear the rest of this one because I'm certain there's a lot more to it than what you've just told me."

"See? Not only are you smart and beautiful, with great taste in literature, but you're also very perceptive."

I laughed and said, "And you really know how to charm the pants off a lady."

He grinned and helped me up and we walked into the foyer of his enormous home. I could see right away that it was a renovated Victorian, with some modern touches, like pot lights combined with sconces. Oddly, I couldn't see a stick of furniture anywhere. I looked at him and asked, "How long have you been living here?"

"Nine months."

"Are you a minimalist or have you been too busy furnishing other parts of this beautiful mansion?"

"You know, I never bothered to think about furniture. When my mother shows up, she'll put her stamp on it." He turned to me. "Would you like to pick out your room before I take off for forty-five minutes?"

"Is it okay if I just stay down here and wait for you to come back?"

"Absolutely. Let me just go change and find you something to sit on." He ran up the winding staircase and in about two minutes he reappeared wearing a beat-up jogging suit and carrying a blanket and a folding chair. He opened the chair, I sat down, and he was out the door.

I took in the massive front hall, with its high ceilings and intricate plaster moldings, until the sheer scale of the space left me feeling dizzy. I closed my eyes and waited for the vertigo to pass. As the room slowed to a stop, I tried to think. I couldn't help asking the most basic of questions, even though they seemed both ungrateful and necessary. Questions like, Who is this man, and how did I end up here? I thought about the other models at the party. Any one of them would kill to be in my place. All of those beautiful women, salivating over this man, and who does he take home with him? The broken Barbie with the hole in her face. It made no sense.

I got up from the chair and walked out onto the patio. Nick was there, a supine figure lying on a blanket, contemplating the stars and the universe. Suddenly he stood up, folded his blanket, and walked back toward the house. I got so excited at the thought of seeing him after he'd been gone a whole forty-five minutes that I started feeling lightheaded again, and after about thirty seconds, my world went blank. The last thing I remembered was him walking toward me, smiling, with his hand raised in a gesture of greeting.

# CHAPTER EIGHT

I woke up in an incredibly comfortable bed, under a duvet that reached up to my chin. My first thought was: *This man may not own any chairs, tables, or couches, but he sure knows how to pick a mattress.* High above the bed, a ceiling fan with long, wooden blades rotated slowly, sending cool air down to me. I could hear and smell the ocean, and when I turned toward the sound, I saw Nick sitting in the folding chair, next to a large window, reading Toni Morrison's novel, *Jazz*.

"What happened?" I asked.

"You fainted."

"Oh."

"I thought about calling a doctor, but you were breathing normally, and your vitals were perfect, so I carried you up here and put you in bed."

"How long have you been watching over me?"

"Not sure. Long enough to finish *Beloved* and most of *Jazz*. What an amazing writer. You have great taste, my beautiful Alicia. She reminds me of Conrad, with a touch of early Capote, and yet her style is uniquely her own."

"Thank you," I said, still dazed. He stood up and felt my forehead with the back of his hand. Then he placed his index and middle fingers on my wrist to check my pulse.

"All normal, I'm glad to report."

"Do you have a medical degree, along with everything else?"

"No, but I learned some basics in the field."

"Handy. So you're not my doctor, but you definitely seem like my guardian angel."

"That's right!" he said. "I'm your guardian angel. Don't you think we all need one?"

"Probably."

"Definitely."

I pulled myself up and sank into the pillows. "Who's your guardian angel?"

"As hard as it is to believe, especially given how she behaved when I was growing up, I'd have to say my mother."

"Not your nannies? What were their names?"

"Ginevra and Francesca. They come in a close second. If God ever made individuals in his own image, it's those two sisters. They're perfect in every way. They moved back to Italy when I went off to college, but we still talk every week."

I should have said "I'd love to meet them someday," but a little jealous voice in my head won over, and I said, "Maybe, one day you'll see me as a guardian angel." Nick didn't flinch.

"That would be great. Another guardian angel … what could be better?" He lowered his face and kissed me on the forehead. Then our eyes met and we started kissing passionately, until he pulled away, saying, "You need rest."

"Oh no I don't," I said, pulling him back and throwing my arms around his neck. For the first time since the attack, I actually wanted a man to touch me, and I wasn't thinking about the left side of my face. Not once. And from the way he looked at me and stroked my hair and dove at my mouth with his, he didn't seem to be thinking about it either. If this was a dream, I prayed that instead of waking up I would simply be allowed to die, blissfully, and stay in this warm bed, with this beautiful man, until the end of time.

# CHAPTER NINE

After we cleaned up, we ordered lunch from a nearby Greek place and ate our souvlaki over a delicious bottle of wine — what Nick called "a crisp dry Riesling," with a laugh at himself for that mildly pretentious description.

"Hey," I said, "as long as you don't start describing its nose, we're alright."

"Now you've asked for it," he laughed, launching into an impersonation of the world's snootiest sommelier. I can't remember all of it —something about jasmine and apricot, with "hints of honeycomb and petroleum wax." I was still laughing when I took the plate out of his hands and went to submerge it in his enormous double sink.

"Oh no you don't," he said, pushing me aside with a hip check and handing me a dish towel. "I'll wash." While I dried the dishes and put them on the marble island, I asked him about the mansion's history, and whether they used to do a lot of entertaining.

"Yes, and it's quite a story. Why don't we open another bottle of wine and I can tell you all about it?"

"Are you trying to get me drunk and take advantage of me?"

"I would never take advantage of you. But if we had a mutual understanding, I would have no problem living up to that understanding."

"You little pig," I said, as I slapped him with the dishcloth.

"Now was that nice?"

"Probably not, but you deserved it."

He laughed as he opened another bottle and re-filled our glasses, and then we went outside and sat on the patio. I stayed in the shade because I had been told to avoid the sun as much as possible until I had the surgery.

As we settled into his outdoor couch, Nick reached across and touched his wine glass to mine. "To fateful meetings at terrible parties," he said, with a smile that made me feel weak at the knees again, even though I was sitting down.

"I'll drink to that," I said, gulping audibly on a tiny sip.

"So you wanted to know about the history of this place."

"Sure. Hit me."

"Remember I told you this stretch of property was purchased by the military right after the end of World War Two?" I nodded, and he said, "Well, the mansion was built by military contractors, and the owners were never disclosed, not even in the public registry.

"At the time, the Air Force, the Navy, and the Army owned and operated more property in the state than any private organization or corporation, and they probably had as many civilian employees as any business outside of the movie industry. From San Diego straight up the coast, one was never very far from a military base. The area was perfect for marine landings, navy maneuvers, tests flights, pilot training, and so forth."

"So the military owned the house, but it was kept a secret?"

"That's right."

"And who lived here?"

"Military brass and their families. There would be one top commander from the Air Force, Navy, Army, and the Marines living here at all times, usually with their spouses and kids. Supposedly each commander was a strategic wizard, but after reading their position papers and analysis of potential threats I would swear they were all smoking opium. At least once a month, top-ranking military leaders from around the world, NATO members, Canadians, and Australians, would gather for weekend festivities, which seemed to include everything except constructive military planning."

"So the families would all live here at the same time, and they were basically using it as party central, while pretending to get work done?"

"Exactly. I'm told by a reliable source that there was a lot of drinking and drug use, and that they used to hold orgies down by the waters' edge … though how they managed that with families around I have no idea."

"When there's a will, there's a way. They probably sent the wives and the kids away so they could play."

"Something like that. And this was all happening on the taxpayer's dime."

"Wild. I wonder how much of our money they blew."

"It had to be a huge sum. There were maids, servants, cooks, chauffeurs, tutors for the children, repairs to the property, and so on. But the Pentagon's budget is so huge that it wouldn't have made a dent."

"How do you think they kept it a secret?"

"The mansion was so isolated that unless they were shooting off cannons it would be hard to hear what was going on behind closed doors, or by the pool, or on the beach. And apart from the fact that there were armed guards in civilian clothes stationed all around the property, there was no indication that the U.S. military owned the mansion. Guests were told never to wear military uniforms.

"Then out of the blue, after some seventy years, a couple of investigative journalists paid off the guards, and as luck would have it, it was on a weekend where the festivities were going full tilt. Bottles of expensive champagne were being passed around like beers. Scantily clad girls were sitting on the laps of middle-aged military men from around the world. People were having sex down on the beach. The journalists took hundreds of photos, and overheard conversations that only military personnel would be taking part in.

"The journalists thought they had a major scoop, and it should have been one. But there was little outrage, even from liberal and progressive citizens of Malibu, and the story just died."

"Why do you think that is?"

"Because the military and the companies and contractors they do business with make up so much of the California economy that nobody wanted to ruffle any feathers. It wasn't until several years later when a few senators discussed the mansion during closed-door meetings with top Pentagon officials that anything was done. The tenants at the time were evicted, along with most of the staff, except for a few housekeepers and the gardener. The auction wasn't advertised, and my bid went in before a notice went out to potential buyers. It was quickly accepted, and they could finally wash their hands of the property and all it represented."

"The Pentagon did that even though they could have made fifty million easy from any number of billionaires or real estate moguls?"

"Fifty million dollars might sound like a lot to us, but to the Pentagon, it's a pittance."

"Oh, there's a lot more to this story. Could I read the papers your mother sent you?"

"No, Alicia. I've already told you too much. The more you know, the more danger you could be in, and I would never put you in a situation like that. Besides, I burned the papers."

I smiled and shook my head. It was Nick who broke the silence when he said, "How about a tour? I wasn't joking when I said I hadn't seen most of this house."

"Let's go, then," I said. "We can see them together."

# CHAPTER TEN

The tour opened in a dimly lit wine cellar. Whereas the rest of the mansion seemed modernized, the wine cellar looked like it was in its original state, apart from a temperature-control system blinking away in a corner. The air was cool and dry and smelled faintly of cedar and vanilla.

Nick held my hand and pointed a flashlight at a section of very old, very expensive red wines. As I dropped his hand and wandered ahead of him, I could tell from my shadow that Nick had lowered the flashlight and was pointing it directly at my backside. I turned and stopped.

"Inspecting the merchandise?"

"Mmm-hmm," he admitted cheerfully.

"Why do I suddenly feel like a bottle of wine that you're considering adding to your collection?" Then I had a bizarre thought. "You don't have a supermodel cellar, do you? Are we going to turn a corner and come across a room filled with models, organized by type and year?"

He pulled back and looked at me intently. "Alicia, wow. That's dark! And no. You're the only supermodel I have any interest in."

I held his gaze and finally hooked my arm around his as we ambled along the wall of crates. When we arrived at a section of Argentinian reds, he leaned in and whispered, "I was really just thinking that you have a world-class butt."

"Well, if anybody should know, it's you. That was some marathon we had this morning."

He laughed as we came to the end of the cellar. As I was about to turn around, he backed me slowly against the wall and held his mouth so close to mine that I could feel the warmth of his breath on my face. He hovered there, just out of reach, until I lunged across and kissed him, and he gathered me in his arms and kissed me back. When we came up for air, I could feel a lump in my throat as I fought back tears. Even I didn't understand why I was so close to crying. We walked with our fingers interlaced until he stopped to look at me.

"What's wrong?" he asked.

"Nothing, really. It's just—"

"Was it the butt comment? I knew it—"

"No! It's fine. I love that you love my butt."

He smiled. "Then what?"

I didn't know how to answer him, but I tried. "It's just … yesterday, I was sitting on that crappy couch in my apartment, crying like a child. Now I'm here…" I gestured around wordlessly. He nodded and loosened his grip on my arms, and I saw him go somewhere else in his mind. When he finally spoke, it was as if he was tuning in from far away.

"Yes, it's amazing how things can change so drastically from moment to moment."

"Please, don't let this be just a dream, a moment in our lives," I said.

He looked into my eyes and said, "It's not. It's already much more than that."

***

The tour continued upstairs, with Nick announcing that we needed to decide which room would be my bedroom.

"I thought I already had a bedroom," I said, referring to the upstairs room where I'd slept the night before. I was already partial to that room, since it was the room where we first ripped each other's clothes off and consummated this speeding train of a relationship.

"We can't make that your bedroom," Nick said. "I'd be worried sick every time you went up or down the stairs alone. I wasn't thinking clearly last night when I brought you up there."

"I don't understand. Walking up and down stairs would be good exercise."

"True, as long as I'm there if your leg goes limp. I've seen plenty of injuries like yours. It takes months of exercising and massages to safely train your leg to function the way it did before those sons-of-bitches did what they did to you."

"I see," I said. "So where am I going to sleep?"

"On the first floor. You choose."

"Are any of the rooms big enough for two?"

"Of course. Why would you ask?"

"Oh, I don't know, maybe in the hope that my room might also be your room."

"I would love nothing more, but that's totally up to you."

I guided him over to a wall and started to kiss him and tug at the waist of his pants. "Does this answer your question?"

"Mmm-hmm," he said. He returned my kiss, but then gently withdrew and took my hand and pulled me along the hallway. He was holding my hand in silence when we reached the first bedroom door.

I pointed to it. "That one."

"You haven't even seen it."

"Is there a bed?"

He laughed. "I think so."

"We'd better check."

Inside the room, like a big nugget of gold, was a king-size bed. I pulled him over to it and playfully pushed him onto the mattress, which was just as plush and comfortable as the other one. Our clothes flew off, and so began another marathon session of love making. He might have been a little slow at picking up the signals I was giving off, but once we got started, he was like a true Olympian.

As we lay back on the pillows, recovering, Nick looked at me and said, "If we keep falling into bed, this tour is going to take a very long time."

"It can take all year for all I care. I think we need to test out every bed in the house."

"Roger that."

For the second time in just a few hours, we took showers and put on clean clothes. I told him I was running low on shirts and asked to borrow one of his. He walked into another room and came back with three dress shirts. I could see right away that they were of the highest quality, and when I peeked at the labels,

I saw the names of three menswear designers known for their exquisite craftmanship: Luigi Borrelli, Ermenegildo Zegna, and Battistoni.

"My God, you have expensive taste," I said.

"What are you talking about? I didn't buy these. My mother sent them to me to wear to important meetings or parties ...like the one where I met the most perfect girl in the world."

"The fabrics are incredible." I touched the sleeve of the Borrelli. It was as soft as the inside of a lamb's ear.

"You can have all three. I have a closet full of them."

I turned around and took off my bra, then reached down and picked up the white Luigi Borrelli and slowly, reverently, slipped it on. I might be five-foot-ten, but in this shirt, I was swimming, and yet it felt perfect. I buttoned it up to just below my cleavage, taking a cue from the many actresses and models I'd seen wearing men's shirts in movies and fashion magazines. I turned and asked, "So?"

I guess I looked pretty good, because he stared at me like he'd just been struck with a frying pan. What is it about women in men's dress shirts? I think of Audrey Hepburn in *Breakfast at Tiffany's*, or Jane Fonda in *Barefoot in the Park*. Instant aphrodisiac. Nick walked over and ran one finger from the base of my throat down to a spot between my breasts. And while I really wanted to get him back into bed again, I thought I'd better restrain myself, so I gently took hold of his finger and led him out of the room.

"Could it be time for food?" I asked.

"Mmm, I suppose."

We ordered Chinese for dinner. I would have been happy to cook something, but all he had in his huge, commercial refrigerator was Budweiser beer, peanut butter and jelly, and sliced white bread. I was ready to ask him if he was waiting for his mother to drop by with some groceries, but I kept the thought to myself.

When the food arrived, Nick chatted with the delivery person for nearly fifteen minutes. When he finally placed the order on the kitchen counter, I asked, "A friend of yours?"

"Yes, a wonderful gentleman, Mr. Wang. He left Hong Kong with his uncle over twenty years ago, just before the British handed it over to China. He was just bringing me up to date on his efforts to get the rest of his family to join him in the US."

"Is he having a lot of trouble?"

"Yes. The last five years have been rough. The Chinese government in Beijing has brutally cracked down on the citizens of Hong Kong, and one of his cousins joined the protests, so there have been some consequences for the family. Mr. Wang has been trying to get his family approved to join him here for years, with no success."

"Is it China or the US that's the problem?"

"From what I understand, it's not so much the Chinese government at this point as it is the lack of a visa program in the U.S., to allow citizens of Hong Kong to come here. And so many people are leaving Hong Kong now, for places like Singapore and the UK, that the visa system there is totally backed up. He's sounding pretty frustrated."

"I'm sorry," I said as he walked out to the patio and brought in two chairs and a folding table. I started to unpack the food as he set the table.

"We really do need some furniture in here," he said, looking around. "Do you know anything about furnishing a kitchen and a living room the size of a baseball field?"

"Not specifically, but I do love to spruce up a room, and could probably help."

"Great! I'll give you my credit card and you can go shopping or buy the stuff online."

"Okay, but before I make any purchases, we're going to be in total agreement on what we buy. So be prepared to sit right next to me when we shop online."

"Works for me," he said. "I like being next to you."

"It would have been nice to meet your friend."

"Seriously Alicia, in that attire? I don't think so."

"I could have changed!"

"Why would you to do that? Then I'd just have to beg you to change back."

I shook my head as he picked up a bottle of wine that he'd brought up from the cellar. He wiped off the dust and read the label out loud. "Petrus Pomerol, 1972. Huh."

"Seriously?"

"Yes. Why, is it any good? I'm more of a beer and shot type of guy."

"It's a three-to-four-thousand-dollar bottle. You might think twice before opening it."

"Why would I do that, when I can have the pleasure of seeing you enjoy it?" When I could think of nothing to say, he added, "You know you're perfect, right?"

"You really are trying to get to dessert before dinner, aren't you?" As soon as the words came out of my mouth, I questioned them.

He slowly eased the cork out of the bottle and looked at me. "As delicious as dessert might be, it has never been, and will never be, my main objective," he said. "It's not just your beauty that draws me to you, Alicia. It's all of you. Your wit, intelligence, goodness, and courage."

I started to cry. He wrapped his arms around me and said, "Okay, none of that."

"Why? It's the one thing I'm an expert in." He wiped the tears away and I asked, "Where were you when I was getting talked into signing up for that stupid beauty pageant?"

"I was in a place and situation I wouldn't wish on anybody." As he said the words, a deafening silence enveloped us, and I looked down at his battered hands.

I felt unworthy, undeserving. To cover my shame, I made a bid for humor. "Now that you've had a cheap look at my bare breasts, would it be too much trouble for you to pour Ms. Perfect a glass of that wine?"

He laughed and kissed my cheek, then went behind the counter and grabbed two glasses. He poured a tiny amount of wine into mine and I swirled it around and took a taste. I could hardly speak, it was so perfect, but I managed to say the one word that came to mind — "divine" — before raising the glass to my lips again.

# CHAPTER ELEVEN

After we finished our second bottle of wine, whatever sense of shame and worthlessness I felt went flying out the door like a caged bird let loose. When I was beautiful, from top to bottom, powerful men treated me like a Barbie doll. I can't remember having a single intelligent conversation with any of these supposed power brokers, sheiks, kings, or politicians; they may have been movers and shakers, but they couldn't see past my looks, and they were convinced I was a simpleton. I shiver at the thought of being close to any of these creatures, never mind having them inside me.

And there I was, after nearly a year of feeling hideous, sitting across from the kindest, sexiest, and most attentive man I had ever known. A man who saw me as a complete person, despite my disfigurement. What was it he saw in me? I had to wonder if being around so much brutality — exploding bombs, gunfire, the butchery of fellow human beings — might have left him a bit deranged. What if he was only attracted to me because a part of his brain wasn't functioning correctly?

We cleaned the table, disposed of the empty bottles, and washed and cleaned our plates and glasses. This time he let me wash while he dried. With the wine still warming my cheeks, this small gesture made me feel so welcomed that I almost cried into the sink. There we were, a couple, doing the normal things couples do. One night I wash, the next I dry. I worked in silence, gently wiping each dish with the soapy cloth as though tending to a relic.

"Oh," he said, as he dried one of the wine glasses, "I forgot to mention. I called the supermarket today and cancelled your appointment."

"What?"

"Your job interview. Remember?"

"Oh. Funny, that feels like a million years ago."

"I know what you mean," he said, pulling me towards him as he leaned against the sink, which was now draining. I stared at him, and had to force myself to adopt a joking tone.

"And just like that, my career as a cashier went down the drain."

"Should we call them back?"

"No, let's let fate take care of this one."

"Agreed."

Then he told me he'd called a moving company to go to my apartment and get whatever I wanted to keep. All I had to do was tell him what I wanted them to pick up, and they would retrieve it the next day. I told him I only needed my clothing and my books from the living room. The place had come pre-furnished, so nothing else needed to be moved.

"Why don't we just drive over there and get it ourselves?" I suggested.

"We could, but I'd rather give them the work."

"More friends of yours?"

"Kind of. They moved me into this place, and we shared a few beers. They told me some horrifying stories about life back home in El Salvador."

"And did you tell them any of your horrifying stories?"

"No. I figured they'd already experienced enough pain. Some of them had seen family members killed as young as five and six years old … just babies."

I immediately felt my eyes welling up. "Of course, then, we must give them the work," I said. One tear escaped along my left cheek, and he wiped it away. I didn't know if I was crying at the thought of these distant families being torn apart by violence or at the generosity of this man who seemed to want to help everyone, rescue everyone.

He took my hand. "Time for some retail therapy," he said. When I looked at him quizzically, he added, "Furniture shopping." Then he pulled me into the hallway and opened the door across from the bedroom where we'd spent a good part of the afternoon making love.

We walked into a room that could have been beamed in from an English manor. It was a breathtaking library, housed within a room about the size of a tennis court. Every wall was covered with mahogany bookcases that reached from floor to ceiling, and there were six movable ladders, for access to the upper shelves. The only furnishings in the windowless room were a gorgeous Oriental rug, a massive wooden desk, and black leather recliner that was being used as a desk chair. A silver laptop sat open on the desk, next to twelve small globes, each with a built-in clock showing the time in a different part of the world.

I turned around slowly, taking it all in. On my third rotation, I noticed an army cot in a far corner of the room. It was made up, and on top of it was a folded green blanket and a pillow. I pointed to the cot and cocked my head at Nick, who smiled and shrugged. I decided to ignore this for now, even though I suspected that this was where he slept most nights. I resolved to change that, even if I had to throw the stinking cot into a bonfire myself.

"Whoever designed this room had fabulous taste," I said. "It's stunning."

"I designed it," Nick said proudly.

"No way! Maybe your mother, but not you."

"Yes, me. This was originally two bedrooms. I had the wall taken down and brought carpenters in to build it just as I had designed it. I think they did a wonderful job."

"More friends of yours?"

"By the time the work was finished they were."

I wandered over to the nearest bookshelf and started looking at spines. I wanted to pull out a book and start reading, but I suddenly felt sleepy. "So many beautiful books," I murmured.

When Nick sat down on the chair, I walked over and lifted myself onto the desk next to him. I was still dressed only in his shirt and a pair of panties, and I might have flashed him slightly — on purpose — as I crossed my legs and rearranged the shirt ends along my thighs.

"Aren't you cold?" he asked, drawing a finger along my left leg.

"Not too bad," I said, breaking into a yawn. "Excuse me."

Nick smiled and got up to leave, and I was suddenly scared. I tried to move, but my limbs felt like dead weights. "Nick," I called out, and then he was back again, wrapping a blanket around my shoulders. As he held me, I lowered myself onto the desk and lay on my side, with my upper body wrapped up like a tortilla and my bare legs arranged along the desktop. Nick sat in his chair and positioned his face close to mine.

"Comfy?"

"Yes," I slurred. I probably should have asked him to carry me to bed, or even the cot, but I stayed put and tried to make conversation.

"Are all of your friends…"

"Are all of my friends what?" Nick was laughing now, but softly, under his breath.

"… working … class … heroes?"

"Are you sure you're going to be awake long enough to hear the answer?"

I opened one eye and he chuckled.

"The ones I can trust, yes," he said. I nodded with both eyes closed, and he said some other things about being a newspaper reporter "in the field" — a war correspondent — as opposed to a news anchor, whose only job is to "read from a monitor and hang out at fancy restaurants." Then he said, "I doubt I gave more than a dozen TV interviews in all the years I was a reporter."

"You would make the best … news anchor," I said, sounding almost drunk. "I would tune in every night just to look at you." I freed one hand from the blanket and waved it around, reaching for him. He moved his face closer to me, until his jaw was resting in my palm.

"I'm sure my mother felt the same way," he said softly, next to my ear. "You two should get along swimmingly."

I laughed and repeated the word, "swimmingly."

"Alicia?" he said, as my eyes fluttered open. "I was thinking I could put another desk in here for you. What do you think?"

"I like this one," I said, eyes closing again. With a floppy hand, I knocked on the desk twice to illustrate my affection. "Can't we share it?"

"We could, but I doubt I'd get any work done. It would be like putting a bowl of chocolate in front of a child and expecting him not to gorge himself on the stuff."

This woke me up a little, and I said, "Are you comparing me to chocolate?"

"No, you are way better than chocolate. Much more delicious."

"Piglet," I cooed.

He turned the monitor toward me and asked, "So, are we going to go shopping?"

"Mmm…" I started to say, but it was game over. The last thing I remembered was his hand lingering on my bare thigh before he covered it with the blanket.

# CHAPTER TWELVE

When I woke up hours later, I was still on the desk. My right hip and arm were sore, and the first thing I saw was the cover of Toni Morrison's novel, *Sula*, with Nick's face behind it. When I said "Hello," his eyes popped above the pages, and he said, "Hello, sleepyhead."

I pulled myself to sitting. "How many of her books have you read so far?"

"Five, not including this one. I'm almost done."

"You've read six of her books in a day and a half?"

"They're not very long, but they're really great. Never judge a book by its size."

He looked at his watch and said, "I have to be on my way. It's almost midnight. I think you should go back to sleep in our bed. I can carry you if you like."

"No! I want to go with you," I said. The idea of him being away from me even for forty-five minutes was setting off alarms. What if he suddenly came to his senses about me?

"Well, if you want to come, I recommend putting on more clothes."

"Very funny," I replied as he stood up.

"Stay there a moment. I'll grab your jeans, some socks and a jacket."

He was back in less than five minutes, and I quickly dressed myself. He then put some type of large, puffy jacket on me that I nearly disappeared into, and zipped it up.

I looked down at the parka, and before I could ask him if we were headed for Canada, or possibly Siberia, he said, "Don't argue. It's cold out there and I don't want you getting sick."

He then put on a spring jacket, grabbed two blankets, and took my hand. "No talking while we're out there. Concentrate on the beauty of the universe. It's very comforting."

"Can we at least hold hands?"

"Yes, but no talking."

The moment we stepped outside he turned to me and lifted the jacket's fur hood over my head. "There," he said. "Now you look like a beautiful Eskimo."

"I feel like a fool."

We started to walk down to the beach, holding hands, and I was immediately grateful for the jacket. Without it, I would have run back to the house. It was freezing.

We stopped about ninety feet from the water. He put both blankets on the ground, side by side, and we sat down. He looked at me and raised his finger to his mouth as a reminder that the no-talking rule was in effect. Once we were on our backs, I grabbed his hand and looked up at the star-laden sky and admired the three-quarter moon hanging over the water. Flashes of light kept crossing the sky. I wasn't sure if they were shooting stars or fighter jets. I was just about to ask him when I remembered the cone of silence and kept quiet.

I did sneak a look at him. I couldn't help myself; he was too gorgeous. His eyes were closed, and after a few moments I realized he was asleep. I was about to try to wake him when I realized that this was the first time I had seen him asleep. Even after making love, he never slept; during breaks, I could always feel him caressing and kissing my neck or running his fingers through my hair. I wondered if this was the only time he was able to sleep without nightmares.

Exactly forty-five minutes later, he woke suddenly, as though an alarm had gone off. He looked at me, stretched a little, and asked, "Did you find it relaxing and comforting?"

"Yes," I said, and for the first time since meeting this amazing man, I pitied him. I didn't mention anything about him being asleep. I just smiled and said, "Very relaxing."

We stood up and shook our blankets and rolled them up. Then, as I stood up straight, my left leg went numb, and I toppled over, ending up face-down in the sand. Like a toddler, I held my breath from the shock of suddenly finding myself on the ground, then burst into tears. Nick was already beside me, holding me and comforting me and saying, "It's been a long, tiring day. We just overdid it."

"We spent half the day in bed!"

"But we were very active in bed," he said. I tried to smile but kept on crying.

He tightened his grip around me and said, "Let me carry you."

"No!" I screamed as I pushed him away. "Just let me lie here. Hopefully I'll catch pneumonia and die."

"Alicia—"

"Don't you have enough to worry about? Why do you even want me here? I'm a broken doll. An albatross. I'll pull you down! I'll drown you!" Sand stuck to my tear-streaked face.

He stared at me for a moment or two, and then he picked me up like a feather. There was nothing I could do. He had me five feet off the ground, and he looked angry.

"If I *ever* hear you talk like that again, I'll put you over my lap and slap your ass so hard … you'll never have to worry about your leg going numb again, because the nerves will be permanently on fire. Do you understand?"

"You would never hit me."

"You don't think so? Well, let me tell you, I'll go to great lengths to protect the ones I love, and I already love you as much as anyone possibly could. Just try me, the next time your leg gives out and you go off like that again."

"I don't believe you."

"Just wait and see!"

"It's not in you to hit someone you love."

"Okay, maybe I won't slap your butt, but I'll lock you in a closet."

"What good will that do?"

"It'll cause you to think before spouting total nonsense."

"What if I have to go to the bathroom?"

"I'll put a chamber pot in the closet."

"That's disgusting. I wouldn't stand for it."

"Then I'll lock you in a bathroom."

I paused. "Would I be able to take any books in with me?"

He shook his head and said, "Please, Alicia, never talk like you did tonight. Can you at least promise me that?"

"Yes, but only if I get a kiss first."

"You are openly manipulating me."

"True."

"I'm not sure you deserve a kiss."

"I probably don't, but can I have one anyway?" I said.

He rolled his eyes and leaned down and kissed me.

"Now say the words."

"What words?"

"Promise to never speak that way about yourself again."

"I promise to never speak that way about myself again."

"Good. I'll hold you to that."

# CHAPTER THIRTEEN

Nick carried me into our bedroom and gently placed me on the bed. He unzipped my jacket and helped me off with it, then carefully removed my jeans. He touched my left leg and asked, "Is it still numb?"

"Yes."

"Tomorrow we can put a hot compress on it," he said as he started to massage my leg.

"You know, it works better if you start low and work your way up."

"How could that be?" he replied as I started to laugh. "Oh, good one. And you have the nerve to call me a pig."

"I can't help it. You're too hot!"

He shook his head and I looked sternly in his direction. "And by the way, if I ever catch you sleeping on that cot in your study when I'm in this bed, I'll be the one whipping your butt."

"I haven't slept on it since you've been here."

"Good."

He continued to massage my leg as I thought back to us lying on our blankets on the beach. I wanted to mention him falling asleep out there, but I kept quiet. What if he didn't know? What if those forty-five minutes were the only time he got any peace?

I covered his hand with mine. "That's enough, Nick. The circulation is back. Thank you."

"You're welcome."

"Coming to bed?"

"I thought I'd stay up and read for a while."

"Please, Nick, come to bed with me and just hold me. Please."

He took off his shoes and pants and got into bed beside me. I turned on my side and he wrapped his arms around me.

I started to cry, silently, not for myself, but for the man holding me, protecting me, and all the while fighting demons that would not let go.

***

I woke up with Nick's arms still around me and his chest warm against my back. Naturally, when I turned over, he was wide awake. I wanted to ask him if he'd slept at all, but I just smiled and said, "Good morning, handsome."

"Good morning, beautiful."

"I don't think I've slept that well since I was a little girl. Were you holding me all night?"

"Yes. I'm glad you slept so well. How's the leg?" I tested it by standing up and it felt better.

After we showered, I asked to wear one of his other dress shirts, but he said he didn't think it would be appropriate because the movers were coming over. He also told me that he'd changed my address at the post office so that all my mail would be coming to the mansion.

I didn't know when he had the time to do all this, especially since we never seemed to be apart. It occurred to me that he might get up and do things while I was asleep, but I didn't want to think about that.

We skipped breakfast and went for a walk along the beach. He stayed on the side closest to the water, shielding my face from the salt spray. When we stopped for a break, he broached a subject that must have been on his mind since we'd met.

"When did the doctors say you could start skin regeneration cell therapy?"

I froze at the question. "You mean, plastic surgery? Facial reconstruction?"

"Not unless that's what you want. I think you're perfect the way you are, but I understand that you'll be more prone to infections and irritation as long as the wound is exposed."

"The doctors said facial reconstruction was my only choice."

"Well, your doctors need to read up on the options available now for people who've suffered extreme facial injuries." He touched the right side of my face and said, "They take small samples from your healthy skin, and inject them with facial skin cells taken from fetuses with a similar skin type as yours."

"Why fetuses?"

"Because babies in the uterus are the only humans in which the process of actual skin growth takes place."

"So, you're talking about stem cells taken from aborted fetuses."

"In some cases, yes, but in most cases it's when the doctor performs amniocentesis and sticks a needle into the fluid surrounding a fetus to check for genetic disorders. That fluid also contains the cells responsible for skin growth."

"And how long does the treatment take?"

"Sometimes as little as a few weeks, but I imagine it varies depending on the wound."

I looked out at the ocean, at its vastness and mysterious beauty, and imagined the many hidden treasures buried deep beneath its surface. I sat down and lay back, with my eyes closed, and listened to the wailing of the gulls and the crashing of the waves against the beach. I remembered, as a child, being too scared to go in above my waist on those rare occasions when my parents took us to the beach. Now I couldn't even dip my toes in the water because the salt spray could cause a dangerous infection.

Nick stretched his body above my mine and hovered there while I kept my eyes closed. "What are you thinking about, Alicia?"

I opened my eyes and looked directly into his. "Just how lucky I am to have you."

"That's not what you were thinking about."

"It's not?"

"No."

"Is that so? Should I add mind reader to your already impressive resume?" When he didn't laugh, I sat up and said, "Now that you've allowed me to move in, I no longer have exclusive rights to my thoughts, dreams, and nightmares?"

"No reason to get defensive, Alicia. If the fact that I worry about you is a crime, then I plead guilty."

"Don't be silly. It's just that when we started talking about treatments and surgeries for my face, I realized how useless it all is."

"Useless? How? These are cutting edge techniques—"

"I'm sure they are. But how am I supposed to afford them? I have very little money and no insurance. I've been working since I was twelve years old, and I made a lot of money as a model, and all I have to show for it is eighteen thousand dollars in a bank account." I lowered my eyes, expecting him to say something, but he kept quiet.

I looked at him and said, "If I tell you something, do you promise not to get mad?"

"I promise."

"That five-thousand-dollar check from the real estate guy is probably already in the mail, and instead of ripping it up, as I promised, I was going to put it into my account."

"And now do you promise not to get mad at me when I tell you the real reasons I wanted you to rip up the check and sent it back?"

"I promise."

"That real estate mogul has been working closely with one of my film producers for years, and believe me, you don't want to take a cent from that man."

"Why?"

"Besides treating young women like whores, before becoming a producer, he made his fortune manufacturing sport shoes and athletic wear in countries like El Salvador and Nicaragua. It's all driven by child labor — kids working ten-hour days for ten cents an hour in conditions not fit for rats. He's one of the reasons so many countries in Central America are always at war, and so many of their citizens are trying so desperately to emigrate to the U.S. There are only two classes in many of these countries, the two percent who are super rich and corrupt and the dirt poor who are lucky if they have running water.

"When I signed with his company for the movie rights to my first three books in the series, I had no idea that he was a major stockholder in the company. When I found out, it was too late to break the contract. I had just been released from the Russian prison, and I didn't do my homework, but you can rest assured that if any of my future books are made into movies, it won't be with his companies."

I sat in silence, letting that sink in, but he wasn't finished.

"I have one other thing to tell you, but you have to promise not to get mad." I nodded and he continued. "I was always going to reimburse you for the five thousand and I'm planning to put another hundred thousand in your account when you give me your account number. As for the treatment, if that's what you want, I already have a specialist in the field that I highly recommend. I met him in Syria, where he specialized in facial reconstruction and regeneration of facial cells ... helping soldiers and civilians who had terrible facial injuries."

I looked at him and started to cry.

"Hey, hey," he said, putting his arm around me. "What's wrong? Are we okay?"

"Are we okay?" I repeated, staring at him. His eyes filled with worry.

"I should never have mentioned the facial reconstruction—"

"Nick," I said, "these are happy tears."

"Oh." He looked relieved but still confused.

"To think that a person like you exists," I said, hardly able to get the words out. "I truly am the luckiest girl in the world."

# CHAPTER FOURTEEN

At exactly eleven-thirty, Rolando's Moving Company pulled up to the mansion. Nick and I walked outside to meet them, just as Rolando stepped down from the truck. He was in his mid-forties, with dark skin, thick black hair, and broad shoulders. Nick and Rolando embraced like old friends, and Nick introduced me to Rolando and his nephews, Juan and Marco, who were both in their late teens and quite shy but respectful.

They opened the side door of the truck and took down a garment rack with all of my dresses and boxes full of sweaters, shorts, jeans, and shoes. With Rolando supervising, Juan and Marco rolled the rack into our bedroom, and they hung all of my dresses in a large walk-in closet. They wanted to unpack the boxes, but I told them I still had no idea where anything was going. Walking out of the closet, Rolando asked, "So have you and Nick been together long?"

"Not long, but we really do get along well," I said, not wanting to tell him that we'd been together, if you could call it that, for approximately forty-eight hours.

"Of course you do. Nick is a great guy, and the two of you make a lovely couple."

Like a dope, I pointed to the left side of my face and said, "We would have made a lovelier couple before my accident."

As soon as the words came out, I regretted them. Why couldn't I stop apologizing for my appearance? And why say such a thing to a person I just met?

Rolando was unfazed. He looked at me and said, "Oh yeah, that's a pretty deep wound." Then he lifted his blue shirt to reveal a long scar below his ribcage. "Look at us. Twins."

He flashed me the sweetest smile, and I started to cry and apologize for crying all at once. Rolando lowered his shirt and faced me, and I'll never forget the look in his eyes. Not a trace of pity there — only kindness — as he said, "You are exceptionally beautiful, and no accident can take that away from you."

I stood there, not knowing what to say. He gave me a quick hug and cupped my shoulders with both hands. "You've got this," he said, and I nodded as bravely as I could. Then he and his nephews got back to work, rolling my boxes of books into Nick's study. I wiped away my last tears and forced my mood up a notch.

"Think we have enough books in here?" I joked, and the nephews laughed and said no, we could probably use a few hundred more. They wanted to unpack the books, but I told them I needed to figure out what order to put them in.

Nick was outside on his phone, ordering pizza, when Rolando and his nephews and I returned to the front of the house. Nick looked up from his call and scrutinized my eyes, which must have still been red. "All good?" he asked, to which I said, "Of course." He grabbed a few more chairs from the patio and we all sat around the table. Nick and Rolanda were drinking beers while Rolando's nephews and I stuck to bottled water.

Nick asked, "How's business been?"

"Not great," Rolando said. "The pandemic hit us hard, but things may be starting to pick up."

"And your wife and two little girls?"

"They're well, but my wife, all she does is pray from the moment she drops the girls off at school until she picks them up and brings them home. She won't even let them go outside and play. It's no way to live.

"When we moved here from El Salvador, I thanked the Lord for giving us the opportunity to live in a free and safe country where my daughters could grow up and become doctors or scientists or teachers. "But now when I look out my window, or turn on the TV and see that demon, that pumpkin-head ex-president, at rallies where thousands of people cheer him on like he's a God, it reminds me of my old country."

Nick nodded and looked down at his beer. "It's a cult," he said. "Far too many of my fellow citizens have lost their minds. I'm sorry you and your family are feeling less secure because of it."

"I know, my man, I know," Rolando said.

Nick turned to him and said, "You know, my offer still stands."

Rolando nodded and said, "I know, my friend."

"I — we — have so many rooms. You and your wife and your daughters can move in here any time. Right, Alicia?" He looked at me, and I nodded emphatically, even thought I was mostly just amazed to be consulted. "We'll find a school — one that's safe and academically excellent. You won't have to pay rent, and I'll pay for the girls' schooling. All I ask is that you wash your dishes and keep the rooms you use clean."

"I appreciate that, my friend, but all of my wife's friends and family live by us, and she wouldn't want to leave them."

"They could visit as often as they like and stay over. Just think about it."

"Thank you, my friend. *Gracias, mi amigo.*"

The pizza came and we ate. Nick and Rolando talked for another hour and had a few more beers, and then they excused themselves and disappeared into Nick's study for another twenty minutes.

Rolando and his nephews drove off about ten minutes after they came out of the study. We waved goodbye, and I turned to Nick and said, "What a wonderful man."

"Yes, he is."

I was tempted to ask what they talked about behind closed doors, but decided not to. I wasn't quite confident that any of this was really happening, and I didn't want to tempt fate by asking too many questions. If I was dreaming, I would rather stay asleep.

Nick took my hand and we walked into the study. He sat down in his chair, and I sat between his legs, which might not have been the best idea, since my libido was off the charts. He logged into his bank account, then asked for the name of my bank and my account number. When I hesitated, he said, "You know, I can find it out without your help."

"I have no doubt about that," I said as I gave him the information. I knew my account number better than my cell number, since I had looked it up so many times in recent weeks, in the hope that a check from a previous shoot might have been deposited into my account.

In the blink of an eye, I saw my account balance go from eighteen thousand to one-hundred-and eighteen thousand. I looked at him and said, as gently as I could, "I hope you don't expect me to repay you anytime soon, because I won't be able to."

"It's not a loan, or even a gift. It's simply yours for being so perfect and loving," he said. I turned around and looked at him and shook my head in amazement. Before I could speak, he said, "We need to get that furniture. It's kind of embarrassing to use patio chairs and a table as our dining room set."

"How much do you want to spend?" I asked.

"I don't care, as long as you're happy with it, and as long as my mother likes it," he said. That froze me for a second, but he added, "She's from West Virginia, so she hates anything that resembles the modern styles of the last twenty years. She's more into colonial."

"Like me, even though I'm from Long Island."

"Great! I'd hate to think of the two of you not getting along over something as simple as furniture."

I sat still and silent for a moment, trying to understand his relationship with his mother. He'd lived a life that put him in mortal danger every day for ten years, and he was as independent as any man I'd ever known, yet his mother, who flat-out neglected him as a child, had a hold on him that seemed uncanny.

I decided to let it go for now — knowing full well that if I was going to be a part of Nick's life, I would have to deal with his mother, one way or the other. I clicked on a link to a store that sold colonial-style furniture. Nick started twirling my hair as I navigated around the website. Within ten minutes I had picked out a beautiful hand-carved couch and two wingback chairs. I asked, "What do you think?"

"Great!" he replied as he continued to play with my hair. I turned around and said, "You didn't even look at them."

"Please, Alicia, if it's a choice between fondling your lovely, glistening hair or looking at furniture, what do you honestly think I'll choose? I totally trust you."

I continued shopping and bought enough furniture to comfortably accommodate at least fifteen guests in the living room, and a table large enough for the dining room to sit twenty people. I bought a kitchen table, with added extensions, that could sit up to ten people, and then added two

LG Ultra HD televisions. Nick made it impossible for me to continue as he started kissing my neck, and so before I lost what I had in the cart, I asked for a credit card number. The cost, including shipping, came to ninety-three thousand dollars. He rattled off a credit card number and needless to say the price tag seemed to be the last thing on his mind. I filled in the relevant information and received an estimated delivery date of ten days.

I turned around to look at him and before I knew it, he had lifted me onto the desk and was leaning in, with his powerful arms on either side of me as I hungrily accepted his kisses. We didn't have time to make it to the cot, let alone the nearest bedroom. It was time to christen his mahogany desk, and christen it we did. Twice.

# CHAPTER FIFTEEN

I sat naked on top of Nick's desk as he handed me a refreshing glass of white wine. He sat back in his chair, fully clothed, and took a drink from his own glass.

"Do you plan on staying like that the rest of the day?" he asked.

"I don't see why not. I can't see the point of putting on clothes when at any time you just might rip them off again."

"You make a valid point."

"Did you look at the furniture I bought?"

"Not really. I was looking at something much lovelier and certainly a lot more tasteful."

"Was that meant as a compliment?"

"I would hope so."

"It sounded more like a line you might have used on one of your many conquests."

"My many conquests? Please, enlighten me about these supposed conquests."

"Oh please, how old were you when girls started throwing themselves at you? Fifteen, sixteen?"

"I'm sorry, Alicia, but I think you might have mistaken me for someone else."

"Seriously? Nick, every supermodel at that party was drooling over you."

"That's all very well, and I'm sure most guys would get a real buzz listening to a lovely girl like you talk about them like that, but that's not me. You fell into my arms, remember? I chalk that up to an act of God."

He picked up the bottle of wine and refilled our glasses. I found my clothes and put them on, and we started to take my books out of their boxes and find spots for them on the shelves. As we worked, Nick set aside at least fifteen books he'd never read and added them to the Toni Morrison books that he'd already borrowed from me.

Later that evening we ordered Chinese food from Mr. Wang's restaurant. This time I made sure to be at the door, fully clothed, to meet Mr. Wang. He arrived with two helpers: an elderly Chinese man who turned out to be his uncle, and a little girl who could have passed for an angel, except that she was real. The girl's light brown hair was tied back in a ponytail, and her dimples seemed to catch the light as she smiled.

"Hi, I'm Alicia," I said, sticking out my hand. Her face brightened and she shook my hand and told me her name was Bee.

"Like the precious little creature that wears a yellow and black coat and carries pollen from flower to flower and makes honey?"

She beamed and said, "Yes. Just like that. B-E-E."

Over the next few minutes, I learned that Bee was ten years old and lived down the road from us. I also found out that she was adopted, and that her mother, Annie, was the sole owner of S&A Studios in Burbank, while her father, Joe, was a writer and a big Yankees fan "who also watches Knicks games, even though they never win."

When Bee had given her potted life story, Nick chimed in to say that Joe had just published a bestselling biography of Annie's brother, Simon, who founded S&A Studios, but who passed away.

"Simon was a very good man. A wonderful man," Mr. Wang said, and Nick and Bee and Mr. Wang's uncle all nodded in somber agreement.

"I will have to read that book," I said. Then I turned to Bee and said, "And do you work in the restaurant business full-time or part-time?" She laughed and looked at the floor and said, "I can't really work. I'm in the third grade." We all laughed as Mr. Wang explained that he and Annie and Joe were good friends and that Bee, who was also his friend and dance partner, liked to come along on deliveries sometimes.

"Dance partner?" I said, needing more information. Mr. Wang took the cue. He passed the bag of food in his hands to Nick and stood in front of Bee with hands raised. She reached up and clasped his hands, and they performed a quick dance move in the front hall — a twirl followed by a dip — and the rest of us gave them an enthusiastic round of applause.

"It's better when the Beach Boys are playing," Bee explained.

Nick invited them all in and they sat down with us as we ate. Mr. Wang, who was middle-aged, polite, and utterly charming, had a beer, and his uncle and Bee had bottled water. We offered them food, which they laughingly declined, yet when I picked up a dumpling, Bee looked at it as though it was a nugget of chocolate. I asked, "Would you like one, sweetheart?"

She looked at Mr. Wang who said, "Bee, you've reached your quota for the day. I promised your mom. You wouldn't want me to break that promise?"

"But wouldn't it be rude to say no to such a nice lady?" Bee reasoned. Mr. Wang smiled and I handed her the dumpling. She polished it off in two bites and said, "Thank you."

"Would you like one more?" I asked.

"No, thank you, Alicia. I wouldn't want Mr. Wang to break his promise to my mommy."

"…any more than I already have," Mr. Wang said, with a look of mock sternness.

"Bee is a very good negotiator," I said, and he chuckled in agreement.

After we finished eating, Nick switched to beer and handed Mr. Wang another beer, and then the three men started talking about Hong Kong and the corrupt, brutal regime on the mainland. I looked at Bee and said, "How about a tour?"

She bolted from her chair, took my hand, and off we went. Our first stop was the study. I chose it because it was the one place I knew that looked like a finished room, even though it still needed more furniture. She looked around and said, "It's beautiful. It reminds me of my daddy's study in our Studio City house."

"Do you have a study or library in your home here in Malibu?" I asked.

"Yes, but I'm only allowed in it if I'm with my mom or dad. It's so big, you need to climb a ladder to get to the books. My parents worry I'll swing from the ladders and get hurt."

"I understand. I wouldn't want anything to happen to an angel like you."

"Can I sit in the chair?" she asked.

Just before I was going to say okay, I remembered what went on in that chair and on top of that desk not long before. I said, "Just give me a minute so I can clean off any polish residue I left on the chair and desk when I cleaned it before. I don't want you to soil your clothes."

I picked up the rag I used to clean my books before we placed them on the shelves and walked over to the desk and chair and cleaned it off as best I could, and invited her to sit down. She sat in the chair and swiveled back and forth while I pretended to clean a speck of dust off the desk. She suddenly touched the left side of my face and asked, "Did someone hurt you?"

I nodded and she said, "Someone really mean?"

I hesitated, and said, "Yes. Some bad men hurt me last year. I was in the hospital for over two months." If she had simply asked me what happened, I would have spared her the details and said it was an accident. But she seemed to know, without knowing, that this was no accident.

"I'm so sorry," she said. "Can the doctors help?"

"Maybe. Nick was telling me about a new procedure. But it's very expensive."

"I'm sure he'll make sure you see really great doctors who will make that side of your face perfect again, like the rest of you."

"And what makes you say that?" I asked.

"Because Nick looks at you the way my daddy looks at my mommy. My daddy loves my mommy so much and Nick loves you just as much."

"You could tell all that from just watching us downstairs?"

She nodded and said, "When you're a kid and you've lived on the street, you learn a lot."

I stared at her, and finally asked, "Have you lived on the street, Bee?"

She nodded again. Then she told me the story of how she met the man who would become her father.

"He was sitting on a park bench in Studio City, watching some boys play basketball," she began, as I listened in stunned amazement.

"I had run away from my foster parents, who used to beat me, and I was living on the street for three days. I was so dirty, and I asked him if I could clean up and sleep at his house for the night because I had been sleeping outside.

"He let me into his house and gave me my own room. He bought me everything I wanted and promised he would never let anybody take me away from him. Then one day we went to visit his friend Simon who is buried in Forest Lawn cemetery, and while we were reciting Simon's favorite poems, a beautiful woman parked this really cool car behind our car. She was Simon's sister, Annie, who had also come to visit Simon. I didn't know it at the time, but Annie and my daddy knew each other and had planned on getting married before they lost touch with each other. Annie fell in love with me, and then my daddy and Annie got married and the first thing they did was legally adopt me. I got very lucky."

"I think your mommy and daddy got very lucky to adopt such a beautiful and loving daughter as you," I said, trying not to cry. "And how did you get to know Mr. Wang?"

"He was my daddy's friend, and his family owned a Chinese restaurant in Studio City that my daddy used to order from all the time. He and Mr. Wang became really good friends, and he was invited to every party my mommy threw and to their wedding. I love Mr. Wang. We dance to the Beach Boys all the time."

I laughed at that and asked Bee if Mr. Wang and his uncle moved their restaurant to Malibu, but she shook her head.

"No, my parents bought them the restaurant in Malibu. Mr. Wang is a member of our family, and he and his uncle sleep over at our house all the time, but they still share the money they make from their restaurant with their family in Studio City. I know I said I couldn't work, but I actually do a bit of work for Mr. Wang. I help with deliveries, like tonight, and I'm learning how to make some of the food. Mr. Wang gives me a small salary and lets me keep the tips, but I give the money back to him and he gives it to the homeless people we pass by all the time."

"That is so sweet of you."

"I don't need anything. I have the best parents in the world, and Mr. Wang."

"And what school do you go to?"

"I'm home-schooled by my daddy, who is very smart, like my mommy. After everything I went through with foster homes, they thought it would be better for a couple of years to be taught at home."

"Is your daddy a tough teacher?"

"Not really, but he makes sure I learn everything I'm supposed to learn, and more. He says by the time I finish grade six I'll be reading and writing and doing math at a grade ten level."

"Do you like going to school at home?"

"I do. It's fun, and my mommy and daddy never get angry."

There was a knock on the door and Mr. Wang and Nick entered. It was time to leave, and Bee hugged me for a long time, and then hugged Nick.

After they left, I turned to Nick and said, "That little girl is precious. Did you know about her life before she was adopted?"

"Yes, she had a tough life before she found those wonderful people."

"Do you ever think of adopting children?"

"All the time," he said. The conviction in his voice took me by surprise.

I asked, "So how did your talk with Mr. Wang and his uncle go?"

"They wanted to know if my mother could pull some strings with the State Department, to try to get their remaining relatives who are in Hong Kong into the States."

"Does she have that kind of influence?"

"She got me out of a Russian prison. I still don't know all the details and she's not one to talk. I'll speak to her about it, and hopefully she can help. Mr. Wang's relatives are mostly elderly, and it would be nice to see them all together again before it's too late."

"You seem hesitant."

"It's not that I'm hesitant. It's the right thing to do, but it seems like every time she does a favor for me, she gains a little more leverage over my life."

"She loves her son and doesn't want to see him get killed, and neither do I."

He looked at me as though I had said something profound, and then switched the subject back to little Bee. "There are so many things to love about Bee, but the thing that really sticks out is how lucky she knows she is to have been adopted by two such loving parents."

"So, you really have thought about adopting children?"

"Yes, Alicia. Why are you so surprised? Do you have any idea how many children I came across who had been orphaned by war? Far too many. And with my job it was impossible to adopt a child."

"But it's not impossible anymore."

"Thanks for the heads up, Alicia. I never would have thought of that."

"Why are you acting like such an asshole?"

He didn't answer, but looked at me before getting up and walking a few feet away. "Are you coming out to look at the stars?"

"I think I'll stay here," I said, then added, "if that's alright." He nodded and walked out to the spot where we had lay down the night before.

After about ten minutes, I crept out to the spot where he lay. I could see from the gentle rising and falling of his chest that he was asleep. I kept watch over him and only left to go back into the house a few minutes before he woke up, exactly forty-five minutes from the time he lay down.

I climbed into our bed, and he came and found me. Soon his chest was warming my back, and his arms were wrapped around me, and I was silently soaking my pillow with tears.

# CHAPTER SIXTEEN

When I woke up at 6:30 a.m. Nick was already gone, but I found a note on his pillow that said, "Back by 7. Walk on the beach?" I watched the morning shadows crawl along the wall and let myself daydream for a while before getting out of bed.

The idea that this could all be a dream was still rattling around in my head. In fact, even if one side of my face wasn't disfigured, I would still have had my doubts. I couldn't help but wonder what this man saw in me that distinguished me from all the other beautiful girls he could have had with a snap of his fingers — girls who could walk without falling down, and whose faces were not packed with silver.

Or was it my wound that attracted him to me? I remembered him saying that he'd known other people with similar injuries. Some of them were probably women that he wanted to help but couldn't. Did being with me alleviate his guilt at not being able to help them? It was a definite possibility, but if it was true, I didn't really want to know. All I knew was that I was madly in love with Nick and I had no intention of letting him slip away.

It was amazing how when I went to bed at night, with Nick's arms wrapped around me, it was Nick who I felt sorrow for, knowing the terrible nightmares he was living with, and then, come morning, it was all about me and how I was going to hold onto him. I had not used any birth control during our sex-a-thons, and I knew I would almost welcome the idea of getting pregnant.

I was off on a fantasy of Nick with his ear to my six-month-pregnant bump when he backed into the room and turned around to reveal a breakfast tray laden with fruit, chocolate croissants, and two cappuccinos. He smiled as he walked over and arranged the tray around my hips, then slid onto the mattress next to me. He pierced a slice of kiwi and fed it to me.

"What happened to going for a walk?" I said, after swallowing.

"We can go soon. I wanted to give you a little treat. Make up for being testy last night."

I held up my hand as if to say it was nothing, and kissed him on the lips.

"You have nothing to apologize for. But I could get used to this level of room service."

I picked up the croissant and fed him a bite, then took a bite of my own.

After we'd picked a little at everything on the tray, but not eaten much, I took a quick shower and got dressed, and we walked down to the beach. My leg felt a little weak at times, but I was able to keep up with him for two miles of slow walking along the shore. At no point did I even come close to falling.

On our way back to the house, I finally met Fernando. He was tending to some rose bushes, and he called to us while he waved a pair of shears in the air. He was short, in his late sixties, and had a friendly smile that immediately put me at ease. Nick introduced us, and asked Fernando how he was fixed for supplies.

"All good, Mr. Nick, all good. I just need to fill in a few perennials along the west side, where we lost those delphiniums."

I could only stay for a short time because I needed to get out of the sun, so I excused myself and went inside, while Nick stayed talking with Fernando.

I walked into the mansion and for some reason I headed straight for the study. It wasn't like I was trespassing, but I felt like I was in there looking for clues and insights into Nick. I walked over to the desk and found his copy of *Heart of Darkness* face down next to the laptop. I sat down and started reading. As the main character, Marlow, was travelling down the Congo River and looking into the impenetrable forest where he was sure they were being spied on by natives who at any time might attack, I could see my Nick in that steamboat, heading down river, through dense fog, in search of the station manager. I was just getting caught up in the story when I turned a page and a collection of photos dropped out of the book and onto the desk. I could tell from the state of the photos that they had just been taken in the last couple of years. I looked at the photos and at the disemboweled bodies of little children, women and elderly couples spread out like pieces of trash across unpaved roads. I dropped the photos as I got violently sick and vomited all over the desk … and I was still spewing up vomit as Nick walked into the room and I felt faint to the floor.

When I woke up in our bed I was totally clean and wearing one of Nick's tailored shirts and a clean pair of underwear. My mouth was so dry that I couldn't speak. Just as I was about to get up and put my mouth under the bathroom faucet Nick placed a straw in my mouth and said, "Drink up." I finished a large bottle of water and was finally able to get out the words, "Thank you, you really are my guardian angel." He took the bottle and handed me another.

"Speaking of guardian angels, you got an important phone call while you were asleep."

"Me, an important phone call?"

"From Bee. She was calling to say how much she enjoyed talking to you yesterday. I told her you were out but that you'd give her a call."

"She's such a little angel," I said as I finally remembered what happened when I lost consciousness. "I'm so sorry for vomiting all over your desk and God knows where else."

"Nothing to be sorry about. It took me a whole fifteen minutes to clean up."

"And how long did it take you to clean me up?"

"Well, that was a more delicate job, so it took longer."

"It was those pictures…"

"I should have taken them out of the book. I'm sorry."

"I had no right to even be reading your book."

"That's not true, Alicia. You have every right to read any book you want to read. Especially that one."

"I was getting so caught up in it when the pictures fell out. The main character, Marlow, reminded me of you."

"How so?"

"Because he senses what's behind the impenetrable forest and the veil of fog. He's like you. You look beyond the surface of things."

I got up and walked into the bathroom to see if any vomitus remains were lingering on my body, but he had done a superb job. I rinsed my mouth and brushed my teeth twice. I looked into the mirror, sideways, of course … still avoiding my left side. Then it occurred to me: I was the one obsessing over my wound. Nick didn't seem to care. In fact, I wasn't sure if he got more turned on by my disfigured side or my beautiful side, or simply the whole Alicia.

Nick had walked back into the study and I sat on the bed and called Bee. We spoke for a few minutes before she had to go back to her math lesson. I blew her a kiss and she blew one back, and I walked across to the study to find the door open and Nick at his desk, working. I knocked on the open door, and he looked up and smiled and asked, "Why are you knocking? This is your house, too."

"I wasn't sure if you ever wanted me near your study again."

"Don't be foolish. When you enter, it becomes the most beautiful place on earth."

I walked around the desk and stood in front of his chair, and he made a place for me to sit between his legs. "Did you talk to Bee?"

"Yes, she was excited because we're officially friends. There's her mom, her dad, Mr. Wang, his uncle, her friend Lisa, Lisa's husband, and now me. I asked about you, and she said, 'Do you really think Nick would like to be my friend?' I said I thought you'd be honored. So when you get that all-important call, please don't mess up."

"I'll do my best," he replied laughingly. "Oh — I got an email. Your furniture will be delivered in two days."

"Our furniture," I said. "But then I doubt you could name one item I bought."

"A kitchen table."

"My God, you're smart. What type of kitchen table?"

"There are different types? All I want to know is did you buy yourself a desk to go in the empty space between my desk and that wall?"

"No, I didn't. I don't want to interrupt you while you're working. You need to be able to focus."

"I'm not sure the books I've written required all that much focused concentration. My mother, after reading my first book, said, 'They pay you to write this stuff?'"

"She said that?"

"She did."

"That's not very nice."

"I appreciate her honesty, and her high standards. Her favorite novelists are the Brontë sisters, Jane Austen, Dickens, Byron, Hemingway, F. Scott Fitzgerald and James Baldwin."

"Impressive," I said. "I still don't think that was very nice."

"But I agree with her."

"It's still hard work to write a book. Any book. I don't know anybody who's done it, apart from you."

"I think you should write a book. I know you have fascinating stories to tell."

"Do you seriously think I have that type of talent?"

"Well, you've already achieved one of the requirements of any great writer, and that is a love of literature. I'm so impressed with the books you've read. The second requirement is to write honestly. Write what you know. So please, don't sell yourself short."

I could have kissed him, but for once, I didn't. All I said was, "With you in my corner, I feel like I can do anything."

# CHAPTER SEVENTEEN

The furniture arrived, but not the desk that Nick made me buy to put next to his. That would take another week. I placed the order, figuring that if he did decide to dump me, I'd at least have a piece of furniture worth fifteen thousand dollars that I could sell on my way out of his life.

Besides spending almost all of my time with my adorable boyfriend, my only other communication, throughout the day, was with Bee. She called about three times a day, during breaks from her studies.

I was lying on the couch reading an Agatha Christie novel — an occasional, guilty pleasure — when my phone rang.

"Hi, my beautiful angel," I answered, assuming it was Bee.

"I'm sorry to disappoint you but this is not the lovely Bee I've heard so much about. It's Nick's mother, Christine."

I sat up and held the phone to my ear. "I'm so sorry, Christine. It's a pleasure to finally get to talk to you."

"The pleasure is all mine, Alicia. My son speaks about you in such majestic terms that I thought it was about time we got to know each other."

"I think your son might be mistaken about how majestic I am."

"No, my son does not exaggerate. Nor is he a liar."

"No, of course not," I said. "He's kind of perfect."

"Yes, he is."

"No argument here."

"Let me ask you, Alicia, has my son proposed to you?"

I hesitated for a moment before saying, "Not in so many words."

"Meaning NO?"

"Yes, meaning no."

"Well, I want you to do me a small favor. After we hang up, I want you to go talk to my son and tell him we spoke. When he asks what we talked about, you tell him that his mother wants to know why you two are not married yet. He'll say something along the lines of, 'I'll marry you right now, if you like,' and you simply say yes. At that point you take his hand and drive to City Hall and get a marriage license, and hopefully in a few days I'll have a daughter-in-law. Do you think you can do that for me?"

"You make it sound so easy."

"What's hard about it? You love each other, right?"

"Yes."

"And you want to marry him?"

"There is nothing in the whole world I wouldn't do to marry your son."

"Great! He's told me a lot about you, including what happened to you on your twenty-third birthday. I'm so sorry. Men are disgusting pigs — and the ones you encountered are simply evil — but my son is not like the rest, and you'll do well to marry him. He's lovely."

"He is. I've never met another man like your son."

"As you probably know, I married very young and had Nick before I turned eighteen. I was basically a mother in hiding, still pretending to be a teenage girl. The nannies we hired to take care of Nick were more like mother figures to him than I was. I remember him telling me that when he grew up he wanted to play for the New York Yankees. So my husband and I decided to put him in the local little league here in D.C. He was so excited, and according to the nannies he was the best player on his team. In the three years he played, my husband and I never went to any of his games.

"After my husband took a nosedive into the Potomac, I decided it was time to become a better parent, and for a year or so the two of us got along wonderfully, until I re-married. Nick went off to college, and after a year he told me he got a job as a reporter and would be leaving school. Of course, I wanted him to finish his degree, but he told me it was an opportunity he had to take, so I said I'd support his decision.

"The next time I heard from my son, he was in Iraq covering 'the surge.' After that he was in Afghanistan, Syria, and Ukraine. It was like having a dagger stuck in my heart, and I so deserved it. I lived ten years waiting for a phone call telling me my son was dead. Instead I got a call from our State

Department telling me that he was being held in a Russian prison. I got my second husband, who is a high-ranking member of the Navy, to work with a few well-placed politicians to put pressure on the Russians to get him released. Some money changed hands, and he was out. When we landed at the airport in D.C., I told him that if I ever heard of him trying to leave the country again I would have him arrested for espionage. Since that day, our relationship has flourished, and I want to make sure it stays that way. That's why I want you to go to him after we hang up and tell him what I told you. And after you get the marriage license, please give me a call."

"I absolutely will. Will you be at the wedding?"

"I wish I could, but tonight my husband and I fly overseas and will be gone for two months. When I return I'll make an extended visit out there, and I can't wait to see my son and my lovely, majestic daughter-in-law."

After hanging up I sat there a moment, stunned. Then I immediately followed his mother's directions. I knocked on the study door, even though he'd told me I never had to, and slowly walked in, feeling his eyes on me the whole time.

"What is it, my beautiful Alicia?"

I sat on the edge of the desk and looked directly at him.

"I just got off the phone with your mother. She called me, and we had a lovely conversation."

"What did you talk about?"

"Lots of things. She expressed surprise that you hadn't asked me to marry you yet."

"I would marry you right now. I just wasn't sure if you wanted to marry me."

"I wanted to marry you within about an hour of meeting you."

"Funny, that's how I felt."

"Is that so? Then I think we should gather up our passports, birth certificates, and driver's licenses and head to the courthouse and get a marriage license."

"I have everything I need right here," he said as he opened the top drawer of his desk and took out a file. "The only thing I'm missing is an engagement ring."

"We're not going to be engaged long enough for me to need one. I'd like to be married by Saturday."

"Great! Let's get a move on."

"I'll be right back. I just need my documents."

I walked out of the room, happy yet perplexed, and stood for a moment in the hallway. Nick had behaved exactly like his mom said he would. I didn't know whether to be impressed or concerned. On the one hand, Christine clearly wanted me in the picture, as a hedge against her son even attempting to go back into a war zone. On the other hand, she could obviously manipulate his every thought and feeling with pinpoint accuracy, and that was more control than any mother should have over her adult son. It was definitely more control than I wanted my future mother-in-law to have over my future husband.

I got my paperwork together, and within five minutes we were sitting in the truck, heading to the courthouse. As I looked down at my hands, I noticed they were shaking, and when I looked over at Nick, I could have sworn that he was trembling a little, too.

# CHAPTER EIGHTEEN

We only hit one red light on the way to the courthouse, and it changed to green almost immediately. As he put his foot on the gas, Nick turned to me and said, "Did I mention that I'm Catholic?" I laughed out loud and told him no, he hadn't mentioned that, but that as life and luck would have it, so was I. It was funny to be finding this out the day we decided to get married.

We found the line at the courthouse to apply for marriage licenses. We were the only couple in that line, and yet the line to file for a divorce stretched out the door. We completed the paperwork, submitted our documentation, and after forty-five minutes, we were walking down the steps of the courthouse with our marriage license in hand. My phone rang, and it was Bee. I told her the great news and she got so excited that at first I could barely understand her.

"Come to Mr. Wang's restaurant in an hour," she said, when she'd settled down slightly. "I'll convince Daddy to let me out of school early. This is a special occasion." We hung up, and two minutes later she texted me that she'd reserved a table.

I informed my future husband, who said, "She's impossible to refuse, isn't she?"

"It would be a mortal sin," I said, then added, "Call your mother right now."

"Right now?" I nodded emphatically and he took out his phone and called his mother. I watched him pace back and forth as he told her that we'd picked up the marriage license. Then he stopped suddenly and looked at me, with the phone to his ear.

"You want a what?"

He lowered the phone and said, "She wants a picture of the license." I laughed and took a selfie of the two of us holding the document and texted it to her. They talked for a few more minutes and he handed the phone to me.

"Alicia, I am very impressed. You got the job done."

"Thank you. I was only too happy to carry out your instructions."

"Nick is right. You're majestic. I can't wait to meet you."

"I can't wait to meet you," I said, and we chatted briefly before hanging up. Nick stared at me during the entire, short conversation.

"What did she say?"

"Not much. She wants us to take lots of photos at the wedding. And she reminded me that she won't be able to attend, but that she'll be there in spirit."

"Like a ghost," Nick muttered.

I looked at him closely and said, "You know, I can't always tell how you feel about your mother."

He raised his eyebrows but said nothing. We were walking back to the truck when he added, "Did she mention her plan for after the wedding?"

"No."

"As soon as she and her husband get back from Europe, she's coming to stay with us for a while.""

"What's a while?"

"Based on past visits, around three to six months."

I imagined a sudden drop in the number of spontaneous sexual encounters around the house. What I said was, "I really look forward to it. She sounds fascinating."

"Oh, she is."

We drove to Saint Joseph's Catholic Church, where we met Father Dolan and told him of our plans. We apologized for the short notice and asked if he could marry us that Saturday at noon at our home. Nick handed him a contribution of five thousand dollars and everything was arranged accordingly.

Half an hour later, we were back in the truck, heading to Mr. Wang's restaurant. It had a small, red-themed dining room with only three tables, and one had a white card on it that said *Alicia and Nick*. The other two were empty. This wasn't a surprise, since Mr. Wang had mentioned that almost all of the business was take-out orders. Bee was there, dressed in a waitress outfit. She tackled me with a hug and wouldn't let go, and kept saying, "I told you, Alicia, I told you!"

"Yes you did, my beautiful angel, and now I want you to be my maid of honor. Could you do that for me?"

"Yes, yes, yes, yes!!" she exclaimed as she started jumping up and down and buzzing all around like a bumble bee. "Oh my God, oh, My God. Mr. Wang! Mr. Wang…"

Mr. Wang came running from the back and asked, "Bee, what's wrong? What's wrong?"

She flung out her arms, with the menu in one hand. "Nothing! Nothing is wrong. Alicia wants me to be her maid of honor. Can you believe that? I'm going to be a maid of honor. I have to tell my daddy and mommy." She walked outside and started to make phone calls, never staying in one place for more than a second.

"Well, there goes my waitress," Mr. Wang said as he looked at both of us and hugged and kissed me and shook Nick's hand. "I am so happy for the two of you. When's the wedding?"

"In three days. You and your uncle are definitely coming, right?"

"Oh, we'll be there all right, unless I want to piss off my favorite part-time occasional waitress and her parents. Please, sit down. Bee reserved the table for you." We sat down and Mr. Wang brought a third chair to the table.

"We're only going to be two," I said.

"I wouldn't count on that," Mr. Wang said as I watched the child jumping up and down outside the window.

Mr. Wang came back with steaming cups of green tea and freshly made dumplings, and my future maid of honor walked back in and sat down at our table. Before she could say a word, I placed a dumpling in her mouth. If you had any doubts about the existence of a God, looking at this little angel took all doubts away. Only a kind and loving God could create such a creature.

"My mommy and daddy are so excited," she said when she finished chewing. She looked at Nick and said, "You're very lucky, Nick, to get such a beautiful and loving wife as Alicia."

"I feel blessed," Nick said. "And my beautiful future wife and I feel blessed to have you in our lives."

After we had sampled a few more dishes, a trim, attractive man in his early sixties suddenly appeared behind Bee's chair and put his hands on her shoulders. She spun around and said "Daddy!" and hugged him from her chair. Nick popped out of his chair and gave the man a quick hug, and then turned to me and introduced him as Joe.

"I've been hearing a lot about you," the man said, in a heavy Bronx accent. I stood up and shook his hand and said, "And I feel like I already know you and your wife because I've been hearing so much about you from this little angel."

Joe picked Bee up, sat in the chair she'd just been using, and plopped her onto his lap. Then he turned to me and Nick and said, "I understand congratulations are in order! Bee has not stopped talking about you two, and now she tells me you've chosen her as your maid of honor."

"Yes, I have, and I have no doubt I've picked the most beautiful and loving maid of honor in the world."

"I couldn't agree more," Joe said as he squeezed his daughter's hand. "She is the most precious gift my wife and I could ever have imagined receiving." He wrapped his arms around her and hugged her and she let out a delighted giggle.

Mr. Wang walked over to table with more food. "Joe, I didn't see you come in," he said. "I'm sure our lovely Bee has told you the great news."

"She has. The next one we need to get married is you, Wang."

"No! No! Much too old."

"Nonsense, you're younger than me." Joe turned to me and said, "Wang and I have known each other for over twenty-five years. We've spent many a Christmas Eve together drinking beer and eating his delicious food."

Bee's phone rang and she looked at the screen and said, "It's Mommy!" She answered the phone and talked excitedly to her mother and then asked, "Alicia, my mom wants to know if it would be okay if we all got together tonight."

"Yes, that would be great. How about our place?"

Bee talked a little longer with her mom, brokered a meeting time of five o'clock, and then hung up.

Nick turned to Mr. Wang and said, "And I expect you and your uncle to come along."

"You haven't eaten enough Chinese food for the day?" Wang replied.

"There's no such thing. Besides I'm inviting you and your uncle as my friends. I have plenty of Budweiser in the refrigerator."

"I know you — lots of beer, no food in that giant fridge of yours! I'll bring food. Don't worry."

Even with that plan in place, Mr. Wang would not give us a check. It was on the house, and he insisted. Nick took out five one-hundred-dollar bills and placed them on the counter, and said, "I greatly appreciate your generosity, but you have a business to run. Thank you for offering to bring food tonight. I'll happily accept that as a gift." He then turned to Bee and handed her a hundred-dollar bill, which Bee then handed to Mr. Wang. She turned to Nick and thanked him and explained that all of her tips and salary go back to Mr. Wang, who gives the money to the homeless.

While Nick was praising her generosity, Joe seemed to be deep in thought. Bee looked up at her father and said, "Let me guess. Social studies?"

"Yes, I think so," her father said. "You can give me three hundred words on homelessness and the role of philanthropy in addressing social inequality. And your math for today can be an accounting of how much you've earned this month, compared with how much a person would have earned if they were making minimum wage."

Nick laughed and said, "Tough teacher."

"You think so?" Bee asked. "This is an easy week. Last week I had to create a business plan for a new restaurant and write a short story from the point of view of a waitress who's saving to go to medical school."

"I just want the best for my little girl," Joe said, and we all laughed.

# CHAPTER NINETEEN

As we were driving home from the restaurant, Nick suddenly pulled over and parked across from a high school baseball field. Two high school girls' teams were playing against each other to a sparse crowd. It was the middle of the day, and despite the ocean breeze, it was hot. I was only half kidding when I said, "Are you checking out the competition before you say yes to me?"

"There's no competition. In a couple of days, I'm marrying the most beautiful girl in the world. I would have married you the first day we met."

"Well, if you'd asked me, we would already be married, and we wouldn't have spent those days living in sin," I said with a laugh.

"I didn't think you'd say yes."

"Really? Even after I told you every supermodel at the party was drooling over you?"

He turned to me and said, "The term supermodel doesn't mean anything to me, Alicia. I'm not putting down your profession. I really don't know anything about it."

"Then what made you fall in love with me so quickly?"

"Your strength and determination, and naturally your beauty. I thought I'd have to go back to a war zone to find a girl like you. Instead, I found that girl at a party I almost didn't attend."

"I'll be forever grateful to the person who insisted you go to that party," I said, then asked, "How could you tell I was strong and determined?"

"I knew the injuries you suffered were especially painful, and difficult on a woman's perception of herself. I've seen men and women who ended up with similar wounds after being tortured. When I talked to the women, many of them were ashamed to lift their heads. I didn't have the means I have now to help restore what was taken from them … all I could do was offer heartfelt encouragement."

"When the Russians picked you up and threw you in prison, was it your intention to go back and find and help one of those girls?"

"No! I did get very close to a young nurse who was perfectly healthy and worked in a hospital in Kiev. She was going to come back to the States with me. When I was released, the first thing I did was get in contact with the hospital she worked at as a nurse. The lady who answered started to cry when I mentioned the girl's name. She'd been working in the children's ward when a Russian missile struck that part of the hospital." His voice cracked and he couldn't continue. I put my hand on his and waited.

Eventually, I asked, "Was she killed?"

He nodded and said, "Along with all of the children and several doctors." He flung a tear off his cheek with one hand and looked away.

"My God." I thought for a few moments, then asked, "Did she have a facial wound, like mine, before being killed?"

"No. My point is only that I've seen injuries like yours, and I knew that you had to be one fierce lady to put on a cocktail dress and come out to a party, given what you've been through."

Nick looked back at the girls playing and said exactly what I was thinking. "Don't for one minute think you're a substitute for that girl. You are unique, and you happen to also be the type of girl I've been attracted to my whole life. Your courage and caring and love of literature simply made you perfect inside and out."

I had to change the subject from me and this other girl. She might be dead, but I really didn't want any competition, physically or mentally, so soon before the wedding. I was sure this girl loved him, but I was also certain that I loved him more. The question of who Nick loved more was none of my concern at this moment, and I simply took him at his word that he felt I was perfect inside and out.

"Your mom mentioned your love of baseball and told me about your little league career. She also said that she and your dad never made it to any of your games. Do you think you might have chosen baseball over journalism if they'd showed more interest?"

"No, I don't think so. I was like a million other boys, dreaming a dream that was nearly impossible to achieve."

"Still, they could have shown more interest."

"Sure. But my mother was so young that I can't really hold it against her. How was a teenager supposed to care for a little kid? I was lucky to have exceptional nannies."

"That's an incredibly mature attitude," I said, but Nick barely heard me. He was off on a tangent and almost seemed to be speaking to himself.

"Whatever I might have been if my parents were different is neither here nor there. Did I choose to go into journalism to punish my mother? I would seriously hope not, but I can't rule it out."

I settled in and listened, with my hand on his knee, as he kept talking.

"About a year after my father died, things were pretty good with my mom. I wouldn't have called it a strong relationship, but we at least were communicating, which was a big step forward."

"Do you think she loved your father?"

"I really couldn't say. I never saw my parents laugh or tease each other or show affection. She did all the appropriate things at his funeral, but I don't know if she shed a tear."

"What about her new husband?"

"What about him?"

"Do you think she loves him?"

"I have no idea. When she re-married a year and a half after my father's death our much delayed yet promising mother-and-son relationship fizzled out, and she was back to her old self.

"When I told her I was leaving college and taking a job as an assistant to a reporter, she said she understood and believed that experience was even more important than a degree. When she received my first letter from Iraq, she went ballistic."

"You didn't tell her your first assignment was covering a war?"

"Of course not. Do you think she would even have let me leave the country?"

"Probably not."

"She contacted me constantly for the next two years. I'd get two or three letters a day, along with calls, emails, and texts. She went on and on, blaming herself for being a terrible mother, then blaming me for throwing my life away. She was convinced I was trying to punish her. She couldn't sleep at night, and she was losing weight at an alarming rate. I knew that if she died, I would carry the guilt around with me for the rest of my life.

"This went on for years. I changed my email addresses but that was pointless because her husband was able to tap into my communications and easily got my new addresses. And then one day, when I was stationed in Helmand Province with the Marines on the Pakistan–Afghan border, honestly believing that I could be killed at any moment, I wrote her a letter. I told her that I loved her more than anyone in the world, and that was the truth. In a sense, she was all I had during that time in my life. I told her my career choice had nothing to do with her and that I felt lucky to have been raised by a mother and father who never denied their child anything. I wanted to say 'except empathy and love,' but I left that part out. I apologized for any pain and suffering I'd caused her and said I hoped she would forgive me."

"That was very gracious. Was she happy?"

"She was. That letter turned our relationship around. She stopped complaining about what I was doing to her and started to open up to me. A lot of our correspondence over the next few years revealed things about her that I knew nothing about. Her letters and emails had a profound effect on me, and while reading them I would get emotionally choked up."

"Were you scared?"

"Of course, I was scared," he said. He started the engine up and began driving off. "It was the quiet moments that were most terrifying…" He looked out at the girls playing and said, "I expect one day there will be young women playing in the big leagues, and I truly think that would be a wonderful thing."

# CHAPTER TWENTY

At first glance Nick seems confident, courageous, and in control. Yet he is also a child in search of an elusive mother — one who has shown him both neglect and deep love. Now that he has her full attention and her devotion, he's willing to do almost anything to make sure he is never again deprived of that relationship.

She tells him to buy this mansion, and he signs on without even looking at the property. She buys his clothes and he wears what he's told to wear. She gets a message to him, through me, that it's time for him to settle down, and suddenly we're off to get a marriage license.

Given the pattern, I should have seen it coming, but I didn't.

Nick sat me down on our newly acquired couch and held out a small gift box. He opened the box, and inside was a simple but beautiful wedding ring. I immediately thought, *Oh my God, how romantic — as soon as that ring goes on my finger I am going to rip off his clothes and straddle him right here on the couch!* But instead of proposing, he cleared his throat and said, "This was my mother's wedding ring. My father gave it to her. I know how much it will mean to her if you wear it as your wedding ring." He slipped it on my finger, and it fit perfectly.

I don't know how long I sat there with my mouth hanging open, but I must have covered for my shock pretty well, because he didn't seem to notice. I pretended to get emotional and hugged him, all the while thinking, *You son-of-a-bitch, the next time you'll get between my legs will be on our wedding night, and that will only be to make sure our marriage is consummated.*

Not surprisingly, my bravado was short lived. After holding the ring out to examine it this way and that, I let him take my hand and meekly followed him into our bedroom, where we ripped off each other's clothes and made love repeatedly.

So he has mommy issues. Don't most men? It's not like I was competing romantically with his mother, and she seemed lovely when I talked to her. Moreover, we were allies, with a strong mutual interest in keeping Nick out of war zones.

The doorbell rang, and when I opened the door, it was Bee, standing at the head of a group that included Mr. Wang, his uncle, and Joe and his wife, Annie. I suddenly felt dirty as I flashed back to Nick and me, an hour earlier, going at it like two ravenous animals. Even though I had taken a shower, I felt like jumping back in and scouring every part of my body again.

Bee handed me a bouquet of white lotus.

"White lotus symbolizes purity," she said, and I brought the flowers to my face and inhaled their scent, hoping some of the purity would rub off on me.

I hugged her and thanked her for the beautiful flowers and invited everyone in. Mr. Wang and his uncle greeted me briefly and warmly before heading toward the dining room, calling Nick's name and looking for instructions on where to put the food they'd brought from the restaurant. Joe and his wife Annie hung back with Bee. Annie, who was draped in a fabulous, flowing ensemble of white linen, leaned in and shook my hand.

"Here she is, the famous Alicia I have been hearing so much about. It's so lovely to finally meet you."

I grasped her hand and returned the greeting, as I marveled at how polished and gracious she seemed. Annie was in her early sixties and could easily pass for her early forties, and there was something about her manner — civility and sincerity, delivered with what remained of a British accent after decades of living in California — that drew me to her and instantly made me like her.

Bee was buzzing around, helping me put the right amount of water into the vase and giving the flowers enough space to breathe. She told me the story of how Mr. Wang gave her a bouquet of white lotus, and how it became her favorite flower. "Isn't that so, Mommy?"

"Yes, my sweet angel," Annie replied and kissed the top of her head.

I looked at the two of them and was suddenly, unexpectedly, pricked by jealousy. I knew, then and there, that Nick and I would *never* find a child to adopt who was a fraction as amazing as Bee. There was only one, and she was taken.

As soon as this thought crossed my mind, I blushed and tried to banish it.

I handed Bee the vase and said, "Since you're the white lotus expert I want you to pick the perfect place for such beautiful flowers."

She thought for a minute and said, "Your bedroom, beside a window. That way when you wake up you'll see them and smell them and feel good all day."

Our bedroom, I thought — *the place where Nick and I, only an hour ago, were going at it like two animals.* I had no doubt that the scents from our adventure were still lingering in the air.

"I love that idea, but before I put them in the bedroom I think it would be a good idea to keep them out in the dining area so everyone can enjoy them."

"Great idea, but don't forget to take them into the bedroom after everyone leaves."

"I promise, angel, I promise!"

***

For the first time since the new furniture arrived, we ate in the dining room at our new table. After we'd enjoyed the wonderful food brought by Mr. Wang and his uncle, the men gathered in the living room and put on the Yankees game, each one with a cold beer in their hands. Bee sat next to her father, sipping a soda.

"So, your lovely daughter is a serious baseball fan?" I asked Annie.

"She and Joe never miss a game. Every time a Yankee gets a hit or scores a run she cheers like crazy, and by the fifth inning she is sound asleep on his lap."

Annie asked if there was a place we could talk in private, and I told her she had a choice of about fifty different rooms, but that I thought I knew which one she'd like best. We picked up a full bottle of wine and two glasses and walked toward the study. On the way, Annie inquired about the house, and I shared a little bit about its history as a party palace for the military elite.

"Goodness, what a tale of decadence," Annie marveled.

"It really was. The Pentagon needed to unload this house and everything it stood for, so the timing was excellent for Nick's mother to scoop it up, with help from her second husband."

We entered the study and settled into two new leather reading chairs. Annie filled our glasses and said, "I hope you don't mind a question about your fiancé," she said. "I'm so curious to know whether he plans to go back to being a war reporter or simply keep writing novels."

"I would love to believe that part of his life is over," I said. "I mean, the part where he's anywhere but here. And according to his mother, he's never allowed back into another war zone. She's threatened to have him arrested on espionage charges if he even tries it."

"Is he guilty of such charges?" Annie asked, looking like she doubted it, but couldn't quite rule it out.

"No, but Christine is the one who got him released from a Russian prison. She apparently has quite a bit of pull inside the intelligence community and the Pentagon. If it meant keeping her son safe, I have no doubt she'd have him arrested and charged."

When Annie asked how Nick and I met, I told her the whole story of how I ended up at the party on the promise of a payout for being a pretty face — even though my face was no longer as pretty as it once was — and how I literally fell into Nick's arms.

"Every model in that penthouse was salivating over Nick, and he picked me — the *ex*-model with the ruined face, who couldn't walk without collapsing."

"Oh now—"

"No, it's true, and yet none of that seems to matter to him at all."

"Journalists and writers have a different way of seeing the world," Annie offered. "They tend to see beneath the surface of things."

"So I'm discovering."

"What happened to the payout?"

"Nick told me that he expected me to rip up the check and send it back to the host. He said he didn't want his girlfriend or future wife taking a payment from a guy like that."

"He said that, within hours of meeting you?"

"He did."

"So romantic. And decisive," Annie said. Then she asked, "What was a guy like Nick even doing at that party?"

"He said he was only there as a favor to his agent, and would never have attended otherwise. The agent wants him to start creating buzz around the third book. But the joke's on the agent, because Nick spent the whole time talking to a bartender, and then he met me."

Annie laughed and said, "Has he already pre-sold the movie rights to the sequel?"

"I'm not sure, but I do know that Nick regrets working with the producers of the first two movies."

"Is that so?"

"Yes. Nick said if he'd known one of the producers was such a lowlife, he never would have signed with him, but now it was too late."

"Interesting," Annie said. "You know, we made an offer on Nick's books, but the agent apparently went with the higher bidder. I know it has worked out quite well for them."

"I can't speak for Nick, but based on what he's said to me, I suspect he would have preferred your studio. He'd just been released from the Russian prison and it all happened pretty fast.

"I can't speak for Nick, of course, but I can promise that if he writes any more books, I'll encourage him to show them to you first."

"That's very generous of you," Annie said. Then she seemed to remember something, and asked, "Whatever happened to the check from the realtor?"

"I received it a couple of days ago. I ripped it up in front of Nick and mailed it back. I tell you, Annie, the last month has been a whirlwind. Never has anyone treated me so well, and asked for virtually nothing in return, except to clean up after myself and make my bed."

"And to rip up that check."

"He even made that easy for me by putting a substantial sum in my savings account," I said. "I know what you said about journalists and writers, but I still find it so strange ... he could have his choice of the most beautiful girls in the world, and he chose the one with the bum leg and the silver bandage."

Annie looked at me serenely. "Well, I would say that he chose the one that was perfect for him, and the one that lives up to his ideals. And you make a beautiful couple."

"Thank you."

From there, we went into wedding planning mode. Annie offered to coordinate everything through her favorite catering company, which happened to have organized her wedding to Joe.

"They're incredible. They handle everything from decorating to seating arrangements, and the food is wonderful. How many people are you inviting?"

"Not many. You, Joe and Bee, and any friends of yours who you might like to invite. Mr. Wang and his uncle and any of his friends, and Nick's friend Fernando, our gardener, and his other friend Rolando and his family. To play it safe, let's say thirty-five." I also clarified that we were not accepting gifts, but that if anyone wanted to contribute to the Ukrainian Refugee Foundation, that would be greatly appreciated.

"I love that," Annie said. "Indoors or outdoors or both?"

"Mostly indoors, because I can't be in the sun for very long. In a month or less, I'll be undergoing a skin regeneration procedure organized by Nick. Hopefully, if it works there will not be such a contrast between my left and right side."

"Was it Nick's idea for you to have that procedure?"

"I told him I would eventually need facial reconstruction surgery, not only for cosmetic purposes but to lessen the risk of infection. He's the one who told me about skin regeneration. It's very cutting edge and not quite approved," I said, in a whisper.

"I think I've heard of this," Annie said. "Does it involve the use of fetal stem cells?"

"Fetal and adult stem cells. The doctor will look for a skin cell that closely resembles my skin type and implant it into my facial muscles. It's supposed to grow like skin covering a cut."

"It sounds very promising."

"To be honest, I sometimes think Nick would prefer I didn't have any surgery, even though the risk of infection is so high that I really have no choice, and he knows that."

"And why wouldn't he want you to remain the same person he fell in love with? You're beautiful as you are."

"Thank you, Annie, but as one woman to another, we know that's not true."

"Well, my daughter thinks you're beautiful, and in my opinion she's an excellent judge."

"She's so wonderful. Nick and I talk all the time about her angelic essence."

"Out of a devastating tragedy, the loss of my brother Simon, I was compensated with an unbelievable husband and a child who could light up the darkest moments in a person's life."

"That's how I feel about Nick. It was at the darkest moment in my life that I accidently fell into the arms of the most loving, intelligent, and caring man I have ever known."

"I guess you can call us two lucky babes," Annie said, suddenly sounding less British and more like a valley girl. I laughed at the phrase and told her I couldn't agree more. Then Annie looked at me almost guiltily, as though she might be broaching a sensitive topic.

"You know, if you like, I can have the makeup artists at the studio come here on the morning of the wedding and work their magic. They can make the bandaged side of your face look just like the other side, without removing the bandage or risking infection. I have no doubt you'll be shocked at what they can do."

"Really?"

"Really."

"That would be amazing, but I'd like to talk to Nick before saying yes."

"Of course."

"I don't know how to thank you for all you're doing for Nick and me."

"You already have, sweetheart, by making my daughter your maid of honor. She's so excited, and I'm thrilled. I'm taking tomorrow off and going shopping with her for a dress. We would both love for you to come along. It can be a girls' day out."

"I would love nothing better."

"Great! I'll get in touch with the caterers and tell them to duplicate what they arranged for Joe and me. That will save a lot of time, and I think you'll love the results. You ask Nick about the makeup and then for the most part we'll be all set."

\*\*\*

Back in the living room, the men were watching the Yankees game and sipping their beers. Bee was stretched out on the couch, with her head resting on her father's lap. Like clockwork, she had fallen asleep by the fifth inning, after a lot of cheering and jumping up and down.

Annie stepped in front of the TV and looked across at all the men, who were suddenly as silent as monks. In her beautiful British accent, she asked, "So have you men come up with a plan for the wedding reception?"

Joe shook his head innocently and said, "We thought that's what you ladies were doing."

"No, my darling husband. We ladies were talking about the upcoming soccer game."

"Strange, I've never once heard you talk about soccer."

"You see, we learn new things about each other all the time. Surely you haven't forgotten that I'm from the British empire, where soccer — or as we call it, football — is the principal sport." She shook her head as she looked at me and smiled. "You see what you get when you leave four men alone, drinking cold beer, and watching a baseball game? You get, 'Oh, I thought you ladies were taking care of that.'" She looked back at her husband and asked, "Are the Yankees winning?"

"They were," he replied, as he looked down at Bee, "until she stopped cheering and clapping and fell asleep two innings ago."

Annie smiled at him and said, "Okay, time to go. We have a big day tomorrow."

"What's on the calendar?" Joe asked.

"Shopping. We need a dress for the maid of honor and a dress for the bride. Invitations need to be sent out. And we need to go over menu options with the caterers." She turned to Nick and asked, "Do you have a tuxedo?"

Nick looked at Alicia and said, "I don't know. Do I have a tuxedo?"

"I haven't seen one. Maybe you should ask your mother?"

"No, that would be too embarrassing," he replied.

"Joe, why don't you take Nick to buy a tuxedo tomorrow? While he tries them on you can talk baseball."

"Great idea, sweetheart," he said as he bundled Bee into his arms and walked over to Annie. Leaning across, Joe kissed his wife and said, "I love you so much."

"And I love you just as much," Annie said, just as Bee opened her eyes and asked, "Did the Yankees win?"

"The game's not over yet, sweetheart," Joe said.

I walked over to the semi-conscious angel and asked, "Do I get a good-night kiss?"

"Of course," she said as she reached up and kissed me, "I love you Alicia, and don't forget to put the flowers by the window in your bedroom."

"I'll do that in just one minute. I promise!"

# CHAPTER TWENTY-ONE

The house felt suddenly empty. Nick settled back in to watch the game and I was fulfilling my promise to Bee by putting the vase of white lotus in our bedroom window. I rearranged the blooms until I had them the way I wanted them, then walked back into the living room and stood next to Nick.

"I want a Bee for myself," I said.

"I don't know if there's more than one in the world."

"I had the same thought. But how will we know unless we look?" I sat down next to Nick and he immediately stretched his beautiful body along the couch and rested his head in my lap. I was about to tell him not to fall asleep, but I knew that wouldn't happen unless he was lying down outside, under the stars.

I ran my hand through his dark, wavy hair and told him about Annie's offer. "She wants to send her own makeup artists from the studio over here on the morning of the wedding. She said it's amazing what they can do. Would that be okay with you?"

"If that's what you want, of course. Just know that in my eyes, you're already perfect."

"I appreciate that so much, but it would mean a lot to me to look the way I used to look on our wedding day. I haven't felt like myself since this happened to me…"

He put a finger to my lips and said, "I understand. Whatever makes you happy is absolutely great with me."

I continued running my hand through his hair and said, "You know you saved me, right?" When Nick turned his head and looked up at me, I added,

"I could never have imagined that a man like you existed, at least not in the world I came from."

"And you saved me."

"From what? Your terrible life as a Pulitzer-prize winning author of two highly successful novels that have been made into blockbuster films?"

"You know what I mean."

"Do I?"

"It's hard to explain ... I mean, to someone who hasn't..."

"Lived under the threat of war?"

"Maybe. Let me try to put it in very basic terms. Before going to that party, it was like I'd shut myself off from the world. I hardly left the house. When my agent talked me into going to that party, I was anxious for days and almost cancelled. I knew the type of people who would be there. Defense contractors who make their fortunes building and supplying weapons that kill more innocent civilians than combatants. Businessmen who become movie producers so they can be in the spotlight and creep on starlets. Clothing manufactures who make huge profits off children working in factories for pennies. Gangsters, money launderers. You name it."

"That does sound bad, but I have to say, you didn't seem anxious at the party. You seemed ... smooth."

"Smooth? That's funny," Nick said. "I mean, it's true that as a reporter, you learn to keep your emotions in check, but I can assure you, I was having a lot of anxiety about being there with that crowd." He stopped talking, sighed, and looked at the ball game on the TV. "You know why I've only been in a handful of rooms in this oversized penthouse?" I shook my head. "Because so often when I opened a door to a room in a heavily shelled and bombed building I encountered the remains of entire families. I've seen the bodies of little children, pets, and parents who were trying to protect their offspring. In a strange way, by not opening a door to a room, I'm protecting myself from the horror. I don't know if I am able to handle what's behind the forest wall, or if I even want to see what's in front of me when the fog evaporates."

"The forest wall?" I asked, confused. "The fog."

Nick tried again, saying, "I don't know if I'll ever be able to simply change the channel or escape the horrific images, but I do know that there has to be a better way. I don't want to go through life with 'eyes half shut,' 'dull ears,' and 'dormant thoughts.'"

"Who are you quoting?"

"Conrad. *Lord Jim*." Nick pulled himself up, leaving my lap suddenly cold as he ran to the library and returned moments later with his copy of the novel. He sat next to me and opened the book to a dog-eared page and began reading.

*"It's extraordinary how we go through life with eyes half shut, with dull ears, with dormant thoughts. Perhaps it's just as well; and it may be that it is this very dullness that makes life to the incalculable majority so supportable and so welcome … Nevertheless, there can be but few of us who had never known one of these rare moments of awakening when we see, hear, understand ever so much — everything — in a flash — before we fall back again into our agreeable somnolence."*

"'Agreeable somnolence,'" I repeated. "Powerful phrase."

"Exactly. I can't fall into an 'agreeable somnolence.' I want to help Mr. Wang get the rest of his family into the U.S. I want to help Rolando and his family reach a place of safety. Teddy Roosevelt once said he 'never wanted to be a man out of the arena but a man who spends himself in worthy causes.' That's me."

"And don't you think what you have done for me is a worthy cause?" I asked.

"I don't know if that counts. I had a selfish motive."

"What was that?"

"Love."

"Love isn't selfish."

"No, but I simply fell in love with you, and I would have done nearly anything to keep you in my orbit, so that hopefully one day you would fall in love with me."

"That's so strange because I fell in love with you the moment I stumbled into your arms, but I never thought I had a chance with you, and to be honest I still have doubts."

"Would I be marrying you if I had any doubts?"

"I don't know."

"No, Alicia. The answer is no. You can put your doubts aside."

I reached my arms around Nick and squeezed him tight, and out of nowhere, he said, "You know, my mother always says the thing that frightens her the most is my returning to a war zone as a journalist, but her real number one fear is that I could follow in my father's footsteps and kill myself."

I pulled back and looked at him in alarm, but he raised his hand to quiet my fears. "There's a big difference between my father and me. I doubt he ever loved my mother. He loved the military, and seeing so many men and women killed under his command proved too much for him. Having a wife and a child wasn't enough to keep him in this world.

"I would never even consider killing myself, knowing that the ones I'd hurt most are the ones who love me the most, and the ones I truly love." He touched my face and said, "In case you're wondering, that means you."

I tried to smile as I looked at his impossibly handsome face, but instead, tears started streaming down my cheeks. He reached across and held me, but the tears kept coming.

He had just revealed more about himself to me than in the entire time we'd been together. I had never even thought about the possibility that he might commit suicide, even though I knew it had a tendency to run in families. I also knew that if anyone ever mentions it, it has to be taken seriously, and never brushed off as just talk.

I grabbed a tissue from my pocket and wiped my tears away. Then I looked at his mother's ring on my finger and suddenly it didn't seem so poisonous. I asked, "Now that we're getting married, do you think maybe I could share guardian angel responsibilities over you with your mother?"

"I would hope so, Alicia, and I'll always be your guardian angel," he said. Then he looked at me and said, "There's something I've wanted to run past you. I'm thinking we should bring the maids back, at least for a couple of days each month."

"I thought you hated having anyone be subservient to you?"

"I do, but they would probably love to have their jobs back, and we do need to keep the house clean, especially now that we have all of this new furniture, and we're starting to use more of the living space."

"I think we're using about two percent of the house at this point."

"Even so."

"I think that's a wonderful idea, but I don't see why I couldn't do that work. It's not like I contribute much around here. You don't take money from me or let me pay for anything. In fact, at times I feel like a spoiled child. I ask, and you deliver."

"Alicia, you are my fail safe, and my mother picked up on it as soon I started talking about you. I cannot tell you how happy she sounds since we decided to get married. I don't want to stop you from doing anything you want, but I won't feel comfortable with you doing certain things until your leg is fully healed. You've made great progress, but you still have a long way to go. So, please make me happy by telling me you are not going to start cleaning rooms until we both feel comfortable that your leg won't give out."

"I promise, but that's almost like telling a child that if they don't do their homework they can eat all the chocolate they want."

He laughed as he reached across and gave me a lingering kiss. During a break in the action, I said, "You know, Annie told me that her company made an offer on the movie rights for your books, but that your agent turned it down."

"Of course, he did. He went for the most money. He got them to guarantee us two million dollars per book, whether or not they were made into movies."

"Well I guess it worked out well for you."

"It certainly did, especially if you consider that I'm getting paid a shitload of money for second-rate books." He lay down again and put his head back in my lap, and I ran my fingers through his lustrous hair.

"Have you seen the movies?"

"No, have you?"

"No, I was too busy crisscrossing the globe, walking down runways, doing photo shoots, partying, and, well — you know the rest."

He looked up at me and ran a finger along my cheek. "You were quite a busy young lady. Were you happy, apart from the way it ended?"

I fixed my eyes on the TV screen and said, "Not nearly as happy as I am right now." I couldn't look down at Nick, and decided to stop talking about my not-so-distant past. I was so close to marrying the man of my dreams that I wasn't about to jeopardize it in any way. I could see myself blowing the whole thing by blurting out that I had no idea how many men I'd slept with, and was lucky if I knew a third of their names. While my brave fiancé was risking his life covering foreign wars, I was off drinking Cristal and Dom Perignon, snorting coke, and waking up next to men forty years older than me.

Nick had enough problems; I didn't want to add to them. If he feared opening doors because of the devastating images of slain women and children that once met him on the other side, I didn't want him also having to imagine his wife, at twenty-two, having sex with a seventy-year-old pervert every time he opened the door to our bedroom. I might have been comparing apples and oranges, but I didn't want to risk it.

Nick was smart. Surely he couldn't be under the impression that I was a virgin before we met. I didn't press him about the poor girl who was killed in the hospital before he could bring her back to the States. I simply let it go. I didn't even ask her name. The last thing I needed was to fixate on that, or to worry about him calling out her name during sex.

No, I would keep my mouth shut and get this man to the altar, if it was the last thing I did.

# CHAPTER TWENTY-TWO

I looked down and to my surprise my future husband was asleep on my lap. It was the first time I'd actually seen him sleeping, apart from his forty-five-minute naps under the stars. The clock on the TV read 1:30 a.m. I couldn't help wondering if this was a show of confidence in his future wife, or if he was simply so exhausted that he passed out. Then it hit me. He was facing the TV and had just been watching a replay of the Yankees game. Baseball had a soothing effect on him, and it didn't matter if it was a major league baseball game or two high school girls' teams.

I tried not to stir, and in a crazy sort of way I pretended he was my baby, totally dependent on me, and not the other way around.

I had to pee so bad, and as the minutes went by it got worse. Finally, I couldn't take it anymore. As gently as possible, I slipped Nick's head onto a pillow. Before I even got up off the couch he said, "Where are you going?"

"I have to pee so bad," I replied as I started running toward our bedroom, with Nick yelling, "Don't run." And am thinking, *Right, I'll just pee right here on the floor.* And with my next step my leg went numb and that's exactly what I did. I fell to the floor and peed right through my underwear, pants, down my legs and onto the floor.

Nick was on top of me within seconds, saying, "Just stay there and let me help you into the bathroom," but as he went to help me up I screamed, "No! This is so embarrassing and disgusting, please just leave me alone."

He ignored me and pulled me to my feet as he said, "Stuff like this happens to everyone, Alicia. Believe me, I know disgusting, and this is not it."

"Don't give me that shit. Just leave me alone," I screamed, and for good measure I screamed again, "Leave! Me! Alone!"

He screamed back at me, "Shut your mouth, Alicia! Do you understand?" Then he scooped me up from underneath and carried me into the bathroom and placed me on the toilet seat like a toddler. When I was settled on the toilet he started to leave and said, "I'll be in the next room. If you need help just yell."

He closed the door as I sat on the toilet seat and cried and cried. It was such a paradox. Just a few minutes before, I was thinking of him as my baby, and now he was the parent, cleaning up after his hopeless child.

After a few minutes of self-pity, I turned the tables and thought, *He's truly amazing. Does he actually think he's the only one who has experienced devastation? I was raped and spent two months in the hospital, and was left disfigured. No, you son-of-a-bitch, you're not the only one who knows about suffering and tragedy.*

*But you're the only jackass I know who would choose to be a war correspondent and stay in the job for ten straight years! Now, that's a jackass! No wonder your mother is so worried about you. Only an unstable person would want to cover one war after another for a decade!*

*Instead of giving you two Pulitzers, they should have given you awards for biggest jackass and jailed you for giving your mother a nervous breakdown—*

There was a knock on the door and Nick asked, "Are you okay, Alicia?"

"Yes, sweetheart. I'm sorry for getting so upset. Just give me a few more minutes."

"Okay. If you need help, just yell."

I peeled off my wet clothes and put them in the laundry basket. Then I stepped into the shower and began slowly scrubbing my limbs with body wash and shampooing and conditioning my hair. When I'd finally had enough, I tied a towel around my body and opened the door a crack. Nick was right there waiting for me, and I asked him to hand me one of his dress shirts and a pair of panties. Just as he handed them to me the towel fell, and I made sure he got a good view of my naked body before I closed the door.

I walked into the bedroom, hair still wet, wearing his partially buttoned shirt. I lay down on the bed and said, "Nick if you don't mind, could you massage my leg? It still feels a little numb." He started down by my feet and as he moved upward I occasionally responded with, "Oh my God, that feels so good."

When he reached my panties, I spread my legs wide and asked, "If you're up to it, I would love nothing more..." And just like that my panties and shirt came flying off and we were at it like two animals. Yes, I admit, at times I was nothing more than a manipulative nympho, always working to get this gorgeous man back inside me. I wanted him so much that the idea of anything coming between us was too much for me to handle. All that mattered was that Nick wanted me back, and in two days, if I didn't screw it up, we would be husband and wife.

# CHAPTER TWENTY-THREE

Annie called me in the morning to say that the caterers would be over at one o'clock that afternoon. They would set everything up for forty guests on the day of the wedding, and would use the same menu and decorations that Annie and Joe had used for their wedding. I told her Nick would be here, and she asked if Joe could join him. I said, "Definitely."

She also arranged for a tailor to come over and fit Nick with a tuxedo. She then told me that a limousine would be driving us ladies around today. That way we could have a few celebratory drinks when we went to Bee's second-favorite restaurant, after Mr. Wang's, and not have to drive home. Annie said that Bee thought I should wear a white dress, and I replied, "Do you think white would be appropriate?"

"Has it ever been appropriate?" Annie laughingly replied. "But it's your wedding, and you should pick whatever color or style you like."

Annie said they would be picking me up in an hour and dropping off her husband.

After we hung up I went into the study and told Nick the plans. He said it sounded like a wonderful day, and then he reached into his desk drawer and pulled out a Platinum American Express credit card with my name on it.

I looked at the card and said, "Is this my wedding gift?"

"I would hope not," he replied. "Please don't let Annie pay for anything, and please be careful. And promise to call me every couple of hours so I don't worry."

"I promise," I said as I turned and started walking out the door without kissing him. Despite another sex-a-thon after he finished massaging my leg the night before, I still felt a lingering sense of guilt at the way I'd yelled at him. It was weighing on me, so I turned around and asked Nick if he was still mad at me about last night.

"Why would I be mad at you?"

"The way I yelled at you—"

"Honey, I get it. You were embarrassed. But you didn't need to be. I've seen it all. That was nothing." When I stared down at my feet without speaking, he added, "Besides, do you think I would give you a credit card with a hundred-thousand-dollar limit if I was mad at you?"

"I don't know. Your generosity is at times baffling even to a girl like me who was used to being spoiled."

He walked over to me and took both my hands and said, "Get used to it."

***

When the limo arrived, Nick walked me out, and Joe and I traded places, with Joe getting out to spend the day with Nick and me joining Bee and Annie. I waved goodbye to the two men as I cuddled up next to Bee, who sat between her mother and me.

"I did what you told me to do with the white lotus, and when I woke up this morning they were the first thing I saw, and I immediately thought of you."

Bee hugged me and said, "I love you, Alicia."

"Have you decided what you want to wear on your wedding day?" Annie asked me.

"I was thinking of a Dolce and Gabbana midi dress. Something to keep him interested after the wedding."

"Why after the wedding?" Bee asked.

Annie jumped in and said, "Because every time he sees the dress hanging in her closet he'll remember how lucky he was to marry such a lovely, charming, and intelligent young lady."

"Oh, that makes sense. He should always remember how lucky he is to be married to you, Alicia."

I smiled as I looked across at Annie and then down at Bee. Then I noticed the glass partition separating the driver from the guests, and suddenly my mouth felt dry. Within about thirty seconds my chest began to feel tighter, and soon I was coughing and gasping for air, while Annie and Bee looked at me in alarm. Annie asked Bee for her inhaler, and the next thing I knew, Annie was holding the inhaler in front of my mouth and telling me to breathe out as much as possible and then inhale. I tried to follow her instructions and managed to get some of the medicine into my lungs. I sat back as I caught my breath and Annie asked, "Feeling better?"

"Yes, thank you so much. That's the first time that's happened to me. I guess it's from all the excitement."

Annie cleaned off the inhaler with a tissue and handed it to Bee, who handed it to me and said, "You keep it, Alicia. I have three at home."

"But you might need it," I said.

"It's okay. I have enough. I want you to have this one."

I looked at Annie who simply nodded and hugged her precious child.

***

The limousine stopped in front of the Neiman Marcus Beverly Hills store and the three of us got out and went inside. Annie was immediately greeted by a friendly customer service representative named Natalie. I knew Annie made a point of remembering the names of her employees, but to learn that she was also on a first-name basis with a salesperson at an upscale clothing store came as a surprise.

"Hello, my dear," Annie said to the young woman. She asked about Natalie's daughter, and learned that the little girl had just started ballet lessons and was enjoying school.

"How do you do that?" I whispered to Annie, once Natalie had settled us into a private changing area.

"Do what?"

"Remember everyone's name and the names of their children? You're amazing."

"That's so kind of you. I suppose it was Simon's influence. He was so mindful of everyone around him. Always so thoughtful and attentive."

"Well, it's a lovely way to be."

Natalie began bringing articles of clothing for us to try on, based on our requests, and on one of her return trips, she brought us two flutes of a good champagne, and orange juice for Bee.

I don't know if we were in Neiman Marcus for more than an hour. They had the Dolce & Gabbana white lace midi dress I wanted, in my size, as though they had already been given my measurements. I was dying to buy a pair of sexy high heels, but I remembered the first night Nick and I met, when he walked out of the party carrying my high heels and commenting that they were the worst type of shoes I could possibly wear, given my injuries. He was right, of course, and even though it pained me to walk away from the strappy stilettos that caught my eye, I knew there was no point trying to argue for a wedding-day exception. So I picked out a beautiful pair of Cinderella flats with blue soles that were lovely, but not at all sexy.

The highlight came when Bee emerged from the dressing room wearing a floor-length junior bridesmaid dress. It was a scoop-neck design in gold lace, and it made her look even more angelic than usual — like a literal angel plucked from a scene by Da Vinci. Natalie brought her a pair of ballet flats covered in ruby crystals, with gold bows to match the dress.

I asked Annie to pick out something for herself, but she graciously declined. I paid for everything with my Platinum American Express credit card, which for some reason gave me a sense of power, even though when the bill came my husband would certainly be paying.

As I was cashing out, it suddenly occurred to me that Nick hadn't asked me to sign a prenuptial agreement. This seemed unexpected, especially considering how much the mansion was worth. Then again, for all I knew, his mother might own the mansion, giving me no stake in it anyway. And even though I had only talked to her on the phone, I had the clear impression that anyone who tried to screw her son would find themselves in a coffin, draped in an American flag and dropped over the side of a Navy destroyer, a thousand miles from land.

# CHAPTER TWENTY-FOUR

Our next stop was S&A Studios. Annie wanted to put in some face time at the office and check her messages. On our way up to her office, we stopped and talked to no fewer than fifteen employees. She introduced me to everyone, and naturally they all knew Bee, and like her mother, she knew them all by name.

Annie's office was large, bright, and sparsely decorated, compared to most executive suites. Her mahogany desk was covered in framed photos — pictures of Bee, Bee and Joe, Bee, Joe, and Annie, Annie's parents, Annie and Bee, and a few more of just Bee. A large, framed photograph of Simon hung on the wall behind Annie's desk.

Annie walked us over to the makeup studio and introduced me to the famous makeup artist Bernardo, who had won more Academy Awards than Meryl Streep. As we entered his workspace, I was shocked to see a large board covered in pictures of me from my modeling days. Bernardo had photographs of me dressed in bikinis, lounging in the surf on the French Riviera, modeling lingerie, and striding down runways in ten-thousand-dollar dresses. I nearly started crying, but I fought off the emotions and kept my composure.

"You're going to have your work cut out for you, attempting to come close to the way I look in those pictures," I said.

"Nonsense! I'll have you looking better than you do in those pictures. I am the great Bernardo!" The way he lifted one arm when he said this made me smile, and I was suddenly more comfortable.

Annie had Bee stay with me as she went back to her office to catch up on work. Bernardo looked at Bee and asked, "And why are you hanging around? Is it to torture me?"

"No, Bernardo, I love you. Why would you think I'm here to torture you?"

"Because every time I see you, I have nightmares that everyone will be born as perfect and beautiful as you, and poor Bernardo will be out of a job."

Bee giggled and said, "That will never happen, Bernardo."

"How can you be so sure?"

"I just know. Besides, my mother would never let you go. She loves you as much as I do."

Bee hugged Bernardo and he kissed her on the head and said, "Fine, my angel. You may stay."

Bee sat a few feet away from me. Bernardo asked to look at my wound, and when I nodded, he gently lifted the silver dressing from my face. He examined me closely and said, "The doctors did a wonderful job resetting the bones in your face, but I'm so happy they waited to do a skin graft."

"They tried to do one, but it didn't take," I said. "And now that seems lucky, because Nick has arranged for me to see a doctor who specializes in skin regeneration. If it works, I'll be one happy girl."

"And I'll be one happy makeup artist, because I've never seen a skin graft that didn't insult my artistic integrity," he said. "You have such beautiful skin. I'm going to match it, so that when you say 'I do,' you'll look even more beautiful than in any of those magazines."

He picked up a camera and started photographing my face, neck, ears, nose, shoulders, arms, and hands. He paused for a moment and asked, "Is your fiancé that hunk of a man that wrote those books that turned into blockbusters?"

"That's him, alright," Bee said. "He's adorable, but Alicia is much more beautiful."

Bernardo looked at Bee and said, "I don't remember asking for your opinion," and she scrunched her nose at him. He snapped some pictures of Bee and said, "I always carry around pictures of my little angel, and when someone asks if I have children, I take them out and they look at her in amazement, and I always say, 'Yes it was a miracle that my husband and I conceived such an angel. It's as though God himself placed her in my womb.'"

"I don't understand. I thought only women could have babies."

"My sweet, adorable child, there is so much you need to learn."

"I guess so," Bee said. "Are you staying for the wedding? You can see my new dress."

"I didn't receive an invitation," Bernardo said.

"Nobody received an invitation," I said. "We just started planning it yesterday. And yes, you're invited. Bring your husband and as many friends as you like."

"My crew will be happy. Few things excite them as much as free food and drinks."

Bernardo started taking measurements of my face as he talked to Bee, saying, "So you got a new dress. How many does that make?"

Bee thought for a minute and said, "Five."

"Wow! I don't think I got my first new dress until I was twenty-five," Bernardo said as he wrote down my measurements.

"You wear dresses?" Bee asked.

"Only on special occasions," Bernardo said. Then he held an instrument up to the good side of my face and asked me if I'd seen one of these devices before.

I told him I recognized it as a colorimeter for measuring skin's redness level and pigmentation.

"Exactly," he said. "Can't get much past a supermodel these days."

"Ex-supermodel," I said, trying to sound casual.

"Do you miss the business?" Bernardo asked, and for a minute I couldn't speak. I was suddenly too warm, and the lights were making me dizzy. When I closed my eyes, all I could see were the faces of my former colleagues — models, makeup artists, designers — and the popping of the flashlights as I strode down the catwalks. All of that was swirling in my head when I blurted out, "If I hadn't met Nick, I probably would have killed myself after what happened. My entire identity and livelihood were tied to my looks. How sad is that?"

# CHAPTER TWENTY-FIVE

Bee was quiet during the limo ride to The Smoke House. As soon as we were inside the restaurant and seated at their usual table, Annie ordered their famous cheesy garlic bread, then excused herself and went to the ladies room.

Bee looked at me and I knew exactly what was on her mind. I reached across the table and took her hand and said, "I didn't mean what I said back at the studio."

"Yes, you did," she said, with conviction. "You know how I know? Because when I was living on the streets, before I met my daddy, I wished I was dead. Sometimes, when I think back to the really bad days, I feel like you did in the car when you couldn't breathe."

I looked at this beautiful child, who suddenly seemed much older, and I felt ashamed. It was similar to how I felt when I complained to Nick and then remembered what he had been through for ten years and the misery and pain he witnessed.

Bee continued, "And now I have both a mommy and a daddy, and Mr. Wang and his uncle and you and Nick…"

Annie reappeared and sat down next to Bee. She looked at my misty eyes and asked, "What have you two ladies been talking about?"

"Your daughter is…"

The waitress brought a basket of cheesy garlic bread to the table, along with two glasses of white wine, and a soda for Bee. Bee picked up a piece of bread and handed it to me and said, "This is the best bread ever, Alicia. Isn't it, Mommy?"

"Yes, my beautiful baby, and you're the best daughter ever," Annie said as she kissed Bee a bunch of times.

***

As we sat in the back of the limo, full from a delicious lunch, Bee asked Annie, "Are we going to visit Uncle Simon?"

Annie hesitated for a moment and said, "Yes, sweetheart, but only briefly."

"Can I read my poem?"

"Not today. In a few days, when we come back, you can read it."

Adam drove through the gates of the famous Forest Lawn Cemetery, where many of the biggest movie stars, musicians, artists, directors, and businessmen and women were buried. He parked beside Simon's tombstone, and then came around and opened the door. Annie got out but told Bee to stay in the car with me.

Adam got back into the driver's seat, and I could hear him lock the doors and windows. Bee's face was up against the window as she watched her mother. Annie's shoulders shook as she stood before Simon's grave with her back to us and her head bowed.

After a few minutes Bee asked Adam to open the door, and he did. She fled the limo and ran to her mother, and just as I was about to follow her Adam turned and said, "Don't, Ms. Alicia. I've witnessed this many times. It's best you stay here."

I stayed as I watched Bee hug her grieving mother. Then Annie reached into her purse and took out a piece of paper, which she handed to Bee.

At first I couldn't hear what Bee was reciting, and then suddenly the words were coming out of her mouth as clearly and audibly as if she was standing next to me. She was reciting Lord Byron's poem, "She Walks in Beauty."

*… And all that's best of dark and bright*
*Meet in her aspect and her eyes;*
*Thus mellowed to that tender light*
*Which heaven to gaudy day denies.*

As I listened to her recite the rest of the poem, I hunted in my bag for a tissue and wiped my eyes. Back in high school this had been my favorite poem, and I swore that if I ever fulfilled my dream of becoming an English professor, it would be the first piece of literature I would teach.

A few minutes later, Bee and Annie got back into the car, and I slid over to make room.

Adam drove me home, and we arrived at the mansion just as the four maids who Nick had hired to clean the rooms were leaving. I introduced myself and told them I was very happy they had agreed to come back and that I would see them tomorrow.

Annie and Bee went inside, and just as I entered the mansion, Annie was walking toward me. She told me that Bee was with her father and Nick in the study, then demanded to know, "What were you and my daughter talking about when I was in the ladies room?"

I looked at her, taken aback by her prosecutorial tone, and said, "She gave me a lesson in humility. She talked about living on the streets, and how Joe took her in and gave her everything a child could wish for, and how because of that she met her mommy and Mr. Wang."

"And what brought this on?"

"Because when we were with Bernardo, I said that if it wasn't for Nick, I might have killed myself. I never should have said that in front of her. I'm so sorry."

"What would have caused you to say that?"

"I don't know," I said, twisting my hands together under Annie's gaze. "Bernardo had all of these pictures of me from my modeling days, and he asked me a question about my career, and I suddenly felt dizzy and overheated, and then it just came out."

Annie looked at me and just said, "Stress," and I nodded and closed my eyes.

"Even so," I said.

"Alicia, it's okay. It's just that any mention of death can be very upsetting for Bee."

"Any child would find that upsetting—"

"Yes, but there's more to her story than you know," Annie said. "Her biological parents were killed in a car accident, with her in the back seat, thankfully wearing a seat belt."

"I'm so sorry…"

"Don't be!" she exclaimed. "I mean, of course it's awful, but they were terrible to her. Anytime something went wrong they blamed it on her, and her mother would say things like 'I knew I should have aborted you.'"

"Oh my God!"

"I try not to be too overprotective of her, but it's hard. Joe is the same. Most nights I sleep with her, and if she and Joe fall asleep watching the ball game, I leave them be. That child is our whole world. She brought me back from the ashes of self-destruction and she did the same for Joe, and thanks to Simon, we became a family. I apologize if I came off a little strong, but when it comes to her there is no holding back. She is so excited that you made her your maid of honor, and that Nick and you are now her friends. It reassures her that people really do love her."

"We absolutely love her, and I'll never say anything like that in her presence again."

Annie thanked me and gave me a hug, then turned to look at the wedding archway that the caterers had set up in the living room.

"Everything is coming together nicely," she said.

"It is," I said. "But do you think we should add chairs?"

Annie thought for a moment and said, "No, I don't think so. You and Nick agreed to the simple Catholic wedding vows. Why have your guests sit down only to get up a minute later and move to the ballroom? A quick service is best, with everyone standing. Then your guests can get down to drinking and dancing."

"Good thinking," I said. Then I looked at her gratefully and said, "I have no idea how this wedding would even happen without your guidance. Thank you so much."

Annie beamed at me and took me by the arm as we toured the rest of the wedding spaces. The ballroom was decorated beautifully, with eight round tables for eight guests each, and one empty vase in the center of each table. On the morning of the wedding, the vases would be filled with white lotus. A full bar had already been set up, and there were three catering stations: one for salads and appetizers, another for main courses, and a third for desserts.

A separate area was reserved for a disc jockey, and the center of the ballroom remained empty for guests who wanted to dance. Annie and I sat down at one of the tables. She asked, "Are you nervous?"

"No, I'm in shock. I've been waiting to wake up from this dream since I met Nick, and living in this mansion, or castle, or whatever you want to call it, has not lessened that shock or the horrifying fear that this is all a hallucination."

"I think it's only natural when you consider the circumstances you found yourself in before meeting Nick."

"I guess," I replied, looking around the ballroom. When I returned my gaze to Annie, she was looking at me so expectantly that I chose that moment to vent about something that I hadn't shared with anyone.

"I'll tell you one thing that seems strange to me," I said, "and that's the amount of influence and control his mother wields over him. You'd think that a reporter who spent ten years covering wars would be more independent."

"Successful men in their forties and fifties often turn into little boys when confronted with their mothers," she said, seeming for a moment to get lost in her own memory. Then she raised her eyes and asked, "What is it that's bothering you about Nick's mother?"

"I — I'm not sure. It's probably nothing."

"Probably, but why not get it off your chest?"

I couldn't help thinking that she sounded like her daughter at the restaurant. I paused, unsure of how much to share. Then I launched in, telling her about Nick's parents, how unsuited they were to the job of caring for a young child, and how neglected he felt. I talked about his nannies, and about how, if not for them, Nick would have been a victim of outright neglect. Then I mentioned Christine's attempts to make it up to him, and how her relationship with Nick improved for a while after his father's suicide, then faltered again when Christine re-married.

"Nick's decision to stay overseas for ten years was a kind of punishment for his mother," I said. "She wrote to him constantly, apologizing for her behavior when he was younger, and begging him to come home. She spent a decade waiting for a knock on her door, informing her that her son had been killed. Then, when he ended up in a Russian prison, she was behind the effort to get him out. Since then, she and Nick have become a lot closer. He wrote her to say that he loved her, and they talk all the time now."

"That sounds like a positive development, doesn't it?" Annie said.

"Maybe, but he's just so ... bound up with her."

"Can you give me an example?"

"I told Nick that he was my guardian angel, and when I asked him who his guardian angel was, he said his mother. The Pulitzers he won, he sent to her, along with the cash. They have joint bank accounts. She buys him his suits, sportscoats, shirts, and shoes. She probably buys his socks and underwear. I figured once she met me it would be game over because she would only want a Miss Perfect for her son."

Annie interrupted me to say, "And who says you're not perfect, especially for him?"

I responded by pointing to the left side of my face and listing the number of times I'd fallen down since coming to live with Nick.

"And yet here you are, getting married," Annie said.

"That's right, and it was Christine's idea that it happen now."

"It was?"

I nodded. "A few days ago I answered my phone without looking at the caller, thinking it was your daughter, and it was Nick's mom. I thought I would die. She said she'd heard so much about me from her son that she had to make sure I was real. She knew about the rape and the surgeries, and she asked me if he'd proposed to me yet."

Annie was listening intently and nodding her amazement.

"She's the one who coached me on getting him to the altar. She told me exactly how to do it, and I followed her instructions, and Nick reacted exactly as she said he would. As soon as he heard that his mother wanted us to get married, he proposed. The first call he made after we got our marriage license was to his mother. Later that night, he gave me his mother's first wedding ring. He said it would make her extremely happy if I wore it, and naturally it fit."

"Ah," Annie said, beginning to understand.

"I ask you, Annie, does this sound like a man who spent ten years covering some of the most horrific wars of the last half century, and whose relationship with his mother ranged from nonexistent to hostile until a few short years ago?"

"I don't know, Alicia. At least she approves of you," Annie laughingly replied. "And she got you and her son to the altar. Does it matter how or why?"

"I don't know," I said, crossing my arms. "Maybe not." Then I looked at Annie, my new confidante, and shared one more secret.

"Nick told me a very disturbing thing the other night. He said his mother wasn't so scared about him going overseas as she was about him committing suicide, like his father. I think she's counting on me to keep him from hurting or killing himself. Me!" I pointed to myself helplessly.

Annie nodded and said, "It's complicated, isn't it? But let's focus on the facts. In a little more than a day, you're going to marry the man of your dreams, and he's going to marry the girl he chose over all others. He has pledged his love to you, not with just words, but with unselfish acts of kindness and understanding. Savor this moment.

"Don't worry about the things you don't know about Nick. Surely, there are things he doesn't know about you. What you do know is that he was there for you during one of the worst times one could imagine, and you were there for him during a trying and difficult transition. And whatever you might think, you are up to the job of keeping *each other* safe."

I could only nod my hanging head and hope that she was right.

# CHAPTER TWENTY-SIX

Annie and her family left just before the Yankees game was about to begin. It was a lot easier carrying the sleeping child from the couch in their home to her bed than from the couch here.

I sat down beside Nick and patted my lap and said, "I swear I won't wait until the last moment to go pee." He lay his head on my legs and looked up.

"Did you have a good time today?" he asked.

"A wonderful time."

"I figured. Is that the reason you never called?"

"You could have called me if you were so worried."

"There was no need. Bee was texting Joe every half hour with updates that he passed on to me." He looked up at me and said, "I want you to have fun, Alicia. I just worry about you."

"Are you always going to worry about me?"

"Of course, but not at the same level. Once your leg stops going numb, I'll be able to relax a bit." Then he looked me in the eyes and said, "I can't help it if I love you so much."

I started to laugh and said, "Wow! Surely, a writer of your ability can come up with a better line of bullshit with which to get me into bed."

"It doesn't necessarily have to be in bed, Alicia."

"You pig! One afternoon without sex and this is what you turn into?"

"No need to be cruel…"

"Keep it up and you'll be lucky if we have sex on our wedding night."

"Now that would be downright mean."

"I'll show you mean," I said as I shoved his head back down onto my lap. "Watch the ball game. Maybe that'll get your head out of the gutter."

Suddenly, my conscience got the better of me and I asked, "Don't you want me to sign a prenuptial?"

"I haven't even thought about that. Would you like to sign a prenuptial?"

"You're the one who has everything to lose. I have nothing!"

"Losing you would be like losing everything for me," he said. "I plan on having a long and happy life with you. I was hoping you were planning on the same thing."

"Of course, I am. I've just never been in a relationship where I've been completely financially dependent."

"It won't be like that for long. I have total faith that you'll be successful in whatever career or careers you pursue next. But please, don't even think of going back to modeling."

"I don't think you have to worry about that. Disfigured, prone to falling, incapable of wearing high heels … it's not really the resume they're looking for…"

"I have confidence that all of those ailments and hindrances will be cured."

"What happened to 'Do whatever you want, Alicia, I'll be there to support you?'"

"Oh, that's still the case, except for returning to runways and dirty old rich men lusting after you, and getting their due at the after-party celebrations."

"When did you become such an expert on the fashion industry?"

"Don't play dumb with me, Alicia. You gave away that little secret the night we met."

"Yet here we are," I said, as I saw my dream turn into a nightmare and be flushed straight into the ocean a few hundred feet away.

"That same night you revealed a lot about yourself. Courage, intelligence, empathy, and a uniqueness I've only seen in women of war-ravaged countries. You're beautiful, inside and out."

"Any more ultimatums?" I asked.

"Why are you getting so defensive?"

"Oh, I don't know. Maybe because you just insinuated that I was a whore."

"If that's the impression you got, I apologize. I'm asking you to give up a profession that's degrading to women and that nearly got you killed. I gave up being a reporter."

"You had no choice," I replied angrily.

"Seriously, Alicia, do you really think my mother's threat would stop me from going to cover a war I thought the world needed to know about? I have enough connections that I could get anywhere in the world without her knowing."

"I think you seriously underestimate your mother."

He thought about that and said, "Actually, you're right."

"I'm fairly certain about that."

"Either way, I gave up the idea of ever being a reporter because I owe it to the woman I love, who will soon be my wife, to always be there for her. As for my mother, I've already put her through enough agony."

"What if I wanted to become an actress? Is that also off limits because there might be a scene or two where I'm showing too much flesh?"

"I think you'd make a wonderful actress, and I'd support you one hundred percent. In fact, Joe told me that Annie was thinking about offering you a job at the studio."

"Seriously?"

"Yes, Annie and Bee love you, especially Bee."

"I want a Bee," I said, wandering off topic and not caring.

"There are many children out there that need a loving home, and we certainly have plenty of room. So, if you don't want to get pregnant or can't, I am all for adoption."

"Don't you want offspring of your own?"

"Honestly, before meeting you I had plans in the next year or two to adopt a number of children, most likely from Ukraine. I know it might sound stupid, but since I'm no longer going to be a war correspondent, I felt that by adopting orphans, I would at least be helping."

"Why would that sound stupid?"

"Because there are orphaned children throughout Africa and Central America that have suffered just as much and are just as worthy," Nick said, then trailed off. Then he looked at me and said, "I leave this totally up to you, Alicia. It's your body, and if you want children of your own, I'm one hundred percent with you. If not, we can adopt as many children as you want, or have two of our own and adopt two."

"Why is it that having children of your own means so little to you?"

"I suppose because for the first sixteen years of my life my nannies were basically my parents. I hardly saw my actual parents. My father was always out, and my mother was always passed out until the next party. We never ate meals together. I used to think that if I passed them on the street, they wouldn't recognize me. I look at the way Annie and Joe treat Bee, and the joy and love they all share, and that alone is reason enough to adopt. Biology has very little to do with parenting. It's your actions and behavior and the love you show that makes the difference."

"You turned out pretty well for a guy whose parents were close to nonexistent."

"That's all thanks to Ginevra and Francesca. It's their morals, kindness, and caring that I carry inside me. I would never tell my mother that, because it would violate many of the core principles they taught me. So I spare her, even though I'm quite certain she knows..." Nick shook his head and said, "I swear, there are times I think that woman knows everything."

Despite everything my gorgeous fiancé was saying about the virtues of adoption and his two wonderful nannies, I was not about to tell him that in all probability I couldn't have children. I had seen my life being flushed down the toilet a few minutes earlier, and as far as I was concerned, Nick could talk about himself, baseball, books, writing, or whatever he wanted, but until we were declared husband and wife and screwed for the four hundredth time in a few months, my opinions and past life would be kept to myself … or so I hoped.

Sometimes it felt like he knew everything about me, while I knew nothing about him. Ten years covering wars. I could only imagine how many women he'd been with. He told me about the one that was killed, but after all our sex-a-thons and the number of new things he taught me, on top of what I already knew and experienced, it was obvious he was no newcomer to the game of sex.

*If that's the impression you got, I apologize.* What a line of bullshit. He wasn't insinuating that I was a whore; he was telling me that outright. I swear, at times I thought I was losing my mind, and at that very moment I was certain I was losing my mind, and on top of it all, I had to pee so bad—

I lifted his head off my lap and said, "Excuse me, I have to use the bathroom. I'll be back in a few minutes. I promise." I got up off the couch and tried to walk as normally as possible.

I got to the bathroom just in time, and as I was sitting on the toilet, I remembered I hadn't changed my silver bandage in four days, despite being told to change it every three days.

I flushed the toilet, washed my hands really well, and put on a pair of surgical gloves. Then I carefully removed the bandage, dropped it in the waste basket, and took out a new bandage and a tube of antibiotic ointment.

As I leaned closer to the mirror to inspect the wound, the hole in my face seemed to warp and expand, like a crater undergoing erosion, until I could see my facial veins and even my bones. I stepped back in horror, and suddenly found myself inside a repeating image as the wound grew and my veins writhed like maggots eating away at whatever skin I had left. I grabbed for the sink to steady myself, and my world went blank.

I woke up in bed with a pair of hands in surgical gloves blocking my view. I blinked and saw Nick placing the silver bandage onto the wound and sealing the adhesive sides with his fingers. He reached down and took off my surgical gloves and then his own.

He walked into the bathroom and deposited the gloves into the waste basket, washed his hands, and walked back out and sat down on the bed.

"How long was I out for?" I asked.

"You were gone for over a half hour and that's when I came and checked on you. I knocked on the door and when you didn't answer I came in and found you on the floor. Thankfully it was your right cheek on the floor, not your left. Do you have any idea what made you faint?"

"The sight of the wound," I said. "It seemed to be almost alive…"

"You've had a long day," he said, in a noncommittal voice. "Try to sleep, Alicia."

He got up from the bed, without kissing me, and started to walk out of the room.

"I'm not cancelling the wedding," I exclaimed as he quickly turned around.

"Who said anything about cancelling the wedding?"

"The way you just walked out of here as though you didn't want anything else to do with me."

"I was just going across the hall to get a book to read while I watch over you. I just worry about you, that's all. Would you rather I didn't?"

"Of course not. It's just that…"

"What, Alicia?"

"I don't know!" I said, too loudly, as the tears began falling, and I started rambling like a drunk. "I just want everything to go right. I'm afraid my leg will go limp when we're dancing, or when we take the vows. I don't want to embarrass you…"

Nick came back and took me gently by the shoulders and looked directly at me. "You could never embarrass me. I love you too much." He wiped the tears from my face and kissed me and said, "Please, try not to worry. I know it can be stressful, but I'll always be here to protect you."

"How do you handle things so easily? Is it because of what you have seen? Is it because of that river?"

"What river?"

"The one in the book. The one Marlow goes down, when he witnesses the brutality that humans are capable of inflicting on each other. 'The horror! The horror!' Is it because of the horrors you've seen that cleaning up after me seems like nothing? Is that what you and Joe talk about in the study all day?"

"We talk about books, and yes, we've discussed *Heart of Darkness*. Joe is a big Conrad fan like me. But your name never came up in relation to any book." His grip on my shoulders tightened. "Alicia, what's going on in that beautiful head of yours?"

"It's just … it's not fair."

"What's not fair?"

"You know everything about me, and I know nothing about you."

"How can you say that? I've told you more about myself than I've told anyone. You know everything there is to know."

"It don't feel like I do, and I have this awful fear … I'm so convinced…"

"Of what?"

"That you're going to change your mind, call off the wedding, say it was all a joke."

He looked at me as though I'd lost my mind. I expected him to walk out of the room. What sensible person would sign up for any of this? The rambling, the fainting, the hallucinations. The face with its own little grave in it, crawling with maggots. He should have been running from me. I fully expected him to turn and run.

Instead, he stood over me, his dark hair hanging across his forehead, and said, "The only way we are not getting married is if *you* change your mind."

I turned on my side and said, "Please don't go. Don't read. Just come to bed and hold me and tell me you love me."

He lay down next to me and pulled me toward him and began stroking my hair softly and kissing my earlobe. "I love you, Alicia," he said.

"And I love you," I answered as I could feel that well-oiled piece of hardware between his legs responding to me and becoming hard. At that moment, sex was the last thing I wanted. I felt ugly. I was ugly. Wasn't that the reason I fainted? He continued to kiss my earlobe and I could feel my skin racing with goosebumps as he softly caressed my back and my neck and then my breasts, and suddenly, I didn't give a fuck about feeling ugly, and all I wanted was this son-of-a-bitch inside me and my legs wrapped tightly around him so that he could never get away.

# CHAPTER TWENTY-SEVEN

The following morning, Nick massaged my leg for nearly an hour. As I lay there, floating in and out of consciousness from sheer pleasure, I became convinced that my gorgeous warrior only felt complete when he was helping someone. How else could one explain this level of loyalty to a woman who was emotionally and physically unstable?

After another romp in bed, we took a walk along the beach. It was early and the sun was just rising from beneath the depths of the ocean, or so the poets would like us to believe. It was chilly, and Nick insisted I wear his parka, zipped up and with the hood drawn over my head. Despite all the precautions, I still felt cold, and I wrapped my arms around his midsection.

It was like a light in my head suddenly went off, and I was back in high school, my senior year, and I was once again the beautiful nerd who had yet to kiss a boy. I thought about those years before I was thrown off course, when I had my life all planned out. The scholarships. The PhD in English literature. My dreams of teaching and writing books.

I was a romantic, though I doubt anyone would have thought such a thing about me, and it was Lord Byron whose poems I cherished and memorized. I hoped one day to share a life with a man who loved poetry, and especially Byron, as much as I did. Instead of saying my prayers before bed, I would recite a different Byron poem from memory.

*In secret we met—*
*In silence I grieve,*
*That thy heart could forget,*
*Thy spirit deceive*

*If I should meet thee*
*After long years,*
*How should I greet thee?–*
*With silence and tears.*

I buried my head further into Nick's chest and softly, very softly, started to recite Byron's "To A Lady."

*These locks, which fondly thus entwine,*
*In firmer chains our hearts confine,*
*Than all th'unmeaning protestations*
*Which swell with nonsense, love orations.*
*Our love is fix'd, I think we've proved it;*
*Nor time, nor place, nor art have mov'd it...*

With the pounding of the waves and the seagulls squawking, I didn't think there was any way Nick could hear me. But he lifted my head and looked into my eyes and said, "Reciting a little Lord Byron?"

"How in the world could you make out the words with all the noise surrounding us?"

"A reporter learns to listen. Besides, when I see the mouth of the most beautiful girl in the world moving, I pay attention, and when the words coming from that mouth are Byron's poetry, I am overwhelmed."

"He's my favorite. When I was in high school, I used to recite his poems every night before falling asleep."

"Well, I think we need to make that a nightly ritual."

I laughed and asked, "And why is that? Do you think we need to add a little more fire to our romance?"

"No, because I could tell it makes you happy," he said as I looked into his eyes and saw a blazing love, an unconditional love that sang out louder that the crashing waves and the squawking seagulls. Then he said the words that I never tired of hearing: "I love you so much, Alicia."

Never had anyone spoken those words to me with such honesty and awareness. My eyes immediately got misty, and he asked, "What's wrong, my beautiful bride-to-be?"

I shook my head and said, "Nothing! Absolutely nothing." I stood on my tiptoes and he bent down to kiss me. My face was covered on both sides by the fur-lined hood attached to the parka, but he managed to find my lips, and we hung there for ages, kissing and nibbling and warming each other with our breath. I felt as if I was being transported into one of the fairy-tale dreams I would have in high school, after reciting Byron and falling asleep.

My memory was being washed clean by the ocean air and the squawking of the gulls as they greeted a new day. All of my doubts, my obsessive anxiety, and my fear of being abandoned were being pulled out of me.

When we finally surfaced from our kiss, we walked in silence toward the mansion, holding hands. Suddenly Nick stopped, reached down, and picked me up.

"Afraid my leg might give out?" I asked.

"Not at all," he said, trudging through the sand, toward the stairs that led from the beach to the estate. "Isn't it customary to carry a beautiful princess up and through the doors of her palace, and maybe have her recite another Byron poem?"

"I think it would be more fitting if the handsome prince recited a Byron poem to his princess."

"You know, I think you're right," he said, and after racking his brains for a few moments, he started up the stairs, reciting Byron's "She Walks in Beauty."

*She walks in beauty, like the night*
*Of cloudless climes and starry skies;*
*And all that's best of dark and bright*
*Meet in her aspect and her eyes…*

My eyes dampened as I remembered being at the cemetery the day before, watching Annie crying at Simon's grave, and little Bee running to her mother and embracing her. Bee had recited the same lines that my prince was reciting to me.

*And on that cheek, and o'er that brow,*
*So soft, so calm, yet eloquent,*
*The smiles that win, the tints that glow,*
*But tell of days in goodness spent,*
*A mind at peace with all below,*
*A heart whose love is innocent!*

Before Nick could ask me why I was crying, I reached up and we kissed, and it was as magical as when we had kissed by the water's edge. With his face so close to mine, the final lines of the poem rang repeatedly through my consciousness — *A mind at peace with all below, A heart whose love is innocent!*

\*\*\*

For the rest of the morning, I was high on Byron. Lines and verses that I hadn't thought about in years were suddenly flooding into my mind. Nick and I were out on the patio, drinking coffee and picking at a communal plate of berries and croissants, when I had a brainstorm.

"I have a game for us to play."

Nick looked up from his latte.

"Intriguing. Does it have a name?"

"It's called the Byron Bonus Round. Or something like that."

"More Byron?"

"Well, you said you know Byron's works really well, and there was a time I knew his works really, really well. Let's see who can recite more poems by Byron."

"What does the winner get?"

"To be decided." Before our walk by the water, I hadn't recited a Byron poem in three or four years. When I was modeling, the cocaine and the booze muddled my memory, and I began to forget them. My mind felt so clear now, and I was so happy in love, that I had no doubt that the rest of the poems I'd once memorized would come back to me.

"Okay, what are the rules?" Nick asked. "Do lines and verses count? And are we allowed to recite the same poems?"

"Good thinking. You're so systematic," I said.

"Stop buttering me up, lady," he said. "This is serious business." I laughed and pulled my chair out from the table and moved my feet to his lap. He had no choice but to shift his chair until he was facing me, and he looked down at my feet as I wiggled my toes.

"Fine. If you want a battle, you've got it," I said, as he rolled his eyes and started to massage my feet. "Partial poems get half a point, full poems get a full point, and yes, we can recite the same poems, but only after we've recited a different one first. If you can't recite a different one, you forfeit."

"Wow, you don't mess around."

"No, sir."

Like a gentleman he allowed me to go first, and I recited "So we'll go no more a roving." He countered with "To Caroline," and as he recited it, looking directly at me, my eyes started to well up, especially at the lines,

*But, when our cheeks with anguish glow'd*
*When thy sweet lips were join'd to mine;*
*The tears that from my eyelids flow'd*
*Were lost in those which fell from thine.*

When we reached seven each, I recited "Epitaph to a Dog," in honor of my beautiful golden retriever, O'Malley, who died at the beginning of my senior year in high school.

I told my prince, "It's your turn," and he looked confused, and I started to laugh. "Can't recite another one?"

"Can I recite something from another poet?"

"Sorry, my prince. It's Byron or bye-bye."

"I guess you win," he said, giving my feet one last rub. "See? You're brilliant *and* gorgeous. How lucky can one man get?"

I moved my feet to the ground and did a little victory dance in my chair. Nick laughed and called me a show off, but of course he leaned across and kissed me, and there was a glow to his face, like when a parent or spouse looks upon the one they love with pride and admiration.

Nick had often said that it was much more than my looks that attracted him to me — that it was what he saw inside me that moved him most. I was starting to believe that what he saw was the girl I used to be — the one who dreamed of becoming a professor and writing books, living happily with a man who loved Byron as much as she did. I was starting to believe that if he could see that girl, she might still exist. And my God, it was good to meet her again.

# CHAPTER TWENTY-EIGHT

Nick and I invited the maids to have lunch with us, and they happily joined us for pizza, calzones, and cannoli. We chatted about their children and about the old days when the mansion belonged to the military, and it felt like they'd been our friends for years. As soon as lunch was over and the maids returned to work in other parts of the mansion, Joe and Bee came over.

Bee was all excited, so we let the men go talk in the study while we went into the dining room. As soon as she closed the door she started jumping around like a bumble bee, and I had to place my hands on her shoulders to keep her in one place. She was all upset because when she looked up the responsibilities of a maid of honor on her computer she realized it was too late to do most of the tasks that came with such an exalted position.

"I never even threw you an engagement party or a bachelorette party!"

"Bee, sweetheart, please, please don't worry about any of that," I said, holding her arms and looking at her directly. "I didn't expect you to do any of that."

"You didn't?"

"No, angel. Those are things a maid of honor does when the wedding is announced a year in advance, not three days before. I'm just honored that you accepted my request. All I ask is that you be in as many pictures as possible, because you're the most beautiful girl I've ever seen."

She hugged me and said, "I'm so relieved," and then, "I love you so much, Alicia. Thank you for being my friend and making me your maid of honor."

I couldn't hold back the tears.

"Why are you crying, Alicia?" she asked. "Shouldn't you be so happy?"

"I am, my lovely angel. They're happy tears. I'm so happy to have you as my friend and maid of honor." I gently ran my hand along her face — a visage so pure, loving, and innocent that it glowed like the brightest star in the sky.

I held her arms and looked at her, and said, "A little fairy told me that besides Mr. Wang's dumplings, and the cheesy bread, your third favorite food is cannoli."

"I love cannoli, but Mommy and Daddy only let me have two at a time."

"Well, it so happens that I have two in my refrigerator, with your name on them."

I took her by the hand, and we walked into the kitchen. I sat her down at the table and placed the two cannoli in front of her, with a glass of milk.

"I have another idea," I said, as she bit into the first cannoli and her face lit up. "How about we write a poem about your mommy? I think that would make her so happy."

She had to gulp before she could speak. "I've never written a poem. Will you help me?"

"Of course, I'll help you. Let me go grab a book and some paper and I'll be right back."

I walked into the library and found Nick and Joe discussing Dickens's *Bleak House*. I sat on the arm of my soon-to-be husband's chair and said, "I have a favor to ask. Could you two charming men drive into town and pick up three sweatshirts? One with the Yankees logo, one with the Knicks logo, and one with the Chelsea F.C. logo. All in your daughter's size, Joe. And if they don't have them in her size, a size or two bigger. We women love to wear clothes a size or two bigger when hanging around the house. Isn't that so, sweetheart?"

"Most definitely, my wife-to-be. The one problem might be finding a Knicks sweatshirt."

"Why's that?"

"Because the last time they won a championship was nearly fifty years ago, and they've been terrible of late, but we'll see what we can do."

"Don't say anything to Bee. It's customary for the bride to give a gift to her maid of honor."

I kissed Nick and grabbed a copy of Byron's complete poems from my side of the library. "Can I please have one of the yellow legal pads I see you using?"

He handed me a clean legal pad and a pen and asked, "Are you off to memorize more of Byron's poems so I can never stand a chance of beating you?"

"Sweetheart, you can lock yourself in here for the next month memorizing Byron's poems and you still won't beat me. But no, I'm teaching Bee about poetry, and where better to start than with Lord Byron."

"She knows some Lord Byron," Joe remarked.

"I know, I heard her recite some yesterday."

Joe sighed as he looked at me and said, "You girls visited Simon's grave yesterday?" When I nodded, he said, "That explains a lot."

I kissed Nick and left the library. Then I stood just outside the door for a short while … listening.

"I never would have taken Alicia for a big Lord Byron fan," Joe said.

"She's very intelligent. Her bookish side went dormant for a few years while she was modeling, but it has been gushing out of her like an open fire hydrant the last couple of days."

"She has that bridal glow about her."

"She's always had that glow, at least, in my mind," Nick said. "I feel like the luckiest guy in the world."

I left on that wonderful note and when I walked back into the kitchen, humming a happy tune, Bee was just finishing her second cannoli. I held up the book and said, "I gather you're familiar with Lord Byron. I heard you recite a poem by him at Simon's grave."

"Yes, when my daddy and I went to visit Simon's grave he told me his friend would love to hear a young lady reciting a poem by Byron, and he picked 'She Walks in Beauty.' A few minutes later, my mommy showed up. That's before she was my mommy. She always carries that poem around with her and when we visit Uncle Simon's grave, she has me recite it."

I used a tissue to wipe some cannoli cream from her chin and said, "What are some things you love most about your mommy?"

Bee thought and said, "That she loves me and my daddy, and that she protects me. That she's beautiful, and treats everyone so nicely, and everyone likes her. She's very smart, and she always tells Daddy and me that we're the two most important people in her life, and that we bring her joy and happiness. I love her so much, Alicia. She's the best mom anyone could ever have." She started to cry and before I could ask what was wrong, she said, "Happy tears."

I wrote down what she told me and opened the book to Byron's poem, "She Walks in Beauty." I had her read the first stanza and asked, "If you had to pick something from nature that reminds you of your mommy, like a plant or flower, or the sun or the moon or the stars, what would you choose?"

"The sun," she quickly replied.

"So how about we begin with something like this: My mother is the sunshine that greets me each morning."

"Ooh, I like that. I love the way she glows when she looks at Daddy and me."

"And does she tell you a favorite bedtime story, when you don't fall asleep cheering for the Yankees?"

"Yes, she tells me about a handsome prince who saves the life of his princess. It's the same story her mommy used to tell her, and she always covers me with a blanket and hugs me."

"Wow! That's quite a lot there," I said as the image of a mother tucking in her daughter at bedtime ran through my mind. "How about something like this: She protects me throughout the dark night with a tale of a prince who saves his princess, and covers me with a blanket of love that shields me from all harm?"

Bee nodded enthusiastically, and I asked, "And when you're out with your mommy at the studio or in a store, what's one thing that sticks out for you?"

"My mommy is so sweet and nice to everyone, and she always reminds me to treat people the way I would like to be treated."

"That's great advice."

"Yes, my mommy is very smart."

"Yes, she is," I agreed.

I suggested a line based on some of the images she offered, and Bee clapped in excitement to see the poem come together. Then I asked a few more questions, and Bee offered more replies, and by the end of the process, we were working on the lines together, and she was really getting the hang of it. After talking and writing and going over the lines together and making adjustments, here and there, we had a poem.

"What do you want to call it?" I asked.

"My Beautiful Mommy."

"I think that's perfect," I said and I hugged and kissed her a bunch of times as Nick and Joe walked into the kitchen. Joe asked, "And what have we here?"

"Your daughter just wrote a poem for her mommy," I replied.

"With a lot of help from Alicia," Bee said.

"With very little help from me."

"Do we get to hear it?" Nick asked.

"That's up to my mommy. She has to read it first."

Joe picked Bee up and kissed her a bunch of times and said, "You're going to make mommy so happy. I'm so proud of you."

Nick came around to me and as he looked at me, it was as though I was the only one in the universe. He wasn't looking at me any differently than all the other times, but now my doubts were gone, along with my disbelief that a man like him could actually love me. He whispered in my ear, "I am so proud of you, my bride-to-be."

The men went off to buy the gifts for my maid of honor, while I went into the library in search of a writing pad that I kept inside a large dictionary. The sheets were all bordered in hearts, and I thought it would make a perfect backdrop for Bee's poem.

I took the pad off my desk, along with a matching envelope, and then I picked up a good-quality pen. I was briefly tempted to look at what Nick was working on, even though he had told me he was finishing up the third and final book in the series about a war correspondent turned warrior, but I walked out of the library without being a nosy future wife.

I sat down next to my pupil and put the pad and the poem we'd written in front of her and handed her the pen. She asked, "Don't you want me to type it on the computer?"

"No, my angel, I want you to write it out. It will mean so much more to your mommy, believe me."

"My daddy tells me I should get more used to writing in case I don't have my phone or computer. He tells me when he grew up, they didn't have computers or cell phones. Did they have computers and cell phones when you grew up?"

"Yes, but I never had my own computer or cell phone until I started working. My parents were very old-fashioned," I replied.

"But you love them a whole bunch?" she asked.

"Of course, sweetheart. A whole bunch," I said as I turned around and felt like vomiting. I remembered researching a used computer that would have cost next to nothing, but that would have helped me tremendously with school, and how they refused to put a penny towards it. Anything I did receive, including essentials, like underwear or a new winter coat, came with guilt and strings attached. They would say, *I hope you appreciate this. It's not like money grows on trees.* Every time my mother and father said something like that, I used to think, *Maybe if you learned how to use birth control, I wouldn't be such a burden. In fact, I wouldn't exist.*

I looked at Bee, as I tried to shake off these bitter memories, and said, "I have a little something else for you when you're finished. I'm so proud of you."

She wrote out the poem, slowly and carefully, and the results were amazingly legible. We put it in the envelope, and she wrote on it: *To My Beautiful Mommy.*

The cleaning ladies came down and were ready to leave when I ran to the refrigerator and took out all the leftovers from lunch to give to them. Bee introduced herself and they were all admiring the beautiful little girl who was ten but looked like she was seven. I reminded them about the wedding and stressed no gifts, just come and have a great time.

Nick and Joe came in shortly after and were holding a couple of bags. I asked, "Did you have any problems getting what you were looking for?"

They both laughed and said, "It took a little driving around, but we finally got it all."

Bee got a text from her mother telling her that she'd left work and was on the way home. Annie asked, *If everyone agrees, would you please order food from Mr. Wang's? I know we've had it three times this week but I am simply dying for it.*

Everyone agreed, and Bee placed a large order. While she was on the phone, I took Nick aside and asked, "Did you have any problem getting the Chelsea sweatshirt?"

"No, we had a harder time getting one with the Knicks' logo, but we finally found an antique store that had some dusty old merchandise from fifteen years ago."

"You're kidding, right?"

"Yes, my beautiful wife. I'm joking. With so many New Yorkers living out here there will always be a market for Knicks merchandise, no matter how pitiful they are."

Annie arrived before the food did, and after kissing her husband and hugging and kissing Bee, she was given the envelope with the poem in it. "And what is this?" she asked Bee.

"A little something I wrote for you, with Alicia."

"Oh! How about we go into the ballroom so I can read it without any disruptions?" Annie took her daughter's hand and they walked into the ballroom and slid the doors closed.

They were in there for a long time, and once Mr. Wang and his uncle arrived with the food, I asked Joe if he could go get his daughter and wife. He knocked on the pocket doors and went into the ballroom. After about five minutes they all came out, and it was obvious that Annie and Bee had been crying.

Annie came straight for me and folded me in a hug. "Thank you for helping my daughter write that beautiful poem." She started to cry, and I handed her some tissues and went into the kitchen and poured us two large glasses of white wine. "Perfect!" she said. "You read my mind."

We all sat down, including Mr. Wang and his uncle, and ate the delicious food. Nick kept the beverages flowing, refilling all our glasses and topping off Bee's soda. As I watched him taking care of everyone, it became clear to me, once again, that this was just who Nick was. He always needed to be making a positive difference, whether he was helping a person, an institution, or a cause. Some might call it a savior complex, but that night, it looked more like a server complex. I smiled as he refilled my glass and he asked, "What are you smiling about?"

"Oh, nothing very important," I said and kept on smiling.

"Feel like sharing?" he asked as he moved over to Annie and refilled her glass.

"Not really," I said as I took a sip.

"She's smiling because tomorrow she's marrying her prince charming. Right, Alicia?" Bee asked.

"That would be a very good reason to smile," I said as Bee bit into a dumpling.

After we'd eaten, the men did the dishes, which left us girls to run off and have a semblance of a bridal shower. I grabbed a fresh bottle of wine and two clean glasses and a bottled water for Bee. We went into the study and sat on the floor. I handed Bee her three bags and said, "It's customary for the bride to give her maid of honor gifts to show appreciation for all the support she has shown leading up to the wedding."

Bee opened the first bag that contained the Yankees sweatshirt and exclaimed, "Oh, my God! Oh, my God!" as she slipped it on over the shirt she was wearing, gave me a big hug, and ran out the door to show her daddy.

Annie looked at me with respect and said, "What a brilliant gift. I would call that a home run." We clinked our glasses and drank up. Bee ran back in the study, sat down, and opened the next bag. When she pulled out the N.Y. Knicks sweatshirt, she repeated the same ritual, putting the Knicks sweatshirt on over the top of her Yankees one, and took off to show her father.

Annie turned to me and said, "The Knicks season is not a very happy time for our household. I can't tell you how many times I've walked in and simply had to shut off the game and march them out of the room."

"No complaints, no arguments?"

"No, they've come to understand that it's better for their health not to watch that pitiful excuse of a team."

Bee came running back in and took off the first two sweatshirts, because she was getting too hot. Then she opened the last bag and took out the sweatshirt with the Chelsea F.C. soccer logo on it. She looked at it and said, "Who are they?"

"That's your mommy's team, sweetheart. They actually win championships, unlike the Knicks," Annie replied as Bee put on the sweatshirt, hugged and kissed her mommy and me, and ran out to show it to her daddy.

Annie looked at me with pure admiration. "Bravo, Alicia," she said. "You are one creative and thoughtful bride-to-be."

# CHAPTER TWENTY-NINE

Our guests left early. Everyone kept telling us that we needed sleep before our big day, and my maid of honor wanted to be at her best. She looked so adorable in those oversized sweatshirts that I had her put them all on again so I could take pictures of her in each one.

I sat on the couch in the living room and Nick stretched out with his head in my lap. I ran my fingers through his beautiful hair and said, "You haven't been doing your meditation lately. I hope I haven't been keeping you from that."

"Sweetheart, if it's a choice between forty-five minutes alone and forty-five extra minutes with my arms wrapped around you, there's no choice. You win, hands down."

"Wow," I said, "I had no idea I was a substitute for peace and enlightenment."

"Always."

I kissed him on the forehead. "Tradition has it that the bride and groom sleep separately the night before the wedding. I say throw out tradition."

"I second that," he replied.

"Tradition also has it that the bride and groom don't make love the night before the wedding. Once again, I say throw out tradition. What do you think?"

"I say, throw both traditions into the ocean."

"Wow! You're one accommodating groom."

"When it comes to you, I'm always accommodating."

"Yes, you are," I said. "Hey, are we going on a honeymoon?"

"That's totally up to you, sweetheart. But if we do, we'll have to limit it to the lower forty-eight states. My mother seems so happy. I don't want to give her any cause for alarm."

"I understand, and personally I'd prefer to spend our honeymoon right here. I think both of us have traveled enough for a while, and living here is like being on a honeymoon every day. That should make your mother happy."

"Absolutely! I've got to give the woman credit. In all my life I've never seen a person do such an abrupt turnaround. She went from being totally absent to being obsessed with her son's well-being."

"She was awfully young when she had you."

"Yes, she was. And her family was dirt-poor. The only thing she had going for her was her looks, and she used that. I don't even know if she went to high school, but I'll tell you something. She knows more about great literature than I do, and more about government, history, and real estate than almost anybody I know."

"Impressive."

"It is, when you think about it," Nick continued. "She wasn't content being arm candy for her current husband. She's a self-educated woman. After reading my first two books she called me up and said, 'Nick, I'm very proud of you and I'm overjoyed that they're going to make the books into movies, but in all honesty, I know you can write better books. Books that rise to the level of art.' I totally agreed with her and promised her that after I finish the final book in the series, my next books will live up to her literary standards."

"Did your two Pulitzers live up to her standards?" I asked, feeling defensive of him.

"If they did, she'd never admit it. Those years when I was a correspondent were pure hell for her." He suddenly had that far-off gaze that I often saw when he thought he was alone, and didn't know I was watching him. "Sadly, my love, there remains a part of me that takes delight in knowing that she suffered. Her reward for being so neglectful early on. I know it's wrong."

"Do you think you might have chosen a different career path if she'd been more loving?"

"I really don't like to think about it because if I'd chosen differently, I wouldn't have met you."

I looked down at him and smiled and said, "It's a good thing we don't believe in tradition because after that remark there's no way we're not making love tonight. In fact…" I started to get up, but he stopped me.

"Just one moment my beautiful, soon-to-be wife. I've talked about my parents, but I know you didn't have it any better. So, if you want to talk, please go ahead."

"No, I don't want to talk about them. As far as I'm concerned, the life I always wanted began the night we met, and right now all I want to do is get you into bed."

And that's exactly how our last night together as an unmarried couple ended, between the sheets of our big, lovely bed, with a cool ocean breeze moving the curtains in tandem with our bodies.

# CHAPTER THIRTY

Nick and I woke up early, and after he bundled me up in his parka with the hood, we went for our usual early morning walk along the beach. He lifted the hood over my head, and I felt like little Bee wearing those oversized sweatshirts.

We stopped about every fifty feet and kissed, for long magical moments, serenaded by the gulls and the crashing waves. We knew that once we went back to the mansion, the caterers and makeup artists would be arriving, and we wouldn't see each other for an ungodly five hours.

Naturally, the mansion had its own makeup room that was nearly as big as the one at the studio. I sat down in a chair and studied my reflection in the mirror. I craned my neck until I could only see my right cheek, and I had to admit it was thrilling to think that I would look like my old self again, even for half a day.

While I waited for Bernardo, I put a clean silver bandage over the wound, even though the one I had on was only a day old, and I could wear them for up to four days. I didn't want to take a chance that the makeup might get into the wound and cause problems.

Bernardo entered holding a number of fashion magazines and a long, thin piece of plastic. He asked, "And how is the beautiful bride-to-be this morning?"

"A little nervous, but very happy," I said.

"Well, if I was marrying your groom I would be over the moon."

I laughed. "You're not planning on stealing him from me at the alter?"

"Well, if there was a possibility that he might run away with me, I would give it a shot, but I have it from a reliable source that he's madly in love with you … so I wouldn't worry."

He held up the piece of plastic. "Remind you of anything?"

I looked down at my arm and then into the mirror and said, "It's the exact color and texture of my skin."

"Exactly!" he exclaimed, then he looked at me more closely. "The silver bandage was recently changed?"

"Yes, five minutes ago."

"Perfect. Now, if you could kindly close your eyes."

I did as he said and could feel him place the plastic over my bandage and gently run his hands across the edges to seal the adhesive. Then I could feel some brushes on my face, and after a few moments, he said, "You can open your eyes."

I opened my eyes and nearly fainted. The applique covered the bandage, with no bulging or bumps, and matched my skin perfectly. As I stared and stared, I realized that this was the first time I'd felt *whole* since that terrible night. "My God, Bernardo, you're a genius!"

"Thank you! That is what they say," he said, and I laughed and reached out to touch his arm and thanked him again.

Bee entered the room and Bernardo looked at her and said, "I thought by now you'd have been walking around with your pretty new dress on, but instead you're wearing an oversized New York Knicks' sweatshirt. At least you could have chosen a better team. Even I know the Knicks are pathetic."

"They're going to be much better this year," Bee said. "My daddy promised me."

"Great! Would you like to make a little bet on that?"

"I'm not allowed to gamble."

"In this case, that's a good thing."

Bee looked at me and started jumping up and down and saying over and over again, "Oh my God, oh my God. Look at you, Alicia."

"I know," I said, clapping like a little kid. "Can you believe it? It's Bernardo. He's a genius." Bee immediately went over and hugged Bernardo.

Then she looked up at him and asked, "Would you like to be my friend?"

"I thought we were already friends," Bernardo said. "I carry pictures of you around and tell people that you're my daughter."

"I know, but I mean my phone friend."

"And why would I want to be your phone friend?"

"So I can send you texts and pictures in the morning to cheer you up," Bee replied as Bernardo took her phone and typed in his name and number.

He gave it back and said, "Now I can say I'm one of your five million followers, and you haven't even started your acting career yet."

"I don't want to be an actress. I want to be a medical researcher so I can find a cure for the disease that killed my uncle Simon. That would make my mommy so happy."

Bernardo turned away and wiped his eyes, and when he turned back to Bee he hugged her and said softly, "You are an angel, and your uncle Simon would be so proud of you." Bernardo then looked at me and said, "Excuse me for a moment."

He walked out of the room as Bee turned to me and said, "I didn't want to make him sad."

"You didn't, sweetheart. Like your mommy, Bernardo also loved your uncle Simon."

Bee's phone rang and it was her mother telling her it was time to get ready and that they were in my room. The first thing that went through my head was, *thank God Nick and I replaced the sheets on the bed because last night was an exceptionally wild one.*

Bee hugged me, and told me I was the prettiest bride ever. She also told me to tell Bernardo that she's sorry she made him cry. She then pirouetted and ran straight into Bernardo, who was coming back in. "Bernardo," she said, "I'm so sorry for making you sad. Please forgive me."

"There is nothing to forgive. I simply loved your uncle like a million other people."

"Thank you, but I have to run now and get ready. My mommy says it's time."

"To put on dress number five?" Bernardo asked as she hugged him and took off running. He looked at me and said, "If one had any doubt about the existence of God, one would only need to look at that angel and all doubt would be erased."

"I doubt you'll get many arguments about that," I replied. Then I looked at him and asked, "So you were very close to Simon?"

"Every employee at the studio was close to Simon. Annie and Simon represent the very best in human beings."

He worked with his back to me for a few moments, cleaning brushes and arranging them on a towel. Finally he turned and said, "You know, it was Simon who helped me come out to my family."

"Really?"

"Really. I had been at the studio for about a year, and he knew I was capable of incredible work, but my performance was slipping. I'd missed a few deadlines and clashed with a couple of clients. I was miserable, and I didn't know why. One day, Simon took me aside and asked me if everything was okay. I gave him some bluster, but he saw right through it, and do you know what that man did?"

I shook my head.

"He cleared his calendar and steered me out of the office and into a café, and we sat there for hours, just talking. And somehow, just by being the lovely, perceptive person that he was, he helped me figure it out. He asked me about all the usual stuff — my family, whether I was dating anyone — and boom, we put it together. I had never told my parents I was gay, and it was eating at me. I swear, one long conversation with Simon was better than six months of therapy.

"He put his hand around my shoulder and said, 'Bernardo, unless you're true to yourself you will never be happy. If they give you a tough time tell them Da Vinci and Michelangelo were gay, and look at what they left the world to admire for the next five hundred years.'

"That night I went home like usual, and my father like usual was watching a basketball game and drinking a beer, and my mother was cooking in the kitchen, and my two sisters were upstairs giggling over God knows what. I gathered them all into the living room, and said, 'I have an announcement to make. I'm gay. I have a boyfriend that I really like, and would love for all of you to meet him.'"

"What did they say?"

"My dad looked at me and said, 'Bernardo, I thought you were going to tell us something we didn't know.' And I said, 'You mean, you all knew all this time?' And he said, 'My God, Bernardo, a blind and deaf person could have figured out you were gay in less than five minutes.' Then he asked me if my boyfriend was into sports, and I said, 'Actually, he loves the Lakers," and my dad told me to invite him over that Sunday so they could treat him to a great Italian dinner. My sisters went back upstairs and my mom went back into the kitchen. My father said, 'Do your old man a favor and go get him another cold beer,' so I went into the kitchen, and before I could open the refrigerator my mother asked me to taste the meat sauce she had made and let her know if I thought it was cooked enough. So I did that, and I told her it tasted great. She kissed me on the cheek and said, 'love you.'

"I took the beer out of the refrigerator and went back and gave it to my dad. It was a commercial break and he said, 'Did you know Da Vinci and Michelangelo were gay?' I told him I'd heard that, and he said, 'Who knows? You might be the next Da Vinci." Then the commercial ended and he went back to watching the game."

I laughed so hard, I thought my plastic skin might peel off.

"I'm guessing you told Simon every detail of that story."

"Blow by blow."

"Naturally."

Bernardo laughed at the memory, then propped himself against the makeup counter, facing me. He looked like he was holding himself back from starting to cry again.

"The day Simon died, the entire studio was swept into a black hole. A dark cloud hung over Annie for nearly a year. It didn't start to lift until she visited his grave and found a little girl there reciting poetry to her deceased brother. Bee was there with her adoptive dad, Joe. Annie and Joe had planned on getting married shortly after Simon passed away, but she was going through a difficult divorce, and Joe was busy with Bee, so it never happened. Bee sealed the deal. Joe and Annie were married two weeks later, and Annie became Bee's adoptive mom. Annie was never able to have children, but I bet if you asked her if the wait was worth it, she would say yes."

"I have no doubt about that," I said, as I desperately tried not to cry.

Bernardo reached down and handed me my makeup kit and said, "Why don't you put on your makeup the way you like it? And don't try to overcompensate around the plastic skin." Before I started putting on my makeup, he picked up the magazines with a picture of me on each of the covers and more inside. "Just for the hell of it, tell me which pictures of yourself you like best. I know everything is photoshopped and cleaned up, but if you had to use three as head shots, which three would you pick?"

I looked at the pictures and quickly gave up. "I just can't, Bernardo. I feel such a sense of disconnect that I couldn't trust my judgement. I'm sorry."

"Nothing to be sorry about," he said as I started to put on my makeup. I kept it light and understated, and when I finished, I turned to Bernardo and asked, "How did I do?"

"You look as lovely as any girl I have worked on."

"Except Bee?" I jokingly asked.

"She's the exception, but then if you pulled up that Knicks sweatshirt she was wearing, you'd see a pair of wings." He picked up a brush and added a touch of blush to both my cheeks.

"I'm so happy for you, Alicia. Yes, I'm jealous I'm not marrying that hunk of a man, but if it can't be me, I'm happy it's you."

"I'll be sure to tell him, and thank you so much."

"I have one more question, but if you don't want to answer it, I understand. Now that you look in the mirror and look as beautiful as ever before, and with what you know now, if the only way you could have Nick was that you had to relive that terrible night in the limo with those two bastards, the extended time in the hospital, and all the pain, would you still get into the limo?"

"Without a second thought, yes, I'd get into the limo and re-live all of the suffering if I knew it would bring me to Nick in the end."

"That's quite a statement," he said.

"It is," I said. "Bernardo, it's so hard to explain. That man reached inside me and helped me rediscover the person I was before I ever did my first photo shoot. He sees me for who I am, and he loves me, inside and out."

Bernardo was getting misty-eyed again, so I changed the subject and asked him if he was still together with the boyfriend he introduced to his family when he came out.

"Oh God, no. That turned out to be an extended fling. Actually, I think he might have fallen for my father. From the moment we walked into my parents' house he was sitting beside my dad, talking sports nonstop. And if there was a Lakers game on, they were like two crazy men screaming at the TV. My father still asks about him."

I couldn't help but laugh and then I asked, "Are you seeing anyone now? Anyone who might be the *one*?"

"Yes, and we've been talking about getting married and adopting a few children. I think it might be the right time."

"Well, when you pick a date, if you'd like, you can have the reception right here."

"That's very kind of you, but I do have a little problem … how do I ask Bee to be my maid of honor?"

"I can take care of that for you. It'll give me the opportunity to explain to Bee that it's just as natural for men to love men, and for girls to love girls, as it is for men to love women and get married."

"Are you sure you are up to it?"

"Well, of all the people in her orbit I am the closest to her in age. That should help."

"I hope so. I love that little peanut so much," he said as he ran a comb through my hair. "I do have one recommendation about your hair. I wouldn't put a drop of hairspray on it. You're so young, and you have a free and loving spirit, and with that type of spirit, my vote would be to let your hair do as it pleases."

"So, no beehive?" I jokingly asked.

Bernardo flung up his hand. "Don't even say it," he said as I got up and hugged him for a long time, then collected my things and went off to the bedroom.

# CHAPTER THIRTY-ONE

I knocked on the door, announced myself, and Annie appeared at the door in an instant. "Come in, come in," she said, as she quickly embraced me and then returned to the full-length mirror to help her daughter with her maid-of-honor dress. Bee was most of the way into her A-line, scoop neck dress that fell to just above her bare feet. She was all excited, and before her mother could finish, she ran to me and said, "Did you hear the news?"

"No. Please don't tell me Nick is leaving me at the altar."

She looked shocked. "Why would he do that? He's so in love with you. No, Nick got Mr. Wang's family approved to come to the U.S. His parents and some other relatives are going to move here and come live with us. I'm so excited, I need to go hug him."

"Oh, no you don't, young lady, you're going to stay right here and finish dressing," Annie said, and Bee walked back over to the mirror. Annie said, "You'll have plenty of time to hug Mr. Wang." Annie then looked at me and asked, "How did Nick do it? I've been trying for over a year."

"Through his mother, probably."

"Does she have that much pull?"

"Apparently so. She's a very pretty and confident lady who'll do anything for her son."

Annie said, "Well, whatever she did, it seems to have worked a miracle." Then she bent down to help Bee put on her crystal ballet flats.

"Christine got her son out of a Russian prison. Absolutely nothing surprises me when it comes to that woman."

Bee twirled around and asked me, "How do I look?"

"Better than Cinderella," I said, and she hugged me and then turned to her mother and asked, "Can I go see Mr. Wang now?"

"Yes, sweetheart, but please don't run." She opened the door and took off and I looked at Annie and said, "I think she only knows one speed."

"Let me guess, Bernardo told you to let your hair hang wild, no spray, not too much combing," she said, and I nodded. "You know, he's right. You're so beautiful, and one can't even see that silver bandage covered with that thin, tinted, plastic."

"He's a miracle worker. By the way, has anyone seen Nick?"

"I think he's with Joe. I asked Nick who his best man was, and he said he'd never even thought about it. He then turned to his literary buddy and asked him if he would be his best man, and of course Joe said yes. So, you have my baby girl as your maid of honor and my husband as Nick's best man. I'm feeling slightly left out."

"Would you like to be a flower girl?"

"I don't think so. I'll just be lost between the two most beautiful girls on the planet. I'll simply stay as a guest."

I hugged Annie and said, "I don't know how to thank you for everything. You made it so easy."

"Oh, don't you worry. I've already thought of a few things, but you might want to run them past your obsessed husband," she laughingly replied.

"Do you really think he's obsessed with me?"

"Yes, but only in the best sense," she said, as she took my wedding dress out of the closet. "The big moment is getting very close, and before you know it, it will all be over."

# CHAPTER THIRTY-TWO

And just like that, Nick and I were in front of the priest, as he proclaimed us husband and wife and said those all-important words: "You may kiss the bride."

Nick leaned in and kissed me, and I, forgetting where I was, threw my arms around him and seriously kissed back and didn't let go, and he didn't pull back either. My guess is that we were kissing for forty-five seconds, which might not seem long, but with an audience, it's an eternity. They finally started clapping and we pulled away. I looked out at our guests and glanced at the priest and said, "We can't help it, we're madly in love."

"Well, this is one marriage that's off to a great start," the priest said as everyone applauded again and a few people sent up little cheers that started ripples of joyful laughter.

My maid of honor was the first to hug me, and she wouldn't let go, so as guests came up to congratulate us, I had to greet them with an angel attached to me.

The guests quickly moved to the reception area as Rolando, the owner of the moving company, and his lovely wife Maria stopped me. Rolando kissed me gently on the cheek and said, "You look so beautiful, Alicia. I can't tell you how happy I am for you. You have married the best man I've ever known." He turned to Maria and said, "Is he not the very best?"

"Yes, he is," she said as she went to shake my hand and instead, I hugged her.

Rolando continued, "Nick bought us the most beautiful home in Studio City. It's a house I could only dream of, and now my children can go to a good school, and we don't have to worry about them getting hurt, and Maria can go shopping and take walks safely around the neighborhood. I don't know how to thank him … or you. You are family now."

"You can thank us by making sure your children get the best education possible, and by enjoying your new home and making sure it's always filled with love and caring."

"That's almost exactly what Nick said. God bless both of you."

"Thank you, and God bless you and your family."

Before I had a chance to turn around, I felt my appendage, my maid of honor, take my hand. "Everyone seems so happy," she said. "It's wonderful."

"That might be because I have the most beautiful maid of honor in the entire world. You're so radiant you could light up Yankee Stadium all by yourself."

"Thank you, Alicia, but you're the radiant one," she said as she took off and seconds later reappeared with Mr. Wang and his uncle. We all hugged and I told Mr. Wang and his uncle how happy I was to hear that their family would finally be reunited. Mr. Wang told me that he had been trying for over ten years, and then just like that Nick got their applications approved. "It's like a miracle," he said.

We talked for a few more minutes and then I asked Bee if she had seen my husband. She took me by the hand and led me to the study, where Nick was sitting behind his desk talking to his mother. He looked up and said, "And here she is."

I took the phone, and I could instantly feel the joy and relief in Christine's voice. She thanked me over and over again for marrying her son, and I told her that I really wished she could have been there. She said she would see us soon enough, and before hanging up she said, "Please take care of my son. I love you both."

"I will," I said. "We love you too." Then I handed the phone back to Nick.

"And so, my handsome husband, are we ready to go join our guests?"

He came around the desk and grabbed both my hands and pulled me toward him. "I wasn't finished with our kiss at the altar," he said, and suddenly we were back at it, until I faked a cough and pointed to Bee, who was looking directly at us.

"Oh, don't worry," she said. "Mommy and Daddy kiss all the time. They tell me it's what married people in love do."

I laughed as I took her hand and the three of us left the study. As we entered the ballroom, the DJ spotted us and said, "And will the newlyweds give us the honor of the first dance?" Nick and I looked down at Bee, who let go of my hand, and then Nick and I stepped onto the dance floor. As soon as he heard the first notes of "Oh! Darling," by the Beatles, Nick looked at me with surprise and said, "Is this your song choice?" and I nodded. It was the perfect song for dancing a minuet — a slow dance popular a few centuries ago. Because of my leg and Nick's limited dancing skills, it was a safe bet. We had practiced a few times, but not with this song, because I wanted it to be a surprise.

"How did you know I loved the Beatles?" Nick asked.

"Your mother told me."

"Did you even know who the Beatles were?" he asked.

"Husband of mine, everyone knows the Beatles."

"My apologies. I didn't mean to be reverse-ageist."

"That's fine. I *am* very young, and I didn't really know this song, but as soon as I heard the lyrics, I fell in love."

"I'll bet you did."

"Now, tell me again, why did you fall in love with me? I can never hear it enough."

"I fell in love with you … because you're the most beautiful, intelligent, caring and sensitive girl I've ever met."

I threw my arms around him and we kissed as we danced cheek to cheek.

"Why did you fall in love with me?" he asked.

"Oh, it was the sex and the money, obviously. What else is there?" I laughingly replied.

"So you pulled a real scam on me?"

"If there's anything I've learned about you, it's that no one gets anything over on you."

"Is that so, my little scam artist?"

"You had a very busy morning, and you didn't tell me anything about it."

"Tradition, my wife … no seeing the bride on the day of the wedding, until we meet at the altar."

"We had no problems throwing tradition to the wind last night."

"Last night, you made me take a bite from the apple, and that was the end of all inhibitions."

"So I'm the reason?" I jokingly asked.

"I'm sorry, I can't resist a temptation as sweet and delicious as you. I didn't find out about Mr. Wang's relatives until a few hours ago. One of many calls from my mother. I swear, I think she thought I wasn't going through with it."

"It's because she loves you so much," I replied.

"At times, I think she loves you more."

"Well, that's completely understandable. And how about the house you bought for Rolando and his family? Surely, that didn't take place this morning?"

"I meant to tell you, but every time I tried, you tore off my clothes and had your way with me."

"You know, if it wasn't our wedding night, a remark like that might very well have kept you out of my bed."

"Oh please, don't even think such a thing. That would be excruciating."

"Thank you for that tidbit of information. Now, I know how to punish you when you misbehave."

"Like you didn't know before," he replied as I looked directly at him, still unsure if this was a dream, but certain that I was madly in love with him. We kissed, even though the music stopped, and a strange silence descended upon the room as we continued to kiss until I was softly poked in my stomach by my maid of honor.

I looked down at her and asked, "What is it, sweetheart?"

"You're at it again," she whispered.

Nick and I smiled and waved to our guests sheepishly as we walked off the dance floor. Just then, a Beach Boys song came on, and Bee and Mr. Wang took to the dance floor, twirling, whirling, and sliding under each other's legs in a routine that looked like they must have done it a hundred times before. And everyone got to hear the most beautiful sound of all — laughter from the little angel, rising above the dome ceiling and into the heavens, like a choir of celestial beings.

After a couple of songs, Bernardo cut in and started dancing with Bee. He wasn't as athletic as Mr. Wang, but he was more refined. He twirled and twirled the little princess around until I thought she might fly off. All the guests were standing and clapping as Bernardo lasted two songs, and then handed her back to Mr. Wang.

I walked up to Bernardo, who was catching his breath. "You're quite the dancer," I said.

"Thanks! My God, that almost gave me a heart attack."

I introduced him to Nick and said, "Bernardo and his future husband are going to have their wedding reception right here. After the miraculous job he did with me, he deserves a grand wedding and we're throwing it."

"That sounds like a perfect plan," Nick said. Then he looked at me and said, "Bee will probably want to be involved."

"She's going to be my maid of honor, if your lovely wife can talk her into it," Bernardo said.

"That shouldn't take much persuasion," Nick said, and we all laughed.

Once Mr. Wang and Bee were finished with their second set, some of the other guests ventured onto the dance floor. All four cleaning ladies and their husbands danced to several songs in a row. It was obvious that they had been dancing for years, and they looked gorgeous — transformed — in their dresses and makeup.

I spotted Fernando sitting alone and went up to him and sat beside him. "Don't you like dancing?" I asked.

"I used to go dancing with my wife all the time. She loved to dance," he said, looking down at his hands and then smiling at me, with effort.

"I see," I said. Then I reached out and put one of my hands on his hand, and said, "Maybe someday you'll be able to dance in your wife's honor, because she loved it so much. But I understand that it probably feels much too hard right now."

He nodded emphatically and was suddenly close to tears. In a voice choked with emotion, he said, "Since she passed away, I cannot go on a dance floor without feeling like I'm betraying her. I know that might sound silly, but it's just the way I feel."

"It doesn't sound silly. It sounds like undying love."

"Thank you, Señorita," he said, wiping his eyes as he made a sudden bid to compose himself. "You are a beautiful bride, and you and Nick make a lovely couple. He never stops looking at you, even when he is talking to other guests. He's very protective of you and that is because you are very special."

I had to keep myself from crying and when I finally felt back in control I said, "Thank you, Fernando." I squeezed the hand of this gentle and loving man and said, "Thank you for being a part of our family." Then I stood up and walked back over to Nick, who was still speaking with the Academy Award winning makeup artist.

"Are you trying to steal my husband?" I teased, as I wedged myself between them.

Bernardo laughed and said, "Oh sweetheart, I don't stand a chance. This one only has eyes for you, and well he should." He shook Nick's hand and kissed me on the cheek and went off in search of food and drink.

"A very nice gentleman," Nick said.

"And amazingly talented," I replied. Nick had not mentioned the plastic facial covering, and in all honesty, it didn't surprise me. I knew he must have noticed; he noticed everything. He had told me from the beginning of our relationship how beautiful I was, and at first, I doubted his sincerity, but no more. For him to admit that the facial covering improved my appearance was, in his mind, to admit that I wasn't beautiful without it. And he wasn't going to admit that.

I looked across the ballroom, up at the fresco-painted ceiling, and then out through the arched windows overlooking the ocean. I remembered my first night in the mansion, and the nights after that, when I doubted Nick's love for me. I remembered looking through the living room window and thinking that if I walked straight into the ocean, the salt might wash clean the poison that had crept into me after that terrible night on my twenty-third birthday. The night I felt my life end, even as my body, stubbornly and stupidly, remained alive.

Today, I was not only a true survivor but also the princess inside the mansion, and as for the future that I allowed Nick to take control of, with no objection, it turned out to be the best and wisest choice I ever made.

I took his hand, and we walked over to one of the arched windows and looked out at the ocean. Filtered sunshine passed through the stained-glass, and it was as though we were alone, protected by a nimbus of light.

I looked at him and asked, "Do you believe in miracles?"

"I must, because I never thought I could be so lucky as to meet and marry the girl of my dreams." He looked at me and asked, "Do you?"

I nodded as I ran my hands through his dark, wavy hair and along his chiseled face, until we were kissing again.

I knew then that my dream of meeting my ideal man and falling deeply in love had come true. I was not a prisoner of a dream, as Anne Brontë had written about in her haunting poem "Dreams," but an escapee who was living her dream in real time.

*To know myself beloved at last, to think my heart has found a rest, my life of solitude is past!*

# CHAPTER THIRTY-THREE

I stood in the empty ballroom as the last rays of sunshine filtered through the bottom layers of the windows. Nick and I had been married for almost seven hours. The guests had started leaving a few hours earlier, and from the looks on their faces they all seemed to have had a wonderful time. Even Fernando looked happy, and he thanked Nick and me for inviting him and for making him feel like a part of our family.

The caterers had done a superb job. The food and the service were exceptional, and Nick tipped every member of the team generously, remembering their names from when they first arrived early in the morning and introduced themselves. Once a reporter, always a reporter, except that mine would never go on any more dangerous assignments, as long as his mom and I had our way. Fortunately, he was one to keep his promises.

I walked out of the bedroom and into the living room and was immediately joined on the couch by my maid of honor, who could not stop talking about how much fun she'd had. But before I could get a word in, she was out cold, dead asleep, with her head on my lap.

Annie handed me a glass of champagne and sat down next to us.

"She'll be sleeping in that dress tonight," she said. "It's a tradition with her, ever since the first party we had for her, when she wore her first dress. The first dress she ever had."

I smiled and said, "She's a gift from God. It's the only way I can describe such a luminous creature."

Annie nodded knowingly, then asked, "Would it be rude of me to talk a little business?"

"Not at all," I said as I gently ran my hand across the little angel's hair. "What would you like to talk about?"

"I wanted to know if you might be interested in coming to work for me. The job would be to tutor Bee at the studio. I hardly see my daughter five days a week, and I can't stand it anymore. At least if she's at the studio, I can drop in and visit her every hour or so and have lunch with you two. We'd drive down together in the morning and come back home together."

"I would love to! But I'll have to talk to Nick first. We're a married couple now, don't you know," I said, flashing my ring. "But it should be fine. He's repeatedly said that he'll support anything I want to do as long as it isn't modeling."

"I'll pay you quite handsomely."

"For tutoring and getting to spend entire days with an earthly angel? I should be paying you."

Annie smiled. "I wouldn't expect you to start until after your facial surgery."

"I don't see why I'd have to wait that long. If Nick is true to his word, I should be able to start on Monday."

"But your honeymoon—"

"We've been honeymooning since we met," I said with a laugh. "And from what the doctor described, there's very little recovery involved in the facial surgery. They attach two pieces of my skin, injected with my DNA, to opposite sides of the open wound, and hopefully the skin grows and covers the wound like it was a cut. The skin might not be a perfect match, but with a little makeup, no one should know the difference. I might have to miss a day, but that should be about it."

"So you'll talk to Nick and let me know?"

"Absolutely," I replied as I looked down at Bee. "Is Joe okay with all this?"

"He totally understands. Like me, he loves having her around, but now that he has a new friend who loves talking about books, history, politics, medicine, and science as much as Simon did, he'll be able to fill in some of that alone time."

Annie texted Joe to ask him to come pick Bee up and carry her out to the car. The little angel stirred in her father's arms but stayed asleep, and Nick and I walked them out to the limo, along with Annie and Mr. Wang and Mr. Wang's uncle. We stood on the threshold and waved goodbye to our little chosen family until the limo was out of sight. Then I turned to Nick.

"What do you think we should do now?"

"First, get out of these clothes?"

"But you look so much like James Bond in that outfit, even though I don't think anybody who played Bond was nearly as handsome as you."

"Nor do I think any of the Bond girls were half as beautiful as you. So what do you say? A little champagne, poetry, and see what that leads to?"

"Sounds wonderful," I said as Nick opened the balcony door.

"Just one more thing before we go inside," I said. He looked at me and I threw my arms around him, and we kissed passionately, under a starlit sky, to the sound of the crashing waves, without any interruptions.

# CHAPTER THIRTY-FOUR

I slipped my dress off and put it on a hanger and hung it on a rack in the bathroom, along with my bra. I kept my panties on and looked in the full-length mirror. I was torn between keeping the plastic facial piece on or taking it off and going back to the silver bandage I'd worn since meeting Nick.

I didn't think there would even be a choice. Bernardo had said that I should not keep the plastic on longer than ten hours, since there was always a chance that some of the material in the facial mask could seep through the bandage and cause problems.

I stared at my reflection, thinking, *This is the way I looked before those bastards beat the shit out of me.* I still had the same body, and with the makeup on, I looked as beautiful as ever. It wasn't such a far cry to say that I was as good looking as any of the Bond girls. I skipped the clichéd lingerie that so many brides supposedly wore on their wedding nights, and simply went with one of Nick's large dress shirts. I knew that was what really drove him nuts, and of course my vanity won out and I kept the mask on.

I walked out of the bathroom just as my gorgeous husband was popping the cork out of a bottle of Cristal champagne. He turned and said, "Just in time," as he handed me a flute and he filled up his own. We tapped glasses and he said, "To us," and I repeated the toast.

We both drank up and then he looked at me strangely and said, "Alicia, what are you doing still wearing that plastic covering? Bernardo told me you shouldn't wear it for over ten hours, and it's past that by now."

"A few more hours won't matter," I said as he reached over and took the flute out of my hands.

"Please take it off. I could help you if you like."

"No, I don't need help," I said as I walked back into the bathroom. I looked in the mirror and couldn't help feeling that what just happened was like a slap in the face … a slap I knew I deserved. I wondered how far I'd really come since my days strutting down runways, posing for photo spreads, snorting coke, and screwing men old enough to be my grandfather.

I needed to realize that Nick was not like most men. He was a reporter. You couldn't lie to him. He saw past the surface of things.

I took off the plastic patch and changed my silver bandage. I suddenly felt anxious, like a virgin bride on her wedding night, despite the fact that Nick and I had been sleeping together every night since I moved in.

I walked out of the bathroom and sat down next to him on the bed. "I'm back!" I exclaimed as though I had been missing for months.

He looked at me as though I'd lost my mind. "Yes, you are, my gorgeous bride." He handed me my flute of champagne and I downed the contents in two gulps.

"Are you anxious about something?" he asked as he refilled my glass.

"A little…"

He laughed and I asked, "What's so funny?"

"You're having wedding night nerves. It's adorable."

"You know, you're a real ass."

"Well, this ass just got married to the girl of his dreams, so if being an ass is what made it all come true, then I embrace the title."

"You really do have an answer for everything," I said. I couldn't help smiling.

"I don't know about everything, but I do see what's right in front of me, and that's a dream come true."

"Try all you like, but sweet talk isn't going to get you very far. Remember, a little romance, poetry?"

He reached over and touched my ear and said, "You have the cutest little ears. Have I ever told you that? You'll never be mistaken for a rabbit or be a member of their select group."

"I do love carrots. Maybe if I eat them for breakfast, lunch, and dinner my ears will grow."

"I don't think so. I think that ship has sailed."

"Ships, rabbits. Pick a metaphor, mister," I said, and Nick laughed and said, "Fine."

As I brought the glass to my lips, I noticed that my hand was shaking. Nick took a sip of his champagne and looked directly into my eyes, but I glanced away, tapped my flute, and asked for more champagne.

"It was a lovely reception," I said. "I think everyone had a wonderful time."

"It was perfect."

"I was worried my leg would go limp and I would tumble to the floor like a drunken clown. But I didn't need to worry. You had an eye on me the whole time."

"Like a dragon guarding its treasure," he said in a saucy tone, as I sat back on the bed and rested my head on a pile of soft pillows.

"So I'm a treasure. Exactly how much am I worth in today's market?"

"Impossible to say. It would be like putting a price on Da Vinci's *The Virgin of the Rocks*."

"Interesting comparison, especially on our honeymoon night."

He lay his head on my lap and looked up at me, then reached up and ran his fingers around my lips. "You have the softest, most flawless lips."

I moved his fingers away from my lips and said, "Getting a little ahead of yourself, aren't you, my gorgeous warrior?" The anxiety I'd felt since taking off the plastic facial mask was seeping out of me, replaced by a tingling sensation that began in my toes and worked its way up. I was a little drunk, and I wanted my husband badly, but this cat-and-mouse game was fun.

Nick's fingers slowly started making their way down the middle of my chest and I said, "I don't remember giving you permission to venture down river, you dirty old man."

"Seriously, have I ever acted like a dirty old man?"

"No," I had to admit, "you've always been the perfect gentleman. But one never knows how marriage might change a person."

"Oh, so what you're saying is that I should be on high alert when it comes to you?"

I laughed and said, "Who do you think you're kidding? You're always on high alert when it comes to me."

"True," he said, as his fingers continued to make their way down river. When he reached my belly button he circled it twice and said, "You know, you have the cutest little belly button. Has anyone ever told you that?"

"No, you're the first," I said as he licked my belly button and I said, "Stop that, it tickles."

He laughed as he pulled himself up and looked directly into my eyes, and said, "Alicia, you make me feel whole, and I never thought I could feel that way again."

It was the truest thing anyone had ever said to me, and I probably would have started crying if he hadn't shot his hand up and said, as sweetly as possible, "No crying on our honeymoon." I nodded and threw my arms around him, and from there it was heaven, as we dove under the covers and made love, for the first time, as husband and wife.

# CHAPTER THIRTY-FIVE

The sun was already up by the time I finally opened my eyes on the first full day of our honeymoon. Nick was out in the hallway, talking to his mother on the phone.

"Yes, we took lots of pictures," I heard him say, and then he listened for a bit, and said, "She's fine. She's doing well."

I looked out the window and remembered his words from the night before: *Alicia, you make me feel whole, and I never thought I could feel that way again.* I could easily have said the same about him. He glued me backed together and reawakened the person I was striving to be before being thrown off course.

Nick walked into the bedroom and said, "Good morning my lovely wife," and I could swear my heart skipped a few beats.

"Good morning my handsome husband."

He lay down beside me and kissed me gently on both cheeks. Then he asked, "So what were you thinking about when I walked in here and broke your concentration?"

"You mean you can't just read my mind?"

"Nope. Too much going on in there," he said, giving my temple a soft tap.

"I was just thinking about how I feel like the luckiest girl in the whole world."

"That's funny. I was just talking to my mom and telling her that I feel like the luckiest guy in the world being married to you."

"How is she?"

"Terrific. I think she's as excited about us being married as we are."

"That's because she loves you so much. She might not have been the greatest mother while you were growing up, but she's working overtime to make up for that now."

"Don't I know it," Nick said. "Listen, don't get mad, but I've been wondering — should we call your parents and let them know we're married? They might like to know that someone has made an honest woman of their daughter…"

I slapped his arm. "What a piggish statement," I said.

"Oink."

I rolled my eyes at him and said, "No, I don't think my parents need to know. They would just ask us for money. I'm half expecting to receive a bill for all of the expenses they incurred while I was a child in their care. Toothpaste, a dollar fifty, shoes, thirty-five dollars and fifty cents…"

"Were they really that stingy with you?"

"They were. I never gave them any trouble, or asked for anything the slightest bit extravagant, yet they always found a way to make me feel guilty about providing me with the most basic things a child needs. The first couple of years as a model I sent them money every month, and never once got a thank you call. When I needed them most, when I was in the hospital, they couldn't find the time to make a twenty-five-minute drive into the city to see me."

"I'm sorry sweetheart."

"It's okay, because out of that tragedy came the best and most wonderful gift I could have ever imagined."

He pointed to himself and said, "Me? You're talking about me, right?"

"Yes, silly, I'm talking about you."

He reached over and kissed me ever so gently, ever so softly, as he wiped away a few tears that had rolled down my cheeks. I turned over and looked back out the window at the majestic ocean. I asked, "So do you really think your mom is going to visit? When I first talked to her, she said in two months, but hasn't mentioned it since."

"Her perception of time is different than most people's. When she said she'd be here in two months, she might have been talking about from the time we got married, or two months from the Fourth of July, or two months before Christmas. But one day she'll show up, and she might end up staying for a day, or months, or years. We won't know until we know."

"She sounds very … spontaneous."

"She can't stand uniformity. She likes to laugh and have a good time, and — you'll see this when you meet her — she's a real flirt."

"Doesn't that upset her husband?"

"I really don't know. It helps that my mother inherited a rather massive fortune from my father's family. That affords her quite a bit of freedom."

"How lovely for her," I said.

"This feels like a good time to give you an accounting of the family finances, if you think you can stay awake for it."

"I can stay awake," I said, snuggling in and resting my head on his chest.

"I was left a good amount of that fortune, and at twenty-five, while covering the war in Afghanistan, I was notified that a small fortune was deposited into a separate account in my name. I had all that money transferred into a joint account that I held, and still hold, with my mother. Almost all of my paychecks while working as a correspondent were automatically deposited into that account, along with the money I received for the Pulitzers.

"I receive a monthly statement, and the account continues to grow. I told my mother she could do whatever she wanted with the money, and that as far as I was concerned it was all her money. She naturally went ballistic, and that was the last time I brought the subject up. The only money that has ever been taken out of that account was used to buy this mansion. So in reality, she owns half the mansion, and you and I own the other half."

"I don't own the other half of anything. It's all your mother's and yours. Haven't I sponged off you enough already? I literally brought nothing to this union."

Nick leveled me with his gaze. "Please don't make me scold you on the first full day of our marriage."

"Go ahead and scold me. I doubt you're capable of it," I said.

Nick raised his finger menacingly but he couldn't find the words.

"You really don't have the nerve, do you. Scold me, please, scold me, please, please, please."

"Okay, stop the nonsense. I'm not scolding anyone. It's our honeymoon. You have been granted a reprieve."

I laughed and said, "A reprieve, how generous. Should I feel blessed?"

"Yes, you should feel blessed, because when I get angry it's not a pretty scene."

"I imagine not. I pity the man who makes a pass at your lovely wife or insults your mother, but when it comes to the people you love you're a real softie."

He smiled as I turned over and lay flat on the bed with my head atop two pillows. I asked, "How would you like to massage your lovely wife's leg? I'm a little sore after last night's calisthenics."

"And where would you like me to start, up by your thigh or down by your feet?"

"Well, if you start up by my thigh we might not get very far, so why don't you start down by my feet."

As he began to rub my arches, I said, "Tell me something about yourself."

"What do you want to know?"

"So many things," I said, stalling. "Okay, I have it. If you could go back in time for one day and talk with one person, who would it be, and when and why?"

He stopped massaging my feet and said, "President Lincoln at the height of the Civil War. I would love to hear him explain how he was able to still see the good in humanity, when the White House was filled with exhausted, wounded, and dying soldiers who lived with him and his family. Up until the night he was assassinated, he never sought vengeance or reparations from the defeated Confederates, but only unity. He wanted a united country."

I wriggled my feet and he started up again, massaging and talking. "It might seem odd in this day and age, but we did have presidents who our children could look up to, such as Lincoln, Washington, Teddy Roosevelt, and Harry Truman. Who would you choose to visit?"

"Eleanor Roosevelt. In my senior year of high school, during Christmas break, I read two biographies on Mrs. Roosevelt. In many ways, I came away with the feeling that she was a better human being than the great FDR. She championed so many causes that would greatly enhance not only the people of the United States but the people of the world. At a time when her husband's administration didn't want to hear about the Jewish problem in Germany, she begged him to take up Hitler's offer to ship all the Jews in Germany to the United States. If her husband and the Congress had listened to her, there might never have been a Holocaust. She fought for women's rights, against segregation in the South, against segregation in our own military during World War Two, and she was a powerful force in the United Nations."

I diverted my eyes from Nick as I felt like a silly girl who had done nothing of importance and was simply left to idolize a woman who had championed major causes and improved the lives of millions of people. "I admire her," I added, "but she also makes me feel like a massive underachiever. I guess I'm not off to an auspicious start."

"What are you talking about? Eleanor Roosevelt didn't become the great crusader she's remembered for being until she was in her fifties and FDR was president. You're in your early twenties. Your potential is limitless."

"Do you really believe that?"

"I've been telling you that since we first met. You don't need to be Eleanor Roosevelt to make a difference. You just need to be yourself and use your potential to its fullest."

He had worked his way up to the middle of my calf and was making it feel so good. I turned over and looked up at him, and as he continued to massage my leg, I told him about Annie's offer.

"She wants to spend more time with Bee, so she asked if I would tutor Bee three or four times a week at the studio. I would be leaving with Annie and Bee at about eight in the morning, and coming home at around six at night. I'd really like to do this, Nick."

"I think you should. It seems like a perfect opportunity to ease back into something that I know you enjoy."

"She's also hinted at the possibility of me becoming a permanent employee at the studio. Conducting interviews for magazines they own. Talking with actors and actresses, and occasionally appearing in photo spreads, wearing costumes from upcoming period pieces they plan on making. Would that be okay with you?"

"Of course it would. Why are you making it seem like this is all up to me? Like you need my approval?"

"Did you forget that we're married now? Married people run big decisions past each other before making commitments or accepting jobs."

"True."

"I don't want to keep anything from you, especially since this is going to affect the way we live. For one thing, there won't be as many sex-athons ..."

"I have no doubt we'll make up for it on days when you're not working, and we'll appreciate it that much more."

"And you have no problem with me doing photo shoots again?"

"As long as you're not parading down runways before an audience of horny old geezers, dressed in gowns that show more flesh than a two-piece bathing suit..."

"We have an agreement — no more war zones for you, no more runways for me. Surely, the man who doesn't forget anything didn't forget that?"

"No, wiseass, I didn't forget."

"Annie told me I could start tutoring Bee after my facial surgery, but I told her I want to start right away … like in a couple of days. Is that okay or will we still be on our honeymoon?"

"No, that's okay. It's better you get back into the groove as soon as possible," he said, and as soon as he did, my mind started running wild with crazy ideas. Was he already bored with me? What was that vile saying I'd overheard once…that "for every beautiful woman, there was a man who was tired of fucking her?" Oh, God. Here I was, telling him that I would be out of the house every day, and he was totally unfazed. Maybe he was happy to have time away from me. *Yes*, I thought, *it seems so obvious. We just got married and the son-of-a-bitch is already clawing back his freedom.* I suddenly snapped out of my insane, baseless reverie as his hands reached under my shirt and tugged at my panties.

I laughed and he looked at me and asked, "What's so funny?"

"I was just wondering if you would be so kind as to fix your loving wife some breakfast?"

"Of course. What would you like?"

"How about a large orange juice and a bushel of carrots?" I said with a straight face.

"A bushel of carrots?"

"Yeah, maybe it's not too late for my tiny ears to grow some if I eat enough carrots. Maybe then I can become an honoree bunny."

"You're my bunny and I like your ears just the way they are. Let me go get you a glass of orange juice, and maybe some scrambled eggs and toast."

He got off the bed and I grabbed at the back of his underwear and said, "You forgot something, didn't you?"

"What's that?" he replied as I pulled him on top of me.

"Married less than a day, and already you've forgotten. When was the last time you massaged my leg and we didn't make love afterwards?"

"So what you're telling me is that you want dessert before breakfast?"

"What I'm trying to get through to my adorable husband is that it would be very nice to make love, unless you're already tired of me."

"That will never happen, my lovely wife," he said as we kissed passionately and made love for the fifth time as husband and wife.

# CHAPTER THIRTY-SIX

After we cleaned up and ate breakfast, I looked at my phone and saw that I had five messages from my maid of honor. The earliest was date-stamped at 6:30 a.m. Apparently, my precious angel did not understand the concept of a honeymoon. I called her back, and she picked up on the first ring and said, "Good morning, Alicia. I'm sorry to leave so many messages so early, but since you told me that you and Nick were always up very early and walked on the beach before sunrise I just figured you were up."

"We were so tired from yesterday that we slept in."

"I was tired too, but I was so excited about yesterday and all the fun we had that I couldn't fall back to sleep when I first woke up."

"I understand, and I love hearing from you more than anyone in this whole world."

"Thank you, Alicia. Is it true that you're going to be my tutor?"

"I believe so, sweetheart."

Annie's voice suddenly came through the phone and she said, "I apologize for my daughter. Sometimes her excitement overtakes her and she fails to comprehend her mother's words. I told her at least four times not to call or text you because you and Nick are on your honeymoon and need some alone time."

"That's okay, Annie. I was going to give you a call anyway. I spoke to Nick about tutoring Bee at the studio and he thinks it's a great opportunity. I can start whenever you like."

"And you're sure, sweetheart?"

"Positive," I said, then made arrangements for Annie and Bee to come over at 2 p.m. to review Bee's recent schoolwork and to make a plan.

"Afterwards we can all have dinner together," I said.

Annie paused as I heard her tell Bee to go tell her father that he would be watching the Yankees game by himself. "You wanted to see Alicia, and you're going to get your wish."

"Can you tell Daddy? If they lose it will be my fault for not cheering them on."

I heard a heavy sigh on the other end and Annie saying, "Okay, I'll tell him."

She got back on with me and said, "Alicia, we'll see you at two. Now it's time for me to do my daughter's dirty work."

"She's a hard one to say no to, isn't she?"

"Yes, and I wouldn't have it any other way."

Nick had disappeared into the study while I was on the phone. I knocked on the door and walked right in, and as soon as I stepped through the door, he abruptly closed his laptop. I looked at him and said, "What were you looking at, porn?"

"Why would I be looking at porn when I'm married to the most gorgeous girl in the world."

"Because men are like wild animals when it comes to sex."

He shook his head and said, "Not this one."

"Then why did you shut your laptop as soon as I walked in?"

For the first time since I'd met him, Nick was frozen and speechless.

"What's wrong?" I asked. "Did something happen to your mother?" That brought him back to earth, and he said, "No, thank God."

"Then what?"

"I … just got a video from two detective friends on the New York City police department."

Now it was my turn to freeze. I stared at him and just knew, but asked anyway.

"Is it about my case?"

Nick nodded somberly, and I began to feel like a thousand squirrels were running around inside my head. My knees went weak, and Nick scrambled out of his chair and rushed to help me. He walked me back to the desk and sat in the chair and I sat on his lap. Once I was in his arms, he said, "The scumbags that attacked you are no longer on the loose."

"They found them?"

"They found them."

"Do I have to go to New York to pick them out of a lineup or something?"

"No, they're on a slab in a morgue, unrecognizable. An unidentified woman, standing outside a fancy restaurant in the Hamptons, supposedly waiting for a cab that didn't come, was offered a ride in their limo. She agreed, slid into the backseat, and what happened next is as brutal as anything I've witnessed. She taped the entire thing and left the video behind for the police."

I pointed to his laptop. "You have the video?"

"Yes."

"I need to see it," I said as Nick averted his eyes and didn't speak or move to open his computer.

"Nick, I need to see it." I reached across to open his laptop and he grabbed my wrist.

"Alicia, please! Stop! I don't want you seeing this video."

"It's not up to you!" I was almost screaming now, and hanging off the edge of his lap.

Nick looked at me for a long time. Finally, he got up from his chair and motioned for me to take his place. I sat down, and he opened the laptop and started the video from the beginning.

The unidentified woman was about my height, and wore a Canada Goose parka with a fur hood that covered her head and a good part of her face. She was undeniably sexy and wore high heels, black gloves, and a short skirt that was almost completely covered by the coat. From what I could see, she had long blond hair that fell just beyond her shoulders.

She stood beside the restaurant as the limo pulled up. Scumbag #1 asked, "Can we give you a lift?"

"That depends," the woman said. "I'm staying on the other side of the park."

"That's exactly where we're going."

"Great! That would really be nice."

Scumbag #1 opens the back door and she slides in as she places what I imagine is a small camera on the roof directly above them. Scumbag #2 opens the other back door and slides in next to her, as his partner slides in on the other side of her and closes the door. He gives the driver directions, and the driver pulls away from the curb.

"Cold out there tonight, isn't it?" Scumbag #1 says. "How about some vodka to warm up?" He pours three shots and hands one to the woman and one to his friend. "To warmer nights!" he says, and they all drink up.

He places his hand on the woman's leg and works his way up. She says, "Did I give you permission to touch me?"

"Do I need permission?" he says, continuing up her leg and under her skirt.

She grabs his hand and flings it aside. "No permission means no touching, no fucking."

The driver turns into an empty park and turns off the engine. "Did you hear this ungrateful bitch?" Scumbag #1 asks his friend, who says, "Mmm-hmm."

"Like I need permission to fuck her," he says as his friend grabs her from the back and attempts to hold her down. That's when a handgun slips down from under the arm of her coat and into her hands.

Nick presses pause and says, "That's a Ruger SR40c. It's one of the most powerful compact handguns on the market." He asks me again if I'm sure I want to see the video, and I nod. He gently wraps his arms around my shoulders and presses Play.

The woman shoots Scumbag #1 in the stomach and he goes flying backwards as she elbows Scumbag #2 in the face, then turns and shoots him in the stomach. A barely audible click sounds as she turns to Scumbag #1, who pleads with her as she says, "Sorry, but I only believe in consensual sex." She points the gun higher up and shoots him in the face, erasing him from the world.

She turns to his partner, who, despite bleeding profusely from his stomach, is trying frantically to unlock the door. "Don't waste your time," she says. "It won't open."

He looks at her and pleads, "Please, don't, don't…"

"No means no," she says, as she shoots him in the face. The video image glows red, like an abstract painting by Rothko, until a hand approaches the lens and wipes it clean. Then all you see is the entire rear of the limo awashed in blood as the men lay in their gruesome poses, their faces gone, their inert bodies splayed out on the long leather seat.

Up front, the driver is desperately trying to open his door. He starts kicking at the window as the woman takes a tiny electronic device from her coat pocket and hits the button, causing all of the doors to unlock. She detaches the camera from the roof of the limo and attaches it to the lapel of her coat. She opens the door next to Scumbag #2 and kicks his body out of the vehicle. Then she steps out of the limo and looks at the driver, who is still kicking the window, unaware that the doors are unlocked. She opens his door, and he scrambles out and starts to run past her. She trips him with her foot and he goes flying across the pavement, thudding to a stop a few feet from her.

She walks toward him. The clicking of her high heels against the pavement sounds like seconds ticking away on a clock. I'm wishing I could see her eyes as she stands directly over him, but all I can see is the terrified look in his eyes. "Please, I didn't have anything to do with those boys. I have a family and children. I'm begging you…"

She turns and starts to walk away, then turns around, looks down at him, and says, "I hate liars." When the first bullet hits him in the crotch, his screams echo through the dark and abandoned park like a flock of birds stalking their prey. She then shoots him in the upper stomach and bends down close to his face and says, "Surely, you didn't think I would let you live." She steps back and shoots him directly in the face.

She walks back to the limo, stepping over Scumbag #2, and removes the tiny camera from her coat. Then all you see are her gloved hands placing it on the seat, next to the Ruger. The video and audio end and Nick closes the laptop, yet I can still hear the demented Morse code of her high heels tapping against asphalt.

Nick tightened his arms around me and waited for me to speak. My whole body was trembling. I looked at Nick and asked, "Was she a hired assassin?"

"That would be my guess, especially considering the way she handled herself."

"It looked personal."

"It might very well be, but she handled herself like a professional."

"Do the detectives have any leads?"

"They didn't say, but considering how many women have identified those men as their assailants, I doubt the detectives will waste time looking for her. The two rapists were cousins from extremely wealthy families in Westchester County in New York. The driver had been the chauffeur for one of the families for the last fifteen years."

When I closed my eyes, the sound of her high heels striking the pavement continued to ring out. I couldn't tune it out. An agitated tension overtook me, and it suddenly felt like the blood vessels beneath my silver bandage were ready to explode. Nick started to massage the back of my neck, and suddenly the poison that had been circulating all through me since that terrifying night dissipated, and a calm I never thought I would feel again enveloped my being.

"Annie and Bee are coming over," I said. "We're going to go over her tutoring needs."

"That's great, but are you sure you can still—"

"It's the best thing for me."

"Yes, she's like a human palliative."

I lay my head back against the chair and looked up at my husband. I asked, "If I didn't walk in on you, would you have told me about the video?"

"Probably not. I've witnessed that type of gun violence before, and seen bodies obliterated. It's not something I think anyone should see unless they have to."

"I had to."

"I know. And those bastards got exactly what they deserved…"

I nodded, but said, "Yet if not for those bastards, we would never have met."

"Not necessarily. I believe we were always going to meet, one way or another. If we didn't meet at a party or some type of gathering, my mother would have tracked you down, kidnapped you, and introduced us to each other. She knew exactly the type of girl I was looking for. I've described the girl of my dreams to her, and you fit the description perfectly."

I laughed and replied, "So besides all her other incredible traits, she also a sleuth?"

"That woman can achieve whatever she sets her mind to."

Nick lightly massaged the back of my neck as I looked down at the laptop. As much as I wanted to believe that Nick and I were destined to meet one way or another, I couldn't help wondering if the tragic circumstances I found myself in that night had led me into his arms.

Had those two vile creatures given me the best gift I would ever receive in this life? Could my trauma have delivered me into salvation? Even thinking about it made my head spin, and caused me to sink further into Nick's lap.

I nuzzled his hair and whispered my thanks. "I feel lighter," I said. "Almost relaxed."

"I understand, sweetheart, and I couldn't be prouder of you for facing these demons head-on."

# CHAPTER THIRTY-SEVEN

Annie, Bee, and I sat in the dining area as I went over Bee's schoolwork for the last year that she was home schooled by her father. I was still reeling from the video and could feel my mind jumping around. I had to force myself to focus, and while I managed to take in most of what I was reading, I could feel Annie's eyes on me, and my hands shook slightly as I moved Bee's papers from one pile to another after reviewing her work in each subject.

"Is Joe going to miss home schooling Bee?" I asked Annie, who said, "Yes and no."

"Yes, because he loves being around Bee. No, because it's time for Bee to have a teacher who isn't her father, and it's time for my lovely husband to get to work on other projects."

Annie then told me some things about Joe that helped me to understand why he would have wanted to home school Bee in the first place. "He seriously loved college," Annie said. "He went to so many different colleges and took such an array of courses that he got scholarships to graduate schools all over the country. His grade point average wasn't the best, but the grad school administrators had never seen a student with such a diverse course load, from physics to English literate, chemistry, theater, computer science, sociology, criminal justice and more."

"Wow! It sounds like he had a real thirst for knowledge."

"He did, and if you ask him what it all got him, he'll tell you honestly, 'A twenty-five-year stint in the restaurant business.'"

"And a best-selling book," Bee added proudly. "My daddy and mommy are very smart."

"I know, and apparently you're following in their footsteps," I said.

"I hope so. My daddy wanted me to play for the New York Knicks, but after a lot of practice I still couldn't get the ball through the hoop, unless he picked me up and I was able to lay the ball in. So now I want to become a scientist and find a cure for cancer, which is what killed my uncle Simon."

I remembered Bernardo's emotional response when Bee mentioned Simon and so I immediately changed the subject and asked Annie, "So what famous college did you graduate from? Cambridge, Oxford…"

"Oh, God no. I was accepted at USC and when I arrived for my freshman year Simon picked me up at the airport in a limo, with a bottle of champagne, and two flutes. He told me there'd been a change of plans, and that our parents had agreed. College was out, and I was to undergo an apprenticeship at his studio, with him as my mentor."

"Oh my God! What did you think?"

"Well, I was so jet lagged from flying ten hours from London to Los Angeles that I just went along without any objections, and after my first glass of champagne I was in no condition to mount a logical argument against the new plan. Then I saw where I would be living, and all doubts evaporated. I mean it wasn't even a choice. I could live in a mansion in Malibu a few hundred feet from the beach or in a dorm with two hundred other girls. And really, Simon was the best teacher I could have asked for. He assigned more reading, and better books, than I would have read in ten years of seminars at USC. I was lucky."

Suddenly Annie lowered her head, and as tears started flowing down her cheeks, she excused herself and left the room. Bee looked stricken. "I never should have mentioned Uncle Simon," she said, then started to cry and ran off to be with her mother.

As soon as I was alone in the room, it was like a switch had been flipped, and I was back in the limo with those two monsters, and the pain and the terror were as alive in me as they were on that terrifying night. I was tethered to those two vile creatures; they might be dead now, but their evil actions lived on inside me, scratching at me from inside my mind.

While I waited for Bee and Annie to come back, I started to put all the paperwork back together, tapping the worksheets into neat piles, according to subject, then re-tapping them into even neater piles as I stared at the door. When no one came, I gathered the books and put those into piles. After a few minutes there was a soft knock on the door, and when I looked up I saw Nick walking toward me. Instead of my heart skipping a beat, the one thought that ran through my mind was, *If anything happened to him I would kill myself.*

He sat down next to me and searched my eyes. "Where's your student?" he asked. It surprised me to have him treat me normally. Couldn't he see into my mind?

"She ran off to comfort her mother."

"Simon," he guessed.

"Yes."

I felt so sorry for Annie that I started crying — or I might have been crying for myself. If I was forced at gunpoint to explain why I was crying, I could not have teased out all of the reasons. Nick moved closer to me and held me and stroked my hair.

***

Joe came over between innings of the Yankees game. I was sure that Nick had called him up after leaving the dining room when Annie and Bee came back. I had gathered myself somewhat by the time they returned, and we talked some more about the tutoring arrangement. I told them I was fairly certain I understood the parameters of the home school program and the direction and progress that Bee had already achieved and would continue to achieve under my tutelage.

Joe knocked on the door of the dining room and walked in and sat next to his wife and daughter. He asked, "So Alicia, do you think you can handle my little genius?"

"We're going to make a great team. What do you think, sweetheart?"

"I think so, Alicia, but probably not as good as my daddy and me."

"Oh, no one could replace your daddy, but we'll do our best, and maybe even write a few more poems."

Joe reached around Bee and touched his wife's hand and asked, "Are you okay, sweetheart?"

"Yes, Joe, just thinking how great it's going to be to see so much more of my little girl, and to have Alicia around."

"Well, if you girls are done, can I steal this little angel to watch the game? They need a miracle, and it might help to have their most devoted cheerleader."

"Can I, Mommy?"

"Yes sweetheart, go cheer on your team," Annie said as Bee kissed her numerous times.

"Joe, can you please tell my husband that Annie and I would love a couple of glasses of white wine?"

"Actually, just tell him to bring the bottle," Annie said as Joe and Bee left the room. Once we were alone, she turned to me and stared. "You've been crying."

When I opened my mouth but couldn't speak, Annie reached across and said, "It's alright. Take all the time you need." I did some deep breathing, in and out through my nose, until I could feel my heart rate slowing down.

Over the next few minutes, I told her about the video, and about the mysterious woman behind the brazen executions.

"She taped the entire thing," I said, "and she left behind the gun, two cameras, and a pair of gloves. Nick thinks she's a hired assassin, but I think it was personal … that either she or someone close to her were previous victims…"

I stopped talking as Nick entered the room with a bottle of white wine and two glasses. He kissed me on the cheek and said, "You two having an interesting conversation?"

"Yes," Annie said. "I was just telling your lovely wife … that I hope she can talk you into giving us a first look at publishing your next book."

He uncorked the bottle, filled our glasses, and left the bottle on the table. "I'll tell you what," he said. "You promise to keep a close eye on my wife and make sure she doesn't run off with some big shot movie star, and I promise you a first look at the book. If you like it and want to publish it I will accept any offer you make."

Annie smiled and said, "Deal." She took a sip of the wine and asked, "And is my lovely daughter helping the Yankees come back?"

"Actually, since that angel started cheering for them they have tied the game up."

"She's Joe's lucky charm and my savior. I don't see any reason why her cheering wouldn't help the Yankees."

"Enjoy, ladies," Nick said as he walked out of the room.

When we were alone again, I looked at Annie and mouthed the words "Thank you."

"No problem at all. You could have cancelled today. I hope you know that."

"I know," I said. "I didn't want to disappoint Bee or delay your plan. And in an odd way it's helping…"

Annie looked at me intently. "Is it a relief, at all? To know that your attackers have been wiped off the face of the planet?"

I thought for a while before answering.

"There's some relief, yes. But there's something else, too. I had put that night away in a box, in my brain…"

"…and now that you've seen the video, the box is open."

I nodded and we sat in silence for a while. At last, Annie's face brightened, and she wrenched us onto a happier topic.

"That man, right?" She pointed to the door through which Nick had just come and gone. "That husband of yours is so in love with you."

"Amazing, isn't it?"

"Oh, I can see it," Annie said. "Especially the way you've held yourself together on this most challenging day. You are one strong young lady."

"Thank you."

Gently changing the subject again, Annie asked, "Does Nick ever talk about his time as a reporter or a prisoner?"

"In very general terms … he never gives me a full picture of his experiences. Does he talk to Joe about any of it?"

"Yes, but Joe promised Nick he wouldn't tell anyone, and my husband is very good at keeping his promises. Any personal experiences I know about your husband are through you."

"And I know so little," I said. "All I have are theories. For example, I don't think my husband feels complete unless he is helping someone in need. That might explain his response to me. And it's the main reason I feel uncertain about our future. If the facial reconstruction works, I won't look any different than I did as a model. As strange as it sounds, I'm wondering if he'll still want me if I'm whole again."

"Don't even think of it, Alicia. You need that surgery."

"I know, and since he's the one who recommended it, I know he understands how important it is for me to be done with this silver bandage and have the protection of real skin. It's just that your mind can play crazy tricks on you. Imagine being paranoid about looking normal?"

I shook my head and took a gulp of wine and refilled our glasses. "I'm sorry for talking only about myself," I said. "I've seen the way you react when people mention Simon. If you'd like to talk about it, please go right ahead."

"It's okay, Alicia. I don't want to burden you. Like Nick, my husband is a great listener. My daughter knows very little about Simon, but she sees the way I react when we visit the cemetery or when his name comes up, and she only wants to help. Who knows? One day she might become a scientist or researcher and get us closer to a cancer cure. That would make her uncle Simon happier than she could ever imagine."

"Did he suffer very badly at the end?" I asked.

"I don't know. He never told anyone he was sick, except for Joe."

"And how did they know each other?"

"Joe was a waiter at Simon's favorite restaurant, the Palm, and they got to be great friends over the years that Joe waited on him. Joe was the one person Simon could talk to about anything: Aristotle, Da Vinci, Newton, the best and worst U.S. Presidents, climate change, the opium wars, and of course literature, but never about movies.

"Simon checked himself into the hospital two weeks before he died, and Joe was the only one allowed to visit. He brought him dinner from the restaurant every evening, and they talked late into the night ... Joe was at his bedside when he died.

"I finally got to meet my future husband when the hospital called to tell me the news and asked me to come down and identify the body. Joe was waiting for me. Simon had talked so glowingly about him for so many years that I couldn't figure out why he didn't just offer him a job at the studio. The reason was much bigger than I could have ever imagined. Four people were invited to the burial, his two daughters, Joe, and me. He picked Joe to speak, and to recite whatever poem Joe thought Simon would like. Joe picked, "Sailing to Byzantium," and as he recited the poem it was like I was listening to Simon. The poem Simon had recited to me probably a hundred times.

"After the burial, I took Simon's two daughters and Joe to The Smoke House for lunch. After his daughters left, Joe and I spent the next five hours in the restaurant, segueing from lunch into dinner and getting very drunk. It was during this time that I saw in Joe the only other man I can say I truly loved.

"We got into the back seat of the limo I came in, and as we approached Joe's home in Studio City we started making out like two teenagers." Annie laughed as she shook her head and continued. "Two sixty-year-olds, acting fifteen. I invited him to spend the night in my house in Toluca Lake, and like a gentleman he politely said that if it was any other night, he would love nothing more, but not on the day that Simon was buried. He said it didn't seem right. We talked the next morning and we both agreed we wanted to continue seeing each other…"

Suddenly a super charged cheer echoed through the mansion and Bee burst into the room and hugged and kissed her mom and said, "The Yankees won! The Yankees won!"

She then scampered under the table, and hugged and kissed me and repeated, "The Yankees won!"

Joe and Nick followed her in and she then ran over to her father who easily picked her up and said to Annie, "What can I say? Our daughter is a good luck charm."

Annie's eyes glowed as she looked at her husband and daughter, and I could see that this amazingly successful woman, who had experienced great suffering and loss, had also found all of the joy she would ever need.

***

Annie gathered her family and left the mansion fairly quickly. I knew she felt a little guilty about encroaching on our so-called honeymoon, despite the many times I'd told her we had already been on a two-month honeymoon. She never finished her story about Simon and her subsequent marriage to Joe, but I had a feeling I would hear the rest of it another time.

I took off my clothes and put on a new pair of panties and one of Nick's dress shirts. I looked at myself in the mirror and decided to leave my hair wild and unkempt. I looked sexiest that way, especially in the attire I was wearing to bed.

I walked out of the bathroom. Suddenly, I began to hear the clicking of high heels against pavement. It grew from a soft tapping to a steady hammering, until it combined with a ringing in my ears. I rushed to the window and opened it wide. I let the clean ocean air envelop my body as the waves crashing against the beach synchronized with the ringing in my ears. Nick was behind me, speaking from far away. "Alicia, Alicia." I could not turn around or move my feet. The shoes were ten-foot-tall heels, hammering a dark patch of asphalt in a dark and abandoned park. "Alicia." Nick's voice was airborne, trying to reach me. And when it did, the tapping and ringing were suddenly and completely gone, as though washed away by the receding tide.

I knew that my horrific experience would always be with me, despite witnessing those vile creatures receiving their just punishment. I closed my eyes and continued to let the ocean air wash over my body and the song of sirens beat back against the unceasing past.

"There you are," Nick said. "Didn't you hear me?"

"Sorry, no."

"Not too cold for you?"

"Not tonight."

"Well then, maybe we can sleep with the window open a little wider?"

"Not unless you have different plans than me, I don't think so," I laughingly replied.

He moved around me until we were standing face to face. "What were you thinking about when I walked in here and interrupted your star gazing?"

"If I said *none of your business* would that satisfy?"

"I've always respected your privacy," he said.

"Great! None of your business!"

He reached across and lifted the window up, leaving the top part open just a crack. Then he wrapped his arms around my waist and asked, "Are you looking forward to tutoring Bee?"

"Yes! Are you going to miss me, or will me being away finally give you the time and space to finish your work?"

"First, I'm going to miss you greatly. Secondly, I have not fallen behind on my work, and even if I did, it would have been well worth it."

"I just feel like I need to contribute," I said, looking down. "And at the same time I feel guilty about running off to my new job after being married for only two days."

He raised my chin and said, "You *do* contribute. You contribute to my well-being every minute of every day. You've been my salvation. I was at a low point in my life, and meeting you and falling in love with you gave my life a new and wonderful purpose."

"I could say the same about you," I replied as my eyes glistened with tears and I continued, "And this whole time I've become a first-class cry baby."

He laughed, and then suddenly I started to laugh and we hugged tightly and all I could think of was how much I loved this man and how truly lucky I have been.

# CHAPTER THIRTY-EIGHT

The next morning, we went for our early morning walk along the beach just as the sun was peeking over the horizon and the seagulls were squawking over their breakfast pickings. Nick had dressed me in his parka and lifted the fur hood over my head. I told him I had worn it so many times that it was officially mine. He said he decided that the first time he saw me in it. "Anyone who can make a piece of clothing look that adorable deserves to own it."

I wrapped my arms around him as we walked, pretending to be colder than I was. It was just another excuse to be close to him. When it came to my husband, I had to admit that I was greedy. It wasn't enough to have his arms wrapped around me all through the night; now that we would be separated for hours every day, I needed some Nick time in reserve, to get me through the day.

He massaged my left leg for over half an hour, and because I was running late we couldn't properly finish the session like we usually did. Amazingly, my leg had not gone limp since before the wedding. Maybe all that massaging and the subsequent love making really did help my leg get stronger.

Nick made sure I took extra silver bandages, a small bottle of healing ointment, and extra pain medicine in case I was to suffer from a severe headache, which was another side effect of that tragic night.

Annie and Bee pulled up in the limousine, and before getting in, I grabbed one more quick kiss from Nick, who said, "Please be careful and don't forget to give me a call when you get a chance." He waved to Bee and Annie and we drove off, with Adam at the wheel.

Bee greeted me with a big kiss and a hug and handed me a new asthma inhaler that was still in the box. "But I still have the other one you gave me, sweetheart," I said.

"You should always keep some in reserve. Isn't that right, Mommy?"

"Yes, sweetheart," Annie said as she looked at me with a suspicious but knowing expression.

"I know what you're thinking, so please don't go there. Nick and I talked this over and we both agreed it was the right thing to do. Besides," I said, as I gently ran my hand along Bee's hair, "being next to this angel is the best medicine one could ever hope to have."

\*\*\*

Adam parked beside the front entrance to the studio. On our way to Annie's office, we stopped and talked to at least ten employees, and we did not pass any employee without Annie and Bee greeting them by name. Not once did Annie let go of Bee's hand.

We took the elevator up to the second floor. Inside her office, she glanced at a few notes on her desk, then turned to Bee and me and said, "Follow me, ladies."

She opened a door adjacent to her office and we walked into a room lined with empty mahogany bookshelves that reached from floor to ceiling. In the center of the room was a two-person workstation with matching desks and hutches. On the left side was a desk plate with the name Bee printed on it, and on the right side a plate with the name Alicia. The peninsula was fitted with an iMac computer.

Bee looked around and asked, "Where are all the books, Mommy?"

"I expect you and your lovely teacher to fill the bookshelves as you go," Annie said. "You can start building a library of age-appropriate books." Bee looked at me and shook her head, and Annie looked confused.

"What's wrong, sweetheart?"

Bee reached into her backpack, took out a notebook, and read out loud. "Daddy has me reading *A Christmas Carol*, some of *The Nick Adams Stories* by Hemingway, and Truman Capote's short story, "A Christmas Memory." I love that one, but it's very sad at the end. I'm also reading *Animal Farm* by George Orwell. I love that one, but it's very long and Daddy said I should take my time."

"I'm surprised he doesn't have you reading Dostoevsky," Annie said.

"Daddy said I should be ready for him in about a year."

"But of course," Annie said. "I think I read him for the first time at twenty-two. I don't see any reason why you would have any problem reading him at eleven."

"That's what Daddy's says." I was chuckling a little when Bee said, "So is it okay if I put those books on the shelves, along with all the other books Daddy has on our list, and the ones Alicia thinks I should read?"

"Yes my little Einstein, that would be great," Annie said as she kissed and hugged her daughter and quickly left the room as her eyes glittered with tears.

I gave Bee a few minutes to set up her side of the desk and then I said, "I forgot to ask your mother something. I'll be right back." Bee looked at me suspiciously as I stood up, knocked on Annie's door, and went into her office.

Annie was sitting behind her desk with her head lowered and her eyes still misty. I asked, "Is there anything I can do?"

She shook her head, picked up a tissue, and wiped her eyes. "My whole life, I wanted children," she finally said, "and as God is my witness, I think my first husband had a vasectomy to make sure we never had any. It would have cramped his style. And then out of nowhere this perfect child falls into my lap and I promised myself I would be the best mother ever, and just now I realized how badly am failing."

"How can you possibly say that? That child adores you."

"I have no doubt that she loves me, but it doesn't mean I'm doing right by her in every way. I feel like I'm failing her and even neglecting her in some important areas."

"Such as?"

"Checking in. The first thing my mother asked me when I came home from school was what I had learned that day, and I had to explain to her what I learned and why it was important to know. I don't think I have once asked Bee what she learned. I just took my husband's word that she was doing great."

"But your responsibilities as the head of an entire studio have to be overwhelming…"

"That's no excuse. My mother worked as a nurse during and after the war. Her job was overwhelming. She was saving lives. I'm making movies…"

There was a knock on the door and Bee came in and looked at her mom and asked, "Did I do something wrong?"

"No, sweetheart, why would you even think such a thing?" Annie replied as she put out her arms and Bee ran toward her. Annie picked her up and placed her on her lap and Bee hugged her and started to cry.

"I love you so much, Mommy. I would never do anything to make you mad."

"I know that, my sweet, beautiful daughter. I was simply surprised to find out how far ahead you are in your studies."

"Daddy says that since I probably won't be playing for the Knicks, that if I work hard enough I definitely have the ability to be a genius like my mommy."

"Did he really say that?" Annie asked as her eyes, once again, started to glisten with tears.

"Yes, Mommy, I would never lie to you."

They hugged for a long time, and I couldn't help wondering how different my life would be if I'd had parents like Bee's. Then it hit me like a thunderbolt that Bee was an abused and tortured little girl up to a few years ago before she was adopted by Annie and Joe.

I walked out of the office, letting Bee know that I would wait for her in the study, and gently closed the door behind me. I sat down on my side of the work station and wondered how far ahead Bee might be in mathematics. It's not like that was a subject I excelled in ... history, geography and literature, yes, math, not so much. Yesterday, I had only gone over the grade level she was at and it wasn't much of a surprise that she was a couple of grades ahead. All you had to do was look at who her parents were.

I nearly screamed in pain as a cramp ripped through the lower half of my stomach. I had thought I was finished with menstruating, after the beating I received, and the doctors said it was very unlikely I could ever have a baby because of all the scar tissue around my uterus. I guess I jumped to the wrong conclusion because if these weren't premenstrual cramps I didn't know what the hell they were. I also, in the last few days, had found my panties soiled with small amounts of vaginal blood. I didn't say anything to Nick because, after all, it was our actual honeymoon, and I was embarrassed. I also felt a recurring pain in my shoulder which I simply assumed was because of all the action that took place in our bed and quite a few other places around the mansion.

Bee sat down on her side of the work station and I asked, "Did you and your mommy figure it all out?"

"Yes, Alicia. I love my mommy and daddy so much. If it wasn't for both of them I don't know if I would be alive today."

I softly touched her face and said, "I think they also feel very lucky having such a beautiful, intelligent, and loving daughter like you."

"I hope so, Alicia, but they didn't need me in order to survive. They have plenty of money."

"But they needed you to make their lives complete, and no amount of money can accomplish that ... only a perfect daughter named Bee."

She walked over to me and hugged me and for a few moments the cramps and the pain in my shoulder faded into the background, replaced by pure joy.

# CHAPTER THIRTY-NINE

I gently knocked on the door of the study and Nick looked up and remarked, "Aww, there you are. And how did your day go, Miss Brodie?"

"It was wonderful. Strange that you should use that nickname for me. Did you know I played Miss Brodie in our high school play, *The Prime of Miss Brodie*?"

"No. But weren't you a little young to play Miss Brodie?"

"Makeup does wonders, in case you haven't figured that out yet, and besides, I was the only one in our entire student body able to memorize all the lines."

I suddenly cringed in pain and like the Flash, Nick was beside me. "It's menstrual cramps. I thought I was over this but I guess I was wrong."

He helped me into his chair and as I laid my head back and closed my eyes I said, "I'll be better in a few moments."

"Alicia, you are seriously bleeding."

I opened my eyes and it was like a river of blood was running down both of my legs. I struggled to get up and as I started walking, a sharp pain cut right through my shoulder blades and I fell backwards as I screamed, "Nick, help me. Nick…"

He caught me before I hit the floor and as I fell in and out of consciousness I could hear him calling 911. The next thing I remembered was being put on a stretcher by two paramedics and wildly waving my hand and screaming, "Nick, don't leave me. Don't leave…"

Nick grabbed my hand and said, "I'm right here and I'm not leaving you." I held tightly to his hand before finally falling completely out.

# CHAPTER FORTY

The next thing I remember is shielding my eyes from the sun as it came streaming in through an unfamiliar window. I was hooked up to an IV and a heart monitor and Nick was sitting right beside me in a chair by the head of the bed.

"Where am I?"

"You're at the Malibu Urgent Care Center," he replied as I looked more closely at him and noticed a two-or three-day beard growing and bleary eyes.

"How long have I been here?"

"Two days," he said as the surgeon walked into the room. The doctor was a tall, slim man with slightly rumpled hair. He had a gentle, comforting manner, and his name was Dr. Souter.

"And how are you feeling today?" he asked.

"Tired," I said. "And thirsty." Nick handed me a glass of water from the bedside table.

"Well, that's all to be expected. How's your pain level?"

It was like he had asked me a question about nuclear physics and my brain went dead for a few moments, and then a sharp pain around the area of my vagina snapped me into the here and now. I pointed to the area and replied, "It hurts quite a bit."

"We'll up your dosage of pain medicine and that should bring you relief. You had what is frequently called a tubal pregnancy, an ectopic pregnancy. It's what happens when a fertilized egg gets stuck in the fallopian tube on its way to the uterus. In your case, it was because of all the scar tissue around that area, caused by the sexual assault your husband says you suffered … approximately a year ago?"

I nodded and he continued. "If not for your husband's quick response, this could have been a catastrophe. Your fallopian tubes don't stretch the way your uterus does, and the fertilized egg had grown to the point that it burst, and you were suffering from internal, life-threatening bleeding. We were able to stop the bleeding, and with your husband's consent we tied your fallopian tubes so that this won't happen again.

"You had to be experiencing extreme pain during this period of time. Surely, it had to concern you?"

"I thought it was premenstrual cramps, and since I haven't had a period since the … assault, I simply thought it was an accumulation … I'm such an idiot."

"No, you're not. You've been through a living hell this last year, but the good news is that you are going to perfectly okay."

"Thank you, doctor."

"You're welcome. I'll be by tomorrow to check on you, and I'll tell the nurse to boost your pain medication."

He left the room and I looked at Nick and said, "I guess no one is entitled to so much fun without some pain." I then started to cry as I blurted out, "You know, it's probably not too late to ask for an annulment."

"What?" Nick looked like he was in shock, and I was flat-out bawling when he said, "Please don't ever say anything like that again. Please!"

The nurse came in and increased the level of morphine dripping into my system from a different IV attached to a vein in my right arm.

I could feel Nick's eyes on me, but for the longest time we didn't talk. Finally, I asked him what he was thinking about, but he just shook his head.

"Is it the girl in Ukraine? The one who was killed by a Russian bomb?"

"That's exactly who I was thinking about. I wasn't able to save her, but as God is my witness, I'll do everything possible to protect you."

It didn't take long for the morphine to kick in, and suddenly I was floating and feeling fine. All I thought about were happy things, and it was easy to put everything else out of my mind.

I stayed in the hospital for five more days, and my husband was there almost every minute. If it was any other man, especially one as good looking as Nick, I would have thought he was there to bang his choice of nurses. Maybe it was because I was high most of the time, but all the nurses seemed young and beautiful, and naturally they kept telling me how lucky I was to have such a dedicated husband, and so good looking, too. I swear, I almost gave them permission to fuck him. He was so perfect, it felt wrong to have him all to myself.

What I didn't tell them was that the only way he'd be interested in any of them is if one of them broke a leg, or accidentally stabbed herself in her abdomen, or at a minimum vomited on him. I was convinced that Nick needed to be *wanted*, and my God, he hit the mother lode with me. Fainting, falling down, peeing on the living room floor, vomiting on his desk, spewing blood across his study floor, and now, a tubal pregnancy. I really knew how to make my man happy.

I was convinced that if I looked the way I used to when we met at that party, Nick wouldn't have given me a second look. I picked up Mr. Perfect by being anything but perfect.

# CHAPTER FORTY-ONE

Nick parked by the front door, and as I looked up at the mansion and the vast, surrounding property, it was like I had never been there before. Nick carried me inside and took me straight to our bedroom. The path was bejeweled with bouquets of white lotus in beautiful, decorative vases.

"All from your student and maid of honor," Nick said.

"God bless her beautiful little soul."

He lay me down on our bed and took off my shoes. "Would you like help getting into more comfortable clothes?"

"No, I'm fine the way I am. I'm not an invalid, Nick. I can go to the bathroom and change my clothes all by myself." I knew my tone was a little sharp. The pain medication was wearing off, and I could feel the tension building.

I fixed the pillows behind my back and sat up in the bed. "What I would really like is a glass of white wine and maybe some crackers."

He looked at me as if I was out of my mind and said, "With all the medication you're on, I really don't think you should be drinking alcohol. I'll get you some orange juice."

He started to walk out of the room and I said, "I would like a glass of white wine. If you won't get it for me, I'll get up and get it myself."

He looked back at me, with eyes blazing, and simply nodded. When I could no longer hear his footsteps, I reached into my purse and took out a medicine bottle with fifteen tablets of morphine that I had begged the doctor to prescribe for me. He'd been hesitant, especially with the opioid epidemic out of control, but after I reminded him of the violent assault and the continual headaches and pain from the attack, he wrote out a prescription, and a nurse was kind enough to have it filled for me at the hospital pharmacy. I made sure Nick knew nothing about it.

I put a tablet under my tongue, and the bottle back in my purse, and looked at the bouquets of white lotus. I suddenly remembered what the flower symbolized for Buddhists: purity of mind, body, and spirit, but for one to reach such enlightenment, one had to experience suffering.

I didn't even hear Nick walk back into the room. He waved his hand in front of my face and I snapped out of it as he handed me the glass of wine. The tablet under my tongue had dissolved and the taste in my mouth was disgusting. I drank the glass of wine in one gulp and asked, "Can I please have one more?"

"No, you can't have one more. Please eat some crackers," he said as he handed me a packet of crackers, which I threw across the room. I yelled, or at least I thought I yelled, "I'm not hungry. I would like another glass of wine, pl…

That was the last thing I remembered as my head fell back onto the pillows.

# CHAPTER FORTY-TWO

When I finally opened my eyes, Nick was staring down at me. I closed my eyes again and tuned my mind to the squawking of the seagulls on the beach below my window. Anything Nick wanted to say to me, he could say through them. I could not stand his critical appraisal of his helpless wife who couldn't even spread her legs so he could release some of that pent-up frustration.

Nick was just an impediment, keeping me from my pills. I don't know how many hours or days I was in this state. The one time I woke up and felt somewhat normal, depressed and anxious, I searched my purse like a maniac for the pills and couldn't find them.

Nick walked back into the room and asked, "Looking for this?" He was dangling my pill bottle in front of him. I pulled myself up to my elbows and said, "What are you doing with my medicine?"

He walked over and handed me the empty bottle and I screamed, "Where are my pills?"

"I flushed them."

"Who gave you the right to do that? I'm in pain, you son-of-a-bitch."

"The pain medicine you have in your bathroom cabinet is more than enough to alleviate any pain you have."

"Since when did you become a doctor?"

He looked at me with a wretched expression and I knew, there was no use in lying. He had covered wars for ten years, been in hundreds of field hospitals, and seen the worst of human suffering.

"What did you do, lie to the doctor?"

"All I did was ask him to look at my recent medical history and he gave in. A doctor gave me those pills. A doctor!"

We remained in a silent standoff for what seemed like an eternity. Then he said, "You need to take a bath, Alicia, and then we need to change the bandage on your face and the one on your abdomen, and then we have to get some food into you. You haven't eaten in two days."

He stood up and said, "Stay here. I'll be right back. You can start taking off your clothes."

He walked out as I stood up and all that I could think about was that I was fucked. Totally fucked!

He returned with a medical chair that's used to prevent an elderly or sick person from falling in the shower. I could hear him putting it in the shower stall, and then he was beside me, saying, "Alicia, for God's sake, take off your clothes. You stink."

I swear at that moment I was ready to punch his smug face. I wanted to scratch his eyes out. But he had all the power and I had none. So I took off my clothes and he placed them in a garbage bag, which he tied shut and flung toward the door. I started to get up and when he tried to help, I screamed, "Don't touch me, you son-of-a-bitch."

He stepped back and I made my way toward the bathroom, holding onto the bed and then the door, and just like that my body gave out and I went flying toward the floor, and just as I was about to crack my head open on the tile, Nick caught me and placed me in the chair. I turned to him and let loose a stream of vitriol.

"See what I mean? Totally helpless. But oh, you love this, don't you? You love having a hopeless bitch in the house. How else are you going to be the big strong man who rescues his princess?"

He paused for a second, but didn't look at me. Then he checked the water temperature and lifted the showerhead off its handle and pointed it straight at me and shot me with a powerful force of water right between my breasts. "That's what you get for being a little crybaby. And don't forget to use soap."

He handed me the showerhead and shut the door behind him. I let the showerhead fall to the floor and started to cry like the crybaby I was. I cried as I looked down at the water shooting out of the showerhead and across the floor. I must have fallen asleep for a while, or still been feeling the effects of the morphine. Suddenly a loud knock on the door snapped me back to reality for a moment.

The shower door swung open and Nick looked across at me and asked, "Are you okay?"

I didn't respond as he stepped into the shower, fully dressed, and closed the door. He picked up the showerhead and wet my hair. Then he massaged my scalp with shampoo and rinsed my hair with a conditioner that he left on while he washed my entire body with soap ... carefully maneuvering around the silver bandage on my face and the bandage on my lower abdomen. He then rinsed off the conditioner and all the soap on my body.

He shut off the water and wrapped a towel around my hair and dried my entire body with another towel. He placed the showerhead back on its handle and looked at me. He was soaked. His shirt, pants, and shoes were all completely wet. His wet hair was spread haphazardly across his forehead and water was dripping down his face.

"It's a good look," I said. "Very sexy."

"Yeah?" he mumbled, as he busied himself gathering up towels.

"Yes. I need to remember this once we're able to do what we do best."

He pulled off his shoes and socks and took off his pants and shirt and left them on the floor of the shower.

Only his wet boxer shorts remained on him, and what was behind those shorts seemed to be growing as he came closer to me. I screamed, "Not until I'm healed."

He looked at me, confused, and said, "You're still hallucinating, aren't you?"

"I don't know what you're talking about."

"Well, it's good to know that you're not only a liar when sober and straight but also when you're high as a kite."

He grabbed my robe and helped me put it on, as he warily helped me up from the chair. He picked me up and brought me to the bed. "I'm going to change your bandages," he said as he touched my cheek and I looked into his big brown eyes. "I would never hurt you, Alicia. Never."

*** 

I woke up hours later, fully conscious. Whatever narcotics had been in my system were finally gone. A lamp beside our bed cast a soft glow over the room. The only sound I could hear was the crashing of waves against the shore. I looked over to where Nick would normally be sitting, reading a book, while watching over me, but there was no sign that he'd been there. The room was spotlessly clean and the sweet scent of white lotus filled the room. The clock by the bedstand read 2:30 a.m.

I lifted myself out of the bed while holding onto the metal backrest. I looked out the window into a blanket of bright stars above a turbulent ocean and saw the lone figure of a man sitting cross-legged near the water's edge.

I felt alone in a way that's hard to explain, like I had been given the secret to happiness and then lost it, and was forever rebuffed from receiving its blessing.

I sat back down on the bed and stared vacantly before me. The man who sat by the water was the only man I had ever loved. After that terrible, unbelievable night, when I learned more about depravity than anyone should have to know, the idea of being intimate with any man was enough to make me want to vomit. That all changed in a matter of minutes. It was like a fairy tale, but instead of living happily ever after, I had to search for answers to why I was so fortunate, and when I couldn't come up with any realistic explanations, I threw it all away. I threw away my own happiness. I took the best traits a human being can possess — caring, compassion, forgiveness, and unconditional love — and twisted them until they looked like a sickness, and I threw them back in the face of the man who had saved me.

I hung my head and tried to think. When I looked back up I noticed the arm of Nick's parka dangling from the closet. I pulled myself to standing and slowly crossed over to the closet and took the parka out and put it on. It was even bigger on me now than before. My hands trembled as I zipped up the coat and raised the fur hood over my head. I slipped on a pair of sandals and silently prayed that my leg didn't go limp. I held onto every piece of furniture as I passed through the hallway and into the living room. I opened the door and looked down at Nick, who was about 150 feet away. I tried to focus on my goal as the wind whipped around me. I could feel my leg going limp and I reached down and pressed on it as firmly as I could with my hands, keeping myself upright and as I inched closer to the best thing that ever happened to me.

Finally, I lowered myself down beside Nick and said "Hi."

He smiled and said, "Hi, beautiful." My eyes filled with tears as he took me in his arms and held me close to his chest. I could feel his lips against my forehead as I promised myself that I would never again jeopardize the fairy tale I was currently living.

When the wind picked up, he lifted me in his arms and started carrying me back to the mansion. I told him I could probably walk back and he said, "I have no doubt, but did you forget already that the reason I love carrying you is because I get to grab your butt?"

I smiled and said, "That might be so, but the real reason is because you worry about me…" I started to choke up. "You worry about me because you love me so much, and I don't know why God brought us together but I will always be grateful."

"And so will I, my lovely Alicia. So will I."

***

Nick lowered me onto the sofa and walked into the kitchen to get me something to eat. I didn't want to go back into our bedroom just yet, especially since this was the strongest I'd felt in days. He brought me a tray with Mr. Wong's dumplings and a bowl of wonton soup.

"Your maid of honor says this will make you feel better immediately."

"I feel so guilty. She left so many messages, and the flowers, and I never got back to her."

"She understands. So do Annie and Joe."

I took a sip of the soup and asked, "And do you understand?"

"Yes, I've had morphine on several occasions. Every time, there was a part of me that wanted to stay on it forever. To just close my eyes and believe I was somewhere else, where the pain couldn't touch me."

I looked at him and said, "There's a lot more to my life that you don't know, and I was too frightened to tell you because I thought you would throw me out."

"If you feel that uncomfortable telling me about it I understand. But just for the record, there is virtually nothing you can tell me that will make me love you less."

I bit into a dumpling. "Delicious. Would you like one?"

"No, I had them for dinner, but thank you."

I put down the chopsticks and looked at Nick. "When I was in high school I was not having sex. At all."

"Okay," Nick said.

"There were guys who wanted to, and some I even found attractive. But I wasn't ready, and I was afraid of catching a disease or getting pregnant. I don't remember even seriously kissing a guy, and I wasn't into partying. I wasn't going to blow my future over a stupid kegger or a one-night stand."

I picked up another dumpling and asked, "Are you sure you don't want even a little bite?"

"Okay, just a tiny bite."

He took a small bite and I continued. "That all changed, basically overnight, when I became a model. Suddenly, I was around people who were partying and doing cocaine almost every night. So I did it too. I partied for five years straight, with other models, with actors, politicians, billionaires, and tycoons."

The next part was harder to say. I spooned a bit of wonton soup into my mouth and gathered my courage as I looked at Nick with worried and hopeful eyes.

"I was waking up with guys I didn't even remember going to bed with. I had multiple abortions. So many that after three, I stopped counting. I was completely lost. I would say I was ashamed, but I'm not even sure I knew enough to be ashamed. The night I got into that limo with those two bastards, I had been partying for hours."

I took a deep breath as I looked down at the remaining dumplings. Nick deserved the truth, and if I was ever going to be truly and honestly happy, I had to come clean.

"You married a fraud, a liar, a party happy whore. I don't remember much of what I said in the hospital, but I do remember offering you an annulment or a simple divorce. All I ask is to live here a little longer and for some money to keep me afloat while I search for a job."

I couldn't look at Nick, but when I finally did, he was staring at me. I felt like a mutant under his gaze, but he said, "Alicia, my love, you are an idiot."

"I am?"

"Yes."

"Why am I an idiot?" My face was reddening.

"You're an idiot if you think any of what you just said could change how I feel about you or derail our future together."

"Oh."

"Good comeback," he said. I laughed and stuffed a bit of dumpling into my mouth, almost in an attempt to not cry. He reached across and grasped my other hand.

"I remember everything I said in the hospital," he said. "My reply is the same as it was then. Don't ever ask me for an annulment or a divorce because of a health problem or mistakes you made in your past or circumstances you unknowingly found yourself in as a teenager. Do you understand?"

"Not really, I don't know how…"

"Well, let me put it this way. The next time you mention annulment or divorce I will place you over my lap and spank you silly."

"Really, that doesn't sound like much a threat. I'm so used to you grabbing my butt that the idea of getting spanked sounds like a turn-on."

"Is that so?" he asked as I couldn't suppress a smile.

"Yeah, it's too bad we can't try it out right now. But it's something to look forward to."

"Do you actually think I would ever hit you?"

"Of course not, but then I didn't think a gentleman like you would grab my butt, either."

I snuggled up to him and wrapped my arms around his waist. "Thank you for loving me so much."

"Thank you for loving me so much, my beautiful bride."

A veil of tears covered my eyes as I looked up at him and said, "I'm sorry…"

He put his finger to my lips. "No more apologizing today. I've done many things I'm not proud of, but it's the lessons we learn from our mistakes that hopefully make us better."

I lowered my head back onto his chest and tightened my arms around his waist, closed my eyes, and fell into a peaceful sleep.

# PART TWO

# CHAPTER FORTY-THREE

The day had come for my facial regeneration surgery, and Nick was pumping me up for the procedure. He assured me that this was what I wanted from the beginning, and that in a few more weeks there would be no more bandages, silver or otherwise, on my face. He had total faith in the doctor, and he had no doubt everything would go perfectly.

"And if I'm flying high on medication and I start saying stupid things, you'll know I don't mean any of it?"

"I'll know."

We stopped and he turned his back to the ocean, shielding my face from the salty spray. At five-foot-ten I seldom felt small beside any man, but next to my husband I felt petite.

Nick was better-looking than any man I'd ever seen, on screen or off, yet he seemed to have no idea how attractive he was … or if he did, he never let on. I never saw him come close to flirting with another woman. When he talked to Annie, she did most of the talking and he listened intently. I knew he respected her opinions and accomplishments and especially the way she treated everyone with dignity and caring, but her beauty seemed to have no effect on him.

It was strange, but at that moment, the only woman I felt I was in competition with was Nick's mother. Even when I was in the hospital and then back at home those first few days, flying high on drugs, I could swear I heard him talking to her on the phone at least three or four times a day.

He continued to look at me without saying a word, and I asked, "Is something wrong?"

He shook his head and smiled. "It's just that you're so beautiful, and I love you so much. I never thought I would be so lucky to find..."

Suddenly, a large wave came crashing against the beach, but before the water could touch me, Nick lifted me up like a feather and deposited me some ten feet further back. His entire back side was wet, but before I could process what had just happened, he reached down and kissed me, and I swooned like a teenage girl being kissed for the first time by her prince charming.

***

The next three weeks, like that very kiss, also went by like a dream, and when Dr. Petrenko helped me off the table and walked me over to a full-length mirror, what I saw was my old self. The model on the cover of fashion magazines, walking down runways in fabulous designer outfits, the object of desire of politicians, movie moguls, oligarchs, and sports icons.

The stem cell injections of fetal skin had reproduced a near exact copy of my actual skin and had covered the entire exposed, damaged side of my face. The doctor remarked, "And now you look as beautiful as ever."

"Thank you, so much, Doctor. Thank you."

"And Nicholas, my dear friend, what do you think? Lovely, isn't she?"

"Yes, my friend, she is lovely. You do amazing work."

I looked at my husband with an expression of disappointment, even though his response was exactly what I expected from him. He had been telling me how beautiful I was from the very first moments we'd met, and for him to say that I looked even more beautiful now would somehow, in his mind, be a lie.

I continued to stare at him, and then quickly turned back toward the mirror as my eyes glistened with tears. He came up behind me and wrapped his arms around my waist, and whispered into my ear, "You look absolutely stunning, Alicia. More beautiful than I could have ever imagined."

"Are you sure about that?"

"Absolutely sure," he said, and I smiled, knowing how hard it was for him to say those words.

I was still in my hospital gown when Dr. Petrenko walked over with my clothes. He looked at Nick and said, "Let's give your lovely wife a few minutes of privacy," and then he turned to me and said, "Please, when you're ready, just knock on the office door."

"Are you okay?" Nick asked me. I looked at him, dumbfounded, and said, "Yes, darling, I think I'm quite capable of dressing myself."

They walked into the doctor's office and closed the door behind them. When I realized I could hear a faint mumbling, I stood next to the door and listened.

"Your wife looks just like her," the doctor said.

"Yes, they do look very much alike. They could easily pass for sisters, except that Nastasiya was so petite," Nick replied.

"Petite but fearless," the doctor said, and there was a long silence. Dr. Petrenko spoke with a heavy accent which I took to be Russian, until I suddenly realized that it must be Ukrainian. He continued, "How is your mother?"

"She's doing well. Better now."

"She was very shaken over what happened to Nastasiya. I was working on the other side of the hospital when the bomb hit. They were removing her body from the rubble when your mother arrived the second time."

Nick's reply was garbled, but I could tell he sounded emotional.

"I'm not sure if you heard—"

"Only the barest—"

"She paid for the funerals and burials of everyone who died that day. She had a special tombstone made for Nastasiya. She took pictures to show you. Did you see them?"

"I … my mother has it all."

"Look at the pictures, Nicholas. You owe her that much. She doesn't deserve to be forgotten, especially by you."

"You think I could forget her? I never forget! Not for one hour!"

Dr. Petrenko said something I couldn't' understand, and when Nick spoke again, he sounded calmer. "I like to think she's responsible for my meeting Alicia. They're so much alike, and not only in appearance. I don't think Alicia fully grasps what she's capable of, or the difference she can make."

"She has been through a lot."

"Yes, and she has handled herself amazingly well. A few missteps, but overall, so well. Can I borrow a pen?"

"There's no cost, Nicholas. I put it all through your insurance, under facial reconstruction and skin grafting. Besides her nose being broken, which was easy enough to fix, there weren't any facial bones that were severely damaged, and she was the perfect candidate for stem cell reconstruction. The skin grew over her exposed face as though it was a simple cut healing."

"You didn't put yourself in any jeopardy?" Nick asked.

"None," the doctor said, and then he raised his voice a little, objecting. "I told you, there's no charge." There was a silence before the doctor said, "Nicholas, this is a lot of money."

"It's not for you, though you can take what you want. The rest, you know who it goes to. And please, put a large bouquet of tulips beside her gravestone. She loved them."

There was a long pause and then the doctor asked, "Are you okay, Nicholas?"

"I will be. It's just that I could do so much more if I was a reporter or even an aid worker. My father used to quote Teddy Roosevelt who said something like, 'Act. Seize the moment. Man was never intended to become an oyster.' I think about that a lot."

"You've done more than enough. You're no good to any of us dead. Besides, you already promised…"

\*\*\*

I walked away from the door and finished dressing. I looked in the mirror and the one thing that had defined me my whole adult life, my beauty, was back … and yet at that moment it seemed unimportant.

I knocked on the office door and entered. Nick stood up and made room for me to sit in the chair next to his. I looked up at him and said to the doctor, "Always a gentleman."

"Yes, you complement each other so wonderfully."

"He's done all the heavy lifting. I've simply been the lucky recipient."

"That's not what he tells me," the doctor said.

"That's because he's modest to a fault."

The doctor stood up and said, "I would love to spend more time with you both but I have to pack and catch a plane that I really can't afford to miss."

"Are you going somewhere fun?" I asked and a deafening silence descended upon the office. Nick walked over to the doctor and hugged him and said, "Please take care of yourself."

I hugged the doctor as well and said, "I don't know how to thank you."

"You already have, in more ways than you know. I'll see you both when I return."

Nick and I were heading to the elevator when the doctor said, "One second, Alicia. I have some products to give you."

I looked at Nick and he said, "Go ahead. I'll wait right here."

I walked into the doctor's office and he took me back into the patients' room, where he handed me a bag filled with ointments and creams and told me to apply them before bed. Then he grabbed my hand and looked at me and said, "I don't mean to alarm you, Alicia, but you need to keep a close eye on your husband and keep him occupied. If you search the globe ten times over you will not meet a better man, but he has witnessed things that simply don't go away ... things too appalling for any one person to live with."

# CHAPTER FORTY-FOUR

In the span of a few minutes, my life was turned upside down. Yes, I was happy that people would no longer be looking at me with pity in their eyes, or gawking at me like I was some sort of deformed clown. And in a pathetic way, I was happy that Nick thought I looked so much like Nastasiya, since I now knew he was still obsessed with her.

It was the doctor's words that threw me for a loop. I'd long suspected that Nick was suffering. It seemed obvious from those first few nights on the beach, when he fell asleep in the bitter cold and woke up with a jolt after forty-five minutes, that he was struggling to keep his mind in balance. Ten years of living and working in war zones, followed by nine months in a Russian prison, would wreak havoc on any mind.

I smiled as I walked toward Nick, who was holding the elevator door open for me. Once we were traveling down to the garage, he asked, "What did the doctor give you?"

"Just some ointments to promote healing. He said to use them before bed. Such a nice man. When he comes back, can we invite him to dinner?"

"Of course," he said as the elevator doors opened and he took hold of my free hand as we walked over to his truck. He clicked the truck doors open and helped me onto my seat, then reached over and fastened my seatbelt.

I smiled at him and said, "You know, I'm quite capable of putting on my own seatbelt."

"I know," he said as he looked right at me and smiled.

"Just another excuse for a cheap grab, isn't it?"

"Maybe." He kissed me on the forehead, then got into the driver's seat and drove.

"How can I ever thank you?" I asked after we had been in the truck for a few minutes without saying a word.

"You already have, a million times over."

"That's what you always say, but according to my calculations you are way off, and while I might not be Einstein, I'm fairly good at math."

"I have no doubt about that," he said as we came to a stop at a red light. He turned toward me and gently caressed my face.

The light changed and he turned onto the highway that leads to our house. I stared straight ahead, my minding buzzing with the warning the doctor had given me about my husband and I suddenly cried out, "You promised."

"What did you just say?"

"You promised you wouldn't go back to reporting!"

"And that's a promise I have every intention of keeping. Why would you think otherwise?"

"I heard you."

"Heard me where? When?" He turned to look at me. "Were you eavesdropping on my conversation with the doctor?"

"Yes," I said, stubbornly. "That's what loving wives do."

"Okay, I can't argue with that ... or maybe I can. I don't know. Anyway, you misunderstood what you heard. I have no intention of ever going back to being a war correspondent, unless of course you decide to divorce me and take me for all my money."

"You know, you're a real asshole at times. I love you so much, it hurts."

"And I love you so much it hurts, but let's not forget your promise."

"I wouldn't go back to modeling if they offered to pay me a hundred times what you pay me for doing nothing."

"You really are good at math?"

"I'm great at math, just don't let anybody know. It was tough enough being called a nerd all through high school."

"The 'beautiful nerd,' if I'm not mistaken."

"Beautiful or not, I didn't like it," I said, as I looked at my drop-dead gorgeous husband and asked, "And where is Dr. Petrenko going?"

"You mean you don't know? Some spy you are."

"That's the second time you're talking like a complete asshole in the span of a few minutes."

"He's going to Ukraine to help out in the hospitals." When I crossed my arms and stayed silent, Nick parceled out a few more details. "I originally met the good doctor in Syria as part of a United Nations mission. At that time the Russians were mostly killing innocent civilians — women, children, the elderly, and people from religious sects that didn't embrace the dictatorship. They hadn't moved on to Ukraine yet."

"Is he originally from Ukraine?"

"Yes, but he moved to the U.S. years ago and attended Harvard Medical School. He's been a practitioner and researcher for most of the time when he's not doing volunteer work for the Red Cross and UN."

"Please tell me he didn't let me jump to the front of the line in a research trial that could have helped much more serious cases."

"I would never allow that, Alicia. The procedure he used isn't even legal here. The use of fetal stem cells is still a very polarizing issue in this country. The stem cells he had hidden in his lab just happened to be a near-perfect match with your skin. By this time tomorrow he'll be in Ukraine. God forbid anything happens to him there, he didn't want his colleagues to be held responsible for his unsanctioned research. So he put your procedure down as a normal graft."

"He still has family in Ukraine?"

"His entire family is there," he said. "At least … the ones that haven't been killed."

We turned into our driveway and out front I saw a number of vehicles. "I think we have visitors," I said.

"We do. Your maid of honor wanted to be present for your unveiling today, so once I was sure everything went well I called her and told her she could come over. She was so excited and said that you're the most beautiful girl she's ever seen, except for her mother, and that I should consider myself 'so lucky to be married to such a beautiful and intelligent girl.' I agreed with her, of course. She then asked if she and her parents could come over because she's dying to see you. There was no way I could say no."

"That I totally understand. Besides, I can't wait to see her."

He parked the truck and reached over toward me. We kissed, and at that moment I felt like an angel, inside a large rose, who had just received God's grace and blessing.

# CHAPTER FORTY-FIVE

Nick got a phone call just as he helped me out of the truck. I walked into the mansion as he stayed outside talking.

I could hear music coming from the ballroom as I stepped into the living room and was greeted by Joe, who was sitting on the couch watching a ballgame, with a book beside him.

I asked, "Are we having a party?"

"Oh my God, Alicia, you look absolutely stunning." He stood up and couldn't stop staring at me. "Simply amazing."

"Thank you, Joe. I have the doctor and Nick to thank. I never would have believed…"

I was suddenly interrupted by a loud scream from the ever classy and fashionable Annie, who was striding toward me. "Oh my God, I can't believe it! It's as though nothing ever happened to your face. It's a perfect match."

"I was just saying the same thing," Joe said.

Annie took me by the arm and slowly walked me toward the ballroom where I could hear the sound of Bee's favorite group, The Beach Boys.

She asked, "Did you ever wonder where your husband got his amazing looks from?"

"Is this a trick question?"

"No."

"From his parents, I imagine."

"Well, you are about to meet one half of that combination."

"Nick's mother is here?" I nervously asked.

"Yes. You've never met her before, or seen a picture?"

"No, but we've spoken many times."

"Are you old enough to know who Lynda Carter is?" Annie asked.

I thought for a moment. "The actress who played Wonder Woman?"

"Very good, Alicia. Who says the younger generation knows nothing about the past?"

I looked at her and said, "You're in a good mood today."

"Of course I am. I was so worried that everything wouldn't turn out as well as we were all hoping, but it turned out better than I could have imagined. You look stunning."

I started to cry as I turned and hugged Annie and said, "Thank you for being so supportive. I love you so much."

"And I love you so much, and I have a little girl in there that is so anxious to see you that she had us drive over here an hour before we knew you would arrive."

She took me by the arm as we walked into the ballroom. "Good Vibrations" was playing, and Bee was there, down at the other end of the long room, dancing with a strikingly beautiful woman who looked about thirty. As soon as Bee noticed me, she started running toward me and Annie stepped in front of her and was nearly run over. "Remember what I told you, my darling girl," she said. "Alicia had a very serious operation on her tummy and she's still healing. So you have to be gentle."

"Yes, Mommy," she said as I knelt down and spread my arms and received a gentle but ecstatic hug from the world's most beautiful angel.

When I looked up I saw Nick embracing his mother in a way that actually made me feel jealous. They seemed to be glued together, and not in the traditional mother and son sort of hug.

"I still can't believe she's Nick's mom," Bee whispered.

"And why is that, angel?"

"Because she looks so young." I nodded as Bee continued. "But she's very nice and she loves to dance. I can't wait for Mr. Wang to come over so we can all dance together."

Finally, mother and son separated, and as they came walking toward us it was apparent that they had both been crying. That at least made me feel better. When she was just a few feet away from me I could clearly see that even with irritated eyes and tracks in her makeup, she was one of the most beautiful women I'd ever seen. At nearly six-feet tall, and wearing a sexy, draped pantsuit with ivory flats, she had the type of body that made even the most powerful men genuflect before her.

She took both my hands and said, "Finally, Alicia, we get to meet in person."

I hesitated and said, "Yes, finally."

We hugged as she whispered into my ear, "Thank you for taking care of my son."

I whispered back, "It's more like he has taken care of me."

"Well, I am forever grateful," she said as we continued to hug. I started to wonder if this was my cue to start crying, but then she moved away and gently touched my reconstructed face and said, "Doctor Petrenko does amazing work. He is truly a saint."

"Yes he is, and now he's off to Ukraine," I said. She looked directly at me, as though I'd revealed a secret, and said, "Yes, he is."

Nick stepped forward and asked Christine, "Have you picked out a room yet, Mom?"

"No, sweetheart, there's plenty of time for that. Besides, I've been dancing with this beautiful angel." She knelt down beside Bee and asked, "Is Bee short for Beatrice?"

"Yes," Bee responded, as though hypnotized.

"How appropriate. Don't you think Nick?"

"Yes, quite appropriate," Nick replied.

"Are you really Nick's mom?" Bee asked.

Christine looked up at her son and said, "She doesn't believe I'm your mom. That might be the nicest compliment paid to me in a long time."

Nick laughed as he helped his mother up. "Yes, Bee, she is definitely my mom. She's simply blessed with great genes."

"I guess so," Bee said, and everyone laughed.

Christine looked around the ballroom at the thirty-foot-high Italianate ceiling, arched windows, and marble floors. "I still can't believe how enormous this place is," she said. "The military certainly has no qualms about spending the taxpayers' money." She looked at Annie and said, "A little pompous, wouldn't you say?"

"Not for a lady born and raised in London," Annie said as she wrapped her arms around her daughter.

"My son sent me a copy of your husband's biography on your brother and the great company you both built. A truly remarkable achievement."

"Thank you, but without the exceptionally creative individuals working for us it never would have been possible."

"I guess not, but it says so much about you and your sibling that so many of your employees stayed with your company throughout their careers."

"My parents taught us to treat everyone with respect and gratitude."

Christine lowered her eyes as Bee turned around and hugged her mother.

"Maybe if I'd had parents like yours I would have been a better mother. At the very least, I would have been present and paying attention while my son was growing up."

Nick reached over and took his mother's hand and said, "How about we get you something to eat. You must be starving."

"No, I'm fine. My beautiful dance partner has already taken care of dinner arrangements. She put in a call to Mr. Wang and ordered enough food for twenty people. Mr. Wang, his uncle, and family will be joining us. I hope that's alright?"

"Of course. It's Mr. Wang's family who you helped get into the U.S."

"Oh, that was nothing. A few minutes flirting with the Chinese Ambassador and another few minutes with a man I know at the State Department, and voila, six visas."

"It might not seem like much to you, but to Mr. Wang and his family you're a goddess," Annie said as her daughter turned around and walked over to Christine.

Bee excitedly said, "Mr. Wang and his mother are teaching me Chinese."

"So, not only are you an angel and a dancer, but you're also becoming multi-lingual. That's very exciting."

"Thank you, I think so, too."

Nick took his mom by the arm and said, "How about we open a couple of bottles of wine. We have a lot to celebrate. My beautiful wife's successful surgery, and the long-awaited visit from my amazing mother. You are staying for a while?"

"Yes, I plan on staying for a long time, if that's okay with Alicia and you?"

"That's more than okay," I said enthusiastically, and while the smile on my face might have been plastered on, I was quite sure it was only the stem cells, still settling into their new homes, that were making me feel like a big fake.

# CHAPTER FORTY-SIX

While Nick, Joe, and Christine sat in the kitchen drinking wine and talking politics, Annie, Bee, and I set the dining room table for eleven. We figured it was easier to set up than to clean up.

Nick checked on me every five minutes, despite me telling him that I felt perfectly fine. I finally said, "You need to stop. What, do you think if I faint, Annie and Bee are just going to let me lie there? Go talk to your mother, but first why don't you bring us another bottle of wine and a soda for Bee."

"Are you sure you should be drinking so much?" Nick asked. I looked at him so sternly that he finally planted a quick kiss on my lips and left the room.

"He loves you so much," Bee said.

"And I love him just as much," I said, "but I can't have him, or his mother, thinking I'm helpless."

Annie piped in, saying, "I wish *my* husband would drop in once in a while to check on *me*." It was a simple gesture of solidarity from her to me, but Bee spun around, looking stricken.

"Why, Mommy, is something wrong?"

"No, my sweet child…"

"Then why does Daddy need to check on you?" Annie looked nervous, and I could see the wheels turning in Bee's head. "You're not feeling sick, are you?"

"No, honey, not at all. How could anyone feel sick when they have you as a daughter? I feel better than ever."

Joe suddenly arrived with an open bottle of wine. He looked at me and said, "Your husband said you're sick of him hovering, so he sent me instead."

"Clever workaround," I said.

Joe laughed and refilled our glasses and left the bottle on the table. Annie jokingly asked, "Did you forget about your daughter? She would also like something to drink."

"I'll go with you, Daddy," Bee said, taking her father's hand.

"Aren't you going to help us finish setting up?" Annie asked.

"Yes, Mommy, but first I have to speak to Daddy about something."

Annie turned to me as Bee and Joe left the room. "She's going to ask Joe if I'm sick."

"Why would she ask that?"

"Because she's terrified of anything happening to either of us. She's worried she'll be left with no one again, like before Joe took her in."

"Poor angel," I said.

"When she first met me, Joe had to rush her to the emergency room because she was hyperventilating and couldn't stop crying. The doctors had to give her a sedative. It turned out she was convinced Joe was going to give her up to marry me. Joe and I go out of our way never to bring up anything around her that she might misinterpret, but sometimes things slip out."

"It was such an innocent comment," I said, but Annie shook her head, downed her entire glass of wine, and started to cry. I handed her a napkin and said, "Careful, she might come back. Best not to let her see you crying."

Annie nodded and wiped her eyes and asked, "Do I look okay?"

"As beautiful as always."

"As beautiful as Nick's mom?" she said, and we both laughed. Then her face lit up. "I almost forgot, with all the confusion around here, to ask you a very important question. Would you and Nick consider being Bee's godparents? My non-practicing Catholic husband has suddenly decided that she needs to be baptized. Bee's fine with it because we promised her a new dress for the ceremony, and in all honesty it would make me feel better knowing that the two of you were there for her if, God forbid, anything happened to us."

"I would be honored, and I'm quite sure Nick would, too."

# CHAPTER FORTY-SEVEN

Mr. Wang, his uncle, and his newly arrived family showed up with enough food to feed fifty. Mr. Wang's parents were adorable, and his grandmother and other relatives were as sweet as pie. They only understood a few words of English, but Wonder Woman knew enough Cantonese to get through a basic conversation. She was stronger in Mandarin, which she had used to speak to the Chinese Ambassador.

When Mr. Wang told his family that Christine was responsible for getting them into the U.S., they crowded around her and thanked her repeatedly. She insisted that it was her honor to help such a beautiful family be reunited.

Nick and Annie were also able to communicate with them, and of course my future godchild even knew enough words to get by. It was only Joe and I who could not speak a word of Cantonese or Mandarin, and when I looked at Joe for reassurance he said, "Don't look at me, I'm lucky I can speak English."

Joe and Nick served dinner, and when I offered to pour the wine my husband said, "Why don't you sit down, sweetheart, you don't look so good." I was tempted to kick him in the shins, but then like a good little girl I simply sat down. In truth, I was very tired. If ever there was a time I could have used a couple of hits of cocaine, it was right then.

Halfway through dinner, I turned to Nick and said, "I need to lay down, I'm sorry."

Nick stood up and addressed everyone in Cantonese and English, and told them that I'd had surgery and needed rest. There was a collective sigh of understanding from Mr. Wang's family and before I knew it Bee was by my side saying to Nick, "I'll go with Alicia."

Annie sprang to her feet, wine glass in hand, and told Nick to sit down, and that she would see her daughter and me to the bedroom. When Nick tried to respond, she said, "Don't even think of it! Stay here with your mother."

To my surprise, Nick backed down like a little child and sat next to his mother.

Annie had Bee hold her wine glass as she took my arm and the three of us walked toward the bedroom. I asked, "What was that all about?"

"I didn't like the way he spoke to you, and I especially didn't like his tone when he spoke to Mr. Wang's family about your condition."

When we reached the bedroom, Annie and Bee helped me put on a pair of pajamas I forgot I even had. I lay back on the pillow as Annie gently ran her hand through my hair. Her touch was like a soothing balm that I imagined only a loving mother could possess. As I dropped into a state of pure relaxation, I either said, or dreamed that I said, "Thank you, Mommy," but there was no reply.

\*\*\*

When I woke up it was still dark outside. I was very groggy, but I forced myself out of bed and walked into the kitchen, where Nick and Christine were standing at the sink with their backs to me, washing dishes.

Suddenly, my husband smashed his hands against the sink and yelled, "It was all my fault. I should have waited in Kiev and then taken her back with me. That's what her father wanted. As usual, I fucked up."

"Shut up, you son-of-a-bitch, and stop blaming yourself for everything," Christine yelled.

"And tell me, Mom, how is that working out for you?" Nick asked.

Christine threw the dish towel she was holding into the sink and started to jab her finger into Nick's chest. "Don't you go there. Do you understand?"

"Yes," my husband replied meekly. That's when Christine turned around and saw me. She looked shocked and said, "Alicia, what are you doing up? My God," and then she ran toward me and helped me sit down.

I was silent as I let her settle me into a chair. She gently caressed my face and touched my hair, the way Annie had earlier. "Sweetheart, are you okay?" she asked.

"I'm just so tired. Sorry for being so much trouble."

"You're no trouble at all. In fact, you're perfect," she said as she stood up and pulled my hair back and tied it into a ponytail. "Did the doctor give you ointment for your face?"

"Yes, but I haven't used it yet."

She started to help me up as Nick said, "I'll take her into the bedroom."

"No!" Christine exclaimed. "Why don't you finish the dishes. I know how upset you can get if everything isn't cleaned up perfectly before going to bed."

Christine helped me into the bedroom and propped me up against the headboard, amid a bunch of pillows. Then she went into the bathroom and came out with the bag from Dr. Petrenko. She read the instructions on the tube of ointment and gently started applying it to my entire face. She said, "The instructions say to spread it across the entire face so it will match your original skin more perfectly. You are so lovely, my dear, so very lovely."

"Why were you and Nick yelling at each other?" I asked.

"I have no doubt you're married to the best man possible, but occasionally when my son's morals and virtues come into conflict with his actions, his memory is affected, and I simply have to correct it."

"You're not leaving, are you?"

"No, sweetheart, you're going to have me here for an extended visit."

"I hope you never leave," I said, and that was the last thing I remember before falling back to sleep.

# CHAPTER FORTY-EIGHT

When I woke up again it was definitely morning. The sun was filtering through the window and the gulls were squawking. When I turned toward the window I was taken aback by my husband, who was sitting in a chair beside the bed looking directly at me. He asked, "What's wrong, my love?"

"You scared me," I said as I moved farther away from him.

"I thought by now you'd be used to having me beside you."

"In bed, yes." I took in a deep breath and shook my head and said, "I can't believe I could get so tired so suddenly."

"I think the anesthesia was still in your system, and you had a delayed reaction. Besides, you and Annie polished off two bottles of wine."

"Was she okay?"

"Yes, but then she didn't have anesthesia in her. When Joe and I came in to get Bee it was like you were stuck together. It was a delicate operation, ungluing the two of you."

"I remember Bee coming with me, but that's all. Did I get up during the night?"

"Yeah, you came stumbling into the kitchen while my mother and I were doing the dishes. She brought you back here and applied the ointment Dr. Petrenko gave you to your face."

"Did we talk at all?"

"I imagine we did but I don't exactly remember what we said."

The man who remembered everything couldn't recall the argument he'd had with his mother, which he had to know I overheard, regardless of how tired I was. "Would you like to go for our walk?"

"Not today. I feel really dirty and need to take a shower."

# CHAPTER FORTY-NINE

I walked outside, feeling like a new person after showering and getting dressed, and found Christine on the terrace. She was reading the *New York Times* and drinking a cup of coffee.

She greeted me with a big smile and said, "And how is my favorite daughter-in-law?"

"Much better than yesterday. Sorry for being such a mess."

"There's no reason to apologize, sweetheart." She reached over and gently ran her fingers through my hair. She was so breathtakingly beautiful. It was as though her features were made of Italian white marble; from afar, one might mistake her for a statue.

"Have you ever done any modeling?" I asked as her glistening green eyes remained fixed on me.

"Oh, God no! I'm just a lucky redneck from West Virginia. No catwalks for me."

"You're so beautiful, you could have modeled if you'd wanted to," I said.

"That's so sweet of you to say, but of course I had my hands full."

I asked her how she met Nick's father, and she told a short, passionless story about catching the eye of the lieutenant general back in Virginia, during celebrations for the 125th anniversary of the Battle of Philippi, the first land battle in the Civil War.

"He was in town with the Air Force, and I was a fresh-faced seventeen-year-old out for a night on the town. It all happened real quick."

"What did your parents think? Wasn't he more than double your age?"

"They were overjoyed. One less mouth to feed, and snagging a lieutenant general was a *big* step up from marrying a local guy from the mines."

"I can't even imagine how many suitors you must have had."

"And not one of them mattered one iota to me," she said as I looked out over the water.

"Did you love him?" I asked, and she thought about it.

"No," she said, "no, I can't really say I did. He was handsome and all, but it's not like he ever confided in me. In truth, I never knew the man."

"That's what Nick said. That he never knew the man."

"It was a sad truth of our marriage that we were two islands in a big sea," she said. Then she smiled at me and asked, "What about you? Are you madly in love with my son?"

"Yes, although I'm not sure 'madly in love' captures all that I feel for your son. I never knew men like Nick existed. All the men I knew before him were pigs." I looked away as my eyes glistened with tears. "I'm not stupid. I know I'm not his first choice. That honor goes to Nastasiya, the beautiful nurse killed by a Russian bomb."

"Did my son tell you that?"

"Not in so many words, but I overheard a conversation between Nick and Dr. Petrenko, and last night I heard you two arguing … and people say that Nastasiya and I could pass for sisters."

"Well, you could, except that she was petite and you're tall and full-figured."

"And while I was strutting down runways, she was saving lives."

"My son knew Nastasiya for about a month. I guess you could call it love at first sight for both of them. After they became engaged, she gave the normal ten-day notice at the hospital she was working at. She also agreed to work double shifts each of those days. They were going to fly back to the States right after her last shift.

"Nick decided that during those ten days, since they weren't going to see each other much, he would take a trip to Crimea. She begged him not to, and he knew the situation between the Russians and Ukrainians was seriously heating up. Nick didn't listen, told her not to worry, and he went. On his third day there, he was picked up by the Russians on suspicion of spying. His media credentials were no help. Thankfully, the Russian soldiers were not above taking a bribe, and so he was able to communicate with Nastasiya and me. Nine months later, with the war in full bloom, I was able to bribe the top Russian officer in Crimea to have my son released."

"And how much did that cost?"

"Half a million U.S. dollars. I expect the Russian officer took the first flight to Switzerland and is watching the destruction of Ukraine and the deaths of his fellow soldiers on a TV in an upscale bar in the Swiss Alps.

"I promised my son that before picking him up I would stop in Kiev and pick up Nastasiya. I visited her in the hospital. She was so busy, but she managed to get an hour off and we sat down outside and talked." Christine's voice cracked with emotion and tears began flowing down her cheeks. "She was so petite, and with her nurse's uniform on, she reminded me of a doll. She knew why I was there, and she immediately told me that there was no way she could leave with me and desert her country and people at such a time. I couldn't argue with her, especially as one ambulance after another pulled up with seriously wounded children and civilians. She asked me if I could come back tomorrow because she had certain things in her apartment that she wanted Nick to have. Then she ran off and started helping unload the wounded from ambulances."

"You never saw her alive again, did you?" I asked, and she shook her head.

"The next morning when I arrived at the hospital they were carrying her body out of the building. The entire wing was still smoldering from the bomb the Russians dropped on the hospital. A couple of her neighbors were kind enough to take me to her apartment, and there beside her bed was a box labeled *Nicholas*. My relationship with my son had improved remarkably up to that point. I finally felt like I was making up for my early negligence. But at that moment, Alicia, I felt no love for my son, only hostility, because I knew that if he had listened to Nastasiya and stayed out of Crimea, she would never have been killed. He was the reason that such a beautiful and caring child was dead."

I looked at her in confusion and sadness. I knew I needed to speak up for my husband, but the pain of Christine's grief beat down upon me. Her use of the word *child* to describe Nastasiya was the proverbial nail in the coffin.

Christine lifted a section of the newspaper from the table and below it was the box labeled *Nicholas*. She opened it and took out one of many photos and handed it to me. It was a photo of Nastasiya in a nurse's uniform. She undeniably looked like me but she was even more beautiful. She was petite and her smile was genuine and betrayed an innocence and happiness that one usually only sees in children. She reminded me of my beautiful Bee, and with that reminder I started to cry as I handed the photo back to Christine.

"Nick would never purposely hurt anyone. It's a crime that she had to die, but to blame him isn't right."

"My son was a wartime journalist for ten years and it wasn't like he took vacations. I doubt you will meet another person with more knowledge of world affairs than him. He knew that the Russians were going to attack Ukraine. They had already started stationing troops, tanks, jeeps, and all different types of weaponry along the border. Nastasiya begged him not to go, yet he couldn't resist. There was plenty to do in Kiev to keep him busy for ten days."

"How old was she when she was killed?"

"Twenty-two," Christine angrily replied as she handed me another picture of Nick and Nastasiya from just before Nick left for Crimea. Nastasiya's smile was forced as she looked up at Nick and cuddled up to him on a park bench.

I handed the picture back to Christine and she put it back in the box. She put the cover over the box and placed it right in front of me.

"I don't want to see any more. This is between Nick and Nastasiya."

"You don't have to look at anything else in the box, but you are going to give it to Nick."

"Why? It was given to you to pass onto your son."

"Because you're his wife, and what's in this box and how he responds to it will give you a much clearer picture of his mental state."

"No!" I said, pushing the box back to Christine. "You're the one…"

"How many times has he told you that you're his savior?"

"I don't know. We say it to each other all the time."

"How many times? Ten, twenty, a hundred, two hundred?"

I looked at my mother-in-law and finally started to connect the dots.

"If you love my son as much as I think you do, you'll give this to him." She pushed the box back in front of me, and I looked down at it and started to cry. As my tears splashed the top, anointing the treasures of a courageous and caring young lady, the term *savior* took on a whole new meaning.

# CHAPTER FIFTY

As I walked toward the study, I could feel my heart thumping, and I was reminded of how I used to feel moments before a fashion show. My palms were sweaty and I had to take care not to leave marks on the box. The contents told a story that could very likely foretell the future of our lives, marriage, and well-being.

The study door was open and yet I still knocked. Nick looked up from his desk and said, "Hello, my beautiful bride. Feeling better?"

All I could do was nod. I walked toward him as he started to stand up, but before he could make a move I reached out and handed him the box. He looked at it and placed it on the desk and asked, "Did my mother give this to you?"

"Yes."

"What did she tell you?"

"That doesn't matter," I said as he sat back down and nervously tapped his fingers across the top of the box.

"Well, whatever she told you..." he said, as he stopped tapping and looked at me, "is one hundred percent true."

"I'll leave you alone," I said as I turned and started walking toward the door.

"No, Alicia, please stay. This concerns you as much as it concerns me."

I turned back around and sat in a chair, directly across from him, on the other side of the desk. He opened the box and took out the first picture of Nastasiya dressed in the nurse's uniform. He looked at it for a long time as he smiled distraughtly.

He passed the picture to me, without a word, and I glanced at it and carefully placed it on the desk next to me.

He looked at every picture, gently passing his fingers across each one. Except for a few pictures of just her, all the others were of the two of them, standing together in front of famous Kyiv landmarks: Saint Sophia Cathedral, St. Andrew's Church, and the Prince Volodymyr the Great Monument, with the prince overlooking the Dnieper River, holding a cross.

He handed me the last picture as he sat back in his chair and said, "It isn't easy living my life knowing that I killed that beautiful, caring, and loving angel."

"Please, don't talk like that. You didn't kill anyone."

"I might as well have, and to pretend otherwise is insulting."

"Do you actually think she'd want you to go on living with this unjustifiable guilt?"

He reached into the box and pulled out a copy of *The Great Gatsby*. He opened it and read an inscription she'd written on the inside cover, in Ukrainian.

He handed me the book and I asked, "What does it say?"

"It says, *Why did Gatsby have to die at the end? I don't like that. Love you, love you, love you, your Nastasiya*."

I handed the book back to him, with the last photo, and he returned them to the box.

"Thank you for sharing that with me. I know it couldn't be easy," I said.

"Being with her helped me forget the sound of artillery shells being fired, the cries of the wounded, the stench of the dead and dying … she laughed like a child and bounced around like the Energizer bunny. She was the first girl I fell in love with…"

My husband suddenly stopped talking, but pain and anguish were etched so deeply in his face and eyes that they seemed to pass directly into me.

"What can I do to help?" I asked as he looked up and smiled.

"If not for you, Alicia, I might not be here right now. Meeting you was like a sign from Nastasiya that I needed to keep living, keep making a difference … that she'd forgiven me and wanted me to be happy."

"And how much of a difference did it make that Nastasiya and I resemble each other so much?"

"I imagine it made some difference, but girls who look like you and Nastasiya have always been the type of girls I've been most attracted to … and that's the truth."

I suddenly had a flashback to those sessions down on the beach, when he would lay down and sleep for forty-five minutes.

Nick looked at me and said, "What are you thinking about, Alicia?"

I folded my arms and placed them on the desk. "I don't want you to keep Nastasiya a secret. Please put pictures of her anywhere you like. We can frame some of them, and put them up where they'll be seen. She shouldn't be hidden. Her story deserves to be told."

I got up from the chair and leaned over the desk to kiss my husband, and he reached out and grabbed my hand and pulled me closer. We kissed softly and he said, "I never want you to doubt…"

"I don't," I said as I turned and walked out of the study.

I walked back out onto the terrace and sat down beside Christine, who was still reading the paper.

"How did everything go?"

"He asked me if you had told me anything, and I told him that didn't matter. Then he said whatever you told me was one hundred percent true."

Christine's expression remained unchanged, and I said, "You don't seem surprised."

"My son possesses very strong ethical and moral principles. I imagine he received them from the nannies who cared for him as a child. They were very religious and they both loved him like a mother. Rest assured, I had nothing to do with my child's upbringing."

"You weren't much more than a child yourself."

"That's no excuse. I was old enough to grab onto the one high ranking military man who couldn't take his eyes off of me. Yes, he was more than twice my age, and I wasn't at all attracted to him, but he was my ticket out."

"Your relationship with Nick has improved so much. When I asked him who his guardian angel was in this world, he named you, without hesitating."

"You mean, he didn't say his wife?" she jokingly asked.

"We'd only known each other a couple of days, but I have no doubt that's still the way he feels."

"And who is your guardian angel?"

"Your son."

"And how long did it take you to come to that conclusion?"

"One hour from the time we met."

Nick walked out onto the terrace and pulled up a chair and sat down between his mother and me. He took his mother's hand and said, "I'm sorry about last night."

Christine didn't respond. She simply ran her fingers through her son's hair as tears rolled down her cheeks. I looked away and I swear I felt like screaming, *while you're passing around blame, why don't you blame the sons-of-bitches who dropped the bomb on the hospital that killed Nastasiya. If not for them, Nastasiya would still be alive and I would be working as a cashier.*

I walked into the mansion and into our bedroom and retrieved a floppy beach hat from the closet. I looked in the bathroom mirror as I put on the hat that was large enough to shield the reconstructed part of my face from the sun.

I walked back onto the terrace where Nick and Christine were still sitting at the table, talking. Christine looked up and said, "I love the hat."

"Thank you. I have a bunch, and you're more than welcome to take one. They're great for blocking out the sun. I'm going to take a walk along the beach now."

"If you wait a few minutes I'll go with you," Nick said.

I pulled out my cell phone from my pocket and waved it at him and said, "If any of my body parts give out I'll be sure to call you. Promise. Stay and talk with your mother."

I turned and started walking down the path to the beach. I stopped just before the water's edge and started walking in the direction that Nick and I usually took. I was quite certain my husband was watching where I was going, and I didn't want to worry him by taking a different route. Having lost his first choice, he had no intention of losing his back-up.

After a few moments, I shook my head in disgust. My thoughts were racing. *Nastasiya probably had more courage and compassion in her little pinky than I have in my whole body. She's the one who should be walking along this beach, not me.*

A flock of seagulls seemed to be following me. I stopped, and to my surprise, they also stopped, like a well-disciplined regiment. Their webbed feet were planted firmly in the wet sand. I looked down at them, yet not one of them looked my way, and then in the blink of an eye they flew off, like fighter jets, their white and black wings spread wide as they rose in formation, out to sea, then circled back and landed about a hundred feet from where I stood. They squawked loudly as though sending me a message, a cryptic message that I could not decode.

The birds scattered as I continued walking, aimlessly, and it struck me how few people I ever saw on this section of beach. I guess it wasn't that unusual, considering the California coastline ran over eight-hundred miles long, but it felt strange, as though civilization was forbidden from entering and polluting this virgin stretch of sand and shore.

I climbed atop a flat rock about fifty feet from the water and looked out over the majestic Pacific. I remembered a few lines from the Yeats poem, "Beggar to Beggar Cried," and recited its opening couplet to myself:

> "Time to put off the world and go somewhere,
> And find my health again in the sea air…"

I lay back on the rock, took off my hat, and placed it over my face. As tiny flashes of sunlight shone through its fibers, I recited the poem's final line, "*The wind-blown clamour of the barnacle-geese*," and marveled at its odd beauty. Was it the music? The meter? The surprise of jamming together something so small, sharp, and inert with something so expansive and free? I heard the same line again and again, like a mantra, and felt it pulling me into a tunnel. The *wind-blown clamour*. The *barnacle-geese*. What were they?

I was back in the study, transported, dreaming, with Nastasiya seated next to me and Nick sitting behind the desk in his usual chair, across from both of us. We looked like twins, with our hair done the same way — long, parted down the middle, with long, curly locks down our backs. We giggled and ran into the next room, and changed into identical outfits and yelled, "Close your eyes." We sat back down, told him to open his eyes, and to pick which one of us he would choose to marry. He chose Nastasiya not once, not twice, but ten times in a row.

I looked greatly disturbed and Nastasiya turned to me and said, "Don't you understand, Alicia? I'm just a memory, and memories fade … sometimes for the better, sometimes for the worse … but I'm only an apparition."

I heard my name being called, "Alicia, Alicia…" My hat was lifted from my face, and when I opened my eyes, Nick was crouching over me.

"Sweetheart, you've been gone for hours. I was worried sick. I tried to call but you didn't answer."

I pulled my phone out and handed it to Nick. He looked at it and said, "Your battery is dead."

"I'm sorry. I lay down and before I knew it I was asleep."

He sat down next to me on the rock. "And what were you dreaming about? A dashing prince lifting you onto his white stallion and the two of you riding off into Paradise?"

"That's so strange," I said. "That's exactly what I was dreaming about, except the dashing prince was choosing between me and another girl, and he chose the other girl."

"Well, apparently there's something wrong with his eyesight."

"Perhaps," I said sheepishly.

"What's wrong, angel?"

"Nothing," I said as I sat up and wrapped my arms around his middle. "I just love you so much."

"And you don't think I love you as much?" he asked as he gently ran his fingers through my hair. "You don't think I will ever get over Nastasiya?"

The look on my face must have made it clear that this was an active worry, because he continued, saying, "And that might have been the case if I hadn't met you. Nastasiya will always hold a special place in my heart, but a larger part of my heart is reserved for you."

I stayed nestled against his chest, listening to the beating of his heart. Then I started to unbutton his shirt, and when I had opened four buttons, I leaned in and slowly ran my tongue up his chiseled wall of a chest. I slid onto his lap and squirmed on top of him, with predictable results. We started to kiss, and then he suddenly, gently, pushed me away.

"What are you doing, Alicia?"

"Surely, it hasn't been that long that you've forgotten."

"You're still not totally healed from the surgery you had a little over a month ago."

"I feel perfectly fine," I said as I took his hand and placed it on my wet panties.

"No, we're not taking a chance," he said, pulling his hand away.

"My God, you are such a boy scout," I said, moving away from him.

"It has nothing to do with being a boy scout and everything to do with loving you more than anything."

Coming from any other man I would have felt spurned, but not from my husband. I knew he meant every word of what he said. I shook my head, rolled off of him, and lay down a few feet away. I put my hat over my face as he said, "Alicia, let's go."

"No! This is my rock, and I am queen," I said as I slapped my hand down on the rock.

"Well, queen of the rock, I see an invading regiment heading straight toward you."

I shot up, looked behind me, and screamed as I jumped into my husband's arms. Thousands of fire ants, literally thousands of them, were swarming the rock's flat surface, just a few feet from where I'd been resting my head.

"Some queen you are, abandoning your rock," he said.

"Oh, why don't you go build yourself a campfire and recite the Pledge of Allegiance?"

"Ouch. Alright, come on, your highness," he said, taking my hand. "Back to the castle."

I surrendered my rock and went with him.

***

As we walked and walked for what seemed like a long time, but only because we were dawdling, he asked, "So how are you and Mom getting along?"

"Great! I love her and have already told her that I never want her to leave."

"Well, be careful what you wish for. She just told me she's divorcing husband number two. She was willing to overlook one affair and even a second, but it recently got out of hand." I had stopped and was gaping at him as he told the story. "She served him with divorce papers and threatened to ruin his military career if he dared to contest her conditions. She kept all of her own money and got him to cough up some of his."

I shook my head. "Men are pigs," I said. "Except you. You're a little piglet."

"What's that supposed to mean?"

"Well, a piglet is still a baby, and its sex drive is dormant … sort of like you, even though your sex drive is more like that of an adult pig, but you refuse to act on it."

"Well then, maybe I'll just have to find myself a hot babe until you're fully healed. Can't have all that sexual energy going to waste."

"Go ahead. Then you'll have the two closest women in your life filing for divorce, but unlike your mommy I'll take you for every penny I can."

"Wow! Your true colors are finally showing."

"I am a rainbow."

He stopped and kissed me, and when we started walking again, I remembered to tell him that Annie and I referred to his mom as Wonder Woman.

"The superhero with the gold bracelets and the leotard?"

"Yes, the one played by the breathtaking Lynda Carter in the late-1970s TV series. Both Annie and I, who have been around some of the most gorgeous women in the world, don't believe we've seen a woman more beautiful than your mom. She really isn't your mom, is she?"

"Of course, she's my mom."

"Your stepmom?"

"You're starting to sound like Bee."

"Well, Bee is very perceptive. And that reminds me, Annie wants to know if you and I will agree to be Bee's godparents. Joe wants her to be baptized."

"It would be an honor," Nick replied.

"That's what I told Annie. Question: Is there a reason why I never see any other people along this long stretch of beach?"

"My guess is that the military forgot to take down signs that warned: *Property of the U.S. Military. Anyone caught trespassing will be shot.*"

"Do you think we should check and see if there are any signs and take them down?"

"Let me ask my mother. For all I know, she might have told them to leave them up to give us more privacy."

"Do you think after your mom divorces husband number two, her relationship with the government and military will come to an end?"

"Sweetheart, do you really think husband number two is the reason she wields so much power? My father opened the door for her and it has remained open ever since. She walked into the Chinese Embassy and the U.S. State Department, and in under an hour, secured six visas for Mr. Wang's family. My mom can use her beauty and body as well as any woman who has ever walked on this planet, and she doesn't take her clothes off."

"She's Wonder Woman, and I wouldn't be surprised if she can seriously kick ass," I said as we suddenly stopped walking and he looked at me pensively.

"I have come to regret the agony I put her through." He looked down at the white foam creeping up toward our feet. "She was still a child when she had me. I doubt she'd ever been out of West Virginia when she met my dad. Her prospects were dim. She has come a long way."

"Just look at the way Mr. Wang's family treated her. You'd think she was a goddess."

"Before I went crazy last night about my guilt over Nastasiya, she told me that she felt very awkward about the way Mr. Wang's family glorified her. They're the ones who've been through hell. All she had to do was flirt with a couple of oversexed sixty-year-old men."

I laughed and said, "I saw your mother's response to your overwhelming guilt. She didn't back down."

"No kidding. I have the bruises from her slamming her finger into my chest to prove it."

"Did Doctor Petrenko arrive safely in Kiev?" I asked.

"Yes. Just before going on my search for you I got an email from him."

"I still don't know how to properly thank him. Between you and him, I've been given back a big part of my identity."

He looked directly at me and at first I thought he was going to give me the speech about how my looks are only a small part of who I truly am, but he didn't. He ran his fingers through my hair, and my entire body was flooded by a tingling, shimmering sensation.

A wave crashed against the beach and suddenly we were up to our knees in water. We laughed as the water receded, leaving our sandals soaked as we moved further up from the shore.

"You still didn't answer my question," I said. "How can I properly thank you and the doctor for making me feel whole again?"

"I've told you, Alicia. You saved me. Your debt, if there was one, came pre-paid."

"I understand that, but it seems like you've done everything for me from the moment we met until just a few minutes ago, when you saved me from that regiment of fire ants."

"I must admit, that was very gallant of me," he laughingly replied.

"My hero," I said. "And what about the doctor?"

He lowered his head as we stopped once again. "I think … the doctor would want you to live the life that has been given to you to its absolute fullest."

I looked out over the ocean and watched the gulls circle over the water and then plant themselves on shore. I wondered what secret messages they communicated to each other with their squawking. Surely their cries had to signal a warning, a source of food, a time to mate…

"Do you think the doctor will be okay?" I asked.

"He doesn't have as much to live for, and that's not an optimal state of mind to be in when you're in a war zone. He tells me he's fine and that his job is the same as it has always been. To reduce suffering and keep people alive."

"I don't understand."

"Nastasiya was his daughter. His pride and joy," Nick said as he seemed to unconsciously walk toward the shore. He took a few steps into the water and stood still.

I followed him and gently touched his arm and said, "I think we need to get back before your mother starts worrying."

I took his hand and we walked out of the water and back onto the beach. The silence that suddenly existed between us was alarming. My husband suffered terribly, and I wasn't sure of anything anymore, except that I loved him so much that it hurt.

In truth, I could not relate in any constructive way to the life he'd lived for over a decade, and he would never allow me in far enough to get the slightest perception of what he actually lived through.

We finally broke the silence when we were directly across from the mansion and he said, "Time to carry my beautiful bride the rest of the way."

"That might not be such a great idea, since you are so intent on remaining celibate. I would hate to have you get excited and have to do something to relieve the pressure."

He simply picked me up like I was a toothpick and said, "You really are looking for a spanking, aren't you?"

"Promises, promises."

# CHAPTER FIFTY-ONE

Christine was watching us from the top of the stairs to the beach, and when she saw Nick carrying me, she started down the steps, calling out, "What's wrong? Is Alicia okay?" We both waved to her and called out that everything was fine, and Nick put me on my feet to prove the point. Then we walked up and met at the top and Nick and I took turns telling her the story of how I fell asleep on the rock, and how Nick found me, and how I refused to go anywhere and declared myself the queen of the rock, and then had to be saved from the fire ants. We kept it PG, leaving out the part where I tried to seduce her son.

"You two are pretty entertaining," she said, and then she announced that since I'd been returned to safety, she was going into town for a little shopping trip.

"What are you shopping for?" I asked.

"Vinyl and lingerie. Vinyl for a dance party with Bee, and lingerie in case I meet a handsome movie star strolling along this famous beach."

"You don't need to stroll along this beach to meet a movie star," I said. "I'll give you a tour of Annie's studio and you'll have movie stars crawling all over you."

"I don't think that came out exactly right, sweetheart…" Nick said.

"What do you mean? She's buying lingerie. It came out perfectly."

"She's right, darling," Christine told her son. "They can crawl all they like." Nick rolled his eyes in defeat.

"And you're having a dance party with Bee?" I asked.

"Yes, We're officially friends. I think she said I was number eighteen."

"I'm thirteen and Nick is fourteen. It's a real honor."

"She's the real reason I'm going into town. She and Mr. Wang are coming over later and we are indeed planning to cut a rug. I'm going into town to pick up some show tunes."

"Can I go?" I asked.

"From the way he was carrying you up to the house, I wondered if you and your husband might have something else planned…"

"No, he's sworn off …" I never got to finish my sentence because Nick pinched me and whispered, "My mother doesn't need to hear this."

"He's right. And yes, I would love for you to come along," Christine said.

***

Before driving into town with Christine, I dropped into the study to say goodbye to my husband. He was talking on the phone with his agent, and mouthed a silent apology to me for not seeing me off to the car. I blew him a kiss and met Christine outside.

I climbed into the SUV and sat on the passenger seat across from her. She asked, "Would you prefer to drive?"

"I don't even have a learner's permit, never mind a license."

"Oh forgive me, I forgot you supermodels get driven around in limos," she said. As soon as the words came out, she apologized. "Please forgive me. I feel terrible."

"It's okay. You're right, we did get driven around in limos. And you shouldn't have to walk on eggshells."

"Still. I would never want to say anything to remind you of that terrible night."

"I appreciate that," I said. "Now I hope I'm not going to be the one to touch a nerve … Nick told me about your impending divorce."

"That's alright. And it won't be pending for long. It should be finalized next week."

"How are you feeling about it?"

"Resigned," she said, then looked at me. "You know, I knew my first husband was fooling around on me all the time, and for all I know I might have cheated on him. I was usually drunk from early afternoon to whatever time I fell out at night.

"But it was different with my first husband because he held all the cards. If we had ever divorced, I would have been lucky to get child support and a small allowance. When he took a nosedive into the Potomac, I thought I was destroyed. But the military ruled it an accident instead of a suicide, which meant that I would be receiving his pension and death benefits. The real shock came at the reading of his will. It was then I found out that he was the last remaining member of an extremely rich family. He left Nick and me a massive fortune. In all the years we were married, I knew nothing about his family or their immense wealth. It was not until the reading of the will that I found out he had a younger sister who was killed in a car accident at eighteen.

"It was the first year after my husband's death that Nick and I finally started to bond as mother and child. I sort of sobered up, stopped with the martinis at lunch, and limited myself to two glasses of wine with dinner. I told my son all the details of the will, and even though he wasn't supposed to receive any money until he was eighteen, I gave him a hefty allowance. I figured he had a harem of good-looking girls chasing him. Instead, I found out that the only ladies he hung out with were our nannies, and nothing perverse was going on with them.

"It was also at this time that I realized how exceptionally intelligent he was. He's the one who got me into reading, and together we read the same books and had great discussions about the authors, the characters, the plots, different writing styles … you name it.

"It was also around this time that I met my second husband. He was good-looking, my age, and moving up the military ladder. I kept the relationship a secret. I never brought him home. We met in hotels. Very classy. I had no intention of marrying him, and I took every precaution not to get pregnant, but it happened anyway, and then I made the biggest mistake of my life. Instead of following my first instinct and going straight to an abortion clinic, I told the sperm donor, and he insisted we get married and have the baby."

She suddenly stopped talking as she gripped the steering wheel so hard that I thought at any moment she might tear it out. I said, "It's okay, Christine, you don't have to go on … I understand."

It was like she didn't hear a word I said and just as suddenly she started talking again. "We got married and he moved in with us. A month later I had a miscarriage, but by then it was too late. The bond I had finally formed with Nick was shattered. Instead of spending my evenings with my son discussing books and world politics, I was out on the party circuit with my ambitious new husband.

"Then my son went off to college, and you know the rest. It was like he stuck a knife in me, and for the next ten years he slowly twisted it back and forth."

"Did you ever tell Nick about the pregnancy?"

"No, and please don't tell him. The last thing he needs is another deposit of guilt."

"He told me you were moving in with us."

"I haven't decided on anything yet," she said as we came to a stop sign.

"Can I make a decision?" I asked.

She looked at me, smiled, and said, "Yes sweetheart, you can make as many decisions as you like."

"Please, please, move in with us. I beg you, please."

"What are you, the only daughter-in-law in the world that wants her mother-in-law to move in with her?"

"Sure, if you want to put it that way. But it feels more like you're my sister."

"That's bananas, but okay," she said, as the light changed and we started moving again.

I leaned back in my seat and asked, "How about one hard, cold fact? Could that help you make up your mind?"

She quickly looked at me and said, "It might."

"When we left Doctor Petrenko's office, he called me back under the pretense that he forgot to give me something. Nick stayed by the elevator. The doctor said he didn't want to alarm me, but that I need to keep a close eye on Nick and keep him 'occupied.' He said Nick had witnessed things that simply don't go away ... things 'too appalling for any one person to live with.' I think we need two sets of eyes on him to keep him safe. One isn't enough. I can't do it by myself. Please, Christine—"

As the words tumbled out, it was like a stone wall came crashing down upon me. I started crying hysterically and panting and gasping for breath. I bent over as I suddenly felt the car swing over and come to a stop. The next thing I felt was Christine taking hold of me and sitting me upright and calmingly saying, "Try to take long, deep breaths." I tried to do as she said but I couldn't. She then gently ran her fingers through my hair and said, "I would never abandon you or my son. That's a promise. I'm moving permanently into that oversized hotel you live in and you could beg me to leave but it won't work. I am a stubborn bitch and I plan on staying."

"Promise?" I asked as I started to breathe normally and my crying slowed down.

"Yes, I promise. I love you and my son way too much…"

That was enough to appease my anxiety for the moment, and suddenly I felt depleted, closed my eyes, and fell asleep. When I finally woke up we were already halfway home. Christine had called up the record store, put in her order, and paid with a credit card by phone. She then pulled up in front of the store and the owner of the store came out and handed her the records and off we went.

"I'm sorry I was so much trouble," I said.

She turned toward me and put her finger in front of her mouth. I looked out the window at the beautiful ocean as the sun started its descent into its mysterious, unfathomable depths.

"Can we please not tell Nick about my meltdown?"

"My lips are sealed," she said. "I'm just so grateful that he has found someone who cares and loves him so very much. Thank you, Alicia … my beautiful, darling daughter."

# CHAPTER FIFTY-TWO

Nick met us at the front door and said, "You're back. I was starting to worry."

"Why is that?" Christine asked as she looked at her son and smiled.

"Yeah, why would that be? Afraid we ran off?" I jokingly added.

"Have you two been drinking?"

"Not a drop. But now that you mention it, why don't you be a gentleman and open a bottle of white wine for your wife and me. Picking out records can be exhausting."

We started walking toward the ballroom when Nick pulled me aside and asked to speak to me for a second. Christine continued into the ballroom, and I walked over to my husband, who asked if I'd been crying.

"I'm always crying over something. Face it. You married a crybaby."

"That's not true. You might cry a lot, but it's always over something that you find hurtful or sad. A crybaby cries for no reason. You have reasons. What's your reason this time?"

"You need to stop being a reporter. Your mother told me a moving story about the family of a young marine. I cried. That's all."

Nick eyed me suspiciously, then said, "I only asked because I love you so much, and because I so want you and my mother to get along."

"Your mother is great. She's amazing in ways I could never had imagined. I've been begging her to move in with us permanently, and she just said she would, and I'm so happy."

Nick processed this news and we looked at each other for a long moment. I wrapped my arms around him and kissed him as tears suddenly began rolling down my cheeks.

"What are you crying about now?" he asked.

"Nothing. I don't know," I said, bawling. "Because I love you so much. If anything ever happened to you, I would—"

He put his finger to his mouth and said, "Please, don't even finish that sentence! Nothing is going to happen to me. I promise!"

I stepped back from him and tried to smile as the tears continued to fall.

When Nick left to get the wine and the wine glasses, I walked into the ballroom and found Christine removing the plastic from the album for the musical *Chicago*.

She slid the record out of its sleeve and held it up by its edges. Then she looked at my red eyes and said, "Oh, sweetheart, again?"

"When am I not crying, I ask you? Never."

"It's okay, my darling," Christine said, with a smile. "It's your party and you can cry if you want to."

"I know that's a song."

"Very good," she said, grinning, as she held up the vinyl record and asked, "Have you heard many of these?"

"A few," I said, "but you know my generation. It's mostly MP3s."

"You really haven't listened to music until you've heard it on vinyl," Christine enthused. "The vinyl record offers up a pure, naturalistic sound like the song of a nightingale with the occasional wisp of wind between its notes."

"So poetic," I said, as Christine placed the album on the turntable. The needle moved over and dropped onto the vinyl, and suddenly "All That Jazz" was in the air.

Christine took my arm and gently twirled me around, then stopped and asked, "Is your leg strong enough?" When I nodded and said I thought so, she flipped off her shoes, and I flipped off my scandals, and we went back to dancing.

Nick walked in at just that moment with two bottles of white wine and three glasses.

"There he is," I said, "My knight in shining armor. If I start to fall, Nick will catch me."

Nick nodded and Christine twirled me around a few more times as her son sat drinking his wine and watching us. "Are you just going to sit there?" she asked.

"Oh, you don't want me out there," he said.

"How do you expect to get better if you don't practice?" Christine asked as Nick poured us a glass of wine each. Christine turned down the music as we sat opposite him, sipped our wine, and looked directly at him. "Am I under surveillance?"

"No, why? Do you feel like you're under surveillance?" his mother asked.

"Maybe a little."

"Could it be that you're intimidated by being around two beautiful women?" I asked.

"That wouldn't usually do it, but when one of them is my mother, I do feel a tinge of anxiety."

"Only a tinge? I must be slipping," Christine said.

"Not from what I can tell," I said.

"Well, thank you, my lovely daughter." She looked at Nick and said, "Do you know how lucky you are to be married to her?"

"I thank the gods every day."

"As you should."

I raised a glass to "the two queens of the castle, Queen Christine and Queen Alicia." Christine laughed and took a big gulp of her wine. Then she looked at her son with lowered eyes and asked, "Do you ever … would you ever … thank the gods for me?" The aching need in her eyes was unmistakable, but Nick didn't catch it.

"Are you fishing?" he said with a laugh, then turned to me. "She's fishing."

Christine swatted her son on the arm, and said, "Just answer the question."

"I thank the gods for you all the time. And like my wife, I never want you to leave."

Christine became misty eyed as she reached over and touched Nick's hand and said, "That's exactly what I want. Besides, we still have so many books and authors to discuss late into the night."

Mr. Wang, Annie, Joe, and my precious little princess, Bee, walked into the ballroom. Bee looked even more angelic than usual in a ballet dress with a long-sleeved leotard.

She started running toward me with Annie reminding her to be careful and not run into me. Bee stopped just before me and I grabbed her and pulled her closer. I hugged and kissed her and spun her around so everyone could get a good look at her dress.

Annie remarked, "I see the party has already begun."

"Well, not exactly. We've been waiting for the little princess and Mr. Wang to show up before the festivities really start," Christine said as she looked at Mr. Wang and asked, "Do you usually show up to a dance in your work clothes?"

"No, but Bee said I didn't have time to change because we were already late. Besides, who is going to be looking at me when so many beautiful ladies and one princess take to the floor?"

"And where is the rest of your lovely family?"

"They don't want to be too troublesome," Mr. Wang replied.

"Nonsense! You call them up and you tell them that I insist that they come."

"I think it might be better if you told them," Mr. Wang said as he took out his phone and called home. After saying a few words in Cantonese, he handed the phone to Christine, who took less than a minute to convince them that it wouldn't be a party without them. When she hung up, she turned to her son and said, "Would you please go pick up Mr. Wang's family? They'll be waiting outside."

Nick looked at me as though I was the one who she was talking to, and Christine asked, "Why are you looking at her? Do you think I'm going to kidnap her while you're gone?"

"Of course not. It's just…"

I looked at my husband and just knew: He was concerned that if he wasn't there and I was dancing and my leg gave out, no one would be quick enough to catch me.

I hugged him and whispered, "I won't do any dancing until you come back. I promise."

I kissed him and then he and Joe left to pick up Mr. Wang's family. I turned to Christine and said, "Your son is concerned about my leg going limp. So I'll sit out until he comes back."

She gently took me by my arm and said, "I'm sorry, sweetheart."

"It's okay," I said. "I'm still getting used to the fact that anyone could care as much about my welfare as your son does. The men I used to meet all treated me like garbage, to be disposed of after they were satisfied."

Christine hugged me and whispered into my ear, "As long as I have a say, no one will ever treat you that way again."

I whispered back, "I think the little princess is ready to rumble."

Christine dropped the needle onto the record and "All that Jazz" rang out again, and everybody brought out their dance moves. What started out as a lesson in expressive individual body movement turned into a ragtag collection of dances from the waltz, to hip-hop, to ballroom, to Irish dance and improvisational dance. Before long everyone joined in, including Nick and Mr. Wang's entire family, Bee, Joe, Annie and me. After about an hour and a half the only two left dancing were the princess and Wonder Woman, with the princess's joyous laugh reaching beyond the cathedral ceiling and into the oceanic atmosphere.

We then sat down to a traditional Chinese dinner that Mr. Wang's family had made. It was absolutely delicious and included rice balls, wonton soup, spring rolls, vegetables mixed with fresh seafood and bite-sized portions of meat and poultry and of course dumplings made especially for Bee.

We all helped clean up, except for Bee, who was dead asleep on her mother's lap.

# PART THREE

# CHAPTER FIFTY-THREE

I leaned in close to the bathroom mirror and applied the ointment to my skin. Except for occasional headaches and some ongoing numbness in my leg, I was starting to feel almost like my old self. But to say I was emotionally healed would be a lie. I still had nightmares, and every so often I could hear the sound of that lady assassin's high heels on the pavement as she exacted gruesome, methodical revenge on those sons-of-bitches.

Nothing, though, compared to the anxiety I felt over my husband. Dr. Petrenko's warning was like a red light continually flashing before me. Maybe it was because I had never been in love before. The only true romance I had experienced was in my imagination. Then, at the lowest point in my life, imagination aligned with reality, and the prince I'd always dreamed of literally picked me up and carried me to his castle.

Love is blissful, but like any narcotic, it comes with a heavy price. The idea of any harm coming to my husband was enough to stop me in my tracks and cause me to go pale and sweaty, no matter where I was or what I was doing. Between Dr. Petrenko's warning and the things Nick said to me to relieve my anxiety, my concerns were actually heightened. He had lived a life where consequences and memories didn't simply go away when you walked off the battlefield, but lingered in the mind, ready to strike.

***

After my tubal pregnancy and surgery, I stopped wearing Nick's dress shirts to bed, and wore pajamas. I had tempted him to have sex with me once too often, and needed to make life easier for both of us. It was only for another two weeks. He was more interested in my health and welfare than I was, and it was wrong of me to keep pushing to resume old habits before I was physically ready. He was just so delectable…

I walked out of the bathroom and lay down beside my husband on the bed. He propped himself up and said, "I'm sorry to keep harping on this, but I have to ask. Why were you really crying when you were out with my mother?"

"You have the best memory of anyone I've ever known. You know exactly what I told you earlier," I said. "Are you calling me a liar?"

"No, it's just that I so want for you and Mom to get along."

"Actually, I like her better than you. If we were both lesbians I would marry her."

"Now, that's a lie."

"Only the first half. The second part is true. Your mother is stunning. I knew there had to be a reason you were so gorgeous. One look at her answered that riddle."

"My father doesn't get any credit?"

"Sure he does. I'm thankful to him for supplying half of your DNA."

"He was actually a very nice-looking man."

"I'm sure he was," I said and started laughing so hard that I repeated myself, "I'm sure he was."

He smiled and looked directly into my eyes and said, "I think you're the most beautiful woman I have ever seen."

"Well, thank you so much, my dashing prince," I said as we looked at each other in a way that usually meant the talking was over and the love making would begin … but I had made a promise to myself and intended to keep it. Suddenly I asked a question I wish I could take back. "Do you ever wish you could go back to being a reporter?"

He thought for a moment and said, "No. I'm proud of the work my crew and I did, but I don't want to go back."

"Really? It's such important work. And I heard you telling Doctor Petrenko that you wished you could be more useful."

"You mean you *over*heard me?"

I blushed and said, "I invoke the concerned wife defense."

He laughed, and then he got serious.

"You're right that it's important work. Everyone should know about the horrific conditions people in war-torn counties have to live under. And the soldiers, too … most of them younger than you, bunkered down for months, if not years, protecting and holding on to territory that is under constant attack … Where your life isn't measured in years but seconds. Where the indiscriminate killing of children is not the outlier but the norm."

He lowered his eyes and shook his head. "I was happy that no members of my crew were killed. A few were wounded, but none seriously. I never allowed them to get too close to the actual fighting. I was the one who took the chances, not because I was so brave, but because my death would have had the least impact. Besides my mother and the two saints who took care of me, I had the least to lose."

"Why did you leave journalism? Was it … for Nastasiya?"

He looked at me, and I had the sense he was surprised that I would bring her up. Doing so seemed to open a door to a longer conversation that I was instantly unsure I was ready to have.

"No, she wasn't the reason. I'd decided months before meeting her. I met her father years earlier, while I was covering the war in Afghanistan and he was working as a volunteer doctor for the United Nations. We got along really well and stayed in touch. He insisted that I visit Ukraine, where he was from, and he especially wanted me to see Kiev, where his daughter Nastasiya worked as a nurse. During my last assignment, I decided to take a few weeks off and visit Kiev. The good doctor picked me up at the airport and our first stop was at the hospital where Nastasiya worked, and by mere coincidence she was scheduled to start a two-week vacation the next day."

He laughed and suddenly became very quiet as a mist formed around his eyes. "Please, please don't continue," I said.

He looked at me and said, "I really don't need to, because you already know the rest of that story. But, let me continue just a little longer because it might help to explain a lot."

He waited until I nodded. "It was during my last assignment that I started remembering something really odd from when I was seven or eight years old. My mother was drinking a lot at the time, but I guess she was also becoming conscious of how she had failed me as a mother, because she started coming into my bedroom late at night and seeking forgiveness. She would sit at the head of the bed, next to my pillow, and start crying. I would wake up from the tears hitting my face and she would apologize and beg me to forgive her for being such a terrible mother. Then she would vow to do better. I would always tell her it was okay, and she would say, 'Promise?' and I would reply, 'I promise.'"

"It's so hard to imagine your mother like that now."

"I know."

"Do you think she meant all those things and wanted to change?"

"Not enough to do anything about it, or at least not at the time," he said. "I would knock on her bedroom door the next morning, full of hope about what she'd said, but she'd be passed out on the bed, wearing the same clothes from the night before, oblivious. This went on for months, with her visiting three or four times a week. I started locking my door at night, and I'd hear her trying the handle. Sometimes she would knock and call my name, but I never let her in."

"Did you ever mention this to her?"

"No! I was eight years old. I told the nannies and they spoke to her, but nothing changed, except that she stopped trying to enter my room. It was during my last assignment that it hit me like a thunderbolt. My father had literally married a child. She was begging for help and I shut her out."

"But you were only a child, yourself."

"Yes, but I carried those memories for another five years before shoving them down into my unconscious. I hated her, Alicia. I wanted so much to get back at her, not only for her midnight confessions but for pretending I didn't exist the rest of the time. She barely spoke to me when she wasn't drunk and crying in my room at night…

"I knew better. The ladies who raised me were religious. When I was five, they taught me Christ's teachings and the guidelines he put forth in the Sermon on the Mount, about how to treat your fellow man. 'Judge not, that you be not judged / Blessed are the merciful, for they shall receive mercy / So whatever you wish that others would do to you, do also to them…'

"They used to give me pop quizzes to make sure I hadn't forgotten, and they still occasionally quiz me when I call them up. I've tried to live most of life by those rules, and yet when it came to my mother, I threw them out the window."

"Again — you were a child," I tried to say, but he held up his hand.

"Yes, but later, I should have known better. I can't say for sure that I became a war correspondent to spite her, but it certainly played a role. My replies to her letters were brutal. I would say things like, 'Why would I come home? You never even knew you had a son for most of my life…'

"Despite everything, she continued to write to me. Telling me how sorry she was, begging me to forgive her … telling me how much she had changed. It took me nine years to hear her and accept that she meant it. Then I became the one asking for forgiveness and granting her wish that I resign and come back home."

"Why did you have all your paychecks sent to her?"

"Out of pure malice, and because I knew she would never spend any of it but put it into our joint account. My mother might have been many things back then, but she was never cheap and certainly not a thief."

He stopped talking and gently ran his fingers through my hair as tears rolled down my cheeks and he asked, "And why are you crying?"

"Because it's what I do best these days," I said, as he wiped the tears from my face.

"It's kind of funny," he said, "because when I see how much fun she has with Bee, it tells me that if she hadn't been a child bride she most likely would have been a wonderful mother."

"She is a wonderful mother, now, and now is what counts most," I said, almost angrily.

"I know that, Alicia. That's why I am so happy she's staying and that the two of you seem to be getting along so great. This is the happiest time in my entire life. I have you, my mom, and all these wonderful people around us who have become more like family than friends."

I kissed him and said, "I love you so much."

"And I love you so much," he said as he wrapped his arms around me and accidently, or not, placed one of his hands on my breast.

"Unless you plan on breaking your vow of celibacy, I'd move your hand. That's not playing fair."

"Like you've been playing fair?"

"I haven't taken a vow of celibacy."

He took his hand away from my breast and I asked, "Can I tell you something?"

"Of course, whatever you like."

"I know how difficult it was for you growing up … and I'm not trying to compare, but there are parallels …"

Nick raised himself up on the pillow and said, "What kind of parallels?"

"From the time I was little, my parents made me feel like I was a major inconvenience. I was the reason they couldn't take vacations or go out on dates to fancy restaurants. Every dollar they had to spend on me was depriving them of something. They didn't treat my older siblings like this. Only me. I was apparently the accident that destroyed their lives, like I forced them to get drunk that night, fuck, and conceive the monster that would bleed them dry."

Nick reached across and pulled me into a warm hug. "That's terrible," he said. "I'm so furious, I want to go find them and give them a piece of my mind."

When I hugged him back he said, "And I know that this isn't the worst of it. I'm really glad you brought this up. I've asked you about your family a couple of times, and you never seemed to want to talk about them before now."

It was so strange that my eyes were dry for once, when talking about the most difficult thing for me. It was as if I had cried myself dry, and had nothing left. "You're right that I haven't wanted to talk about this," I told Nick. "I'm telling you parts of the story now, so that we can talk about it … so you know you're not alone."

Nick sat with that for a while. Finally, he reached across and took my hand.

"Parents," I said jauntily, trying to lighten the mood. "They screw us up, don't they?"

"They can, for sure."

"And there is always a worse story than your own. Annie told me that Bee's biological mother used to say to her all the time that the worst thing she did was to not abort her. Imagine a mother telling a child something like that. Especially Bee! Well, in the strangest way I'm sure that's how my parents felt, even though from the age of twelve I always had a part time job, and a full-time job during summer vacations."

"When I think of you as a young girl, trying so hard to please those ingrates and avoid being a burden on them, it makes me a little crazy," Nick said, his eyes wild.

"I know!" I said. "I feel the same way about that little boy, knocking on his mother's bedroom door, hoping to find out that her promises from the night before meant something."

We clung to each other like two children lost in the woods. I had never felt so close to him. We were like orphans, except that one of his lost parents had returned to him, very much alive, and changed. And I was going to be able to enjoy her as well. A little piece of my heart was telling me: *She can be the mother we never had.*

We lay on our backs next to each other, like kids at camp, looking up at the stars. Only our fingers were touching.

I said, "I never once dreamed of becoming a fashion model, and maybe if my parents had been more supportive I would have avoided that clown car. I could have finished my master's by now and be starting a PhD. But the idea of being totally independent from them was so strong, and the idea of making my own money was so strong, that I jumped at the first dumb job that came alone. And I ended up living this totally inauthentic life, and behaving in ways that I am truly ashamed of."

"Listen to me," Nick said, rising up on his elbow and looking at me. "You have *nothing* to be ashamed of. You were doing your best, with no support, no guidance, and a lot of blame placed on you, for absolutely no good reason."

Nick lay back down and faced me. He kissed me on the shoulder, and I continued with my story.

"The first year I was a model I sent money home to my parents and siblings every month. I think I got one thank you, and not a particularly sincere one. They all just seemed to expect that I would pay them back for having been a burden all those years. But, what hurt the most was that they never once came to visit me in the hospital. And it was a short forty-five-minute drive from their home."

"I have to say, ever since you told me that they never visited you in the hospital, I've been wondering what kind of parents could do that. I didn't want to push you to talk about this, but really, who, other than a monster, leaves their child to fend for herself after she is viciously raped? How did they explain themselves? Did they even try?"

"Oh, they were full of excuses. My mother has always complained about having to work because my birth made it impossible for her to retire, so all I heard about was her schedule at the auto-parts store. My sister had some sort of extended dog-sitting obligation for a colleague. I can't even remember. I gave up on them."

"Dog-sitting. My God."

"Right? Annie was the first lady who ever behaved like a mother toward me, and then today your mom and I bonded in a way that I imagine a loving mother and daughter might connect. She is so super that when you talked poorly about her before I really got angry, even though I knew you were speaking from experience." I started crying softly as I turned away from him and lay there, curled up in the fetus position. Nick held me and said, "That's exactly how I hoped my mom and you would get along, and for the record, whenever I think I couldn't be more in love with you than I already am, you always find a way to push my love for you to the outer limits."

# CHAPTER FIFTY-FOUR

Early the next morning, just as it was getting light outside, Nick and his mom went for a run. Afterwards, Nick helped me into his parka and placed the hood over my head, and we went for our morning walk.

"Good run?" I asked, and he reported that his mother had left him in the dust, but that he had every intention of catching up to her, and hoped I would one day be able to join them.

"I hope so too," I said, then thought of something I'd been meaning to ask. "You and Joe have been spending a lot of time in the study together. Are you having heavy literary discussions when you're in there?"

"Sometimes. It's unusual to find someone with similar literary taste as me, but Joe's one of those people."

"And how about me?" I asked in a miffed tone.

"I've thought about asking you to join us, but you're usually too busy with Bee. And any time spent with Bee has to be a million times more rewarding than talking about authors who lived a couple of hundred years ago."

"Well, you're right about that, but I think Annie, Wonder Woman, and I would be wonderful additions to your group of two. We've all read plenty of books by authors, dead and alive."

"I definitely agree with you, but at the moment that won't be possible because Joe and I are working on a book together."

"Really? How exciting. What's it about?"

"It's about war correspondents and their crews. Actually, Joe's writing the book and I'm supplying him with the material from my time in the field. I've reached out to many of the members of my crews and fellow correspondents who I got to know over the years and they're contributing quite a bit. We've all agreed, Joe, my crew members, fellow correspondents, and I, that all profits from the sale of the book will go to help Ukraine."

"This is so great! I remember Annie saying that Joe's biography on her brother did really well."

"It did. It was on the New York Times best-seller's list for over a year. Annie told Joe that if he behaved and stopped spoiling their daughter she would be very interested in publishing the book we're working on together."

"But she's the one who does all the spoiling," I said.

"She was pulling his leg, sweetheart."

"They're adorable."

"Yes, they are. And when he talks about her it's like he's talking about a saint. Of course it doesn't hurt that their daughter is an angel."

"And when you talk about me do you describe me as a saint?" I asked.

"No, I describe you as an oversexed supermodel who is trying to kill off her older husband and inherit his fortune."

I pushed him so hard that he went tumbling into the water and re-emerged completely drenched. He asked, "Was that really necessary?"

"Yes, you pig."

"So I've graduated from piglet to pig. What's next, wild boar?"

"No, neutered boar," I replied as we both laughed.

He stood beside me and I said, "You know, you look even sexier wet than you do dry."

"You know, if it wasn't for your minor ailments I would be picking you up right now and depositing you in the water. But I'll be patient, and when you least expect it I will exact my revenge."

"Wow! I can't wait. We've done it everywhere else, it's only right that we do it in the ocean."

I pushed him into the water again, and this time he seemed slightly upset when he stood up and looked at me. So, I stuck my tongue out at him and without thinking I started to run around in the sand, laughing. Then I suddenly stopped as I realized that this was the first time I had actually run since that tragic night. I turned and smiled, and Nick, who was a few feet behind me, stopped and asked, "Are you okay?"

"Yes," I said. "Do you know this is the first time I've run? I'm getting better!"

He gently touched my face with his wet hand, and even though he was soaking wet, I could see his eyes turn misty and fresh tears roll down his cheeks. He said, "You've been perfect since the moment I met you, and still you never fail to inspire and amaze me."

We passionately kissed to the celebratory applause of the squawking gulls.

# CHAPTER FIFTY-FIVE

By the time Nick and I made it back to the house, Wonder Woman was in high gear. She had already read and signed her divorce papers and returned them to her lawyers in D.C.

She felt a moment of guilt over the settlement in which she gave up nothing and got a pretty penny out of husband #2. She turned to Nick and said, "That's what the son-of-a-bitch gets for cheating on me, not once, but multiple times. Remind me to celebrate later."

She had also spoken to Annie, who was sending a couple of sound engineers over to the mansion to help set up a state-of-the-art sound system throughout the lower half of the house and outside on the patio. I asked, "I thought you loved the console in the ballroom."

"Yes, Alicia, for the ballroom it's wonderful, if you like all your music coming out of a piece of furniture. But for real music lovers, there's nothing like surround sound. Isn't that so, son?"

"If you say so," Nick replied. "It's not like I know anything about it."

"I thought you knew something about everything?" she asked.

"You overestimate me."

"Oh no I don't. Do I, Alicia?"

"You most certainly do not."

"Thank you, sweetheart. I've also been in touch with my real estate agent and put our house up for sale. The agent thinks it'll sell in a flash. Between the army of lobbyists and corrupt politicians she believes we'll get a lot more than the asking price. So if you had any doubts about me moving in here you can put those to rest."

"Oh my God, that's the best news ever!" I exclaimed as I hugged Christine. "Now that's a reason to celebrate."

"I told you; you married the best and most beautiful girl imaginable. A daughter-in-law overjoyed about her mother-in-law moving in. That belongs on Ripley's Believe It or Not! And how about you son, what do you think?"

"Did you forget, I'm the one who begged you to move in," Nick said as he kissed his mother.

She stood back from him. "Did you fall into the ocean?"

"I tripped and fell in."

"Funny, we run every morning before the sun comes up and you've never even stumbled. What happened? Did you say something stupid and your beautiful wife pushed you in?"

"That's exactly what happened," I said excitedly. "Twice in fact. Why don't you tell your mother what you said?"

"Some things are not worth repeating, sweetheart."

"Well, if it wasn't so embarrassing I would tell her," I said.

Christine laughed. "Maybe, I should start going on these little walks with the two of you. They seem rather eventful."

"We do have exciting news to share. For the first time since leaving the hospital in New York, my lovely wife was able to run without numbness in her leg."

"That's wonderful! I'm so happy for you."

"It wasn't for very long, but it did feel good," I said, and just then my handsome husband reached over and kissed me.

"And will there be another dance lesson today with our lovely Bee?" I asked Christine.

"But of course. The first email I received this morning was from that adorable angel. Mr. Wang and his family won't be able to come, but Annie and Joe will be here with her."

Nick left to take a shower and clean up as I walked over to Christine and hugged her and said, "Thank you so much for coming to live with us. It means more to me than you can know."

"I should be thanking you. If someone had told me just a couple of years ago that I would be living in this colossal house with my son and his darling wife, surrounded by all these lovely people, I would have said they were dreaming.

"I think you know how much this means to me. I spent a decade terrified to answer the phone, because I was sure it would be about Nick. He could so easily have died on the job, just like his predecessor. And he was so angry with me, so justifiably angry. To be here now, with both of you, and to know that my son is safe and happy, in love and loved, is a dream come true."

I started to cry and Christine reached over and wiped my tears away and said, "Please don't cry, sweetheart."

"But I have become so good at it," I replied and she laughed.

"I am so glad to be out of D.C. I know they talk about all the phonies out here, but I think per capita, our nation's capital easily tops this town when it comes to phonies. Sadly, our government is up for sale, and the lobbyists are in charge."

"Who knows, maybe you'll meet Mr. Right out here," I said.

"Do I look like I'm looking for Mr. Right, or for that matter, any man?"

"Forgive my assumption. After what happened to me, the thought of a man ever touching me again made me nauseated. And then I met your son. So I tend to think there's hope."

"My son is one of the exceptions. So is Joe. The way he and Annie and you and Nick look at each other is a testimony that true love, though rare, does exist. Neither of my husbands ever looked at me that way, and when I catch other men eyeing me I can guess what they're thinking. News flash: it's not love! They look at me the way a child looks at a bowl of chocolate. No, if I ever crave intimacy, it won't come with attachments, or a ring."

I looked at Christine, and didn't doubt a word she said.

# CHAPTER FIFTY-SIX

Annie, Joe, and Bee came over later in the afternoon, after the sound engineers had been and gone and taken down all the information they needed for the wireless system they planned to install. Bee was dressed in a white ballet dress and leotard. Christine and the little angel got right down to dancing, while Joe and Nick disappeared into the study. This left Annie and me at a table outside the ballroom, where we had a perfect view of the dancers.

Annie opened a bottle of white wine and filled our glasses. "I talked to your mother-in-law earlier and asked if she would be interested in doing some modeling and a little acting for our publicity department. She said she'd been acting for the last thirty years, pretending to be in love with her two ex-husbands, and was frankly tired of it all. And how are you feeling health wise?"

"Well, I'm just about there."

"Really?"

"Yes, and if the job is still open I would love to tutor Bee."

"That's what I was hoping you would say. The job is still open, but the location has changed. I've decided to drastically cut back my work schedule and do as much as possible from home. I don't want to miss these years with Bee. Would you have a problem coming over to our home for about four hours each day during the week?"

"Not at all," I said.

"Wonderful! That'll allow Joe to come over here and work on the book with Nick."

After dinner, Nick, Joe, and Bee sat inside and watched the Yankees game, and while the men enjoyed a few beers, Bee cheered the Yankees on nonstop until she crashed and fell asleep on her daddy's lap.

Christine, Annie, and I took our party outside to the patio where we drank Cristal Champagne out of engraved flutes. Christine was celebrating her divorce, her move, and her new home.

The blue, cloudless evening sky turned quickly into a star-filled night. Christine suddenly stopped speaking and turned to face the sky, then looked at Annie and me and said, "An F-35 fighter jet just flew by."

"Are you sure?" I asked. "I didn't hear a thing."

"That's because it's a stealth aircraft with the engine built inside the belly of the plane."

"And I didn't see anything," Annie remarked.

"Even better. You've been in the movie business your whole life and are more likely to see things ordinary people don't see."

"So you did learn something from being married to two military men," I jokingly said.

Christine laughed as the three of us touched glasses and drank up. Christine asked Annie, "Did your parents ever talk about the German Blitzkrieg of London during the war?"

"No, whatever I learned was from my brother Simon, who was about five years old at the time," Annie replied.

"You've never read your husband's biography of your brother?" Christine asked.

"No, except for the first few lines," Annie replied. "I just ... couldn't." I reached over and took Annie's hand.

"I understand. I totally understand," Christine solemnly replied.

I picked up the bottle of champagne and filled everyone's glasses. I then turned to Annie and reported that I'd run for the first time that morning without my leg giving out or going numb. "I was so excited," I said, and Christine and Annie raised their glasses.

"Now, that's something to toast to," Annie said. "To Alicia's leg, getting better by the day!" We touched flutes and drank up.

I then turned to Christine and asked, "And how is your star pupil doing?"

"She is doing wonderfully. I don't know what I enjoy more, her rapid progress or her joyous, contagious laugh. She is simply a joy, better than any antidepressant."

"She's all confused," Annie laughingly said. "She doesn't know if she wants to play for the New York Knicks, or become an Olympic swimmer, a doctor and researcher, or a professional dancer."

"I don't know why she shouldn't be able to do all of them. She certainly has enough energy," Christine replied as she finished her champagne, then refilled all of our glasses and placed the empty bottle in the ice bucket. She then called Nick on her phone and asked, "How much do you love your mother? Great, I love you just as much. I'm out on the patio with Annie and Alicia. Can you please bring us two more bottles of Cristal? Thank you."

"I could have gone to get them," I said.

"Why? My son, your husband, is the definition of a gentleman. We don't want him getting sloppy."

Nick opened both bottles, filled our flutes to the top, and placed the bottles in the ice bucket. Then he deposited the empties in the trash and went back inside to watch the game.

I looked at Christine and then at Annie and remarked, "I introduce her as my younger sister, and not one person expressed the slightest disbelief," I said. "What's your secret, Christine?"

"It must be the pepperoni rolls I ate for lunch and dinner nearly every day of my life in West Virginia and the moonshine they had us drinking instead of sodas and lemonades."

I drank to that and said, "Starting tomorrow, I guess it's all pepperoni rolls and moonshine for me. Surely I can do without these overpriced champagnes and fancy wines."

"How old were you when you started modeling?" Christine asked.

"Eighteen."

"So since the age of eighteen, all you've known is expensive champagnes and wines, lobster dinners and caviar."

"It goes with the job," I said.

"And look what it got you. A mansion in Malibu and a super-hot, extremely intelligent, caring husband."

"Good point, sis. I think I'll stick with the good stuff."

Christine turned to Annie and asked, "Are you sure you want her tutoring your precious daughter? I'll be glad to take over for her."

"But you're already her dance instructor."

Christine laughed as she lay back in her chair and looked up at the sky. "It's such a lovely night," she said. Then after a few reflective moments, her eyes scanned the sky and she began to recite a poem.

*The stars are forth, the moon above the tops*
*of the snow-shining mountains. — Beautiful!*
*I linger yet with Nature, for the night*
*Hath been to me a more familiar face*
*Than that of man, and in her starry shade*
*Of dim and solitary loveliness,*
*I learn'd the language of another world.*

"Lord Byron," I said.

Christine smiled as she gently ran her fingers through my hair and said to Annie, "On second thought, she's the perfect tutor for your daughter."

Annie raised her champagne flute and said, "A toast, to the perfect tutor!"

# CHAPTER FIFTY-SEVEN

For the first time since I met my husband, I didn't feel like I was living a dream from which I might wake up at any time. I was living my life and it felt so good.

Christine was undeniably larger than life. Besides being stunningly beautiful and intelligent, she seemed to have the energy of a thirty-year-old. After she had her sound system installed, she decided to convert two upstairs bedrooms into her own library and study. Like ours, it was fitted with floor-to-ceiling bookshelves, but painted in red, with gilded detailing. Her study also included a fireplace with a blue-and-white marble surround and a large bay window that looked out onto the ocean.

Sitting in front of the window was a large mahogany desk, similar to Nick's. I couldn't help wondering if she would ever invite a lover up there and have passionate sex on top of the desk, the way Nick and I did in our study. I could imagine them whispering sweet nothings into each other's ears as they looked out onto the ocean.

She moved only a couple of pieces of furniture from her house in D.C., a few pictures, and ten thousand pounds of books. The rest of her furniture she had her real-estate agent sell for her. The boxes of books were all labeled and arranged in alphabetical order, according to the author's last name. It took us six hours and three bottles of wine to get all the books onto the shelves. Christine ran a damp rag over each book to make sure it was free of dust.

The only time I saw my husband during this process was when I brought a bottle of wine into the study for either Joe or him to open. When I asked,

"Aren't you going to ask how it's going?" he replied, "No, I'm fairly certain I know how it's going."

And I couldn't help thinking, *But of course you know. You're one and the same. Thank God you're mother and child, or I would have a serious rivalry on my hands.*

When I walked back into Christine's study, she was looking at a framed picture of Nick and me from our wedding day. She held it out and asked, "Have you ever seen a better-looking couple?"

"I've never seen a better-looking man."

She looked at me seriously and asked in an uncompromising tone, "I asked, have you ever seen a better-looking couple? There is only one correct answer, Alicia, so please don't get it wrong."

"No, I have never seen a better-looking couple," I nervously replied.

"That's my girl. I love your modesty, but occasionally you need to throw a bone to your mother-in-law. Thank you."

She stepped onto a small stepladder and hammered a hook and a finishing nail into the wall above the fireplace mantle. I handed her the picture and she hung it dead center.

"Wow! Perfect on the first try. Have you done that before?" I asked.

"Sure. It's easy. You just measure the area and put a tiny pencil mark in the center."

"You sound like Nick."

"Like mother, like son," she said with a big smile. "Of course, it also helps that he's the son of a military man. My first husband might not have been much of a father, but he still passed along a few useful traits."

"I'm sure that's true, but the more I get to know you, the more alike you and Nick seem," I said. "So I think some of it must just be good genes. Like, *really* good genes."

Christine flashed me a smile as she stepped off the ladder and went to refill our glasses. She turned to me and said, "I'm so happy here, Alicia, and you're a big reason for that. You're even more perfect than my son described."

I started to cry, and before I could say anything she said, "Go ahead and cry. As you always say, you're good at it, and while you may be joking, there is some truth to that."

"What do you mean?" I asked, through tears.

"Only that not everyone has a heart as big as yours, or wears it on their sleeve as well as you do." She put down her glass and hugged me and said, "I love you so much, so very much."

\*\*\*

After working all day and sharing three bottles of wine, we left her beautiful study and went downstairs, where we were greeted by Bee and her lovely mother. Bee looked excited but a little tired, and Annie, who was lagging behind her daughter, looked exhausted.

Christine took Bee by the hand and whisked her off to the ballroom, as Annie and I sat down and I opened another bottle of white wine and poured each of us a glass. I looked at her and gently asked her if she was feeling alright, and she gave me a wan smile and explained that she'd been up all night with Bee, who was having nightmares.

"It was the worst I've ever seen her. At times she screamed so loudly that Joe came running into the room, frightened that something serious had happened.

"I would have stayed home this morning but I had a number of important meetings. If I had told Bee to stay home with her daddy, she would have thought I was angry with her, and that could trigger her panic attacks." Annie took a large sip of her wine and added, "It doesn't seem to matter how much love we bestow on her. Her fears of abandonment always win out."

Annie started to cry. "My poor little baby…"

I reached out and took her hand and said, "In a couple of weeks I'll be her full-time tutor, and I can help watch for patterns or triggers." I paused before continuing. "I have some personal experience in this area."

Annie looked at me curiously, and I added, "Nothing like what Bee experienced, but I know what to look for. I can watch for signs, head off issues as they arise, and reinforce what you and Joe are doing to make her feel calm and supported."

Annie smiled at me gratefully, and as I looked into the ballroom at her dancing and laughing, it was easy to forget what this sweetheart had been through in the nine years before she met Joe and found her forever family.

# CHAPTER FIFTY-EIGHT

Two weeks later, I had a night of strange dreams. In one of them, I was sitting alone at the back of a giant auditorium, listening to Sigmund Freud give a lecture. He was pacing in his tweed suit, smoking a cigar, as he explained to the mostly empty hall that all human instinct falls into two classes: the life drive (Eros) or the death drive (Thanatos). Partway through his talk, the father of psychoanalysis spotted me at the back of the room and stopped speaking. He put down his papers and walked all the way to my seat, as the sound of his leather-soled shoes echoed through the hall. When he reached me, he rested his hand on my forearm and looked into my eyes and said, "An albatross is a large seabird, and birds can fly."

My eyes popped open, and I immediately started to laugh. I half expected Nick to hear me and ask me what was so funny first thing in the morning, but he was already up and gone.

I rolled out of bed and put on my running outfit. I'd been running a little further every day since discovering that I could do it again, and I was excited to get out on the road that day. I put on Nick's parka, which I wore for a bit every morning while stretching, and before I started my run. Then I walked out to the patio.

Christine was there, seated before an untouched cup of coffee, staring off into the distance. I asked, "Christine, are you okay?"

She looked up at me with flushed eyes and said, "My God, I didn't even hear you sweetheart."

"What's wrong?" I asked as I moved closer to her and she handed me a piece of paper. It was a certified letter, from the Office of the President of

Ukraine, and it read, *Dear Nicholas: I am sorry to report that Dr. Petrenko was killed a week ago while working at the hospital. A Russian bomb struck the building overnight, while he was assisting in the oncology wing. He was one of four doctors and twelve patients killed that night. It was his wish that you not be notified of his death until seven days had passed, and that under no circumstances were you or your mother to visit our country until we have defeated the invaders.*

*All of Ukraine joins you and your mother in grieving the loss of this great man, and the loss, not so long ago, of his daughter, Nastasiya. They are buried in the same plot, and on their tombstone it reads, In Death they were not parted.*

*The support and contributions we have received from your mother and you are greatly appreciated. I hope when we have finally repelled the invaders that you, your wife, and your mother will visit our beautiful country as our guests.*

I put the letter down and asked, "Where is Nick?"

She pointed to the ocean and to Nick sitting on the sand about twenty feet from the water. I turned and started walking toward him as Christine called, "Alicia…"

I stopped and turned toward her, and for the longest time she said nothing. I looked at her and was ready to ask if I could do anything for her when she shook her head and said, "Go to your husband," and then, "Go, sweetheart."

I walked toward Nick as an eerie silence settled over the beach. The seagulls were quiet and the waves crashed noiselessly against the shore. The sun beat down upon me, and yet I was shivering. When I reached Nick, I sat down beside him and wrapped my arms around his body.

He looked down at me and ran his fingers through my hair. I asked, "What can I do?"

He shook his head helplessly, and said, "There's nothing to do, angel, but keep his memory alive." He touched my left cheek, where Dr. Petrenko had healed me.

Nick looked out at the water and when he spoke again, he seemed to almost be speaking to himself. "I've seen bloated bodies floating down rivers, innocent families burned alive, women raped and disfigured, cowering in mud huts—

"I protected my crews, so I wouldn't have to grieve their loss." He looked back down at my flushed and teary eyes and tenderly wiped away the tears that were rolling down my cheeks.

"But I didn't know them. Not really. With the doctor and Nastasiya—" he broke down, bowing his head and sobbing into the space between his knees.

I held onto my husband and tried to console him, as we sat there in the sand, shaking. "With the doctor and Nastasiya, you made a connection—"

"I did," he said, his voice cracking.

"I know," I said. "It's the price of loving. It's a terrible price."

Nick looked back out over the ocean as I wrapped my arms even tighter around his waist. I felt so cold, under a blazing sun. He wiped his tears away and asked, "What did the doctor tell you when he called you back into his office to give you the ointment he supposedly forgot?"

I closed my eyes and pretended not to hear the question. A few moments passed as I remembered the look on the doctor's face as he warned me to keep a close eye on my husband.

"Your silence speaks volumes, sweetheart, but I would still like to know."

"He told me I needed to keep a close eye on you because you had seen things that no one should ever have to witness. And he said I was married to the best man he had ever known."

I could suddenly hear the seagulls squawking and the waves crashing against the beach and the beating of my husband's heart. And then it was like the changing of a channel on a television set, and I was once again in the back of the limousine, kicking and swinging my arms at those two sons-of-bitches, fighting for my life, as metal met flesh and tore a hole in the world, and the blood of a thousand innocents comingled in the air.

"Alicia! Alicia!" Nick was screaming and I opened my eyes and I found myself on my knees with my hands beating fiercely against Nick's chest.

"Oh my God! Oh my God!" I repeated as I tried to move away and Nick pulled me back and I continued, "I'm so sorry, so sorry."

"I understand, believe me, I understand," Nick said and as I looked into his eyes I had no doubt that he did. I wrapped my arms once again around my husband and cried … for Dr. Petrenko, Nastasiya, Nick's father, my husband, Christine, Bee, and Annie. Finally, I truly understood what my husband had been telling me — that we were each other's saviors, and that this required constant vigilance.

Suddenly all went quiet again and all I could hear were the sobs and snuffles of a husband and wife.

Nick and I walked back up to the house and sat down at the table on the patio beside Christine. Nick picked up the letter, folded it, and put it into his pocket. He took his mother's hand and asked, "How are you holding up?"

She shook her head and said, "He was such a good man, and Nastasiya…" She started to cry and wheeze as Nick gently held her head against his chest. When she finally pulled away, she picked up a napkin and wiped her face, and said, "Don't worry about me, I'll be fine."

Her cell phone dinged and she looked down at the message and said, "It's the little angel. She wants to know if we're dancing tonight. I hate to break her heart…"

I reached over and touched Christine's hand and said, "Please, Christine, don't cancel. She's been having terrible nightmares."

"Nightmares?"

"…about the abuse she suffered before Joe took her in." Christine listened with her mouth ajar to the story of Bee's first nine years, of her escape from the foster home, and her time on the streets before her eventual adoption by Joe.

"She looks so forward to the dancing," I said.

"I had no idea. She's always so happy," Christine said, and then typed her message out loud: *Of course, we will be dancing tonight. Love you.*

"Thank you so much."

Nick left and came back with a chilled bottle of Ukrainian Horilka, an infusion of herbs, berries, or roots in alcohol. Nick placed a rocks glass in front of each of us and poured about an ounce into each glass.

"You need to be careful, Alicia. It's very strong," Christine cautioned me.

"You make the toast, Mom."

We raised our glasses as Christine said, "Za nas, za vas, i za Ukraine! To us, to you, and to Ukraine."

We laid the glasses down as the seagulls squawked and "Za nas, za vas, i za Ukraine!" reverberated all around us before a receding tide carried the message out past the horizon and into the heavenly palaces of benevolent deities.

# CHAPTER FIFTY-NINE

Life proceeded normally under difficult circumstances. I got out of the shower, put on my panties and a bra, and looked into the mirror at the face I have been looking at most of my life, except for the time I wore the silver bandage on the left side. At that moment, I would have gladly worn the bandage for the rest of my life if it would bring back Dr. Petrenko.

I walked out of the bathroom and there was my husband, passed out on the bed. It was the first time I'd seen him asleep during the day.

I padded softly over to my closet and picked out a simple white sundress and put it on. I looked into the full-length mirror as I straightened the shoulder straps and smoothed down the A-line skirt.

I turned back toward the bed and Nick was sitting up, looking directly at me. "Wow!" he said, "Don't you look like the picture of innocence."

"Really, after what's gone on in that bed, I didn't think you could ever look at me and think of innocence."

"I don't see what one has to do with the other. We're married."

"That we are … forever and forever," I said as I walked over and kissed him. "Time to go greet the little princess."

I started walking toward the door and then turned back around and asked, "You like it best when I dress in white?"

"No, I like you best in any color."

"But white is your favorite?"

"No, white is not my favorite."

"Oh I get it; you like me best in the nude."

He got up off the bed and walked over to me and took both my hands and looked directly into my eyes. "Nude would be my least favorite."

"Oh really. I need to remember that when you start ripping off my clothes."

"*My darling, my darling, my wife and my bride,*" he recited, "you are undeniably beautiful, but that's only a fraction of why I find you so irresistible. It's all the other traits … your empathy, intelligence, knowledge, courage, and your easy acceptance of people and cultures that are vastly different from ours and, of course, your little bouts of jealousy."

"Oh, you had me, right up to the last line. Sometimes you need to know when to quit."

I turned back toward the door as he reached out and took my arm and turned me back around. He kissed me gently on the lips and said, "I love you so much, Alicia. So much."

I wrapped my arms around him and buried my head in his chest and we stayed that way until the chatter of voices in the hallway rang out like an alarm clock in the middle of the night.

\*\*\*

I greeted the army of guests. Mr. Wang's entire family had arrived, bringing food, and of course my soon-to-be-godchild and Joe and Annie were there. Joe and Nick disappeared into the study, and the bags of food went into the kitchen. Then Christine started preparations for the dance portion of the event, which she began to call a *recital.* Mr. Wang was invited to join Joe and Nick, but he decided to stay with his family in the ballroom, where they talked and laughed amongst themselves. Annie and I stood just outside the pocket doors, next to a small table and a new mini-fridge that Nick had recently installed, for wine and beer service in the ballroom and living room.

At the far end of the ballroom, Christine was working with Bee on a new dance move that looked like a plié. Mr. Wang had pulled one of his aunts onto the dance floor and was executing some sort of waltz.

Turning to Annie, I asked, "Do they even bother to ask us to join in anymore?"

"Nope, I guess they're too advanced for us amateurs," she replied, a hint of amusement in her eyes.

"You seem more relaxed. Did the princess have a good night?"

"Perfect. But there's been a new development. You have to promise not to mention it to anyone."

"I promise!"

"Joe seems to think there's a link between Bee's good nights and the Yankees winning, and her bad nights and the Yankees losing."

"Wait, what? But how would she know? She always falls asleep during the fifth inning!"

"Joe lets her sleep on his lap until the game ends. He thinks it's good luck."

"Why not just put her to bed when she falls out?"

"Because he goes into her room and kisses her goodnight and she always wakes up and asks 'How did the Yankees do?'"

"Why not just tell her they won, for the sake of a good sleep?"

"He can't do that. She'll just figure it out in the morning when she looks at the scores, and the trust will be broken."

I stared at Annie helplessly, trying to wrap my head around this mystical convergence and offer another solution. "So ... the Yankees losing is what triggers her nightmares?" I asked, as Annie looked at me, trying desperately to conceal a smile.

"What's wrong?"

"Nothing," she said. "Not a thing."

"Annie."

"It's just that you're so adorable. Please, oh please, never change, and please never stop loving my daughter as much as you do."

She was giggling maniacally when the penny dropped that I had been pranked. I rolled my eyes at her and said, "Very funny, Annie. What is it, April first?"

"Not that I know of."

"I learn new things about you every day. Today I'm learning that you can be an absolute imp." Annie laughed uproariously, and I added, "And as far as me ever stopping loving your daughter, that's something you'll never have to worry about." Then I looked at her and asked, "So, Yankees superstitions aside, you don't really believe they're the cause?"

"No angel, I don't, but your reaction solidifies why we picked you as her godparents. If it were true, the Yankees would be banned from our lives in a heartbeat."

"That would be tough on Joe."

"True, but if he thought for a moment that the Yankees were triggering our little girl's nightmares, the team would never be mentioned in our house again," she said. Then she added, "All joking aside, it's clear that Bee needs to see a professional therapist, but for now that's completely out of the question."

"You think she's too young?"

"I think it would terrify her. We've seen how fragile she can be. The first time she met me and heard that Joe and I were planning to get married, Bee became so upset at the thought of losing Joe to me that she ended up in the emergency room with a severe panic attack.

"By the time he got her to the hospital she was turning blue. In her traumatized state she thought Joe was going to kick her out, or put her into another orphanage, so he could be with me."

"Poor angel."

"I know. I think about that day often and wish I'd known how to avoid triggering her."

"You couldn't have known. You had to learn from experience."

Annie nodded appreciatively. "When she's a little older we'll find her a great therapist. But at this stage, even mentioning it could be catastrophic. She would see it as a sign that we think there's something wrong with her and are thinking of putting her in a home."

I nodded in silence as I walked over to the refrigerator and took out a bottle of white wine. Then I picked up a bottle opener that sat on top of the unit. Annie watched me as I fumbled with the foil and nearly sliced my finger with the corkscrew.

"Please give me that bottle of wine before you seriously hurt yourself," she said. "I guess they didn't teach this skill at modeling school."

"Nope," I said, as Annie removed the cork in seconds and filled our glasses.

I raised my glass and said, "To our beautiful Bee."

"To our beautiful Bee," Annie repeated as we both drank.

"You really had me with that Yankees prank," I said, poking Annie gently on the arm.

"Sorry," she said with a laugh. "I suppose that was cruel."

"It's fine. I appreciate your attempt to wring humor from a brutal situation."

"What else can we do? We have to just keep showing Bee how much we love her, and putting her in situations like this, where she gets to laugh and play and dance, and hope that, in time, her mind and body settle down."

"Exactly. It'll just take time for her system to realize that she's safe. Time, love, and — when she's older — therapy."

"Time, love, and therapy," Annie repeated, raising her glass. I clinked her glass and we drank, and Annie suddenly looked pensive.

"I remember growing up in the early fifties, and any time there was a loud noise my mother would instinctually pull me down to the floor and cover me with her body. It's exactly how she would try to protect Simon when London was being bombed by the Germans night after night during the war. Nearly ten years later, all it took was a loud noise to trigger her instinct to protect her child."

Annie stared into her glass as though she could see her mother jumping to her defense. "Some things you just can't bury. That's the way it was for my mother, Simon, and my sweet baby. You can be on top of the world, and then one night when you fall asleep it re-emerges as though you're living it for the first time … or it might be an innocuous voice or a stranger walking down the street that triggers the life-changing event that refuses to die."

Annie refilled our glasses and looked directly at me and said, "And what about you, Alicia? How are you able to handle it, when the past comes rushing in?"

# CHAPTER SIXTY

I was relieved when Bee chose that moment to run across the ballroom, waving at Mr. Wang and his family as she streaked past, and came out to see her mother and me. Christine had called for a five-minute break, and the little girl had gulped down a glass of water before racing over to see us.

"Whoah," Annie said, as the little ball of energy came at us. "Slow down, or you'll have nothing left for the second half of your lesson."

"Are you going to come in and watch?" Bee asked, and Annie held onto her daughter and said, "Of course, we are. We're just talking for a few minutes first."

Bee eyed us both suspiciously and said, "What are you talking about?"

"Well," Annie said, "we've covered the Yankees, and when you came over, Alicia and I were just talking about history."

Bee looked like she was about to say something when the music started up again and Christine called her back into the ballroom. She hugged her mother and gave me a quick embrace before running back to Christine for the next part of her lesson.

Annie looked at me expectantly and said, "You were just about to tell me how you handle intrusions of the past into the present."

I lowered my eyes and shook my head. "I'm not sure how to answer that. I do know that if not for Nick, I might not be alive at this moment.

"I was saved by a prince. He looked past my bandaged face and broken body and saw the person I didn't think existed anymore. He resurrected that girl who used to read poetry and novels every chance she got, and who would write love letters to herself and sign them Lord Byron, and…"

I stopped as I took a large drink from my glass. "If it wasn't for Nick I would have killed myself. At that point in my life, dying seemed like the easiest option."

Now it was Annie's turn to get misty eyed. "Well, I'm as happy as hell you didn't, as is my baby girl, my husband, and everyone who has been blessed to come into your orbit."

"Thank you," I said, as my own eyes welled up and tears started streaming down my cheeks.

"My goodness, you really are an expert crier," Annie said, and I laughed.

We were smiling at each other through tears when Annie added, "And do you know who's the happiest of all that you're still around? Your adorable husband. That man has seen the worst of humanity. He never fails to tell Joe that if it wasn't for you, he never would have had the courage to continue. So if he's your prince, you are most certainly his princess."

"I sometimes feel like one of his projects. He has this powerful need to always be helping people, whether it's me or his friend who was living in Hollywood, who feared for his children when they went to school, or someone else…" I turned my attention to the ballroom and watched the esteemed dancers. Christine was twirling Bee around under her slender arm.

I looked at Annie and said, "She's amazing, isn't she?" You couldn't have picked a better nickname than Wonder Woman."

"It does seem to fit," Annie said.

"At times it's like she and Nick are of one mind. They're both so … systematic. They pick a project, study it, and then get right to it. When I asked her about the similarities between them she credited her first husband. She said being the son of a military man allowed Nick to pick up certain traits, even if they were passed along unconsciously.'"

"So Wonder Woman and Daddy played some positive role in the raising of their son after all?"

"Not that I'm aware … from what I've heard, they were about as absent as two parents could be. Wonder Woman attending social events with other military wives seven days a week, drunk by noon, while her husband was off flying fighter planes and cheating on his wife."

"Cheating on Wonder Woman!" Annie exclaimed. "Was he blind?"

I laughed and said, "Maybe Wonder Woman isn't so great in bed."

"Blasphemy! The only logical explanation is that Wonder Woman is too much for any one man to handle."

"That must be it. I should be whipped for suggesting otherwise."

"How about we skip the whipping and you just go get us another bottle of wine."

I walked to the refrigerator and grabbed another bottle, which I handed to Annie, who opened it like a professional. She filled our glasses as she said, "Well, Christine must have done something right. Nick turned out exceptionally well."

"That's the work of his two amazing nannies, Ginevra and Francesca. Italian sisters. They raised him, and he adores them still. They're responsible for his moral character. They taught him the difference between right and wrong. They had him read and re-read the Sermon on the Mount and told him that if he truly wanted to live a good life he should practice Christ's ideals. They made sure he got to his little league games on time and they were his biggest cheerleaders. They helped him with his homework, taught him Italian, and made sure he got the gifts he wanted at Christmas. He's invited them to come and live with us, but after so much time away they're finally back in the little village where they were born and raised, surrounded by family and friends."

"A toast to the Italian sisters," Annie said as we lifted our glasses.

"To the Italian sisters."

# CHAPTER SIXTY-ONE

After everyone had gone home for the evening, Nick, Christine, and I met on the patio for a nightcap and a bit of star gazing. It was a beautiful, clear night, and Nick was telling funny stories about Dr. Petrenko and how he found ways to communicate with mothers and children in war-torn countries on the continent, despite language barriers.

"There were plenty of times when he was without a translator, and so he started to use hand gestures and little bits of sign language to get his message across," Nick said. "During a work trip to Central Africa, he was treating a young lady of about fourteen or fifteen for a fungal infection, and he made a sign that the patient took for a marriage proposal."

Christine and I started laughing as we could see what was coming next.

"Suddenly he had all the women in the village congratulating him, and the young lady was smiling admiringly at the good doctor before she disappeared and re-emerged in a beautiful African wedding garment. The parents were about to give him a goat when he realized…"

Nick was in mid-sentence when Christine suddenly stopped laughing and looked up at the sky, and he stopped talking. Nick and I looked up just in time to see a luminescent banner streak across the sky, with a message that read, *We see you, Christine.*

"What, do you have stealth bombers keeping an eye on you?" Nick asked as the banner disappeared as quickly as it appeared.

It was as though Christine hadn't heard a word her son said. It was as if she had left us. Nick touched her shoulder and asked, "Mom? Are you okay?"

She stood up and said, "I'm fine, sweetheart. I'll be back in a few minutes." She walked into the mansion, and Nick sat there, looking pensive. He finally said, "I need to go check on her," but when he started to get up, I put out my hand to stop him, and said, "Let me go."

He sat back down with a confused look on his face and said, "Okay, you go check on her. Thank you."

***

I walked into the mansion and heard music coming from the ballroom, and noticed that the pocket doors were closed. I slid one side open and slipped into the room. The lights were off, but I could see Christine on a settee near the console. She was listening to a song I'd never heard. The music was mesmerizing and the lyrics, which were beautiful and haunting, referred to spirits dancing in a dream from long ago.

The stars shone through the stained-glass windows, creating a rainbow of colors so magical and breathtaking that it felt like I had entered the sanctuary of deities.

I walked toward Christine, who sat with her back to me. Suddenly all I could hear were her anguished sobs. I stopped a few feet away from her and said, "Christine, can I help?"

She reached her hand out to me without turning around. I took it and sat down beside her. The lady before me was no wonder woman. She was deeply distraught and fragile. Tears streaked her face, and her eyes were smudged black. "What can I do to help?" I asked again.

"Just having you here is a great help."

I got up to grab a few tissues from a nearby box, then came right back and handed them to her. She placed her head on my lap like a little child as she continued to cry. I gently passed my hand through her hair as she had so often done to me. She chokingly remarked, "To forget a lover is one thing, but to forget someone you dearly loved, who you planned to spend an entire life with … whose only fault was getting killed in action … is an unpardonable crime."

It was all she said the entire time we were together. Her tears had become silent. Eventually we both stood up and collected ourselves. She dabbed a tissue under each eye and asked, "Do I look too terrible to say goodnight to my son?"

"You look as beautiful as ever," I replied as she laughed. She then hugged me so tightly that for a few seconds I thought I was suffocating. She remarked, "My son and I are very lucky to have you in our lives."

Naturally, I started to cry, and when we finally walked out of the ballroom my husband was standing just outside the doors, ready to come in. His face was blotchy and it didn't take a genius to know that he had been crying, and it was not like my husband to cry. He asked, "Are you okay?"

"Strange, I was just about to ask you that same question," Christine said.

"I'm fine. What happened out there?"

"Oh, nothing too consequential," Christine said. After a pause, she forced a smile on her face and spoke.

"A couple of nights ago I spotted a stealth bomber in the sky, and the next day I wrote jokingly to the high command that they have to do a better job of keeping their bombers under the radar. When I saw that banner in the sky tonight I just got overly emotional. Despite my relationship with your father and my second husband, I have gotten to know so many wonderful individuals in the force, and seeing that they still remember me and were willing to go to a lot of trouble to send that sweet message … well, it meant a lot."

Christine kissed both of us goodnight and then I took my husband by the hand and started steering him toward our bedroom. Just as we were about to disappear around a corner, Christine came back and said, "Don't forget, Alicia, we have a date with Bee and Annie tomorrow."

"Nine o'clock tomorrow, out front," I said, and Christine gave a little salute before turning to walk toward her bedroom suite.

***

The second we entered our bedroom, my husband asked, "Is my mother sick?"

"I wish I was as healthy as your mother."

"You didn't answer the question, Alicia."

"No, your mother's not sick. She's fine."

"Why was she so upset?"

"Nick, sweetheart, your mother is a grown woman. You don't need to know everything about her."

Nick looked puzzled as he tried to process that statement. "Of course not, but did she tell you something that you're not telling me?"

I shook my head and started to walk toward the bathroom as he asked, "Was she telling me the truth about the stealth bombers?"

"Why don't you go ask her?"

"I don't want her to think I don't trust her."

"That's funny, because you don't seem to have any problems questioning my truthfulness."

"That's not true, Alicia. I never would have married you if I didn't trust you. At times, I'll admit, I do get jealous when it comes to you, but that's because I love you so much."

It was hard enough to keep my hands off him in front of other people, but when he talked to me this way behind closed doors, all I could think about was ripping off his clothes, throwing him on the bed, and doing as I pleased. Thankfully, I was able to control myself, and asked, "Do you have a problem with the stealth bombers keeping an eye on your mother?"

He looked at me pensively and said, "It's not like I can do anything about it."

"You didn't answer the question, sweetheart."

"I don't like the idea of a technology with that type of surveillance power circling our property. But then again, it's her friends doing the surveilling."

"Or maybe it's her way of telling you that wherever you might go, she'll eventually find you," I half-jokingly replied.

"For most of my life it was like I didn't have a mother, and I put her through hell for that. I don't plan on doing anything to damage the close relationship we enjoy now."

I looked at him, and it was like I had suddenly lost all of my desire along with my ability to speak. I turned and walked into the bathroom and quietly closed the door.

# CHAPTER SIXTY-TWO

The next morning, Nick and I waited outside with Christine as Annie's limo pulled up and parked. The tension was palpable, and I could feel Nick holding himself back from questioning his mother about the night before. When the limo arrived, Joe got out and greeted Nick, and I slid in beside Bee, while Christine sat beside me. We waved goodbye to the men and Bee turned to me and asked, "Did you bring your inhaler?"

"Yes, sweetheart." I took it out of my purse and showed it to her.

"Good. I always carry mine, and my mother and daddy always carry an extra one just in case."

I looked down on Bee's lap and saw that she had brought along an abridged Catholic Catechism. I asked, "Is the priest going to give you a quiz before your baptism?"

"Yes, my daddy quizzed me last night and I got everything right, but you can never be too sure."

The limo pulled up in front of the studio and the four of us got out and walked through the front gate and toward Annie's office. Naturally, on the way to her office we stopped and talked to at least a dozen people.

Annie gave Christine a tour of the studio and Bee and I went to visit Bernardo. I was pleasantly surprised that Annie was willing to let go of Bee's hand and let me take her to Bernardo's department without her there. This simple action showed that Annie trusted me with the most important thing in her life, and that made me feel really good.

We entered Bernardo's studio and Bee ran right up to him and hugged him. He jokingly asked, "And what brings you here today? Is it to haunt me again with your perfect face? The type of face that could put me out of business?"

Bee giggled and said, "No, I'm here to make sure you come to my baptism in two days."

"Oh, let me guess, a new dress for the occasion?"

"Yes, and it's beautiful."

"How many does that make?"

"Six."

"Six! My God, isn't it great to have parents like yours. I'm fifty years older than you and you know how many new dresses I've had. Four in total … excuse me, make that three. My fiancé dumped me for a younger man, so I had to return my bridal gown. Never the bride, always the bridesmaid."

"I'm so sorry. I can ask my mommy to buy you a new dress. Would that help?"

"No, unless she can buy me a new dress and find me the perfect husband."

"I'm so sorry, Bernardo," I said as he looked at me and gasped. He picked Bee up and placed her in a chair and walked over to me and examined my face.

"My God, it's perfect. Please take a seat."

I sat down next to Bee as he held up a magnifying glass to my skin. He remarked, "This is truly a work of art. Da Vinci would be jealous. You're more gorgeous than ever."

"She was always gorgeous," Bee said.

"Did anybody ask for your opinion, Ms. Nosey Pants?" Bee giggled and scrunched her nose at Bernardo, who scrunched his nose back.

"Who did the procedure?" he asked, and I shook my head and started to cry.

He whispered, "Dr. Petrenko."

I nodded and he said, "I read about it. I'm so sorry."

"Why are you crying, Alicia?" Bee asked.

I glanced at Bernardo and said, "They're happy tears, sweetheart. I'm so happy I am going to be your godmother." I didn't know if I should tell Bee about Dr. Petrenko or not, and I erred on the side of caution, given what Annie had said to me about Bee's worries.

Bee stood up and walked over to me and sat on my lap. "Please don't cry, even if they are happy tears."

"I'll try not to, but sometimes I can't help it," I said as she hugged me.

"Maybe, instead of paying my psychiatrist two hundred dollars a visit, I could just come to you with my problems."

"I think you just need to get married, Bernardo," Bee said. "That might solve a lot of your problems."

"My God, she's a genius. Your…"

Bernardo stopped short as Annie and Christine entered the studio. "Are you joking around with my child?" Annie asked.

"But of course, why would I stop now?"

"This is the famous Bernardo. What is it — seven or eight Academy awards for makeup and costume design?"

"Eight, but who's counting? I'd give them all up for the right man. And who is this gorgeous woman with you?"

"This is Alicia's mother-in-law. Nick's mom."

"You mean step-mother?"

"No! Biological mother," Annie repeated.

"Would you mind taking a seat so I can examine this abnormality? By the way, how old are you?"

"Bernardo, don't you know better than ask a woman her age?" Annie snapped.

"Sorry…"

"I'm fiftyish, and if you want to examine me to see if I've had any plastic surgery, go right ahead."

Christine took a seat and Bernardo started to examine her face and neck with a dermatoscope. Finally, he said, "You are a bizarre specimen. What's your secret?"

"Enough questions, Bernardo. I came down here to invite you to lunch, but I'm suddenly having second thoughts," Annie said.

"Mommy, can you please buy Bernardo a new dress?"

Annie shook her head and said, "Let's talk about that another time, sweetheart."

"Okay," Bee replied.

"Are you really the mother of that serious hunk of a son?" Bernardo asked Christine.

"Yes, I'm seriously the mother of that serious hunk of a son," she replied with a laugh.

"Well, that explains his looks," Bernardo said.

Annie stepped in front of him and asked, "Any more questions?"

"No."

"Great! Because I was thirty seconds away from uninviting you to lunch," Annie said as she took Bee's hand and we all walked out of the studio and got into the limo. Adam drove off as I turned to Annie and asked, "Did you get all the papers and material you needed?"

"Yes, it's all in the trunk, and now I get to spend so much more time with my beautiful daughter and her lovely tutor."

Adam pulled up in front of the Smoke House and we all got out. Annie invited Adam to join us, but he cordially declined. The hostess greeted us and said our table was ready and that two gentlemen were already seated. Annie said, "But we didn't invite two gentlemen."

The hostess whispered, "You won't be disappointed." We followed the hostess to a large table at the back of the restaurant. Nick and Joe stood up as we approached and the hostess asked, "Was I right?"

"Yes, you were," Annie said as she handed the hostess a hundred-dollar bill and thanked her.

"Thank *you*," the hostess said. "If you need anything please let me know. Enjoy your lunch."

I sat down next to Nick and kissed him and said, "What a pleasant surprise."

He looked at me and immediately I could see that his eyes had a teary, red glare to them and I asked, "Are you okay?"

"Yes, sweetheart, why would you even ask?" He picked up a crystal rocks glass filled with ice and liquor.

"What are you drinking?"

"A Macallan 12 single malt scotch."

"I don't think I've ever seen you drink anything other than beer or wine, except when we make a toast."

"That's because beer and wine is what I usually do drink. Would you like a taste? It's quite smooth."

I shook my head and ran my fingers through his gorgeous hair and asked, "So what brought you and Joe down here?"

"Joe hasn't visited Simon's grave in over a month and he was feeling guilty about that. I suggested we surprise you here for lunch, then go to the grave. Joe was very close to Simon."

"Yes, I know," I said. Then I leaned in and whispered, "I'll make a deal with you. You set aside that scotch and I'll make it up to you later."

"What might you have in mind?"

"If I went into detail I might have to drag you to the closest hotel."

"Okay," he replied as he pushed the scotch glass away.

The waitress put a couple of baskets of their famous cheesy bread on the table and then opened three bottles of white wine and filled our wine glasses. When she came back with a soda for Bee, I picked up the scotch glass and asked if she could take it away, which she did. I said to my adorable husband, "You won't be disappointed."

"I'm sure I won't," he said as Bee reached over and grabbed the bread basket and took three slices.

Joe remarked, "Next to Mr. Wang's dumplings, I think this is her second-favorite food in the world. Isn't that so, sweetheart?"

"Yes, Daddy," she replied, as butter dribbled down her chin, and Annie reached over to wipe her child's face clean.

# CHAPTER SIXTY-THREE

Nick and Joe had taken a taxi to the restaurant and once Annie found out they were going to the cemetery she decided we would go with them, even though we had no flowers to lay at the grave site.

Adam drove us to Forest Lawn Cemetery and parked beside Simon's grave. We all got out of the limo and, remembering what happened the last time we visited Simon's grave, I took Annie by the arm. The grave was beautifully neat, and as Bee stepped up to the tombstone she lifted a small rock off the top of the headstone. There were about twenty-five rocks, not very big, on the top of the stone. Bee looked at her mother and asked, "Mommy, why would someone leave all these rocks on top of Uncle Simon's tombstone?"

Annie didn't know, and apparently no one else knew, except for Christine, who took Bee's hand and the rock in her hand and explained. "Your uncle Simon was Jewish, and in the Jewish religion when friends and relatives visit the grave of a loved one they leave a rock to show they were there. So, as you can see, your uncle Simon had many visitors."

"Why would they leave a rock and not a flower?" Bee asked.

Christine bent down to explain. "Because flowers, as you know, wither and die, but a rock is more lasting. It never dies, like your uncle Simon's spirit, and by leaving a rock, relatives and friends are not only keeping a part of Uncle Simon's spirit here but also his guidance and knowledge that they desperately seek. The rock holds down a part of your uncle's being here on earth. Don't you occasionally feel his presence?"

"All the time," Bee said.

"And I bet he is so very proud of you."

"I hope so. I try to take care of my mommy because I know how much he loves her, and my daddy. And when I go into the library at home I always read poems out loud because I know my uncle Simon loves poetry."

Christine handed Bee the rock she had in her hand and Annie turned away and started to cry silently.

Christine saw this and steered Bee back over to Simon's grave. "And now you can put the rock back on top of the tombstone, honey."

Bee reached up and put the rock back on the stone and said, "Should I look for my own rock to put on top of the tombstone, so Uncle Simon knows I was here and doesn't leave us?"

"He knows you were here, sweetheart, and I'm quite certain he's never going to leave you, or your mommy and daddy, or the other people who have come to visit him. But the next time we come, we'll definitely bring a rock from the beach."

"He would like that," Bee said as she hugged Christine.

Joe, Bee, and Annie had brought some poetry to read to Simon, and Nick and I gave the family some private time with Simon to perform their ritual. Bee wouldn't let Christine go, and so she got to read some poetry too. And Bernardo, who had listened to Christine's explanation about the rocks, was now sitting in the back of the limo having a private cry.

Nick held on to me as we walked up to beautiful Memorial Park, at the top of the cemetery. He'd never been there before, and I was excited to introduce him to the artwork that reflected the park's theme of a joyous life after death. But as we walked amid statues of presidents and war heroes and stood back from murals depicting the signing of the Declaration of Independence and other scenes from American history, my husband was strangely quiet. When we finally sat down on a bench across from the mural depicting the founding of our country, I asked, "Why were your eyes all red when I first saw you at the restaurant?"

"Would you believe allergies?"

"No," I said as I looked directly at him.

"You're not only the most beautiful creature I've ever seen but very possibly the smartest. Bee is one lucky girl to have you as a tutor."

"Stop the bullshit! What's going on?"

Nick looked across at the mural, occasionally closing his eyes, as the resoluteness he usually exhibited seemed to be rattled. He shook his head as he looked at me briefly, smiled, and began to speak. "Every day I remind myself about how lucky I am to be surrounded by you, my mom, Annie, Joe, Bee, and Mr. Wang and his family ... and how lucky I've been to meet and befriend so many great people whose unselfish courage, humanity, and sacrifices have made the world better.

"Losing Dr. Petrenko really hurt, but sadly it didn't surprise me as much I thought it would. In a sense, I'm the reason his daughter is dead. He would never admit it, but I couldn't help feeling that he held me responsible. Besides his work, Nastasiya was everything to him."

I wanted to say, *That's ridiculous! Dr. Petrenko loved you! He would never have blamed you for his daughter's death!* In the brief time I knew the good doctor, he had only ever shown genuine love for Nick and concern for his well-being. We both knew that Nick would never intentionally endanger anyone. But there was no point trying to convince Nick of that. From the moment he learned of Nastasiya's death, he must have concluded that the good doctor held him responsible. Nothing I could say would change his mind about that.

Nick looked away and stared at a statue of Nathanael Greene, a Revolutionary War hero who remained with General Washington throughout the entire war. He turned back toward me and asked, "What percentage of Americans do you think have even heard of General Greene?"

"Less than one percent," I said as I gently ran my fingers across his handsome face and asked, "How's the book coming? Are you and Joe working well together?"

"He's a talented writer and a great listener. I often tell him that he should have been a reporter but he just laughs it off."

"Have you finished interviewing fellow reporters and soldiers?"

"We're close. I had two interviews set up for today with two young marines who I got to know pretty well while I was reporting on the fighting in Helmand Province. The fighting in that area was intense, but thankfully these two marines got their discharge orders while I was still there and I actually watched them take off in a plane heading back to the States. They were both married and one had a toddler waiting for him at home with his wife.

"These were two of the sweetest, funniest guys I met in all my time as a reporter. They always managed to tell jokes and laugh, even under the most hellish circumstances. I'm sure it was a coping mechanism, but it made them extremely likeable. I was so happy they made it out."

Nick stopped talking and looked back at the statue and said, "So you think it's less than one percent? I think it's probably a tiny fraction of one percent, but then what do I know."

He turned back toward me but didn't look at me directly. "When I talked to them about two months ago and told them about the book, they were excited to participate. They both said, 'It'll be nice to talk to someone who understands.' I should have realized something was wrong, but they were still telling jokes over the phone and Joe and I were cracking up and everything seemed to be fine. They both said we could call anytime we were ready."

Nick lowered his head and stared at the ground between his knees. I realized that I was holding my breath, and I finally took a big gulp of air and reached out to grasp Nick's hand.

"When I called them today, their wives answered," he said, and paused. "I asked for their husbands, and found out that both of them committed suicide a few weeks ago. One went first, a gunshot to the head, and the other one shot himself a day later."

I gripped Nick's hand tightly and wrapped my other arm around his back as I shook my head helplessly from side to side. He was crying when he said, "They couldn't have been any older than twenty-four or five. They both visited veterans' hospitals for help and had weekly appointments with psychiatrists, but those doctors have zero combat experience.

"Unless you've been in a war zone with death and confusion all around, you can never relate to the problems, the nightmares, these two young marines were living with every day of their lives. With all the money our government wastes, you'd think they could at least get psychiatrists with field experience to help our returning veterans. They give them drugs, like that's going to stop the nightmares. We've lost three times more soldiers to suicide than we've lost on the battlefields. And in almost every case, those suicides happened after they were discharged and back home. It is simply unbelievable!"

He stood up and started walking around aimlessly, mumbling to himself, with his head bowed. I stood up and was about to go to him and try to help him when he walked head-first into a statue and started yelling and swearing, I rushed to him and took him by his arm and yelled, "You're scaring me. Do you hear me? I'm sorry about your friends and I understand the nightmares. I still have them. They haven't gone away. But you know what helps? Knowing that you love me so much, despite all my problems…"

He turned away and wiped his tear-streaked face with his sleeve. When he turned back to look at me, his dark brown eyes were still mostly vacant, but he said, "I'm sorry, Alicia."

I touched a red spot on his forehead where he made contact with the statue and said, "It's okay." Then I wrapped my arms around him and said, "I love you so much, so very much."

"I love you too," he said. "I'm sorry if I hurt you."

"You didn't hurt me. You worried me. It's what people in love do. They worry about each other. You remember how worried you were when I had the tubal pregnancy?"

"Of course. If anything were ever to happen to you I would kill myself."

"Nothing is going to happen to us, and I never want to hear you talk about killing yourself. You promised, remember?"

His vacant look had returned, and he sounded almost robotic as he said, "I remember."

I didn't like the sound of that, and I started jabbing his chest with my finger. "You promised! And you are a man who keeps his promises!" I was almost yelling at him. "Say it! Say you never go back on your promises!"

"I never go back on a promise," he said, and for the first time, I didn't believe him. He looked so lost when he was walking about aimlessly, so very lost, and now his voice and his words rang hollow.

We walked in silence back to the group and got into the limousine, and without saying more than a few words, I buried my face against my husband's chest and wrapped my arms tightly around him. Bee, Christine, Annie, Joe and Bernardo were talking, but they might as well have been speaking Cantonese.

# CHAPTER SIXTY-FOUR

At a little after midnight, I knocked on the open door to Christine's study. She was sitting in a chair, looking out the bay window. The study was dark, and outside, a million stars cast a ghostly glow across the surface of the water. I sat down beside her and she asked, "When did my son start going out at this ungodly hour to lie down on the beach? It has to be freezing out there."

"He used to do it all the time when I first met him. He told me it helped him relax. I went out with him a number of times and yes, it was always freezing. He would fall asleep almost from the moment he lay down, and wake up exactly forty-five minutes later, and we would come back inside. Before tonight, he hadn't done it for a long time."

We both looked down at Nick's prone form. After a while, Christine said, "What happened when the two of you went up to Memorial Park?"

I recounted the heartbreaking story of the two marines Nick befriended in Afghanistan, who were discharged and sent home to their families. I told her that Joe and Nick had made plans to interview them for the book, and that he'd spoken highly of their humor and camaraderie.

"He said they were always so funny and friendly, even back in Afghanistan, and that they were still telling jokes when Joe and Nick talked to them a couple of months ago.

"Today, they reached out to them to make the arrangements and found out that both of them committed suicide, one after the other, a few weeks ago.

"Nick was out of his mind. He started walking around aimlessly, rambling on about the ineptitude of the government and the psychiatrists treating veterans who were exposed to combat. I've never seen him so out of control. Bouncing off of statutes, so lost…"

"I was afraid it was something like that," Christine said. "I knew something was off."

"He was like a different person."

"You don't come back from ten years in war zones and just pick up where you left off. The memories don't go away, and there is a reminder on the other side of every phone call, around every corner, in every bar and restaurant, and especially at night when you lay your head down and fall asleep. My son has been extremely resilient … and so have you," Christine said, looking up at me. "It's not like you haven't also experienced severe, life-altering, trauma. You have. And yet you have fought your way back."

"If not for your son I wouldn't be here right now."

Christine looked directly at me and said, "And he says the same thing about you."

Tears started to flow down my cheeks and Christine reached over and wiped them away as she ran her fingers through my hair. She said, "Remember I told you I lost a pregnancy after a few months? Well, the doctor told me that it would have been a girl, and if she had lived, she would be a few years younger than you. I often think that if I didn't have that miscarriage, my son might never have become a war correspondent. He might have despised me, but I doubt he'd have left a baby sister behind. Today, I have that daughter, and while you might not have been around to change my son's career choice, you're here to help him now ."

"And you're really not going anywhere?" I asked hesitantly.

"Why would I even think of it? The two most important people in my life are right here. Besides, I promised you I wouldn't leave, and over the years I have become fairly good at keeping my promises."

"Good," I said.

She looked down at the beach and at Nick walking back toward the house. "Speaking of promises, you made one to my son today. I think right now might be the perfect time to keep it."

"What are you talking about?"

"At lunch today. That little maneuver with the scotch…"

"You heard that?" I exclaimed, blushing madly, and Christine laughed.

"I have excellent hearing. I think I caught it all. Something about making it worth his while if he put the drink aside?"

I took the nearest throw pillow and scrunched it into my face, but Christine just laughed and said "Oh Alicia, don't be embarrassed." She tugged at the pillow to pull it below my eyes and peeked at me, smiling. "You're married. Married couples have sex. And your husband desperately needs you right now. Consider it medicine for a mind in distress."

I hugged her and said, "I'll try not to be too loud."

She laughed as I hurried out of the room.

# CHAPTER SIXTY-FIVE

A white stretch limousine stopped in front of the mansion. The driver opened the back door and Nick, Christine, and I were greeted by a mixed welcoming chorus of English and Cantonese. Mr. Wang's entire family were present, as were Bernardo, Annie, Joe, and the soon-to-be baptized Bee. Everyone was dressed beautifully, but the child with the lovely dimples, flawless skin, and light brown hair stood out. Dressed in her white gown, she literally looked like a seraph.

Bernardo was very quiet, and I asked him if everything was okay.

"Yes, I'm just a little worried. I haven't been to church in so long I have this terrible fear that God might strike me dead."

"Oh, please don't even suggest that," Annie said. "I really don't have the time to look for another makeup artist."

Everyone laughed except Bernardo and Bee. "I wouldn't worry so much; you could probably replace me before I am even buried."

"That's not so, Bernardo. My mommy loves you too much and so does everyone else," Bee said as she hugged Bernardo.

"I don't even know why you need to be baptized. You're already an angel."

We gathered around the font at the front of Saint Joseph's Catholic Church. Father Dolan allowed everyone to stand and witness the baptism up close since we were the only ones in the church. Nick and I, the godparents, stood on either side of Bee. Joe stood next to Nick, and Annie stood next to me.

Father Dolan smiled down at Bee. He held a piece of paper and started speaking. "It is a tradition in the Catholic Church that older children who wish to be baptized go through a series of classes, known as the Rite of Christian Initiation for Children. In these classes, the children study passages from the Bible. At the end, I ask each child to write down his or her favorite passage, and what they like about it. Beatrice, without a doubt, was one of the best students I've ever had the privilege of tutoring. She chose a passage from the Sermon on the Mount, where our Lord Jesus Christ delivers the moral teachings that he hopes all will follow.

"Beatrice chose the beatitude, 'You are the light of the world.' This passage deals with the question of our influence and how our actions are perceived by others. I usually read aloud what the children have written, but Beatrice's response to this beatitude is so remarkable that I've asked her to read it."

Father Dolan handed the paper to Bee and said, "Take all the time you need. What you have written deserves all our attention."

"Yes, Father," Bee said as she took a deep breath and started to read.

"It was not too long ago that I was living on the streets, eating out of garbage bins, and sleeping behind those large bins you find behind restaurants. I had run away from my foster parents, who were beating me.

"Then one day I saw a man sitting on a park bench, watching some kids play basketball. I could tell there was something different about him, and when I sat beside him I could see it in his face.

"He talked to me for a while, and then he left to go to his favorite bar to drink beer. I told him I would wait outside, but I don't think he believed me. Hours later, when it was dark, he came out of the bar and started walking to his house. I followed him and said, 'You must have had a lot of beers. You were in there a long time.'

"He turned around and said, 'Bee, what are you doing here?' I told him all I wanted was to take a shower and clean up and sleep in a real bed for a night. He took me to his home and gave me my own room. I took a shower and when I came out he didn't even recognize me because I was so much cleaner. We ate pizza and I told him everything that had happened to me, and he told me stories about his family, and about his uncle Tony who had polio as a child but never let it stop him from doing the things he wanted.

"Before I went to bed that first night, the man that took me in promised to adopt me. He is now officially my daddy. He gave me everything I could ever dream of, but more importantly he loved me like only a great daddy could. His uncle Tony would be proud, and I'm the luckiest girl to have the best daddy in the world. He is like the light that God talks about in the Sermon on the Mount. His light shines brightly, and it is because of my daddy that I met Mr. Wang.

"Mr. Wang works with his family in a restaurant that has the best food. I especially love their dumplings. My daddy and Mr. Wang have known each other for a long time, and Mr. Wang and my daddy would sometimes sit around and drink beers together and even celebrate Christmas together.

"The night I met Mr. Wang he was delivering food to us. After he left, he came back and handed me a bunch of fortune cookies and called me an angel. He has become part of our family, and I love him so much. We love to dance to the Beach Boys."

I looked across at Joe and Mr. Wang and both men had tears rolling down their cheeks. I whispered to Bee, "You're doing great."

She smiled at me and continued. "One day my daddy and I went to visit a friend of my daddy's. His name is Simon and he is buried in Forest Lawn Cemetery. While I was reading a poem to Simon, the most beautiful woman in the world pulled up in a car. She hugged my daddy and they kissed. I got worried because I thought this beautiful lady was going to take my place and I would have to go back to a foster home.

"I was wrong, and now I call that beautiful lady my mommy. Simon is my mother's brother, and it just so happened that my daddy and mommy had planned all along to get married but they had to put off the wedding. Simon was the light that brought us all together that day. My mommy has a really big job, but she and my daddy have taught me to treat everyone nicely, no matter their position. I have met so many wonderful people at my mommy's studio, including Bernardo, who loves to laugh and has more Academy Awards than Meryl Streep.

"My mommy is the one that comes and holds me at night when I'm having nightmares. She has started working from home more so she can spend more time with me. She misses her brother Simon so much and I tell her that when I get older I want to become a researcher and find a cure for what killed her brother and my uncle."

Annie suddenly latched onto me and at any moment I thought she was going to faint.

"My mommy, like my daddy, is the light that Lord Jesus Christ talked about. They are the light of the world. The caring and love they show to everyone shines brightly. Sometimes I see my mommy crying and it hurts me a lot. But it's because she loved her brother so much, and loves so deeply, that she cries. I love her so much."

Bee looked at Father Dolan and he simply smiled and said, "Please continue, Beatrice. You have everyone enthralled."

"I drove along on a to-go-order from Mr. Wang's restaurant with Mr. Wang and his uncle. It was the last order of the night and it was at this house that I met Alicia and Nick. Alicia was hurt very badly by some very mean men and she had a silver bandage on her face. Even with the bandage, she was so beautiful. She was a model before those men hurt her.

"We sat in the study, and she told me that if it wasn't for Nick she didn't know if she would still be alive. She said that her leg went limp from her injuries while she was talking to some friends at a party, and she fell into the arms of the most handsome man she had ever seen. The man helped her over to a table, sat with her, and then took her home to her apartment in a not very safe area. He wanted her to be safe, so he took her out of that apartment and invited her to move into his very big house.

"Sometimes when my parents think I'm asleep, I hear them talking. I know it's not right, but I can't help it. My daddy and Nick are working on a book together. It's about war correspondents. Nick was a war correspondent for ten years and it's people like him who shine a light on the suffering of so many innocent people in places where there is war. I know that Nick, like Alicia and I, probably suffers from terrible nightmares because he has seen and written about so many horrible things. Yet, the light that he has shone upon the world is so important.

"Nick has told my daddy many times that if it wasn't for Alicia he might not be alive. Together, they shine a light upon each other and in so doing, they make the world a better place.

"Not too long ago, Nick's mother, Christine, came to live with Nick and Alicia. At first, I couldn't believe she was Nick's mother because she looks so young. She is so beautiful and she is such a wonderful dancer and she gives me lessons. But more importantly, she was able to reunite Mr. Wang's family who had been trying to emigrate from China to America for a very long time. Mr. Wang and his family now live with my daddy, mommy, and me. They are teaching me how to speak Cantonese and how to make delicious dishes. They are so very sweet. Christine used her influence, caring, and love to help Mr. Wang's family to reunite. She tells me what she did for Mr. Wang's family was no big deal but every time I am with Mr. Wang and his family I know how big a deal it was."

Bee stopped reading and simply held the piece of paper with one hand at her side. She bowed her head as tears ran down her cheeks. She chokingly started talking again … no longer reading from her paper. "Sometimes I hear things that I know no one wants me to hear. They're afraid they'll scare me. I heard them talking about Nick's friend, Dr. Petrenko, who fixed Alicia's face so it looks as perfect as it did before she was hurt. He went to Ukraine to work in a hospital and to help heal and save the poor people who were wounded in the war. He was killed when a bomb was dropped on the hospital. His lovely daughter, whose name I can't pronounce, was also killed many months before, when a bomb was dropped on the same hospital where she was working as a nurse. I know how terrible Nick must feel and it hurts me because I don't know how to make him feel better.

"Dr. Petrenko and his daughter are examples of what our Lord Jesus Christ preached about in the Sermon on the Mount. Their spirits are very much alive, like my uncle Simon's, and their love and caring will forever shine a bright path toward…"

Bee dropped the piece of paper, turned and buried her face just below my chest, and cried. I bent down and whispered, "Do you have any idea how very special you are?"

She shook her head and I said, "I'm so very proud of you, and Nick and I are the luckiest two people in the world to have you as our godchild."

She tried to speak but the words came out muddled and then she looked up at her mother, who was crying, and she said, "Oh Mommy, please don't cry. I didn't mean to make you cry."

She embraced her mother, who lowered her face and kissed Bee on her head over and over. "You're the best gift that God has ever bestowed upon me," Annie said as mother and daughter remained as one.

Father Dolan addressed the congregants. "If anyone had any doubts that angels walk beside us, I think our Beatrice has put those doubts to rest."

Bee, like the honeybees in Dante's *Paradiso*, had pollinated the glimmer of light inside all of us and illuminated a path we would all be wise to follow.

The baptism itself went by fairly quickly, with Father Dolan asking Nick and me and Bee's parents a series of questions to verify that we all rejected

Satan, and believed in God, the Father, creator of Heaven and Earth. After the adults answered "yes" to all of the questions, Bee lowered her head over the font as Father Dolan intoned, "I baptize you, in the name of the Father, and of the Son, and of the Holy Spirit," pouring water over her forehead each time.

"God the Father of our Lord Jesus Christ has freed you from sin, given you a new birth by water and the Holy Spirit, and welcomed you into his holy people." Father Dolan anointed Bee with the chrism of salvation, saying, "As Christ was anointed Priest, Prophet, and King, so may you live always as a member of his body, sharing everlasting life."

We all replied, "Amen."

# CHAPTER SIXTY-SIX

We all piled into the limousine and it was Bee's baptismal wish that we visit Uncle Simon's grave. She and Christine had collected some rocks from the beach, and those they deemed desirable they polished and labeled with a person's name.

Bee picked up two rocks that looked like glittering gems and handed them to her parents. "Christine and I decided that these two rocks were the most beautiful, and since you were both the closest to Uncle Simon, it's only right for you to put them on the top of his tombstone."

Annie looked down at her rock and said, "I can see my reflection. You must have put some extra muscle into polishing this rock."

"No, mommy. Daddy told me that Uncle Simon believed you were the most gorgeous girl in the whole world. So it's only natural that your rock would hold your reflection, so when Uncle Simon looks up he will always be able to see the prettiest girl in the whole world."

I thought Annie was going to break down but she held firm and simply reached over and kissed her daughter and said, "Thank you, my lovely child."

Bee handed out all the rocks, leaving no one out. Mr. Wang explained the meaning of the rocks to his family, and they all bowed in Bee's direction, and she bowed at them in return. I looked down at my rock and, like Annie's rock, I could see my reflection but I decided not to say anything. When I looked up I noticed that Christine was looking directly at me. I reached over, took her hand, and squeezed her in between Nick and me.

I whispered into her ear, "I love you so much and I am so happy we are all together as a family."

She whispered back, "Me too, my beautiful daughter. Me too."

The limousine parked alongside Simon's grave and in no particular order we all went up and placed our rock on top of the tombstone. If it was true that the rocks kept the deceased spirit connected to the living and to this world then we could all rest assured that Simon's spirit wasn't going anywhere for a long time.

# CHAPTER SIXTY-SEVEN

The Smoke House restaurant was just down the hill from the cemetery, and Annie put in a large to-go order of their famous cheesy bread.

A waiter brought out a box filled with the bread and placed it on the table inside the limo. Bee couldn't take her eyes off the box and Annie didn't have the heart to deny her angel anything, especially on the day she was baptized. "Go ahead, have a piece now," Annie said to Bee and Bee opened the box and took out a piece and a few seconds later Annie just flung open the box for everyone to enjoy some cheesy bread. Joe uncorked two bottles of white wine and poured everyone a glass.

Bernardo downed his glass of wine and said, "My God, I needed that." He re-filled his glass and Bee said, "You see, I told you God wouldn't do anything bad to you."

"That's because he couldn't take his eyes off you and forgot I was even there."

"That's not true. He knew you were there."

"You think so? Either way, the next time I go to church I'll be taking you with me. Why take a chance?"

About halfway through the ride I felt my husband rest his head on my shoulder. It was the first time he had ever done that. It was usually me holding onto him for support.

Ever since Bee started reading her composition in church it was like a change had come over all of us. It was as if, for a moment at least, we were all free from our tragedies and traumas.

My husband reached around and kissed me and said, "I love you so much," and whereas I might at one time have not believed him, I had no doubt that he was telling me the truth. He, once again, rested his head on my shoulder and fell back to asleep.

I know that this moment in time is just that … a moment in time. I have no illusions that my husband can ever put his past behind him. There will always be plenty of times when he needs to go outside at midnight and sleep under the stars for forty-five-minutes at a time. I plan on being beside him as often as I can. I also have no doubt that I'll continue to have nightmares about my awful night, and forever hear the sound of the avenging angel's footsteps on the pavement when she erased that evil from the world. And I'm certain that Nick's strong and muscular arms will gently wrap themselves around me and whisper in my ear, "No one will ever hurt you again," every time that awful night revisits me in my dreams.

I look across at my beautiful, angelic, godchild and am thankful that her parents are forever vigilant against the past intruding on the present and the future, and that Nick and I and everyone in this limo are there as back-up. I cannot think of a better job than to tutor my precious, loving Bee and, in turn, to learn from her wise counsel.

I hesitate to say that Annie will ever get over losing Simon, but it's comforting to know that if she's feeling down, she only needs to listen for her child's laughter or look at the angel's glittering dimples, embodiments of a light that one simply needs to follow to lead to a better place. And she has a husband, like mine, who will do anything for her.

I look across at Christine, who gazes out at the ocean. I will never pretend to know what is going on in her mind. I would like to know more but I will never cross that Rubicon. If she needs to talk about anything, I will always be there for her. Whether she will ever forgive herself for neglecting her child during his formative years, I don't know. His choice of a career was solely his attempt to get back at her, and it worked … yet if not for her he might still be in a Russian prison, and he certainly wouldn't be the owner of a mansion overlooking the majestic Pacific.

I looked across at my sleeping godchild who was extended across the laps of both her parents. Her lips were a bright orange from the cheesy bread and with her hair pulled back, she looked like a ballerina. I had no doubt that my godchild loved to dance because it made her happy, and it probably also released her from the stress and hurt she suffered before a kind gentleman, born and raised in the Bronx, took her into his home in Studio

City and treated her with the kindness, caring, and love he was treated with as a child by his parents, grandmother, and assorted relatives.

Maybe it was just that type of love and caring that would keep all the demons from all our past traumas at bay … forever lurking but never overcoming.

# CHAPTER SIXTY-EIGHT

Later that evening, after all the guests from Bee's baptism had left, and after Nick and I enjoyed a beautiful walk along the beach, I visited Christine in her study. Sitting in two plush chairs a few feet from the bay window, we sipped wine and looked out at the magnificent vista. The sky was so bright, with a million glittering stars, that we didn't even need to turn on a light.

I asked, "So, there is no part of you that ever wanted to be a model before, during, or in between marriages? I know you had to be asked, considering all the publicity, *paparazzi, and fashion* inside the D.C. bubble."

Christine smiled but didn't move, focusing instead on the breathtaking view of the sky and the waves tumbling against the shore. She finally said, "I might not have loved either of my husbands, but I had great respect for their jobs. For the former wife of a deceased member of the Joint Chiefs of Staff and the recently divorced wife of a high-ranking Naval officer, it would be unbecoming to be seen on the cover of magazines clad in skimpy bikinis and revealing garments."

"But just think of the added power you would wield over foreign diplomats and ambassadors."

"I already wield that power, sweetheart. I don't need to get down any further into the gutter."

"Don't you miss being around the D.C. power brokers just a little bit?" I asked.

"Yeah, like I miss a boil on my behind."

Christine stood up, put her glass on the table between us, and walked out of the study and to the bathroom. I lay back in my chair and closed my eyes. It had been a long day. I could hear the waves colliding against the shore, and just like that I was transported to another place where I was surrounded by a thick, blinding fog. I could hear the whistle of a steamboat and the rattle of its engine beneath my feet. I waved my hands in front of me in a futile attempt to see beyond the fog. The boat shook so hard that it felt like it was about to break apart. I went flying across the splintered floor and hit my head against the deck.

The fog suddenly cleared and I found myself in a small Italian village with cobblestone streets and houses built from quarried stone decked with colorful plants in terracotta pots. A door opened and a lovely lady in her mid-to-late sixties greeted me, "Ciao Bella, Alicia. We've been expecting you."

She ushered me into the house and called out, "Ginevra, it's Nicholas's beautiful wife." Ginevra, dressed in an apron, wipes her hands on a dish towel. Like her sister, she is lovely, and speaks perfect English. She hugs and kisses me on both cheeks and says, "Bellissima!!! Even more beautiful than the pictures Nicky sends to us."

I turn to the sister who greeted me. "And you are Francesca?"

"Sì, Bella," she says as they usher me into the dining area. I sit at the table and in a blink of the eye a large plate of bruschetta appears before me with a glass of red wine.

I look at both sisters and ask, "Aren't you going to eat?"

"No, Bella. We ate earlier," Ginevra says, then looks at her sister. "But we should have some wine."

Francesca leaps up, walks into the kitchen, and brings back two more glasses. She picks up the bottle of wine that's on the table and fills their glasses. "A toast," she says, "to you and our Nicky. We wish you a long life and much love."

We raise our glasses as tears start to flow down my cheeks. Ginevra reaches across and touches my hand. "Please don't cry, Alicia." She gently runs her fingers through my hair. "This is a time to be happy."

"I've never been happier. It's just that Nick has told me so much about you both..."

"He was God's gift to us. He filled our hearts with joy, and the love between the three of us has never diminished. We talk all the time, and he sends us money, even though we tell him we don't need it. We give it to the poor in the village and that makes him happy."

"He tells me that he considered the two of you his mother when growing up."

"No! No! Bella. Christine was always his mother. It's just that she was still a child herself, and so we were blessed with helping raise her perfect, beautiful boy. Isn't that so, Francesca?"

"Oh yes, he was the most delightful little boy, and when he dressed up in his baseball uniform he looked like an angel."

"And he is so handsome. Like a movie star," Ginevra adds. "But it's what's inside him, in his heart, that makes him so very special. It makes us so happy that he and his mommy are back together again. It nearly killed her when he became a reporter."

"It nearly killed *us!*" Francesca cries. "I don't know how many novenas we said over the years…"

"Thankfully the good Lord answered them and he is back home, safe, with his mother and beautiful wife."

"Did you get along with his father?" I asked.

"The general is the one who hired us," Ginevra says. "I went to the interview. Francesca only came along to keep me company. When the general hired me, he asked about my sister who was waiting outside for me. He asked, 'Is she a nanny, too?' I said she was, and that she was also looking for a job. He hired her without even interviewing her.

"I asked, "But you have only one baby boy?' And the general said 'And my wife, who is not that much more mature than our son.'

"He put us in charge of the household. We bought the food, cooked, bought Nicky's clothes, helped Nicky with his homework … We even had our own separate rooms."

"So you liked him?"

"Yes, when he was home," Francesca replied. "First he was in Sarajevo, then Afghanistan and Iraq. He wasn't home much, and when he was home, we could notice the changes in him. Nicky was too young, and Christine…"

"He saw too much killing," Ginevra added, shaking her head. "When we all moved to Washington and he became a member of the president's cabinet we thought things might improve for him. He didn't have to travel much and he was at home more than ever before, but after dinner he would go into his study and close the door. Sometimes, you would hear him crying.

When the general had dinner Christine was still out, and in the morning he left the house five hours before she rolled out of bed…

"At first the family moved quite a bit … and before each move he came to us and asked if it would be problem to move with them. It was never a problem. Besides, it would have been a sin to leave that little boy. When we finally moved to D.C., the general came to us and said, 'I will be forever thankful for all that the two of you have done for our family. I can forgive Christine for acting so reckless and irresponsible. I knew when I married her that she was still a rebellious teenager. I thought by this time she would have grown up, but I was wrong.' Then he paused and said, 'Yet, I seriously believe that one day she is going to shine. I am the one who is seriously at fault. I could and should have been a much better father. I know so little about my son, and that is truly an unpardonable sin.'

"A few days later, the general and his son actually sat down and had breakfast together. They then went to Sunday Mass together. Nicky had always gone to church with us but my sister and I thought this was a sign from God that father and son were on their way to forming a real relationship. Little did we know that this was the beginning of the end."

"The general left my sister and me a substantial sum of money in his last will and testament," Francesca said. "He also thanked us profusely for watching so lovingly over his family."

Ginevra refilled our glasses and said, "For a couple of years after the general's death, Christine and Nicky for the first time began to bond. She started to shine, like the general had predicted." Ginevra choked up and started to cry. Her sister tried to hand her a napkin but she waved it off and continued, "But then she met another serviceman, a naval officer, and just like that re-married and her relationship with her son, once again, became non-existent.

"We left the household and came back here when Nicky went off to college. We kept in touch, talking three to four times a week. And then we didn't hear from him for a long time and so we called Christine and she told us what he did. She was hysterical, repeating over and over again, 'This is his revenge, his revenge, his revenge…' We didn't raise him to be vengeful. Just the opposite, we raised him to be forgiving."

"They now love each other as much as any mother and child can. We're a real family."

"We know," Francesca said. "The general's prediction has come true and Christine shines like the brightest star in all of Heaven."

"Do you know what would make it even more perfect? If the two of you came to live with us."

"No, sweet child. Now is the time for us to be with our family and friends. But please, please tell our sweet boy that his father was a good man and that he truly loved him."

There was a knock on the front door and both sisters got up to greet their guests. I sat, alone at the table, and listened to the laughter and joy as it echoed through the house.

And just like that I was lying on my back on the deck of the steamboat, in dense fog. I felt someone take my hand and help me up. "It's okay, Alicia, it's okay."

"Doctor Petrenko?" I asked.

"Yes, my child, it's Doctor Petrenko. The fog will lift any moment now."

And just like that, the fog was gone. We were standing on the bow of the boat, looking at the sun as it rose in the east out of the depths of the ocean and cast a glorious golden glow across the water.

"People are always looking for miracles, yet every day there is the miracle of the rising sun, and most people sleep right through it," Doctor Petrenko said as another person came up from behind me and took my other hand.

"Hello, Alicia. I'm Doctor Petrenko's daughter, Nastasiya."

"Nastasiya," I repeated as I sadly shook my head and said, "I am so sorry, so sorry."

"So sorry for what?" she asked. "It was my choice to stay both times. Isn't that so, Daddy?"

"Yes, my darling daughter," Dr. Petrenko replied.

"The sun still rises over our country, and as long as that miracle continues to happen, we shall prevail," Nastasiya said as I looked directly at her and then down at the water where the colors of a flag, yellow and blue, emerged from beneath the boat and leaped forward with the tide and carried us toward the rising sun.

I felt fingers gently run through my hair and heard Christine's soothing voice say, "Alicia, I think it's time we get you into bed."

I opened my eyes and looked at my lovely mother, who asked, "Were you having a bad dream, sweetheart?"

I shook my head and said, "No, it was a beautiful dream."

"Then I'm sorry I woke you," she said as she continued to stroke my hair, and I smiled to let her know that all was well.

I got up off the chair and hugged Christine and said, "I love you so much … and if I say that too often I'm sorry, but I can't help it."

"Please, my sweet child, say it as often as you like. It's magic to my ears."

# CHAPTER SIXTY-NINE

The following morning, I held onto my husband's hand as we took our walk along the beach. The seagulls greeted us with their usual squawking and then they suddenly flew off, over the water, in the direction of the rising sun. It was as if they knew I had something important to tell my handsome husband, and they gave me the quietude I desired.

"I need to tell you something, but you have to promise not to call me crazy."

"Have I ever called you crazy?"

"I can't recall, but if you haven't, you probably haven't been listening too closely to what I've been saying."

"You know, that's not true. Your gentle teasing, your acute observations, and your knowledge are just a few of the things I love about you."

"Okay, enough with the groveling," I laughingly said. Then I continued, hoping I wouldn't sound too unhinged. "I had a dream last night … only it didn't feel like a dream. It felt as real as the two of us, walking on this beach. I found myself in the home of Ginevra and Francesca, in the little town where they live. They were so lovely — just as you described them."

"That's because they're angels, guardian angels." Nick said with a smile.

"They told me things that not even you have told me. Ginevra said that she originally applied for the job as a nanny and that Francesca simply came along to keep her company. When your father wanted to hire both of them, Ginevra asked if two nannies wasn't one too many to take care of one baby, and the general replied, 'And there is my wife, who is not that much more mature than our son.'"

Nick looked directly down at me and, I briefly wondered if I had already crossed a forbidden line, but he said, "Please continue, sweetheart."

"They then went on to tell me that for the first ten years they hardly saw your father as he went from one war zone to another, and that it wasn't until you moved to D.C., and he started working for the president, that he was home a lot more."

"My father was definitely in the arena with the men and women under his command. He wasn't like so many of these armchair generals who sit in front of computers and yell out life-and-death verdicts to the soldiers who do their bidding."

"Shortly before his death, he thanked the ladies for everything they had done for the family. And he said some interesting things about your mother. He said he expected her to have grown up by then, and had been proven wrong, but that he fully expected her to shine one day. He also blamed himself for the neglect you received as a child, more than he blamed your mother. He said, 'I am the one who is seriously at fault. I could and should have been a much better father. I know so little about my son, and that is truly an unpardonable sin.'"

Nick's eyes suddenly misted over as he turned and looked out over the water. I gently touched his shoulder and he chokingly said, "I'm okay, sweetheart. I'm okay." He turned and looked at me and asked, "Did they say anything else?"

I thought for a moment and said, "That your father left them money in his will, and that you continue to send them money, even though they tell you that they don't need it. They said they give the money to the poor in the village."

"I would expect nothing less from them, and that's why I continue to send it."

"They also said that you were 'God's gift to both of them,' and that you 'filled their hearts with joy' and that the love between the three of you has 'never diminished.' And they really wanted me to tell you that your father was a good man and that he truly loved you."

Nick looked at me and softly smiled as he ran his hand along the side of my face. I said, "I know it was only a dream but it was so…"

"It wasn't only a dream. You know that and I know that, and Ginevra and Francesca knew that you and I were entitled to my father's side of the story. There is no reason to question their method of communicating that story and they picked the perfect messenger."

"It wasn't always about getting back at your mother that you stayed on so long as a war correspondent, was it?" I asked.

"In the beginning it was, but then I saw things, atrocities so brutal and inhumane, that I considered it my duty to report it to the rest of the world, in the hope that something could be done … some measure of relief … something…"

"So you stayed in the arena, like your father?"

"Yes, like my father, and in the end I don't know how many times I contemplated duplicating his final act."

"But not anymore?"

"Not anymore. It would be the most selfish thing I could ever do. It would devastate the people I love most … Ginevra, Francesca, my mother, and especially you."

He bent down, beneath my floppy beach hat, and kissed me. We then sat down, about fifty feet from the water, and silently looked out over the lovely Pacific as we held hands.

"I think it would really be nice if we went to visit Ginevra and Francesca."

"Yes, it would," Nick said, "except for the fact that my mother has exiled me to the lower forty-eight states."

"Oh, I think I might be able to persuade her to lift the embargo if I promise to handcuff you to me during the entire trip. You wouldn't mind that, would you?"

Nick laughed as he took both my hands and kissed them gently. We then looked out over the ocean and watched as two formations of seagulls, side by side, came flying toward the beach.

They veered off in opposite directions and softly landed on the wet sand, revealing, in the distance, the miracle of the rising sun, emerging from the depths of the ocean, illuminating a passageway to a new day.